"Petrie is a master of orchestrating convincing mayhem."
—*Publishers Weekly*

Praise for
BURNING BRIGHT

"I loved every page of this adrenaline-fueled journey. In fact, a beginning chase scene in the redwoods is not only breathtaking, it's also one of the most original action scenes I've read." —*Milwaukee Journal Sentinel*

"The world of Peter Ash is a terrifying place, and it is expertly drawn by Nick Petrie. . . . A fast-paced thriller."
—*The Washington Times*

"Readers can expect some good twists on the way to a hair-raising finish. Another fine thriller in what's shaping up to be a hell of a series." —*Kirkus Reviews* (starred review)

Praise for
THE DRIFTER

"Peter Ash is one of the most complex characters I've come across in a long time. The pace is like a sniper round, extraordinarily fast and precisely calibrated. The prose is fluid, original, and frequently brilliant, the story heart-wrenching and uplifting at the same time. There is grit in this tale that will stay with you. Perhaps forever."
—David Baldacci, *New York Times*–bestselling author of *Memory Man*

"As I was reading Petrie's exceptional debut, Tim O'Brien's [*The Things They Carried*] buzzed at the edges of my consciousness, casting the newer book as a thematic sequel to O'Brien's classic. . . . *The Drifter* may be about a different war, but it's about the same hell, and in this book it's about the things a vet carries home with him. . . . [The] lean prose, gritty descriptions, and raw psychological depth give the novel a feel that reminded me of early Dennis Lehane." —*Milwaukee Journal Sentinel*

"Nicholas Petrie has written just about the perfect thriller. I haven't read such a well-crafted and gripping story in a month of Sundays. If this is Petrie's first novel, watch out for the second one. But why wait? This one's here now, and it's a home run."

—John Lescroart, *New York Times*–bestselling author of *The Keeper*

"Captivating . . . [Petrie's] main character has the capacity to become an action hero of the likes of Jack Reacher or Jason Bourne." —*Lincoln Journal Star*

"A gripping, beautifully written novel." —*Huffington Post*

TITLES BY NICK PETRIE

The Runaway

The Breaker

The Wild One

Tear It Down

Light It Up

Burning Bright

The Drifter

TEAR IT DOWN

NICK PETRIE

G. P. PUTNAM'S SONS | NEW YORK

PUTNAM
— EST. 1838 —
G. P. PUTNAM'S SONS
Publishers Since 1838
An imprint of Penguin Random House LLC
penguinrandomhouse.com

THE LIBRARY OF CONGRESS HAS CATALOGUED THE G. P. PUTNAM'S SONS
HARDCOVER EDITION AS FOLLOWS:

Names: Petrie, Nicholas, author.
Title: Tear it down / Nick Petrie.
Description: New York : G. P. Putnam's Sons, [2019] |
Series: [A Peter Ash novel ; 4]
Identifiers: LCCN 2018018176| ISBN 9780399575662 (Hardcover) |
ISBN 9780399575679 (ePub)
Subjects: LCSH: Criminal investigation—Fiction. | BISAC:
FICTION / Suspense. | FICTION / Thrillers. | FICTION /
Action & Adventure. | GSAFD: Suspense fiction. | Mystery fiction.
Classification: LCC PS3616.E86645 T43 2019 | DDC 813/.6—dc23
LC record available at https://lccn.loc.gov/2018018176

p.   cm.

First G. P. Putnam's Sons hardcover edition / January 2019
First G. P. Putnam's Sons trade paperback edition / May 2019
First G. P. Putnam's Sons premium edition / August 2019
G. P. Putnam's Sons premium edition ISBN: 9780525542148

Printed in the United States of America
3   5   7   9   10   8   6   4   2

This one's for Duncan, a rocket nearing escape velocity

Tell ol' Pistol Pete to tell everybody he meet,
We gon' pitch a wang dang doodle all night long.

—Willie Dixon

I heard Papa tell Mama, Let that boy boogie woogie.
'Cause it's in him. And it's got to come out.

—John Lee Hooker

[multiple versions]

PART 1

1

At the time, Ellison Bell thought it was a goof, the four of them just talking, having fun.

It didn't turn out that way.

In the dark backyard of the empty, they sat on stolen or street-found chairs, sheltering behind the swaybacked old house. The grass was up to their knees and the bushes had gone leggy and wild, grown together into an unruly green wall hiding the boys from the eyes of wary neighbors.

The boys were feeling good, maybe a little loud, but it was a warm spring night, too nice to be indoors, and they weren't the only ones feeling the weather. Music from distant radios drifted on the breeze, crunk to blues to Beyoncé. Ellison Bell—Sonny to his mama and pops, one dead and the other long gone, and Eli to his friends—could smell meat cooking over charcoal.

If the empty wasn't boarded up with the lights and water off, if the four boys didn't have to piss in the weeds and dig themselves a shit hole with a stick by the back fence, it might have been like having a home.

But it wasn't home, not for any of them. It was just another place to stay, the latest in a long line of empties, even if it was a pretty good one. They'd been there a month, keeping mostly quiet and careful, hoping they could make it through summer if they didn't attract attention or set the place on fire by accident or out of boredom.

Not one of them older than fifteen.

I'm saying, there's something to this." Skinny B poked at the air with the half-smoked blunt. "A serious payday. A chance to build up a roll, get something started."

Skinny B saw himself as a hustler, full of ideas, always looking to move up. Tall and thin, long arms and legs, not much muscle. His head was shaped like a chili bean, and his face was smooth as a baby's. More ambitious than smart, Eli thought. Skinny had quit the trap house in a snit when he got passed over for inside work, but there wasn't much else to do on your own. Now he was hungry. Skinny B wanted the high life, the clothes and the car, money to spend.

Right now they were talking about what he was willing to do for it.

"Man, give me that." Coyo reached out and took the crooked blunt from Skinny's hand. He sucked in a deep hit and the burning coal flared bright orange in the night. "What's the payday?" His voice was squeaky from holding in the smoke. It was the only time Coyo was squeaky. Otherwise he was low-down brown, up for anything and everything.

Anymore Eli didn't know half of what Coyo got into, although he heard stories. Coyo wasn't one to tell.

"You can't be serious." Anthony Wilkinson was middle height, sturdy but not fat, with black-framed glasses that kept sliding down the steep slope of his nose. He pushed them back up with a meaty finger. "Walk into a jewelry store with a gun? They have armed guards. Alarms. Cameras."

Eli Bell was only half listening. He had his old guitar on his lap, the original beater from his dead brother Baldwin that had somehow survived Eli's life so far. The nearest radio was playing John Lee Hooker's "Let's Go Out Tonight," and Eli worked the edges of the song, fingers finding notes on their own, heel thumping time on the hard-packed dirt.

"That's the thing," said Skinny B. "The store ain't around here. It's way out the highway, the rich white people's mall. They got guards and cameras and shit, but they ain't set up for four rough niggas like us."

Coyo snorted at the idea of Skinny B as a rough nigga. But Skinny wasn't nothing. Working outside the trap was no joke, dealing with junkies looking to fix, some of them not looking to pay. Eli had never done it.

"What kind of stuff would we get?" Anthony said. "Some kind of cheap shit we take to King Robbie and hope for a few hundred dollars?" Anthony was the only one with something to lose. He still had people, a place to go when he needed a meal or a shower. Anthony was even going to school most days. The rest of them had quit years ago.

Eli thought maybe Coyo had never gone. That boy was raised by wolves, and the wolves had given him up for wild.

Of the four boys, Coyo was always the most likely. Most likely to cause a ruckus, most likely to carry a gun, most likely to pull it. He was permanently wired on Cokes or Red Bull, would smoke a blunt down to a nub in one long drag if you weren't watching, or even if you were.

It was Coyo had set the empty on fire two houses back, burning broken-up cabinets on the kitchen floor trying to keep warm on a cold night. But he'd also shown up tonight with a paper sack full of hot hamburgers and fries and a box of cold Cokes for everyone, and didn't make a thing out of it.

"Rolex watches," said Skinny B. "Diamond rings. I figure we give a watch to King, maybe Charlene and Brody." King's lieutenants. "Then everybody else be wantin' one, too. In the store they go for eight, ten, twelve stacks each. We sell for a thousand, five watches apiece? Or ten?"

"I like the sound of that," said Coyo. "I'm ready to get paid for real. How 'bout you, Eli?"

Part of Eli was still out there with John Lee Hooker, but not so far that he hadn't been following the conversation.

Like any of these niggas were really going to rob a jewelry store.

But part of him, what Eli thought of as the mathematical part, the part that had kept him alive and fed and sheltered since he was nine years old, wanted to take out the idea and play with it.

"You been there?" he asked Skinny B. "Out to that mall?"

"Hell yes, I have," said Skinny. "I took the bus there, day before yesterday." He pulled out his phone and passed it around, showing them pictures. "They got those police camera trailers in the parking lot, and the mall cops got guns. But the store ain't locked up, you can walk right in. Glass cases full of the good stuff, I'm telling you."

"How far is the store from the mall's nearest exit?" asked Eli.

"See, this why we're talking," said Skinny B. "'Cause you got the brains, right?"

"Brains enough not to do something this dumb," said Eli. But he was imagining the money. A Gibson ES-335 for starters, for that old-time sound, with a big fat amp to really hear himself.

Then thought, Maybe a house. Maybe they could buy a house, the four of them. Something to stay in for real.

Something they didn't have to run from when some neighbor called the police.

How much could a house cost, one of these broken-down old empties? He didn't know how any of that worked. Not like they needed furniture. Eli slept on the floor wrapped in a few old blankets with some cardboard laid out for padding, or on the three-legged couch they'd carried ten blocks in the dark. That was good enough for him.

Not good enough for Nadine, he thought. But it was something. A step in the right direction.

"How far to the exit?" asked Anthony. Maybe he was already spending his share, too.

"Well, it's on the second floor," said Skinny. "So you gotta get to the escalator, let's see, maybe eighty steps? There's a side exit almost right at the bottom. That's maybe another forty steps. Parking right outside. And from the parking lot?" He grinned his gap-toothed hustler's smile. "Half a mile to the highway and we're gone."

"Whose turf is that?" Eli was nobody's idea of a gangster, he'd been fired from his starter job as a lookout at one of King Robbie's traps, but he knew, they all knew, you had to ask permission, pay a commission. Eli even paid over a piece of the small-change tips he made playing guitar on the street or at the Lucky. Cost of doing business, or you paid another price. They took it out of your skin and bones.

"That's the other thing," said Skinny B. "Out there ain't nothing but golf courses and fat houses. Can't be nobody's turf, right?"

"That's police turf," said Anthony. "And a whole lot of white folks."

"Hey, I like white folks," said Coyo. "Get real polite when you point a gun at 'em."

Eli gave Coyo a look.

Coyo gave back a sly smile that told Eli nothing at all.

He was Eli's oldest living friend.

"So we got police," said Skinny. "I dealt with them before."

Anthony raised his bushy eyebrows. "You dodge police

after you take three hundred dollars off that chicken joint last month and now you an expert?"

"I'm saying, police ain't shit. They got rules, only so much they can do. Not like straight-up gangsters. Not like King Robbie."

"So what's the plan?" said Anthony. "Walk in, ask nice, and run? Where we gonna get a car? Or are we taking the bus?"

"I can get guns," said Coyo. "A car, too. No problem."

"Okay," said Skinny, rubbing his hands together. "Now we making progress. Guns for the guards. For the goods, we bring hammers to break the glass on those cases. Reach in, grab what we can, run like hell."

Eli laughed, picturing it. Laughed so hard his fingers stopped moving on the strings.

Skinny looked at him. "What I miss?"

"The four of us walking into the high-tone white folks' mall? Gun in one hand, hammer in the other, wearing white T-shirts and Timberlands and ski masks?" Eli shook his head. "They'll call the police the minute we get out of the car."

Skinny B nodded. "Okay, yeah, that's a problem," he said. "How do you figure it?"

Eli didn't want to think about it. But he couldn't help himself, not now. Even if it was half the money Skinny said it could be, or a quarter, it was still a lot of money. He could eat for months on a thousand dollars, maybe get ahead a little. If he didn't get killed or go to jail.

But it was all just talk.

No way they were going into a jewelry store. No way.

Even though the mathematical part of him knew exactly how they'd do it.

The mathematical part wasn't so much about numbers, not really. It had more to do with the music that filled him, weighing possibilities and balance and proportion, seeing ahead of the present moment.

He could see it now, clear as day.

They were all looking at him.

Eli Bell laid the guitar flat on his lap. "Any of them Cokes left?"

"Do you one better." Anthony fished around in his shirt pocket and held up another blunt. Badly made, the paper barely holding together, but it would do the job.

"We're not doing this," said Eli. "Straight up, I'm saying it now. We're not doing this."

"Sure," said Coyo. "Whatever you say." He tossed Eli a Coke from the box at his feet. Anthony fired up the blunt and passed it over. "But if you were gonna, how would you?"

They stayed up talking late into the night.

Just goofing, that's all.

2

Eli woke on the floor with a start.

Skinny B stood over him, holding out a warm Coke and a paper-wrapped package from Hardee's. "Time to go."

"What?" Eli's head felt like a dandelion gone to seed, all fuzzy and flyaway. He got up on one elbow to make sure his guitar was where he'd left it, the first thing he did every morning. The room had cooled in the night. He had to piss. "Damn, Skinny, I was sleeping."

"Now you're awake. C'mon, eat your biscuit. Time to go."

"Go where?"

Skinny's dumb grin brought last night's conversation back to him.

"No," said Eli, scrambling to his feet. "No way, I told you no."

"We're all set," said Skinny. "I made it up to Hubbard's Hardware in Frayser right when they opened, spent ninety-eight dollars for sledgehammers and work gloves and a big tool bag, just like you said. Anthony's outside kicking the bag around the yard so it don't look brand-new. He also went to that paint store for the other stuff you talked about."

Eli knew about the tools because of Dupree. Dupree was a bass player, a good one, but he also worked on houses, and he was always trying to get Eli to work with him. It was nice to know Eli could get a few days' pay when he was flat broke, but he couldn't get up early every morning after playing music all night, not like Dupree could. Plus scraping paint all day made his hands cramp up. Not to mention it was boring as hell.

Better than jail, though. Eli was not going to jail.

"You go ahead," said Eli. "You got the whole plan anyway. Split it three ways instead of four."

Coyo came in the back door. "Car's down the block. We good for an hour, more or less." He carried a Save-A-Lot grocery bag, the brown paper rolled tight at the top.

The heavy way it swung told Eli what was inside.

"Oh, no," he said. "No, no, no."

Eli had known Coyo since before everything changed. Before Eli's pops went away, before his brother Baldwin got shot in the face, before his mama died with a needle in her arm. Even when Eli went to live with his nana, he'd smuggled Coyo leftovers in a paper napkin, until his nana caught him in the act. Then she fed Coyo at her kitchen table, heaping his plate like he was one of her own.

When she passed from a stroke, neither boy had any place to go but the street. Coyo had never forgotten those meals. He'd looked out for Eli when he could.

Coyo had always been his own man, even at the age of eleven when King Robbie had threatened to beat him with a broom handle to prove a point, or maybe just because he liked it.

Coyo had pulled a gun from his pocket, not a big gun or even a good gun, but he held it firm and calm down at his side. He said, "King, I tell you what. Let's skip the next part and call it even, we both be better off."

Eli had watched King Robbie look at this half-grown wolf with new eyes. Seeing a tool he could use, sure. But never one he could own.

Coyo was unpredictable, half-crazy, impulsive, but he wasn't afraid to step into something. He got things done. And he'd always had Eli's back.

When Eli got fired from the lookout crew, Coyo had told Eli, "You don't got to be that guy. You got your music. You don't got to pick up a gun."

Now Coyo wouldn't look at him.

Anthony pushed in carrying a big red tool bag, newly battered and stained by the dark dirt and pale gravel dust of the driveway. It had a zip-close top, just like Eli had talked about, to hide what it carried. "Time to go. Mall opens in half an hour."

A big smile on his face, happy with the decision made, the course of his life set.

Eli could almost hear him thinking it. Fuck school. Fuck those asshole teachers looking down their noses.

Fuck those shitty little jobs with their shitty little pay and their shitty little bosses talking to you like you're nothing at all. Fuck the endless hustle and grind of finding money, a place to stay, food to fill your belly. Time to get paid and be a man.

The mathematical part of Eli knew there was more to it than that. More than just the wanting, more than hoping finally for something good. Wildness factored into it, the urge to take your life into your own hands. Eli didn't know how it would turn out, none of them did.

He did have a pretty good idea of the odds.

He couldn't help it, where he lived. What he'd seen. What he knew in his bones.

Eli stared Coyo full in the face. His oldest living friend wouldn't look him in the eye.

"You're the man with the plan, Ellison. We need you with us." Coyo was the only one besides Eli's dead brother who'd ever called him Ellison. "We're good to go. We got the car, we got the tools, we got the guns, and the clock is ticking. Your plan, your timeline. Remember?"

"We were just playing," said Eli, his heart thumping. "We weren't gonna *do* anything. How many times did I tell you?"

"About that." Coyo gave Eli a surprisingly gentle smile, although his eyes were still looking anywhere else. "You made a plan too good to pass up," he said. "You want to be hungry the rest of your life? It's time we made a move. Made us some *money*."

Eli shook his head. Set his jaw. "I'm not going," he said. "You gonna shoot me?"

Coyo looked at Skinny. "I told you."

Skinny nodded, then swooped down and picked up Eli's guitar. Cheap and battered but his brother had bought it for him years ago. It was the only thing Eli had left of him. The only thing Eli truly owned.

He felt it like a hunger pang, like a sore tooth, but worse. Like his heart had been yanked from his chest, Skinny's hand on the worn wood neck. Like the neck was his own and he couldn't breathe.

Then he flashed hot and jumped toward the other boy, but Skinny was taller and held the guitar up and away. The strings thrummed discordantly as the body thumped the ceiling, some piece of Eli's soul hanging up there. He bunched his fists.

"Careful now, Skinny." Anthony stepped between them, solid and strong, his meaty fingers wrapped tight around Eli's wrists. "You know we don't want to break it," he said. "We know you love that guitar, and we love when you play it. But right now we need you. Need you with us."

Eli struggled, but he was held in place by Anthony's thick hands, the guitar still out of reach.

Without that guitar, all Eli had were the clothes on his back and a hundred forty-seven dollars stuck in the heat vent. The guitar took him outside of himself, away from the memories of his brother, his mother, his grandmother long passed. It was also his living, how he made what little money he could.

"Come on, Ellison." Coyo shifted the heavy Save-A-Lot bag to his other hand. "Five minutes, in and out. Easy peasy."

Eli looked at him. "You really with these dumb-ass boys?"

Coyo still wasn't meeting his eye. "It's a good plan."

"I've never been to that mall," said Eli. "I was just talking. What the fuck do I know?"

"That's why we need you," said Skinny B. "In case we gotta change up on the fly, like."

"It's okay," said Coyo. "I got your back."

"Is that what this is? You having my back?"

Eli hated how weak he was compared to Anthony. He hated how his voice sounded, the pleading in it. How had he ever thought he could keep himself out of something like this? The mathematical part told him it was just a matter of time before the street life caught up to him. The guitar was too thin and light and fragile to save him.

"Yeah," said Coyo. "It's time for you to step up. Step into your own."

Eli didn't have an answer for that. Coyo knew who Eli's father had been, and his brother too. Eli didn't want to believe that history was in his blood. He wanted to believe he was only the music.

"Think about the money," said Anthony reasonably. "What you might do with a couple thousand dollars. Maybe five thousand. Maybe ten. Maybe more."

There it was.

Hard to argue with that, said the mathematical part. You might not like the odds. But what else you got?

His stomach churned with the thought.

Eli didn't like it. Didn't like anything about it.

But maybe Coyo was right. Maybe it was time to learn how to do this shit. Time to make a living.

He twisted himself out of Anthony's grip.

"All right." He glared at each of them in turn. "But if I get killed doing this, I'm gonna haunt you motherfuckers into your goddamn graves."

3

Coyo had found them an old four-door Buick Skylark, janky as hell with the maroon paint faded and peeling off the hood and roof. The interior smelled like old piss and mouse turds. The first thing they did was roll the windows down as far as they could go.

Eli climbed into the front passenger seat. The engine had something not quite right, a high whine in D minor under the regular noise. "This the best you can do?"

"Don't be complaining 'less you can steal your own car," said Coyo as he pulled away from the curb.

The steering column was broken open where the key was supposed to go. Wires dangled exposed, bare and twisted together.

Eli hadn't even known Coyo could drive.

They stopped behind a boarded-up building and got out of the car as Anthony dug into the tool bag for the white disposable coveralls he'd bought at the paint store. They pulled the coveralls over their clothes, but not all the way. They tied the coverall arms around their waists, like a sweatshirt you took off because you got hot.

And they were hot on the warm spring day, the coveralls made from some paper-plastic material that held in the heat, but that wasn't why they didn't put their arms in the sleeves. Just like stopping here where nobody could see them get dressed, it was part of last night's plan. Eli didn't want anyone in the neighborhood to see four black boys driving around in white painter suits.

Somebody might connect that sight to security-camera footage on the evening news.

Anthony handed out the gloves and the masks and the little paper hats. After they'd put on their gloves, Coyo passed out the guns. "Fingers off the triggers," he said. "You know how they work, right? Any questions?"

Eli examined the rusty little revolver with the tape-wrapped grip. Something you could throw away and not miss, he thought. He looked at the other boys and saw that their guns were no better. Cheap and disposable, none of them shiny. He found the lever to open the thing that held the bullets. Every hole was filled.

His stomach churned. He'd handled guns before, had shot them, too, but it was just for fun. Showing off, making noise.

This was different.

Once they hit the road again they were quiet, feeling the weight of what they were about to do. The only sounds were the engine noise, the discordant notes of the tires on the road, and Skinny B giving directions from the back, watching the map on his phone.

Coyo took the circular ramp to the highway at speed, and the force of the turn pushed them sideways in their seats. The wind battered them through the open windows, the smell of the warming day rich in their noses. Eli looked out at the city flying by from the height of the road. He couldn't remember the last time he'd ridden in a car. Mostly Eli stayed local and walked.

The trip was only twenty minutes but it felt like a different country when they turned the tight loop that dropped them onto Germantown Parkway, a concrete boulevard lined with acres of asphalt parking lots almost empty at that still-early hour. On the far side stood neat buildings of brick and glass, the signs crisp and bright. Green plants in long rows or little islands. This was where the good stores were, Eli thought, for people with money in their pockets. People who could afford more than food and a phone, the bare necessities.

"Over there." Skinny leaned over the seatback, pointing. "By that sign says Macy's. See the door?"

"Not yet." Eli's stomach was not getting better. "Circle around, I want to see all of it."

Coyo looked at him.

"What if there's a damn SWAT team at some donut shop on the far side? We need to see all of it."

Coyo nodded and thumped an elbow into Eli's chest, but not hard. "This why we need you, Ellison."

He stuck to the road instead of cutting across the empty parking lots, all of them very aware of the little unmanned police trailer with its security cameras. Around the wide blank block of the Macy's, then what looked like loading docks with semi-trailers backed up to the building. After Sears and another police trailer, the road looped away and back toward something called Malco with a row of Dumpsters lined up outside.

"What's Malco?" Eli asked.

"It's a movie theatre," said Anthony. "I've been to the one by Overton Square a few times."

Sometimes Eli watched TV at the Lucky, if he got there early or stayed late. Sometimes Saint James let him sleep in a booth if it was cold. He'd never been to the movies.

"Okay," he said. "That's where we're working today. If anybody asks, police or anyone, we're working at the movie theatre. We're late, we're a little lost, we went in the wrong entrance. Got it?"

Murmurs of agreement.

"Say it. Each of you."

They repeated it back to him, one by one.

Past the theatre, a big round glass entrance glittered in the sun. At the far end of the mall, they curved around Dillard's with its arched green entryways. Around JCPenney, then back where they started, on the outer edge of the parking lot.

The pit in Eli's stomach got deeper, like it had a mind of its own, and was not in agreement with the rest of his body.

He couldn't believe he was doing this. But here he was.

"Stop up there," he told Coyo, "while we get ourselves straight."

They already wore the pale latex gloves. They shouldered into the upper part of their coveralls, raised the plastic zippers to their necks. They pulled the white paper painter's hats down over their eyes and set the white dust masks across their faces. Then turned to look at each other in these ghost getups, four different shades of brown skin now almost completely covered with identical white.

"Goddamn," said Skinny B. "We some kind of badass space-age motherfuckers."

Eli just shook his head.

Coyo pulled the car up toward the entrance and left it nose-out in the nearest legal parking spot.

Eli said, "Everybody got the plan?"

"I'm good," said Skinny, bouncing in his seat.

"Me too," said Anthony.

"You know I am," Coyo said.

Eli's stomach roiled and churned, like he'd swallowed a pair of live eels. "Okay," he said. "No, dammit, wait."

He pulled off his dust mask and hat with a single upward shove of his hand, then pushed open the door and leaned out to puke up his greasy Hardee's breakfast. It burned hot in his throat, splashing red and chunky on the pavement. His gut clenched like a fist until he was empty. He spat and ran his tongue across his teeth and wished for water, but he didn't have any.

"Okay," he said. Feeling the jitter in his fingers, a wild energy in his legs. "Okay. Let's go. Five minutes, in and out."

Easy peasy, motherfuckers.

4

They walked through two sets of double doors and down a short hall, looking around them at the bright, shiny space so different from where they lived. Anthony carried the tool bag. They each had their guns tucked into the front pockets of their jeans, which they could reach through slits designed into the coveralls. The mall was lit up and stores were open, but Eli saw only a half-dozen people, none of whom paid them any mind. The place had been open just half an hour.

The escalator pulled them slowly up to the second floor, four boys dressed in white work clothes, Skinny B in the lead, then Anthony, Eli behind him, and Coyo at the back.

The first floor had leafy green plants and benches to break up the wide spaces. The second floor had narrower walkways with clear glass balcony railings. The center was open to below.

At the top, Skinny led them to the right and they gathered against the wall at a blank spot between stores. Anthony opened the tool bag, and Eli, Skinny B, and

Coyo took out the short-handled sledgehammers. Four pounds, said the sticker on the handle.

Suddenly Eli needed the bathroom. Had to take a dump real bad. He tightened up, looked around for a sign.

"Time to move," said Coyo. "Everybody ready?"

Eli wasn't, but when the others nodded, he did, too.

Each boy took out his gun.

Hammer in one hand, gun in the other, except for Anthony, who carried the tool bag.

They stepped off the wall and walked past a shoe store and a perfume store and more shoes. The next place was Crown Jewelry. Two wide glass windows with nothing on display but a big Rolex logo on green velvet, and a wide glass double door without handles in between. Coyo pushed the door, then stuck his fingers in the crack and tried to pull, but it didn't move.

"Goddamn it, Skinny. What the fuck?"

Eli looked down the walkway. A pair of white people walked toward them, gray hair and sneakers and bright collared shirts, carrying white paper coffee cups.

"Shit, they were wide open the other day," said Skinny. "They're supposed to be open right now."

Eli peered at the mechanism and saw that the glass double doors were meant to slide sideways. Probably motors in those little gray boxes.

Through the doors, he saw a big square room with waist-high wood-and-glass display cases on three walls, set up like the counter at the Hardee's, with room behind them for the workers. At the back of the store, a woman stood alone behind a long case.

She was older and elegant in a deep blue shirt with bright pearls standing out against her light brown skin, her straightened hair piled up tall on her head. She held a plastic spray bottle and a cloth. She'd been polishing the glass until she caught sight of the boys.

Now she stared right at Eli, eyes wide.

For a moment Eli hoped they could be done with this. Put the guns back in their pockets and step away. Nobody'd seen their faces, they hadn't done a damn thing.

He looked at the woman through the glass and knew he could make his own choice. Turn and walk, drop the gun and hammer and white suit in the trash on his way out, find his own long wandering path back to the North Memphis empty. Collect what little he had and find another place alone. No matter that he'd said he'd do this, that he'd be leaving his boys here without him. They'd gotten him here by threat, against his own best intentions. He could decide for himself.

Then the mathematical part weighed in.

It wanted to see how the plan played out. If Eli had the family knack.

Not to mention the money. Steady food. Maybe a real place to stay.

So Eli stepped forward, caught Coyo's eye, and said, "Break the door with your hammer. Do it now or this is over."

Coyo looked back at Eli, some live spark passing

between them. Then Coyo nodded once, raised his hammer, and swung it hard. The impact showed in the glass like a spiderweb. He swung again and the cracks spread outward toward the edges. With the third hit, the door fell to the floor in tiny rectangular pieces and Coyo walked through the hole with his gun raised, Skinny B scrambling behind.

"Hands up," Coyo called out. "Stay where you are, don't touch a damn thing. Hands where we can see them. Be smart and you all live through this."

Coyo's voice was powerful and full of authority and Eli could see now what had become of his boyhood friend who had stood up to King Robbie. Maybe all those Coyo stories were true.

Eli was third through the opening, broken glass crackling under his old sneakers, Anthony hard at his heels. Skinny had his gun pointed at a strong-looking light-skinned man behind the right-side displays, shouting, "Don't move, don't move, hands up." In the rear left corner there was an opening to a back room. Eli figured there was somebody back there who'd already hit some alarm or called the cops. Who might come out with a gun.

But that was Coyo's part, and Eli left him to it. Eli went directly to the display cases on the right, found the Rolex watches, and swung his hammer. The thick glass cracked and sagged. He noted eighty shining watches in the case. He swung again and the glass fell in with a thousand glittering musical notes. He moved to the next case and smashed that one, too.

Behind him, Anthony put his gun in his pocket, set the tool bag down, took out a white plastic bag from the Save-A-Lot and fumbled it open. He reached past the shattered glass and began to pull the watches from their snug little nests, dropping them in the bag.

Eli saw a flash of movement and turned to see white-suited Coyo stride through the gap in the display cases toward the back room. Eli looked over his shoulder and saw Skinny B with his gun still pointed at the strong-looking man but watching Anthony harvesting watches. The man wore a dark suit and tie, but his jacket was unbuttoned and his hands were easing down. His face looked more angry than scared.

Eli pointed his gun at the ceiling and pulled the trigger.

It was louder than he expected. He'd never fired a gun inside before. Skinny jumped and swore and turned back to the strong-looking guy, whose color had gone pale, his arms now completely vertical. Anthony didn't even seem to have noticed, focused on his job.

Eli stepped toward the rear of the store, the long display case still between him and the light-brown woman with the pearls, straightened hair, and dark, frightened eyes. She was backed up hard against the wall. "Don't worry," he told her, gun in one hand and hammer in the other. "One more minute and we're gone."

She stared at the strong-looking man with an expression Eli couldn't even begin to decode. So he swung the hammer down and broke open the display case. He needed more hands. He dropped the hammer to the floor, tucked the gun into his armpit, took a white plastic bag from his own pocket and plucked out the chunky diamond rings in their plush boxes two at a time, letting them fall into his sack. He glanced to the side and saw Anthony working the second case of watches. Eli had no idea how long they'd been in there, but it seemed too long already.

"Time to go," he called out, even as his fingers kept picking velvet boxes from the small square shards of glass. "Time to go, time to go, time to go."

"Six more," Anthony said.

"We really leaving all the rest of this?" Skinny looked down into the unbroken display case between him and the young white guy. The signs on the wall behind said TAG HEUER, BREITLING, and DE BEERS.

Eli hadn't even looked into the other cases. That wasn't part of the plan. "Don't get greedy, we're all done here." He cinched up his sack and took the gun from under his armpit. "Police on their way. Time to get gone."

Then Coyo came out of the back room towing a heavyset white man in a gray suit by the knot of his swirly-looking tie. The barrel of Coyo's cheap pistol was jammed into the soft pale flesh of the man's neck. The white face was flushed and he held one crook-fingered hand out from his body like a bird with a broken wing.

"Man had a pistol under his coat," said Coyo, calm in that sometimes way he had, like a firecracker fuse softly burning down toward something loud. "Tried to take it out and shoot me."

"Let him go," said Eli, grabbing at Coyo with his eyes. "Stick to the plan. No harm done. We got what we came for." He turned and whacked Anthony on the shoulder to get him moving, then waved the taped-up revolver at Skinny who was still staring down at the case of watches before him. "Come on, all of you. We're gone." He backed toward the hole where the door used to be.

Coyo pulled the heavy white man close enough to kiss, grinding the rough gun barrel into the man's neck. Blood began to seep through the pale, scraped skin.

Eli felt his feet get slow like he was wading through deep mud, afraid of what would happen next.

Coyo didn't speak. Just stood there, his face up to the white man's. Breathing.

Eli was fully stuck now. Couldn't run, couldn't stop watching Coyo and the white man, waiting to see what his friend might do. How true those stories might be.

Then Coyo shoved the man hard and turned away. Eli's flooding relief felt like a long cool drink on a hot day.

"See, we don't want to hurt nobody," Coyo said to the room at large. "We just want to get paid like everybody else."

Then they were scrambling over the shattered remnants of the door and out into the open mall, and it was all Eli could do not to howl like a wolf seeing the moon for the first time. He looked left down the walkway, but the two gray-haired walkers had vanished. Coyo turned right toward the escalator, and Eli moved to catch up, Anthony close at his heels.

Behind him, Eli heard jangled chords of wrong notes. He looked over his shoulder and saw Skinny B down in the jewelry store's doorway, sprawled on his hands and knees in the spreading rectangles of broken glass. "Wait up." He was scrambling to recover his gun.

"Leave it," Eli called. "Move your ass." He slowed when he saw a figure appear in the doorway at Skinny's back, hands together, arms extended and rising. The older woman in the pearls and straightened hair lifted a bright, shining pistol. Rings glittered on her fingers, her brown face rigid with fury.

Anthony pushed past as Eli stopped in his tracks, mouth open but empty of words. Skinny B found a place for his feet and pushed himself up, red spots showing through the pale latex gloves, but his hands were empty. He didn't look behind him. He took a careful step, then another.

The older woman pulled the trigger three times, *crack crack crack*. Skinny's white coveralls jumped from his chest, splotched red. He stood fixed in place without falling, a surprised look on his face.

The woman blinked. Now she looked surprised, too.

The strong-looking light-skinned man came up in a hurry, slipping sideways to the older woman in the space where the door used to be. He put one arm around her shoulders, his other hand pushing down on the gun.

"Mom," he said. He looked back into the shattered

store, where the heavyset white man stood with his hand to his mouth. "Dad."

Skinny B pitched face-first into the broken glass.

This wasn't part of the plan.

Eli turned and ran.

On the escalator, the mathematical part took the heavy-duty black trash bag from Eli's coverall pocket and snapped it open. He set his white plastic Save-A-Lot sack inside, then held it out for Anthony, who looked stunned but dropped in his own sack of watches. The trash bag was heavy now, and none of it seemed to matter.

Eli looked back but saw nobody there. Coyo was ahead of them walking calmly down the escalator, gun in his hand, looking outward at the broad central hall with its bright skylights and leafy green plants and gleaming floor. A black woman with a double stroller looked over her shoulder as she scurried into a store and vanished. A young black man and a young white woman sat holding hands on a bench, frozen in place, eyes wide. "What the fuck you waiting for?" Coyo called to them. "Get outta here."

They scrambled off the bench and ran away.

Eli gave Anthony a shove and they went down two steps at a time, the ground coming up fast. Coyo stood at the bottom looking the wrong way down the hall, some kind of commotion coming from down there. "Go on, now," he said. "I'm right behind you."

Eli turned the corner at speed and headed for the exit, feet flying, knowing he'd be far faster than thick Anthony, even hauling the big trash bag full of stolen shit.

Behind him, he heard shouting. Then flat echoing cracks, like something breaking. He kept running.

The double doors grew bright with golden sunlight as he neared the end of the hall. He listened for Anthony's footsteps slapping the floor behind him, but he didn't hear them. He didn't let himself slow enough to turn and look. He hit the doors at full speed.

In the space between the doors, Eli forced himself to slow. Fighting the need to sprint, he shouldered the trash bag like one of the bent old men collecting scrap metal, as if it held the weight of the world.

Stepping outside, he made his walk tired and plodding, but still a direct line down the sidewalk toward the access road and the parking lot and the janky old Buick with its windows down. Head down, he tugged the mask to his chin, thumbed the papery hat higher. He looked only ahead, not left, not right, while sirens rose up around him.

Crossing the roadway he heard the roar of an engine. Tires squealed and crunched on the road at his back. Flashing red and blue lights reflected off the car windows ahead of him. He kept walking. He thought he heard somebody bang through the double doors. Anthony, he thought, and Coyo. Coyo had told them to run.

He made it to the car and heard shouting while he stuffed the trash bag through the open back window. He heard the too-familiar flat cracking sounds behind him, again and again. They seemed to go on forever.

He opened the door and saw the wires hanging down from the steering column and realized he didn't know how to start the car.

He didn't even know how to drive.

He got himself behind the wheel and leaned over to peer at the wires. The mathematical part of him took over completely. It examined the thin strands, the colored plastic insulation stripped away, the bare stranded copper crimped and bent. Saw how they might have fit together before. Took the two wires and touched the exposed ends together and felt the engine shudder for a second. He twisted the wires fully together so they'd stay, then pressed the gas pedal the way he'd seen Coyo do.

The engine churned until it was running smooth while Eli's foot learned the feel of the gas. He stripped off the white hat and mask, shouldered out of the paper-plastic suit. The breeze through the open windows began to cool his sweat-soaked skin. He finally allowed himself to look toward the double doors, but the big police trucks blocked his view, lights flashing. No actual police in sight.

He put his foot on the brake the way he'd seen Coyo do, then pulled the lever down until the little line hit the D, like Coyo had done. He put both hands on the wheel, looked both ways, then moved his foot off the brake to let the old car ease out of the parking space and wander down the aisle toward the exit, touching the gas with a feather foot, learning to steer as he went.

He watched the mirrors more than he watched the

way ahead. His heart pounded so loud he was sure the police would hear it and come make him stop.

But nobody took notice of the neglected old car, the skinny black boy driving.

It had not been a good plan, he thought.

Not if he was the only one left alive.

He would not allow himself to cry.

PART 2

FIVE DAYS EARLIER

5

"You're getting restless," June Cassidy said.

She sat with Peter Ash in low backpacking chairs, half-hidden in the high meadow grass that was just coming back from the long mountain winter.

Behind them stood windblown pines and tall tilted rocks fallen long ago from the granite peak to the west. Ahead of them was the waterfall that fell a thousand feet to the teardrop-shaped pocket valley where June had grown up. Beyond that was pure blue sky and the rest of the Cascade range, then the open rolling country of eastern Washington.

"I'm not restless." Peter Ash held her slim, strong hand in his wide, knuckly grip. His dark hair was long and shaggy, like a wolf's winter coat, hiding the slightly pointed tips of his ears. "There's plenty for me to do here."

She waved her hand at the valley below, with its fields and orchards and clusters of buildings. "You've been through every fucking structure on the property," she said. "It only took you three weeks to build the new sleeping porch. Then you upgraded the kitchens in all the cottages, did a gut remodel on half the bathrooms, replaced every piece of rotten trim and cracked siding, and put a new roof on the equipment shed. What the hell is left to do?"

"Rust never sleeps," he said. "Eternal vigilance is the price of freedom."

With her free hand, she gave him the finger. She wore her red hair in a short pixie cut, bringing out the freckles on her cheeks. She had freckles other places, too.

"June, this little valley has fourteen buildings, some of them more than a hundred years old. I haven't even scratched the surface. If I play my cards right, I could have a job for life."

"But you're restless," she said. "Or worse. Bored."

He smiled, squeezed her hand gently, and looked out at the wide blue sky above the mountains. He knew she wouldn't give up until she got an answer. It was one of his favorite things about her, that relentlessness. It made her a very good investigative reporter.

"The pay isn't much," he said. "But the benefits are spectacular."

For most of October, November, and part of December, Peter's leg had been healing after a run-in with a particularly unpleasant asshole.

Aside from the punctured muscle, his thigh bone had broken badly. To repair it, the orthopedic surgeon had driven a titanium rod down the interior length of the femur, from the hip to the knee, then screwed it into place and stapled him up. The screws were temporary, removed with the staples after two weeks, but the rod was permanent.

He'd set off a metal detector for the rest of his life.

The damaged tissue and bone needed another ten weeks to be fully mended, but once the temporary hardware was out, the leg would carry his weight again. The surgeon told Peter not to just park himself in front of the television. Physical activity would help the healing process, limit scar tissue, and improve range of motion.

That wasn't a problem for Peter.

It wasn't in his nature to stop moving.

The day after the screws and staples came out, he found a windfallen limb from one of the big maples that grew behind the black barns. He trimmed it into a good walking stick, and found that he could stump his way around the perimeter of the half-wild little pocket valley, if he took it slow and was careful with the bandages.

It wasn't easy. Slow wasn't in Peter's nature, either.

There was no path to speak of, not at first. It became a path as he walked it, every day, rain or shine. Roughly a seven-mile loop, it was flat and easy at the north edge of the fields, rough and rocky and steep above the orchards to the south.

At first, the walk took him the better part of the day. He had to stop and rest. He packed a lunch.

When he finally made it back to June's little farmhouse, he'd allow himself a pain pill and take a scalding-hot shower, soap sluicing over puckers of scar tissue from

Iraq and Afghanistan. He'd walk to the kitchen, open a beer, and stand steaming in his boxers while he prepped ingredients for supper. His tall, lean body resembled storm-torn branches made into a hard, rough frame. It could carry a heavier load than anyone would think possible.

While he worked, June would come up behind him and wrap her arms around the warm flat planes of his chest and belly, press her cheek against the long muscles of his back.

Sometimes she said, "Guess what I learned this afternoon?" Sometimes she said, "I'm getting closer to those dirty bastards." Sometimes she didn't say anything, just held him tight, and he'd know she'd been digging into a particularly ugly corner of the world. Then he'd turn and she'd grab the waistband of his boxers and tow his battered body to the bedroom.

Together, they made the world go away for a while.

Later, he'd finish supper. Marinated steak tacos, or chicken in mole sauce, or black bean and sweet potato enchiladas. Cinnamon ice cream. June said he must have eaten a Mexican cookbook as a child. He told her his grandmother had grown up in Oaxaca, and his favorite dishes were the ones he'd learned to cook by watching her. His *abuelita* had never used a recipe in her life.

While the weather was still mild, he formed and poured the foundation for the sleeping porch, then laid down sill plates and floor joists. The roof was mostly skylights. The walls were sliding windows that stretched from the tongue-and-groove floor to the pine-paneled ceiling. When everything was open to the wind, it was almost like being outside.

Almost.

His leg had lost strength from the muscle damage, but he hiked the perimeter path faster every week. He was in good shape when he got hurt, so recovery was quicker than it might have been. By the time the snow fell, he was running the path every day. When the snow got deeper, he went out in snowshoes. By May, he ran the seven miles with a forty-pound ruck and a four-foot section of salvaged iron plumbing pipe in his hands. The weight of the pipe was comforting, only slightly heavier than his old M4 carbine. Almost like the old days.

It was easier to sleep inside if he was tired.

Although June didn't always let him sleep much.

June had a lot of energy herself.

Now, in the high meadow, she said, "I know you miss it. Being a dharma bum, out on the road."

"I miss some things," he said. "The scenery changes, for one thing. New people. Plus all those lonely farm-girls, looking for a roll in the hay."

She pivoted in her chair and punched him in the arm. It was a good hit, even from a seated position. She'd really put her shoulder into it. He'd been ready—hell, he'd been asking for it—and still she rocked him sideways in the little backpacking chair. June had gotten stronger over the winter, too.

He rubbed his bicep. "Ow."

"I'm serious."

He nodded. "I know."

"What are you training for, with that backpack and that heavy pipe? You're like a goddamn hamster on a wheel."

She wasn't wrong. And he didn't have the answer she wanted to hear.

He was training to be useful. To be ready for whatever might come.

After seven months in the valley, the longest time he'd spent living in one place since he'd joined the Marines, Peter was more than restless. He was starting to climb the walls.

It was one of the souvenirs from his war, his need to move and work and do. Even sitting in that high meadow, his knee bobbed in time to some internal metronome that never stopped.

He didn't want to screw this up, what he had with June. He'd never had anything like it before, and he couldn't imagine finding anything like it again.

He didn't want to tell her that he was afraid he'd never be ready. That he'd always be tilted toward whatever might happen next, always looking for the next adrenaline hit. Always wanting that dome of open sky above him.

That was his other souvenir, the one that powered his restlessness. It was hard for him to be inside, after the war. His fight-or-flight reflex was on overdrive. He'd done too much house-to-house fighting over there, kicked in too many doors. Lost too many friends.

After mustering out, he'd spent almost two years living

rough in the mountains, coming down every few months for resupply. He could barely manage the grocery store. He couldn't imagine a job. He felt like he'd become allergic to the civilized world.

Post-traumatic claustrophobia, his shrink called it.

Peter called it the white static.

It was the reason for the sleeping porch, so he and June could share a bed that wasn't in a tent.

With hard work, the static was getting better. It was funny, what actually made a difference. Of all things, it was yoga and meditation that helped him learn to turn down that fight-or-flight feedback loop. He'd also found a veterans' group in Hood River. They talked a lot of shit, but they talked about real things, too. About where they'd been, and what they'd done, pride and shame in equal amounts. Helping each other figure out how to move on with their lives.

Peter was still working on that himself.

But he'd learned to cook a meal in June's kitchen without the static sending sparks up his brainstem. He could spend a day setting bathroom tile, or get into a crawl space to fix the antique plumbing, not without the white static, but without the lightning bolts of a full-blown panic attack. The repairs were part of his therapy. They forced him to push past his limits. To practice dealing with the static, to change his relationship to it. More friend than enemy.

He figured it would be with him for the rest of his life, along with everything else from those war years. But he was learning to see it coming, to take steps, to breathe in and out. And also to see its uses, the readiness it gave him.

Still, he'd always rather be outside and in motion.

He and June usually fell asleep tangled up in each other on the new porch, but they rarely woke in the same place. Some nights, even the porch was too much of an enclosure for Peter, and he'd step outside and wrap himself in his sleeping bag in the orchard, warm as toast in a blizzard at ten below. Or the porch was too exposed for June, and she'd migrate to the bedroom, where the wind didn't howl quite so loudly, where the floor wasn't quite so cold.

"June," he began.

"Here's the thing," she said. "I'm afraid you're going to run out of things to fix around here. And you're going to, I don't know, spontaneously combust or some fucking thing." She skewered him with a look. "You need a goddamned hobby."

"I'm sorry." He looked out across the open valley at the rugged terrain beyond. "I'm not very good at this."

"Me neither," she said. "We're experimenting on each other. But I don't want you here because you feel like you have to be. I want you here because you *want* to be."

"I do," he said. "I am."

"No," she said, "you're not. You can't sit still for more than five minutes, and you've always got one eye on the fucking horizon."

He felt the truth like a kick in the stomach. The evidence of his own internal damage, his inability to live a normal life. And another sensation he liked even less, like a cold wind blowing clean through him. A kind of relief.

She pulled her daypack closer and dug inside. "Anyway, I got you something for your birthday."

"My birthday was in March. You already got me something."

She dropped a bulky package into his lap. "Shut up and unwrap it already."

It was an armored vest. A very good one, lightweight with ceramic plates. He looked at her.

She stared across the valley. "I got an email from a friend," she said. "Wanda Wyatt in Memphis. We've worked together on a few things over the years. She's a photojournalist, a conflict photographer. She's worked in Iraq, Africa, Syria, a lot of places. Someone's been harassing her. I thought maybe you could go lend a hand."

Peter felt it already, his heart beating just a little faster. Training wasn't the real thing. Was he that predictable? "You didn't order this vest last night."

"No," she said. "But I knew you'd meet somebody, or someone would call, or some fucking thing would happen, and you'd need to go help. That's how you're built, I get it. But I also know you're too much of a cheap-ass to buy something like this for yourself."

She turned to look him full in the face, eyes bright, freckles spread across her cheeks like a constellation. Something was different there, he thought. Something in her he didn't quite recognize. He knew she was strong, but he hadn't known she was this strong.

"You're throwing me out," he said.

"It's not like that." Her voice was quiet. "I just don't want you to feel like you're stuck here. Think of it as a catch-and-release program. We don't always have to be joined at the hip, right?"

"Well." He looked at her. "Sometimes it's nice to be joined at the hip."

Wide-eyed and innocent, she glanced around at the grassy meadow, fingers pressed demurely to her chest. "What, up here?"

With a wolfish smile, he reached for her. "Come sit on my lap."

"Oh, no," she said. "It's not going to be that easy."

She stood and stripped off her clothes with a few swift, graceful moves.

She wore lacy red underwear that went nicely with her red hair and creamy skin and the spray of freckles across her shoulders and the tops of her breasts.

"You're going to have to catch me first."

She'd always been way ahead of him.

6

In the end he spent four days driving his old green Chevy pickup from Washington State to Tennessee.

He took I-84 through Oregon into Idaho. He didn't like the interstate, but it was the fastest and most reliable way east through the mountains in the spring. He laid out his sleeping bag on a gravel bar beside the Snake River, running cold and fast and high.

He dropped down into Utah, where 84 merged with 80 past Ogden, and he drove partway through Wyoming to spend the night inside an oxbow of the Green River, where a pair of young black bears wandered curiously through his campsite. He got off the interstate at Ogallala the next day, and rode narrower highways east and south through the dry, empty plains of southern Nebraska and northern Kansas into the hotter, greener country of southeast Kansas, then Missouri.

He carried a cooler full of ice and groceries so he could cook himself breakfast and dinner on his little backpacking stove. His midday meal was a peanut butter and apple sandwich, washed down with lukewarm leftover coffee, except for once in a dusty little town in Nebraska, when he stopped at a nameless gas station with old farm trucks and a pair of bug-spattered state police cruisers angle-parked outside. When he went in to pay for his fuel, he couldn't resist a jumbo hot dog with everything.

June had bought him a new phone—he couldn't seem to hang on to them—and had asked him to text her pictures of his campsites along the way, which he did. Twice he called her while he was driving, but his old truck was too loud for phone conversation, and once he got off the interstate, the cell towers were too far apart and kept dropping his calls.

She'd had it all figured out, Peter's trip to Memphis. But he worried that he'd agreed too quickly. After three days alone in the truck, he thought about it a lot.

That third evening, he drove until long after dark, feeling his connection with June growing thinner with each passing mile. He slept with his truck pulled to the side of a gravel road, his hammock hung between his window frame and the limb of a tree, to be woken at first light by a policeman of some unknown jurisdiction telling him there warn't no camping allowed nor vagrancy tolerated and if he didn't get himself gone in ten minutes, he'd find himself in front of a judge.

He got himself gone, and angled south and east through Missouri, where the land rumbled up into the Ozarks, until he dropped down into flat green fields with long lines of trees for windbreaks and he knew he was nearing the Mississippi. He saw the wide, muddy river for

the first time at Hayti, crossed into Tennessee after Ca-
ruthersville, then worked his way south through Dyers-
burg and Ripley and Covington until it was clear he was
in the suburban sprawl around Memphis.

Wanda Wyatt lived in an old brick house on a residential
street off of Ayers in North Memphis. Her block was
crowded with tall trees and shrubs, and lush, semi-wild
gardens. Invasive kudzu vines smothered fences and
sheds, climbed trees and garages. Some of the lots were
empty, with cracked steps and driveways showing where
homes had once stood. The remaining houses had seen
better days, especially Wanda's.

The back end of a dump truck was visible in her
front yard.

The rest of the truck was jammed into her living room.

Her street was clogged with the curious. Cars slowed
as they drove by, or stopped so the drivers could get out
and get a closer look. Several had their phones out to document the disaster, the ruined house and the deeply rutted
tire tracks in the yard. The crash seemed recent. Getting
out of his truck, Peter could still smell the brick dust.

A police cruiser sat flashing at the curb, with a young
officer moving the traffic along. Yellow police tape reading DO NOT CROSS ran from the neighbor's fence, around
the massive rear bumper of the truck, to the side gate.

Wanda Wyatt was a tall, angular woman, and she
stood in the shadow of the dump bed with her back to
the building and a big long-lensed camera hanging

negligently from her fingertips like some sort of permanent prosthetic device. As each car rolled by, she'd raise
the camera as if somehow surprised to find it in her hand,
but Peter could see her index finger twitch, taking shot
after shot. Without anyone else noticing, she captured
each passing car and each person who got out to look.

Then she was taking a photo of Peter as he strode up
her gravel driveway.

"Hi, I'm Peter," he said. "June Cassidy's friend?"

She lowered the camera and looked him up and down.
She saw a man who looked like Picasso's drawing of Don
Quixote, tall and rangy and durable, but without the
horse. Later Peter would understand that she was com-
paring him to the picture June had sent, held in her head
along with many others. Like a lot of professional pho-
tographers, she had a kind of permanent mental file of
images, some kept on purpose, some she couldn't erase.

"Huh," she said. Her pupils were huge, and he could
see her pulse in a vein at her temple. "I wasn't expecting
you. But your timing is excellent."

She shifted the camera into her left hand and put out
her right for him to shake. Her fingers were long and
slender and surprisingly strong. She angled her head at
the dump truck that had crashed into her house. "As you
can see," she said dryly, "things have gotten interesting."

If she was concerned or afraid, it didn't show.

As though the wreck of her home were an everyday
occurrence.

She wore an electric blue T-shirt, vivid against her
dark brown skin, and loose khaki cargo pants that

exposed architectural ankles. Her dark eyes were enormous and slightly offset, her mouth wide in her narrow face. Short dreadlocks stuck out from her head like a hundred seeking antennae, each tuned to a slightly different frequency.

In high school, Peter thought, the popular crowd probably would have said she looked weird. Definitely not pretty.

At thirty-nine, Wanda Wyatt was striking. More than that, she had a kind of shine to her, a radiance. Maybe it was a byproduct of fifteen years as a conflict photographer, working freelance for newspapers and magazines in war zones around the world. Maybe it was what had allowed her to do that work in the first place.

Maybe it was because she was high as a kite.

June had worked with Wanda on several stories for Public Investigations, a nonprofit group of investigative reporters, so they certainly had a lot in common. But it was obvious why they had become friends. The heat of their fire came from the same internal combustion engine.

"When did this happen?" Peter tipped his chin toward her house.

"About four o'clock this morning," she said. "My room is upstairs, in the back. I woke up when my bedframe banged against the wall." She gave Peter an odd smile. "My first thought was a car bomb, until I was awake enough to remember I was back home in Memphis." She shook her head. "Anyway, I threw on some clothes, ran downstairs, and found a dump truck in my workroom." The smile came back. "I got some nice images before I called 911."

"What happened to the driver?"

"I have no idea. I never saw anyone. But it's got to be connected to the earlier stuff."

The harassment had started after Wanda had bought the building as a foreclosure. She'd paid cash at auction, beating out another bidder, but she'd still gotten it for next to nothing because it needed a lot of work. North Memphis had more than a few foreclosures to choose from.

Not long after she took ownership, though, she'd gotten a series of anonymous emails, the sender increasingly angry about a long photo essay documenting civilian deaths by U.S. drone strikes in multiple war zones.

The last email called her a "black bitch traitor who hates America." The sender had attached a video of a burning cross.

"I'd thought it would turn out to be footage someone had found online, but I couldn't find anything that matched." The odd smile again. "I think they burned that cross just for me."

A week later, someone had thrown a rock through her front window. The note wrapped around it had read, "Memphis doesn't want you. Leave town before you end up hanging from a tree."

Wanda had reached out to June, looking for ideas about how to figure out who was responsible. "I've gotten letters before," she said. "I thought it was just a crank. Any idiot can send hate mail and throw rocks, right? Until this." She gestured at the dump truck.

"All because of some photographs?"

"Maybe they don't need a reason," she said. "I'm black, I'm gay, and I'm a journalist, although not necessarily in that order. Any one of those would be enough to light some dipshit's fuse."

"This is Memphis," Peter said. "Half the city is black."

"More like two-thirds of the city proper," she said. "But the outlying areas are mostly white. The police think the whole thing is racially motivated, what with the burning cross and all. They weren't paying much attention before, but they are now. The detective in charge of my case is supposed to call me in the morning."

"Well, I'm sorry for your troubles," Peter said.

"Not your fault," said Wanda. "Unless you're the one who drove that dump truck."

"No." Peter smiled. "But I'm happy to be of use. I can certainly look at the building, see what kind of damage was done, get started on putting things back together."

"The fire department doesn't want me back in the house until a structural engineer comes to evaluate. They turned off the gas, power, and water so it doesn't, you know, explode or whatever. The engineer is coming tomorrow."

"Did you call your insurance person?"

The pulse in her temple ticked faster. "That's a problem," she said. "I just moved in last month, and I hadn't gotten around to getting insurance. So there won't be much money unless the company that owns the dump truck is willing to help."

"Actually, that makes things easier," said Peter. "Your

insurance company would have all these rules and requirements. I'm not licensed as a contractor in Tennessee—I'm not licensed anywhere, actually—so it would be hard to get them to reimburse you for repairs anyway. This way we just get it done."

"But how will you get reimbursed?"

"Don't worry about it," he said. "I'll work it out."

"I can't pay you," she said. "And you're not working for free."

Peter thought of the particular type of asshole who would email a video of a burning cross, and he smiled happily.

"Oh, someone'll pay," he said. "We just have to find him."

She regarded him with a curious stillness, although her short dreadlocks kept quivering on her head. "Why are you here, exactly?"

"To help," Peter said. Not exactly a complete answer. "Do you have any family or friends to put you up? Or should we find you a hotel?"

"I'll sleep in my own house," she said. "I've spent the night in worse places. Besides, if it were going to collapse, don't you think it would have already?"

7

Gray clouds roiled across the sky, and the air was thick with humidity. Rain was coming.

Peter walked out to the young officer directing traffic past the accident. He was short and round, probably pushing the edge of the department's height and weight requirements, but he stood in the road like he owned it. He pointed at an old blue SUV, then pinwheeled his forearm to point down the road. The SUV didn't move. The cop forked his fingers at the SUV, then swung his arm around again, this time more emphatically. When the SUV rolled on, the cop turned to Peter. He looked like he was barely old enough to vote, but he already had those indifferent, matter-of-fact policeman's eyes.

"You're the guy in the green pickup," he said. "What do you need?"

"My name's Peter, and I'll be doing repair work on the house. I wanted to say thanks for being here."

"Just doing my job," said the cop. His name tag said R. MCCARTER. He waved a brown Volkswagen past, then glanced over his shoulder at the back end of the dump truck. "Hope you know what you're doing."

"Me too," said Peter. "Will there be someone on duty tonight?"

The cop shook his head. "I'm only here because this is a possible hate crime, and it's a slow day," he said. "We're short on cars and cops and overtime money. So no, there will be no police presence after shift change. I might end up leaving early, if somebody somewhere else does something stupid, which they probably will."

"Okay," said Peter. "Good to know. Thanks."

He went to his truck, pulled his Little Giant ladder from the cargo box, and unfolded it to walk up Wanda's roof. He wanted to make sure the house would stay dry when the rain started.

Most of the structure was surprisingly solid for a house that old, and the shingles were new, probably replaced by the bank that had foreclosed on the property. There was just the minor detail of the dump truck occupying the living room, and the front of the building collapsing in on itself.

Back on the ground, he stepped back to examine Wanda's house from the street. It was two stories, long and skinny with a steep roof and narrow overhangs. Some would call it farmhouse-style, which to Peter meant the kind of simplicity of form that could be drawn by any child with a crayon, and built by any capable carpenter. Houses like it dotted the countryside over most of America, although this one had slightly strange proportions. Built longer ago than most.

The outside was red brick, the masonry corners softened with age. A series of additions had been put onto the back, the house growing over the years.

It was definitely an old house. How old, Peter couldn't say.

He left Wanda on the porch with her camera and followed his phone to a hardware store called Hubbard's, on the other side of the freeway, where he bought a blue plastic tarp and a hundred feet of rope. By the time he made it back, the young cop was gone and Wanda was nowhere to be found.

Peter unfolded the big blue tarp and tacked one side under the eaves of the house to keep water from coming through the hole where the wall used to be. As he tied the tarp taut over the back of the dump body, he heard the low echoing rumble of distant thunder.

The house's main entrance was on the side, protected by a wood-framed porch, but the door was stuck in its warped frame. A possible sign that the dump truck had shifted the structure, or else just a sign that the house was old. Peter walked down the steps and around a windowed bump-out toward the back, where another side porch sheltered a second entrance. This door opened easily enough.

He stepped into a big room last renovated sometime in the 1950s, judging by the wide pine paneling. The white static flared, but not enough to keep him outside. Not yet.

The ceiling was water-stained and flaking where the roof or bathroom had leaked upstairs, but it hadn't stopped Wanda from moving in.

A long couch and two overstuffed chairs, none of them new, flanked a wide wooden coffee table cluttered with photo magazines and mugs and empty beer bottles. In the center stood a large ceramic bowl with a chipped rim, filled with plastic pill bottles. To his right was the kitchen, a simple L-shaped run of cabinets with what looked like a thrift-store dining table standing in for an island. Someone had screwed diagonal braces along the table legs to steady it.

"I'm not what you'd call domestic," said Wanda, behind him.

Peter smiled. "Me neither. How you live is your business. I'm only looking at the structure." He turned toward the front of the house, walking into a sunny dining room that was probably the original kitchen, before the additions. In the center of the room stood a big worktable made of a pair of unfinished slab doors set side by side on plastic sawhorses, covered with a neat grid of glossy 9-by-12 photo prints. Cheap clamp lights hung down from a board screwed to the ceiling, low-budget but effective lighting, at least when the power was on. There was no chair.

"Was the floor always sloped like this?"

"I think so," said Wanda. "I only moved in a month ago. I've been working nonstop getting ready for a gallery show."

Looking more closely, Peter saw that the window

glass was thick and wavy, distorting the view outside, from a time before modern factory-made glass. There were no broken panes. The winding stairs to the second floor, an intricate puzzle of interlocking pieces, hadn't shifted since their last coat of paint sometime in the Eisenhower era. Any settlement here had probably happened long ago.

The front room was another matter entirely.

For one thing, it was full of dump truck.

The front of the big Kenworth cab had dropped through the floor into a shallow crawl space, wearing the broken rectangular frames of the front windows across its grille like a horse with a wreath of flowers after winning a race. The truck's windshield was cracked but still in place. The top of the heavy-duty dump body had taken out the ceiling joists overhead for a good eight feet.

At the edges of the room, the floor tipped steeply toward the truck. Wanda's worktables and lamps and other office debris had fallen inward around it. Under the truck, the floor structure had collapsed entirely. Broken bricks had collected at the low spots around the front wheels and nose. He noticed that the wall plaster was troweled directly over the brick. This house was *old*.

"Is there a way to get into the crawl space?"

Wanda didn't answer. He turned to see her standing in the doorway, one hand holding the camera to her eye, the other controlling the focus of the lens.

"Wanda?"

"What? Oh, sorry." She edged sideways into the room, her shoes finding purchase on the popped edges of the pine planks, camera still up, her finger still twitching on the shutter. "Is it okay if I shoot you?"

For a fraction of a second, Peter didn't understand the question. He was used to a different context for "shoot."

He didn't want her to take his picture. He hadn't liked it in Iraq, either, strangers documenting him and his men doing a difficult job in impossible conditions, trying to catch them in moments of weakness or failure.

But he figured that the camera was what she could control, her way to make order out of this chaos.

"Fire at will." He stepped past her to look for the entrance to the crawl space.

He found it at the back of the house, a metal hatch with uneven brick steps down into what was once probably considered a storage cellar for home-canned fruit and vegetables.

As he went down the stairs, the white static crackled up his brainstem. Hello, old friend. He reminded himself to breathe deeply, in and out.

The bare bulb didn't light up when he pulled the chain. He remembered that the fire department had turned her power off. He took a small flashlight from his pocket and hit the switch.

The cellar was small, barely ten feet square. The walls were the same old brick as the house, with warped wooden shelves standing empty along the sides. The floor was hard-packed dirt. The ceiling was low enough that Peter had to bend in order not to hit his head. Cobweb sheets opaque with dust hung down like ghostly shrouds.

Nobody had been down here for a long time.

Where the cellar ended, the crawl space began, dirt-floored and dark, smelling of mold and rot. He wouldn't be crawling inside, there wasn't enough space, not even for a combat crawl. No, this would be more like a squirm, flat on his belly, with just his forearms and toes to propel himself forward. He felt the static turn to sparks in the back of his head. He thought of the time he'd gone under a broken-down front porch to remove a large, unfriendly dog.

That little adventure had turned out well enough, he reminded himself. The worst he would find down here was a possum or raccoon, maybe a snake or two. Unless the dump truck decided to fall into the hole while he was inside.

But it didn't matter, not really.

If he was going to put Wanda's house back together, he had to know what he was dealing with.

What, you want to live forever?

He went back to his truck to get the blue mechanic's coveralls he kept for dirty jobs.

Working his way back into that crawl space was like moving back in time. The wood framing overhead changed from 2-by-8 floor joists to rough-sawn lumber to barely squared logs. The center beam went from a rectangular timber to an unpeeled tree trunk, its midsection resting not on a brick pier but on a massive stump with gnarled roots still deep in the dirt. His light showed him the ax marks left long ago.

At the near side of the stump, he found a lumpy section of bricks laid down as a kind of rough floor. Dirt-colored uneven shapes, bricks that had come badly from the molds and were probably just thrown down to keep the mud from swallowing boots during rainy-season construction. Peter smiled at the old-school frugality of it, finding a new use for something otherwise without purpose.

On the far side of the stump, daylight shone through and everything was shattered. The log beam was snapped like a toothpick, the framing overhead turned to splinters. The front bumper of the dump truck had plowed up the dirt, but it hadn't budged that ancient stump from the Tennessee soil.

He saw a flash of light behind him and he knew Wanda was taking pictures of his boot soles.

He turned himself around and made his way out again.

"I ordered a pizza," she said. "I thought you might be hungry."

"Sounds great." Peter was definitely hungry, but he was also thirsty. Her fridge had been without power since early that morning. If she had anything to drink, it would probably be warm.

As if she could read his mind, Wanda said, "I got cold beer, too. On ice."

Peter smiled. "June told me we'd get along."

. . .

After he changed out of his dirty coveralls and washed himself with the neighbor's hose, they sat on the porch steps, ate pizza from the box, and drank Ghost River Gold while Wanda shot the cars driving by.

"I knew an Army major once," Peter said. "After a car bomb or suicide attack, he'd take pictures of the people standing around the blast area. He said some bomb makers like to see the aftermath. Sometimes for pure pleasure, sometimes as a kind of quality control, to inspect the damage and make a better bomb next time. Maybe this guy has the same impulse."

"Maybe I knew the same major," she said. "I was on-site after a market bombing, and he asked me to send him the crowd photos. Since then, it's become a habit. I caught a lot of license plates and faces today."

Wanda was looking a little ragged around the edges. Even her dreadlocks seemed to droop. She'd had five beers, not much pizza, and she'd been awake since the middle of the night.

"How are you holding up?"

"Aside from the fact that we're out of beer?" She raised the heavy camera and waggled it at the end of her wrist. "Long as I have this, I'm fine." She stood, a little unsteady on her feet. "Yeah, I should get to bed," she said. "You're welcome to crash on the couch, but you better pull your pickup around back first." She laughed. "Even before the dump truck, this wasn't a great neighborhood."

Peter got up, too. "I think I'll stay out here. You know, just in case."

She raised her eyebrows. "You're standing watch?"

He was reminded again that she'd been embedded in war zones. Standing watch wasn't a particularly civilian concept. He shrugged. "I don't sleep very well inside."

"Suit yourself." She looked him full in the face for a moment. Then her long arm reached out unexpectedly and roped him into a hug. Just as abruptly, she released him. She smelled of plaster dust, overripe sweat, and stale beer.

"June was right," she said. "I told her I didn't want a big dumb guy here, some bubba I don't even know getting in my way, telling me what to do. She said you weren't like that."

"Give me time." Peter smiled. "I'm dumber than I look."

"Mm," said Wanda. "I don't think so." She wobbled down the path to the door that still opened, and went inside.

Peter backed his truck to the far end of the gravel drive beside her boxy blue Toyota Land Cruiser. She had a small garage, but the green kudzu vines had overgrown it and started pulling it over. No shortage of projects here, he thought.

He dug his phone out of his glove box. June answered on the second ring.

"Hey there, handsome."

"I'm pretty sure you lied to me, a few days ago."

"Who, me?" He could hear the smile in her voice.

"Wanda Wyatt didn't really ask for help, did she?"

"No," June said. "She never would. She's a lot like you that way. But she needs it, right?"

"Oh, definitely," said Peter. "More ways than one. Did you talk to her today?"

"No. Why?"

"Someone drove a dump truck into the front of her house this morning."

"Shit." He heard her fingers flying across the keyboard and knew she was online, searching. June was never far from her laptop. "Is Wanda okay? Did they get the guy? What about her house?"

"Wanda didn't get hurt. The driver vanished. Wanda says the cops don't know anything yet. I got a tarp on the house to keep the rain out, and an engineer's coming to take a look tomorrow. But she's wound pretty tight."

"That's Wanda," said June. "Boy, it's a good thing you left when you did, isn't it?"

He grinned at the night. "Nobody likes a know-it-all."

"Someone does," she said. "I was totally right, by the way. You do need a goddamn hobby."

When they were done talking, Peter found his ground cloth and sleeping bag and rolled under the back end of the dump truck. The rear axle was two feet above his nose, but he could see out on three sides.

It reminded him of the night he'd slept under a burned-out Iraqi tank during a long patrol along the Tigris.

The same soft humidity, the same lush green landscape. The same knowledge that someone out there wanted to do harm to a person under his care.

He slept with part of his mind half awake and tuned in to his environment.

The rest of him slept better than he had in months.

8

Peter woke early to find Wanda lying full-length on the wet grass, the camera blocking her face as she took Peter's picture under the dump truck.

"I don't think I'm ready for my close-up," he said. "At least not first thing,"

"It's not about you. It's that long morning light."

"Did you sleep at all?"

"Sleep is for the weak." She pushed herself up on long arms and stood. Now all he could see were her runner's calves and unlaced red Chuck Taylor high-tops. "I turned the utilities back on. There's coffee if you want some."

"Wait," he said. "Do you smell gas? Are there any pipes leaking? Did any circuit breakers pop?"

"It's fine." Her shoes walked away. "Don't be such a worrywart."

Inside the house, in the bright light of morning, the mess had a different quality. The chemical smell of the wrecked truck had faded, and now he could smell something else, the faint stink of rot. Maybe it was the garbage can left unemptied for too long, or the dirty pans on the stove turning interesting colors. He felt the static rise. Something else was wrong here.

Wanda was in the workroom, her back to the mess. She waved a hand at the kitchen. "Mugs," she called out. "Coffee. Help yourself. Food in the fridge."

The coffee poured like black paint. He opened the fridge and found moldy bread, milk gone chunky, packaged hamburger turned gray. Nothing had been edible in there for a week at least.

He walked into the workroom, carrying the horrible coffee. "You must be pretty stressed out about all this," he said. "Is there anyone I can call for you? Any family or friends? Or maybe we could just go to breakfast, get out of the house."

She stood staring down at the crisp grid of 9-by-12 photographs on the worktable made of doors and sawhorses, her own mug of coffee held tight against her chest. He realized that she wore the same clothes she'd had on the day before. He wondered if she'd slept in them.

"I'm trying to narrow down the images for my show," she said. "These are just placeholders. The real prints will be much larger. But I'm having trouble choosing." She handed him a fat stack of photographs. "See if there's anything in there you like."

The images were striking, and brought the war sharply back to him. The first pictures were obviously taken during active combat, armed men with rifles up and fear in their eyes. Some of the men wore U.S. uniforms, others wore dress shirts or knockoff T-shirts over dirty pants and sneakers. A few more in turbans and *shalwar kameez*.

"You were with the insurgents, too?"

"I was with everyone," she said. "I wanted to capture the war. To show its cost to all sides."

The next photos were of the wounded. Again, some were Americans with blood on their BDUs, some were civilians in primitive hospitals. As he flipped through, he realized that the later pictures included the dead. Fighters from all sides, but also women and children.

"How long were you there?"

"Ten years, on and off. Twelve embeds, each anywhere from a week to a month. Seven of those in combat."

He shook his head. "You're crazy."

"You were there, too," she pointed out.

"I signed up," he admitted. "I wanted to do some good. Now I just try not to remind myself of it every day."

"Well, that's my job," she said. "To bear witness for everyone else. To remind people of what happens when we go to war. It's not pleasant."

"No," he said. "It's not. Nothing else quite like it."

"Yeah, that's fucked up, right?" She shook her head. "You'd think after the first time I got shot at, or my hotel got shelled, or I saw the aftermath of a drone attack or market bombing, I'd never sign up again. When actually, that's the reason I kept going back."

Peter knew exactly what she meant.

The sun never shone so brightly as when somebody was trying to kill you.

The next group of photos showed more ruined buildings, more wounded men and women, more lifeless bodies sprawled in the dirt. But the buildings were small Cape Cods or bungalows. The men and women were mostly black, wearing Levi's or sundresses or sports jerseys or plain white T-shirts. Wanda hadn't taken these in Iraq or Afghanistan.

"That's my new project," she said. "Memphis. A different kind of war zone, but the job is the same. Document the waste and dignify the dead."

"You ever think about shooting landscapes?" he asked. "Maybe flowers? Or butterflies?"

"You sound like my last girlfriend," she said sourly. "Wanted me to do celebrity weddings. I do have some portraits, but those won't be in this show. I have to get this done first."

"When I got here, you said something about talking with the police today?"

"Right." She bent to a laptop on the corner of the worktable, and plucked a small USB drive from its socket. "I already downloaded all my images from yesterday and isolated all the faces and license plates."

"Really, did you get any sleep last night?"

Wanda waved a hand dismissively. "Who needs sleep?"

He looked at her, at the dark suitcases she was carrying under her eyes, at the forward lean like she was walking into a high wind. "Maybe you?"

She drained her coffee mug. "I'll sleep when I'm dead." Then pulled a small black notebook from her front pocket and riffled the pages until she found a business card, which she handed to him. DETECTIVE JAMES GANTRY, MEMPHIS POLICE, DETECTIVE 2ND GRADE.

"He said he'd call, he wanted to stop by this morning." Wanda glanced at her phone, then back to the prints laid out on the worktable. "The thing is, I really need to finish getting ready for this show."

"You need to meet with the police, Wanda. This is a big deal."

"It's an inconvenience. I don't have the time." Her face distorted with the words, and her narrow shoulders rose as if the pain was physical. She clenched her phone tightly in her long fingers. She was practically vibrating in place. "What I need to do is work."

Peter glanced from the smashed front of the house to the clean, ordered worktable with its neat grid of photographs, then to the back of the house with its clutter and mess, the tangled blanket on the couch, the dishes piled in the sink.

Suddenly claustrophobic, Peter felt the white static rising up like a signal flare.

There was definitely something else going on with Wanda Wyatt, he thought.

Something worse than a dump truck in her living room.

"Okay." He pointed at the cell phone clutched in her fist. "They'll call you on this, right?" He reached out slowly, gently, and tugged on the phone. "Let me help, okay? I'll take care of it."

She opened her hand without taking her eyes from the

vivid images of beautiful carnage laid out on the table. "Take it," she said. "Whatever."

Outside, the warm, clean smell of last night's rain on dirt and grass and pavement poured through him like some kind of medicine.

9

Before he did anything else, Peter arranged for the delivery of a heavy-duty thirty-yard Dumpster in Wanda's front yard, and scheduled a lumber drop for later that afternoon. He was going to need to reinforce the frame of her house if they were going to get that dump truck out of there. Right now, it was the only thing holding up the building.

Next, he used Wanda's phone to call the Memphis detective, but got sent to voice mail. The message was barely audible, as if it was recorded on speakerphone while driving on the freeway with the window down.

Peter gave his name, then said, "Wanda Wyatt asked me to call you for a progress report. She's working today and won't answer her phone, so best to call me directly."

He left his cell number, then went to unlock the cargo box on the back of his truck. He hadn't been able to manage more than a single sip of Wanda's paint-smelling coffee, so he parked himself on her porch, unpacked his little one-burner backpacking stove, and fired up the old-fashioned espresso pot June had given him for his birthday.

While he waited for the little pot to do its magic trick, he put a spoonful of brown sugar and a splash of cream into his fancy double-walled featherweight titanium cup—another gift from June, Peter's camp kitchen getting pretty upscale these days—then diced up onions, red pepper, and cured sausage and threw it all into his little Teflon saucepan with a slab of butter. When the espresso was done, he poured it into his mug, gave it a stir, then set the saucepan on the flame to cook.

He'd already used his last eggs on the drive east, but still had some leftover cooked rice, so he dumped that into the pan to soak up the butter and oil from the sausage. He was almost out of groceries. While he was crumbling the last of the cotija cheese on top to glue it all together, Wanda's phone rang.

Peter turned off the stove and picked up the phone. "Wanda Wyatt's office."

"This is Detective Gantry of the Memphis Police." With a crisp cell connection, Gantry sounded like the older, Vegas-era Elvis, the same resonant, Mid-Southern voice, each word sliding into the next. Peter pictured a black velvet pompadour. "Is Ms. Wyatt there?"

"She's not available. This is her assistant, Peter." True enough for the moment. "I left you a message earlier. She asked me to talk with you."

"Please tell Ms. Wyatt I can't make it this morning. Something's come up."

Peter could hear a cascade of sirens in the background.

"Sounds like you're busy. But this thing has gone from simple harassment to major property damage, and I'm concerned about what might happen next. Please tell me you've made some progress."

"Well, we've eliminated a few things," Gantry said. "Things" sounded like *thangs*. "The dump truck came from a black-owned excavation company. It's not a huge outfit, we've talked to all but two of their people. One is in intensive care after getting the crap kicked out of him outside a bar in Orange Mound, the other is in North Carolina picking up his daughter from Wake Forest. The office was broken into and the keys were taken from a locked cabinet. I'm confident the truck was stolen out of their yard and nobody there was involved."

"What about the computer stuff, the email threats and the video?"

"No luck there, either. The guy used a free email account to send the burning-cross video. There were no identifiers on the image or the camera used. The electronic trail ends at an Internet café outside of Oxford, Mississippi. The store manager says they don't have cameras and they don't require ID from people who pay cash. There's no way this guy would use his own credit card to pay for computer time, but the store manager won't even release those names without a court order. We don't have jurisdiction there, and it's not a priority for the locals. So, another roadblock. Maybe that's intentional, too."

"Okay, he's not sophisticated enough to hide behind an Eastern European firewall, but he's not stupid, either," said Peter. "Does it bother you that figuring out how to send an anonymous email and stealing a dump truck are fairly different skill sets?"

"It does, actually." The detective paused, recalibrating. "Tell me who you are again?"

"I'm a friend, trying to help. You know Wanda's house was bought at auction, right? And that she just moved in? Did you talk to the former owner?"

"Golly, thanks for the tip," Gantry said dryly. "Tip" sounded like *teeyup*. "Today's my first day on the job."

"I thought you sounded new," said Peter. Then, "Sorry. I'm worried about Wanda."

"I get you. I'm worried, too. But you really think the guy who lost his house is pissed enough to wreck it trying to kill the new owner?"

"Shit, I don't know. It's the only actual idea I had."

The sound of pages turning. "The previous owner's name is Vinson Charles, he goes by Vinny. A year ago, he was in a car accident. According to the Shelby County Sheriff's Office, he was going something like ninety miles an hour on I-55, lost control, and hit a concrete bridge abutment. According to Vinny, the Devil ran him off the road, trying to kill him." More pages turning. "Vinny was fairly stoned, I gather. Either way, he's lucky to be alive. The investigating officer found enough drugs stashed inside that car—heroin, methamphetamine, and ten kinds of pills—to get the State of Tennessee high for a month. After the hospital, he went to Henning for eight to thirty, and he's still there. So it's probably not him."

"Could he have arranged this from prison?"

"A year later?" Peter could practically hear Gantry roll

his eyes. "Son, you watch too much of that teevee. Vinny Charles is nobody, just a mule moving weight like a hundred others. He had no fancy lawyer, just a Shelby County public defender who pled him guilty. Anyway, along with the sentence came a hefty fine, and to pay it, the State of Tennessee took his house and sold it. He'd inherited the place from his uncle, so he owned it free and clear. The woman who oversaw the sale told me that house was no prize."

"So you've eliminated a few things," Peter said. "You find anything leading you forward?"

"A whole lotta nothin' goin' on," said Gantry, sounding more like Elvis than ever. "Now I got a question. By any chance, are you licensed to carry a firearm?"

"Not in this state," Peter said. "I haven't owned a gun for years." Although, somehow, he kept finding one in his hand, again and again. He was thinking of finding one now. "Why do you ask?"

"Usually in these neighborhoods, violence starts as some kind of personal beef. One guy throws a punch, the other guy pulls a knife, or does a drive-by later. A lot of wannabe gangster stuff. Mostly young men killing each other over territory, or pride, or ambition, or fear. Most of these kids think they got no other options, and most of them don't."

He cleared his throat. "But this thing with Ms. Wyatt, it's different. And like you said, it's escalating. So you need to watch your back, and find Ms. Wyatt someplace else to stay. Because whoever has it in for her, and whatever they want? They're not going away until they get it."

10

Peter went looking for Wanda. He found her on the couch, sprawled out like a corpse, limbs loose, the blanket kicked off onto the floor. He figured her sleeping was a positive development, although the open bottle of Tito's vodka on the coffee table was not. They'd talk about getting her out of that house when she woke up. He left her phone in the kitchen with the ringer off.

The white static was starting to crackle and spark, even though he was back outside. Like a kind of radar, the static had its uses. It reminded him to keep one eye on his surroundings.

He started his truck and sat behind the wheel with the door open and the motor running while he punched in a phone number from memory.

"Jarhead." The answering voice was like motor oil, slippery and dark and latent with combustion. "June told me you were on the loose again. How's that leg holding up?"

"Good as new," Peter said. "How's married life? Dinah and the boys?"

"Nothin' but trouble. Damn kids." That wide, tilted smile coming through with every word. "Where're you at and what you need?"

"I'm in Memphis, and I need a gun."

"Never been to Memphis," Lewis said. "Love that Memphis sound, though."

"What, you don't know a guy?"

Lewis always knew a guy. Usually more than one.

He was a career criminal who had done Peter a big favor, a few years back. Then he'd refused to accept his full negotiated share of the windfall that had come from it, probably because he'd ended up reunited with his childhood sweetheart and her two boys. Despite Peter's attempts to convince him to the contrary, Lewis still seemed to feel pretty strongly that he'd gotten the better end of the bargain. It didn't seem to make any difference that he'd saved Peter's ass several times since.

"Don't know nobody in Memphis," said Lewis. "I'm told it's like Detroit, only smaller. Which means you pick the right corner and stand there long enough, somebody either gonna point a gun at you or try to sell you one. Either way works if you got the right attitude. Or I could bring something down outta inventory, if you want some company."

"You're a married man and a father," said Peter. "You're supposed to be retired, remember? Stay home with Dinah and those boys."

"Some guys go to Vegas, others to spring training," said Lewis. "No reason I couldn't come to Memphis. Listen to some music, eat a little barbecue."

"Maybe," said Peter. "But not yet. I don't want you scaring the locals."

Lewis's laugh was long and deep. "'Cause you such a damn pussycat."

11

Memphis had a few legendary bad neighborhoods, but Frayser was near the top of the list and it was close to Wanda's house. He drove a few blocks east, then turned north on Watkins.

He passed vacant lots, auto repair shops, a trailer park. After Levee Road came a service lot for city buses, then a giant junkyard called U-Pull-It Auto Parts, with a broad dirty swath of water barely visible through the trees on the right. On a long bridge, he crossed a sluggish brown river bounded by trees on both sides. Then under the freeway, past a row of humming high-tension power lines, and into Frayser.

Here, Watkins lacked Midtown's signs of emerging prosperity. He saw a string of run-down gas stations, a pawn shop, a tire shop. Empty buildings and vacant lots everywhere.

Peter needed gas before he could do any more recon. He pulled into a Texaco on the corner of Watkins and Delano, three pumps and a red-brick convenience store guarded by iron grates and steel poles set in concrete. For a commercial street, the area seemed weirdly empty. As if everyone had just left town.

Memphis reminded Peter of some parts of Milwaukee. It had plenty of decent-looking homes, with fresh paint and well-tended gardens, but also more than its share of vacant lots and boarded-up houses. Land was obviously cheap here. Some buildings had clearly been abandoned for years, sagging into themselves while nameless weeds around them grew up into tangled shrubs and misshapen trees.

He ran his card through the slot, then unscrewed his gas cap and set it on top of the pump. As he lifted the pump handle, a boxy red car came down the road. Something from the eighties, Peter thought, with a terminal rattle, trailing smoke that smelled like a refinery fire.

How that car was still running was anybody's guess. Peter imagined some shade-tree repairman with two screwdrivers, a pair of pliers, a spool of baling wire, and a box of used hose clamps. From the smoke and the gasping engine, it was clear that baling wire could only do so much.

When the car slowed for the corner, the driver peered out the side window at Peter. He was improbably young and skinny, with a haunted look on his face that reminded Peter of the kids he'd seen in war zones. Kids who'd seen too many people die, who'd lost family or friends. Kids who might never be quite right again.

Peter happened to agree with Wanda, that the worst parts of Memphis—or Detroit or Chicago or Milwaukee, for that matter—were just a different kind of war zone.

He had friends from the service who'd grown up in those places. Not much opportunity, and people fighting each other over the scraps. The deck stacked against you from the start. Even if you were better than good, even if you were smarter and more talented and worked harder than everyone else, the violence was random and ruthless and could take anyone at any time. Getting out of those neighborhoods was more difficult than anything Peter had ever done, and took more luck than he'd ever had.

The pump ticked off the gallons. Peter thought about Wanda's house and the steps he'd take to shore it up. When he heard the scuff of a shoe behind him, he swung around.

The same skinny kid from the red car stood now between Peter's front bumper and the reinforced steel post protecting the corner of the pump island. The red car was nowhere in sight.

"Nice truck," said the kid. Looking not at the truck, but at Peter.

"1968 Chevy C20," said Peter. "Restored it myself. Very few original parts."

The kid was maybe five feet six, built like a string bean, skin so dark it seemed almost blue. He couldn't have been more than fifteen, but his hollowed-out face looked like it had seen way too much already. He wore a black Fender guitar T-shirt, dirty knee-length denim shorts, and enormous no-name sneakers with a ragged hole above the left big toe.

His T-shirt was soaked at his chest and shoulders, the slender collarbones showing through the thin fabric. He was a good-looking kid, but his face shone with sweat and something else, something darker. Like he was seeing ghosts.

In his right hand, the kid held a black plastic trash bag by its bunched-up neck. His left hand was tucked into his back pocket, out of sight.

He looked the truck up and down. The shining green paint, the mahogany cargo box built onto the back. "How's it drive?"

"It's a little slow to get going," said Peter. "It definitely doesn't corner very well. But once you get it up to speed, it'll go seventy-five pretty much forever. I'm Peter, by the way. What's your name?"

The pump handle clicked, the tank full. Peter turned, put the nozzle back in its socket, and took his gas cap off the top of the pump. When he turned back to the truck, the kid had taken his left hand out of his back pocket and pointed a snub-nosed revolver loosely at Peter's chest.

Lewis, as usual, had been right about finding a gun.

In some neighborhoods, it was just a matter of time.

The revolver was a smaller caliber, maybe a .32, and badly neglected. The bluing was almost gone from the steel, and rust bloomed at the barrel, frame, and cylinder. Peter didn't want to think about the last time it had been cleaned. The effective range of the two-inch barrel was about ten feet. It wasn't a weapon he wanted.

"Hands up," said the kid. "Don't make me shoot you. I'm taking your truck."

Peter sighed and measured the space between them.

He had to admit, the kid had pretty good tactics,

whether by accident or on purpose. He'd caught Peter in the narrow aisle between the vehicle and the pump island. The trash can and the squeegee bin filled the space between the two pumps, so he couldn't go sideways without crawling under his pickup or climbing over a bunch of crap. The only way out was forward, toward the gun, or back, essentially giving up the truck.

Especially when he'd left his keys in the ignition.

Peter really liked that old Chevy.

He screwed the gas cap down tight and held his hands out, elbows bent. "I'd be careful with that little pistol," he said. "You pull the trigger, you might just blow your hand off."

The kid looked Peter in the eye. He was trying for dead-eyed and resolute, but his face still gleamed with sweat, or the thrill of armed robbery, or something else.

"I pulled this trigger not half an hour ago," he said. "It'll put a hole in you just fine."

"Okay," said Peter. He wondered what was in the trash bag. "How old are you, if you don't mind my asking?"

The kid raised his eyebrows, maybe wondering why the white guy wasn't running away. Clearly, this wasn't how he was expecting things to go.

"North Memphis years? Shit, pops, I'm a old man." Then he shook his head, as if shaking off a fly. "Hell's the matter with you, Saltine? This ain't a conversation. This is me stickin' you up. Now empty your damn pockets and step back before something bad happens to you."

"Sure," said Peter. He took his wallet from his hip

pocket and held it out. "Here you go." Hoping to lure the kid closer. The kid would get distracted, would have to put down that trash bag he was holding on to so tightly. Maybe Peter could get hold of the little gun and nobody would get hurt.

The kid just shook his head, not taking the bait, not even considering it. A natural.

"Put it on the seat. Phone and keys, too."

Peter tossed his wallet and phone through the truck's open window. "Keys are in the ignition."

"Now start walking." The kid waved the barrel of the gun in a quick go-away gesture, then pointed it directly at Peter. "I'm not telling you again."

The kid was only seven feet away. The gun had a two-inch barrel, and Peter figured even odds it would misfire if the kid pulled the trigger. Even odds again that if it did fire, the round wouldn't come close to hitting him. At least not someplace important.

Peter weighed his options. Easiest was to step inside and push away the gun hand and take the kid down with a quick strike to the stomach. Most people wouldn't react quickly when faced with an unexpected attack, and most people with guns didn't think anyone without a gun would make a move. It wouldn't be difficult to leverage his own hard-earned combat skills against a skinny, untrained kid. Peter would probably have to pull his punch not to kill the kid outright.

On the other hand, Peter had no illusions about the lethality of youth and inexperience. He'd fought against armed teenagers in two different war zones. Anyone could pull a trigger. This particular kid had decent tactical instincts, and he was wound up very tight.

Peter had no desire to get killed at a Texaco in Memphis, certainly not over a goddamn pickup truck, no matter how he felt about the Chevy.

If the bullet didn't kill him, June Cassidy would.

He certainly wasn't wearing the armored vest she'd bought him. It was still in the back of the truck.

He'd have to hurt the kid. He didn't want to.

Something else held him back, too. Something in that young face, something ravaged and desperate. The kid hadn't lost his soul, not yet. He wasn't dead inside. He should have been learning geometry, trying to kiss a girl. Not taking this wrong road, carjacking a stranger.

"Listen," said Peter. "You ever actually shoot somebody? It's not like the movies."

"You'll be my first," said the kid, his face shining brighter now. Stress and sweat and the other thing, whatever it was. "Prob'ly not the last, the way this day's going."

"Pulling the trigger isn't the hard part," said Peter. "It's what comes after. What you see when you're asleep."

The kid's eyes slipped to the side, just for a moment, and Peter caught a glimpse of what lay beneath the attitude. Some hidden wreckage the kid was managing to float over the top of, at least for the moment.

When the kid could no longer stay afloat, things would be bad for him, Peter could tell. He'd seen it before, too many times, although never on someone so young.

Peter had been there himself.

The kid's eyes locked onto Peter again, and his face changed. Desperation hardened into resolve. His pupils dilated with the spike of adrenaline.

Peter saw the moves he'd have to make.

He saw the way it would end for the kid.

He made a decision.

"Okay." He raised his hands higher. "I'm going." He stepped backward and away. "Just do me a favor, please? Be nice to my truck?"

"My truck now, Saltine. Keep walking." The gun still pointed at Peter, the kid opened the driver's door with the hand holding the garbage bag, then slung the bag inside. Peter could hear a complicated *clank* as it landed.

"Damn." The kid's voice, quieter. Talking to himself. "Three pedals?"

Peter walked around the rear of the truck toward the passenger side. Keeping his distance from the open window, he said, "It's a stick shift."

The kid looked at him, muscles jumping in his jaw. "What's that?"

"Manual transmission, not automatic," said Peter. "You don't know how to drive stick?"

The kid pointed the gun at Peter. It was still in his left hand. "Tell me how."

Peter suppressed a smile. "You're stealing my truck and you want me to teach you to drive it?"

"Forget it," said the kid, his face a mask. "I'll figure it out. You best keep walking."

He turned the key in the ignition and the truck lurched forward with a *crunch*. The engine didn't start.

"Wait, shit," said Peter, walking closer. "Okay. The left pedal is the clutch. When the truck is in gear, you have to push down on the clutch to start the engine."

"What about the other pedals?"

"Gas and brake, just like a regular car. Pushing down on the clutch disconnects the engine from the wheels. So push the clutch and turn the key and give it some gas."

The kid did as he was told and the big V8 roared to life. He gunned the perfectly tuned engine with a faint smile on his face, something changing there. The truck began to drift slowly forward with no foot on the brake, the concrete pitched slightly toward the street.

"Now I let up on the clutch, give it some gas, and go, right?"

Peter imagined his engine overheating, seized pistons, the gaskets blown. He put his hand across his face. "Not quite," he said, following the drifting truck. "You're in first gear now. You have to shift into second if you want to go faster than five or ten miles an hour." The glass ball holding the hula dancer that topped the Chevy's shift lever didn't have the shift pattern printed on it. "Once you're up to speed, push in the clutch and move the lever down, staying to the left, for second gear. That'll get you to fifteen or twenty miles an hour."

Peter liked how the kid's face turned younger, some of the loss and desperation falling away as he thought his way through the problem. "How many gears total?"

"Four plus reverse. Push in the clutch and pull the

shifter out of gear and it'll find neutral. Straight up from neutral is third, for city streets. Straight down is fourth, for the highway."

The kid frowned at the dashboard. "Man, this piece of shit don't even have a radio."

Peter walked beside the truck as it drifted forward faster. "Why don't you let me drive? I'll take you wherever you want to go, no questions asked."

The kid looked at him sharply. The revolver came up again. "You must be stupid or something. Can't you see I got a pistol in my hand?"

What exactly was wrong with Peter was a much longer conversation than he was willing to have at that moment. A whole lot of people had pointed guns at him over the years. He didn't exactly enjoy it, but maybe it didn't bother him the way it should, either. Peter had a complicated relationship with adrenaline.

Regardless, there was something about this damn kid, something Peter didn't want to let go of. What was in that black plastic garbage bag, anyway?

"I'm just trying to keep my transmission from turning into shrapnel," he said. "Take my wallet, take my phone. Shoot me whenever you want. Just let me drive."

"Man, why you want to drive something that's so hard to work?"

"It's the hard that makes it worth doing," said Peter. "And it's not that hard, really. Just takes practice, like anything else."

"Is that all? Practice? Shit," said the kid. "Guess I better get started."

He hit the gas and popped the clutch and somehow managed to chirp the tires on the Texaco concrete.

As the truck rolled toward the road, Peter heard the distinctive sound of grinding gears as the kid searched for second and found it. He was in third by the time he came to the intersection, and didn't even slow for the light as he rounded the corner.

Peter had never told him where to find reverse.

Something told him the kid wasn't going to need it.

12

Peter turned toward the little brick Texaco building.

He was thinking about Wanda, and the Dumpster coming to her house, and the lumber delivery, and the fact that all his tools were in the back of his truck, when he noticed something on the pavement.

Right about where the kid had been standing when he took the gun out of his back pocket.

He bent down and plucked it off the pavement. A deep blue guitar pick. Slightly bent from use, the name printed on it worn and faded. JERRY'S GUITARS, MEMPHIS, TN.

The kid had been wearing a Fender T-shirt.

Maybe the kid was a musician.

When he'd asked the kid how old he was, he'd said something about North Memphis years.

It was somewhere to start, anyway. Peter put the pick in his pocket.

How many places could there be to play music in Memphis, anyway?

Right. He'd just start knocking on doors, looking for young black guitar players.

This was not what he needed right now.

. . .

He opened the door of the little convenience store, and the white static crackled up his brainstem. The flickering fluorescent lights and the bright, crowded shelves always set him off. His allergy to the modern world. He took a deep breath, then let it out and stepped inside.

He saw the usual supplies for beater cars, including motor oil, brake fluid, and radiator-leak-stopper, along with a wide variety of synthetic non-food snacks that would probably outlast the zombie apocalypse. The sales counter was next to the door behind a thick slab of scarred security plastic that had already seen its share of abuse. A curved steel tray was set into the counter to pass your money or card through.

Behind the battered security plastic, amid the pump controls and security monitors and lottery ticket dispensers and high racks of cigarettes, stood a middle-aged man with a sagging brown face and a Grizzlies sweatshirt worn thin with washing. Cradled in his arms was an over/under shotgun with a scarred wooden stock, old and cheap and perfectly functional.

The man looked at Peter, a smile implied in the lines around his eyes. "That's why you pay for gas in advance." He had a slight lisp.

Peter tipped his chin at the shotgun. "You couldn't come out there and give me a hand?"

"Oh, no," said the man, shaking his head. "You chase one off, they just come back in a mob, shoot the place up. Memphis ain't playin', son."

A small television was turned on behind him. It showed a row of police vehicles with lights flashing parked at a large pale building with the Macy's logo. The crawl at the bottom of the screen read, **Breaking News:** *Shooting at Wolfchase Galleria, two dead.*

"I'm starting to get that idea," said Peter. "Can I borrow your phone?"

"Against company rules," said the man. He glanced out the window toward the road, then back to Peter. "They let me call 911, if you want. Nobody got hurt, so the police might be a while."

Peter shook his head. He'd need a police report to collect on his insurance, but that wouldn't bring back the truck he'd found in a barn in central California and spent years restoring between deployments. The project had kept him sane, more or less, and that old Chevy had taken him a lot of places.

In a way, it was his home.

He'd track it down himself. Hopefully before that kid sold off all his tools.

"You ever see that kid before? You know where he hangs out?"

The man shook his head.

"Would you tell me if you did?"

The man cracked a gap-toothed smile, more space than teeth, which explained the lisp. "Depends," he said. "But truth is I never got a look at him." He gestured at the monitors. "I mighta got him on the cameras, but they're acting up again." He shot another glance out the window. "You want to call the police, we can check the tapes."

It was strange, but Peter didn't want to get the kid in trouble. He had the feeling the kid had enough problems already. Peter just wanted his truck back. "Don't bother. But thanks."

"You really don't want the police?"

Peter stopped at the door. "You think they'll help?"

The man shook his head. "That ain't my experience."

"How about a pay phone?"

"They all gone," he said. "Here's what you do. Walk out that door and down to the stop sign. Turn right just like that jacker did. In eight or ten blocks, you'll come to a place called the Wet Spot."

"That's really what it's called? The Wet Spot?"

"They sell ice cream, soda, beer, you know. Tell 'em Fat Rudy sent you, maybe they let you use the phone."

"Thanks."

"Don't thank me yet," the man said. "Piece of advice. They might be some hard people there. Act respectful, you'll do fine."

Outside, the air was thick and threatening rain. Spring in Tennessee. Peter strode across the wide concrete apron toward the road.

Go to Memphis, June had said. Eat some barbecue, listen to music, have some fun.

So far there had been no barbecue and no music.

Was it wrong that he might be having fun?

13

On Watkins, the sidewalk was hard up against the street. Peter had barely reached the crossing at Delano when a sleek black Mercedes SUV, freshly washed, coasted through the red light, pulled a perfectly executed U-turn, and pulled up onto the sidewalk beside him.

A door opened and a brown-skinned man watched Peter from the back seat. He had round cheeks and small ears and a neat tuft of beard at his chin. His hair was crisp on the sides and stylishly shaggy on top. His smile showed a pair of shining gold eyeteeth, slick with saliva. His eyes bulged slightly, like he had a thyroid condition.

"You need a ride, friend? Look like you might be a little lost."

Peter had sidestepped automatically when the big SUV bumped up on the sidewalk, so he stood on the Texaco apron again, looking over a bus-stop bench at the other man.

Thinking that Lewis was right again.

"Actually," Peter said, "somebody just stole my truck."

The man's eyebrows went up. "You don't say. I'm sorry

to hear that." He put his hand to his chest. "My name's Robert Kingston. You don't sound like you're from around here. Where're you from?"

"Wisconsin."

"You don't mind my saying, you're a little pale for the neighborhood." Kingston slid over to make room on the black leather seat. He wore a stepped-up version of business casual, a maroon polo shirt over dark dress pants and pointy-toed alligator-skin boots. "C'mon up in here. I'll get you where you need to go."

Kingston had a half-moon scar on his cheek that got longer as his smile got wider. He wasn't a big man, but he had a charismatic density that exerted a certain kind of gravitational pull. Like a black hole.

Peter felt the first drops of rain on the back of his neck.

He looked farther into the car. A driver loomed large behind the wheel, facing forward. Another person sat in the front passenger seat, mostly hidden by the door column and the deeply tinted window.

He thought about Wanda, at home, asleep on her couch. He remembered what Gantry, the detective, had said about whoever had driven the dump truck into her living room. That they weren't going away until they got what they wanted. He felt the static crackle and spark.

He remembered how the Texaco clerk, Fat Rudy, had kept glancing out the window while he talked to Peter. How the black Mercedes had headed right for him, as if it had been aimed.

The rain began to fall harder. Kingston's smile got wider.

Peter smiled back. Alive, alive, I am alive.

"Thanks," he said. "I could definitely use a lift."

And climbed into the car.

The interior smelled like leather conditioner and stain remover. When the door closed, the sound of the birds went silent. Rain came down harder on the windshield, but without a sound.

Kingston said, "Brody, park us somewhere legal."

The big driver had a shaved head that merged seamlessly with the thickest neck Peter had ever seen. He wore a black track jacket. When he reached forward to put the Mercedes into gear, his jacket tightened on his rounded back. Peter saw two crossed straps outlined under the thin fabric.

Without a word, Brody expertly goosed the gas, threaded the big car through the light poles, thumped down the curb, made the tight right turn around the corner, then back into the Texaco, where he pulled beside the little convenience store.

From the way the leading front wheel sank as it turned the corner and the rear springs bounced off the curb, Peter knew the Mercedes was armored, and expensively so. Which was also why it was so quiet inside.

He could only think of one reason Robert Kingston would have an armored SUV.

But Peter had known as much before he'd climbed inside.

The armor just told him how much money Kingston had, and how many enemies.

"Tell me," said Kingston, tapping his pointed toes on the floor. "What kind of truck was it? Maybe we can get it back for you."

"A green Chevy pickup," said Peter. "With a wood cargo box built onto the back." He figured they'd already have that information from Fat Rudy.

The front passenger turned toward Peter. A woman, mid-thirties, with a narrow, empty face and her hair spiked into sharp twists. Her wrinkled red-and-white seersucker jacket was pale against her brown skin. Where the jacket sagged open, Peter saw a black checkered pistol grip below her arm, snug against her tight white tank top. "What'd he look like, that jacker? How old? What kind of clothes?"

Kingston shot the woman passenger a cautionary look.

"See, this is our neighborhood," he said. "We take this kind of thing personally. The police don't do much for us here, so we have to do for ourselves, if you take my meaning. Why we want to find the person who took your truck, keep our neighborhood safe."

"Is that why your people have guns? You're the neighborhood watch?"

Kingston flashed his teeth again, this time with genuine humor and a kind of recognition.

"Something like that." He looked Peter up and down, getting a better look at the faded carpenter pants worn through at the knees, the paint-spattered T-shirt. Peter's long ropy muscles, big hands on bony wrists. "What are you, exactly?"

"That's a good question," Peter said. "I'm kind of between jobs right now."

Kingston snorted, then took out a purple silk handkerchief and blew his nose. "You got balls." He tucked the handkerchief away. "You're not scared of me, even though you should be. So you think you're a tough guy. You a fighter?"

"Sometimes," Peter said pleasantly. "When I have to be."

"Why don't you tell us about the guy who took your truck?"

"I'll make you a deal," said Peter. "You get me where I need to go, I'll tell you everything I know."

"How do I know you'll tell me the truth?"

"Why would I lie? The bastard stole my truck. If you want him for some other reason, why would I care? I just want my truck back. Can you promise me that?"

"I make no guarantee you'll get it back." Kingston's toes went *tappity-tap*. "Jacker's as likely to wreck it as anything. But if I find it, and it'll still drive, I'll leave it here at the Texaco."

Peter didn't believe him for a minute. And the static was flaring up inside this padded car with its tinted windows. None of it mattered. What mattered was that they could get him closer to Wanda's, and what he'd set out to find that morning.

"I can live with that," he said, and put out his hand. "Drop me on Ayers past Vollintine."

Kingston shook. "Deal," he said. "We'll talk on the way. Brody?"

The armored Mercedes rolled forward.

Before Brody turned left onto the road, Peter saw the kid's boxy red car, abandoned on the street. Visible from the window of the Texaco.

So they didn't know the kid, but they knew the car.

Fat Rudy had seen the car and had called Kingston.

Who'd come on the double in his armored SUV.

The kid must have done something pretty bad to have these people coming so hard on his heels.

Peter pictured his face, that sheen of sweat and desperation, but cool despite all that. Calm and capable and even funny. He reminded Peter of somebody.

"Your turn," said Kingston, still tapping his feet like they had a mind of their own. "Tell me about this jacker."

Peter thought of what Fat Rudy might have seen on the monitors. "He was black, maybe early twenties. Frameless glasses and a black Detroit Tigers T-shirt. And had some muscle, like he worked out."

Pretty much the opposite of the kid who'd taken Peter's truck and phone and wallet.

The woman in the seersucker jacket glanced at Kingston and shook her head. "Light skinned or dark?"

"About like you."

Kingston frowned. "Hair?"

"Short. Nothing fancy."

"He had a gun," the woman said. "What kind?"

"A black revolver, brand-new. He looked pretty comfortable with it. I wasn't going to argue."

"But he took his time," Kingston said. "Maybe he talked to you? What'd he say?"

Now Peter knew Fat Rudy had seen at least some of it on the security cameras. Peter looked out the windshield. He compared the turns the driver had made with the map in his head. They were headed in the right direction. It wouldn't be far now.

"He asked about the truck," said Peter. "What kind of shape it was in. How far it would go on a tank of gas. I got the impression he was headed out of town. He was worried about it breaking down on him."

"And?"

"All the work I've done on it?" Peter shook his head. "That truck will run forever."

"Something else," said Kingston. "He was carrying some kind of sack."

Now he knew what Kingston and his people were chasing. So they knew what it was already.

"A black plastic garbage bag," he said. "Not very full, but it kind of clanked when he set it down."

The woman and Kingston looked at each other.

Peter said, "What did he do, anyway?"

Kingston's face was grim. "Took something didn't belong to him."

They turned onto Ayers and passed Vollintine, four and a half blocks from Wanda's house. It was bad enough that somebody had driven a dump truck into her living room, Peter didn't want to lead Kingston right to her door, too. He figured these three were more dangerous than the dump truck driver. Kingston wouldn't deliver any kind of warning. He'd just take what he wanted.

Brody slowed. Kingston said, "Where we dropping you?"

Peter heard a staccato burp. Then another, longer. It was oddly quiet through the heavy armored glass, but Peter would know that sound anywhere. It would be loud as hell once he got out of the car.

He said, "Brody, step on it, now. Then stop hard at the corner of Joseph Place."

Brody rotated his head to catch Kingston's eye. Kingston nodded, and Brody hit the gas.

The noise got louder. Approaching Joseph, Brody slowed to a crawl. Through the rain-spattered windshield, Peter could see red flashes lancing out of the side of an old station wagon halfway down the block.

Wanda's block.

The woman peered out the windshield. "What the hell. Is that a machine gun?"

Brody stopped the car.

Kingston opened his mouth to give an order.

Peter reached across the seatback, clamped his big right hand around the woman's forehead, and yanked her toward him and into the headrest.

She bucked hard, making a sound deep in her throat, but he held her head tight against the cushioned leather while he used his free hand to pull the pistol from the holster under her left arm.

Kingston leaned back against his door. "Brody, deal with this."

Brody put the Mercedes in park.

With the gun now in his left hand, Peter brought that arm around and trapped her face inside his inner elbow while he dipped his right hand under her right armpit. She clawed at his forearm and tried to bite his bicep. He found a spare magazine in a padded pocket and plucked it free, trying not to touch her breast, but was not entirely successful.

When he released her and reached for the door handle, she turned to come at him over the seatback. "You fuck," she said, her eyes alive for the first time.

Brody slipped one meaty hand into his track suit and reached his other long arm toward Peter. Who held the woman's gun up and pushed open the door with his right elbow. "Everybody stop moving. Don't make me shoot you."

Kingston's face was torqued with fury. "In my own damn Mercedes?"

"Sorry," said Peter, stepping onto the cracked pavement. "Nothing personal. I owe you one."

Then he sprinted through the rain toward Wanda's house, thinking as he did that it was probably a mistake to leave Kingston and the others alive.

It would come back to bite him, he knew.

Right now, however, he had a much bigger problem.

14

Outside, the *thump thump thump* of the machine gun was very loud, even with the dampening quality of the rain. The low, boxy station wagon stood in the street just this side of Wanda's house, with the barrel resting on the windowsill and the gunner crouched out of sight in the back seat.

He sprayed rounds down the exposed side of the building. Windows shattered and brick shrapnel flew into the air. When he aimed his fire back toward the front of the house, the thumping of the gun was joined by a *whangwhangwhang* as the bullets hit the back of the dump truck.

Peter had seen sustained machine-gun fire blast holes through cinder block and concrete. Already the brick was shot away entirely in several places.

If Wanda hadn't jumped out the back window and fled through the yard, Peter hoped she'd thought to run to the living room and slide down into the crawl space. Sheltering in front of the dump truck's engine block was the smartest thing she could do.

If she was still alive.

If the gunman didn't get out of his car and go into the house after her.

Peter ran half-bent along the curb strip, using parked cars for concealment. The station wagon was from the late sixties, long and rectangular, painted a faded canary yellow. Heavy Detroit steel, not modern curved plastic. He still couldn't see the gunner, but now he could see another person in the front passenger seat, gesticulating wildly.

Peter looked back the way he'd come, but the Mercedes was gone.

Probably not for long.

Ten yards away, he stopped beside a little hatchback to check the pistol he'd taken from the woman. It was a black Glock 19, a smaller nine-mil weapon. It definitely wasn't the M4 carbine he'd carried in Iraq, but she'd picked the larger-capacity magazines, and they were fully loaded.

It would have to do. Thirty rounds against a machine gun that was probably belt-fed, given that the gunner hadn't seemed to stop to reload yet. It was either a 249 SAW or, from the sound of it, the beefier 240 Bravo, although Peter had no idea how an asshole in a station wagon got hold of a serious weapon used by heavy infantry or mounted on tanks and aircraft. No telling what else they had, either. Hell, if they had a belt-fed machine gun, they could have hand grenades.

Whereas Peter had no armored vest and no cover to speak of. His Dumpster hadn't showed up yet. That heavy steel box would have been nice. Even the modest pile of lumber he'd ordered would have stopped rounds for a few minutes, unlike the tin-can hatchback he was hiding behind.

He wasn't going to win a pitched battle against a machine gun. His best hope was to put some rounds through the seatback into that invisible gunner.

Aggression and surprise were his only real assets.

Well, hell. No time like the present.

He took a deep breath, then slipped around the hatchback, the pistol raised in his left hand, the butt cupped in his right. As he approached the station wagon, he began to fire deliberately through its rear window and into the seatback. Just foam and springs and a thin metal frame, no match for the Glock.

The window glass starred and fell, and the seatback puffed with the impacts, but the machine gun didn't stop firing. Peter adjusted his fire lower, thinking the man was lying flat on the seat, or crouched into the wheel well. But it made no difference. The gunner didn't even seem to notice him, just kept spraying the house with high-velocity rounds.

The figure in the front passenger seat definitely noticed, however. He rose with some kind of hand cannon and fired wildly in Peter's direction. Peter dropped down under shards of glass exploding outward. Then the hand cannon went silent and the passenger vanished from sight, but the machine gun kept on with its heavy *thump thump thump*.

Crouched on the street in the riotous noise, Peter

dropped the empty mag and reloaded, then rose and stepped closer, placing his shots more carefully now. He saw something odd. Each round made two puffs in the seatback. He looked over the seatback and saw a rust-red line, then another behind the front seat. He fired high and saw a silver mark in the rusty red behind the front seat. It didn't make any sense.

He went to his left, toward the driver's side, and saw another line of rusty red at the door. And he knew what they'd done, whoever they were.

The rusty red was old steel plate, four pieces welded or clamped or wedged into a rectangular box.

They'd made an armored firing position for the back seat of the old station wagon.

The Glock's nine-mil rounds weren't penetrating, they were bouncing off.

Peter circled closer, trying to get an angle at the gunner over the steel plate. He saw a sudden flurry of movement inside the car, then the engine roared.

Peter stepped in, emptying the magazine, the slide locking back.

As the yellow station wagon chunked into gear and lurched forward, the gunner popped his head up above the armor.

Either his face was painted blue, or he wore some kind of skin-tight mask. With pointed teeth.

Then the old car was gone.

PART 3

15

Albert Burkitts had gone to work that morning like nothing had happened.

Like he hadn't picked up Judah Lee at that biker bar outside Byhalia. Like he hadn't driven them both into Memphis after midnight, watched his brother climb the fence at a construction yard, and break down the gate with a big black ten-wheel Kenworth.

Albert had followed in his car, then waited at the curb with his lights off and his windows down, and listened to that twelve-cylinder engine wind up high as the truck accelerated through the stop sign and down two city blocks toward the house.

Part of him had been thrilled to death, another part sick to his stomach.

A third part, maybe the biggest part, hoping Judah Lee would never come back.

Because if he did, there was no stopping him, not Judah Lee, not until it was done. Albert was too old and too crippled up. Albert didn't even know why he'd helped, not really.

There were reasons, but reasons were easy to come by. Albert had known better, or he should have.

The sound of the crash was louder than seemed possible, louder than anything else in that whole big city. Then the wait that seemed longer than it could possibly be, until Judah Lee yanked open the door and pulled himself into the passenger seat. The car settled on its springs, the little Ford Fiesta not designed for the size of Albert's little brother.

"What the hell are you waiting for?" said Judah Lee. "Get us out of here."

Albert was glad he couldn't see his brother's smile in the dark.

A day and a night had passed and now Albert was back in his comfort zone, at the edge of a stand of slash pine, sweating in a rubber apron, up to his elbows in blood.

He was limping around the corral-style hog trap, six pissed-off full-grown wild hogs squealing and grunting as they raced around inside the circular enclosure. They churned up the mud as they ran, slamming their weight against the welded-wire fence and threatening to uproot the metal T-posts that held the corral in place.

Albert had his daddy's old long-barreled .44, taking aim at the big aggressive boar with a bristled back and curved tusks longer than Albert's thumbs. One of the biggest boars Albert had this year, three hundred pounds of angry pig.

The trick was to shoot a hog but once, halfway between

the eye and the ear, and kill it stone dead. A hurt hog, a hog you had to shoot two or three times, would give sour meat, no good for anything but hogburger chili, and over-spiced chili at that.

Albert needed the meat, for himself and for his customers.

Getting the pigs out of the trap was another problem, but Albert had a tool he'd made himself. From a piece of rebar, he'd forged a long, sharp hook like an oversized fish gaff, then welded it to a long pipe handle with a chain on the end. Working over the top of the fence, he'd slip the hook through the hole in the skull, then use the little hand-crank utility crane bolted to his daddy's old Mack stake-bed to lift the carcass up and out of the pen without getting himself hurt.

Albert always killed them one at a time, field-dressing each carcass before shooting the next pig. The meat tasted better that way. He'd already killed and hooked three sows, hung them up by spreader bars, gutted them, cut out the stinky parts, then peeled their skins before he left them hanging to cool and drain. When he ran out of hooks and spreader bars, he'd quarter the carcasses, put them on ice, and start over again.

Judah Lee hadn't shown up, of course. Albert had stopped expecting help years ago. The Lord helped those who helped themselves, that's what their daddy always said.

It wasn't work he liked, not the way he liked sitting half-turned on their daddy's 1950 Farmall, the sun warm on the back of his neck, watching over his shoulder as the plow blades turned the hard winter soil into orderly rows. But killing hogs was work that paid, unlike the home farm. Wild hogs did a lot of damage, and landowners gave Albert cold hard cash to set up his gear on their acreage and trap pigs.

They didn't pay much. But with back taxes unpaid at the farm, and foreclosure letters coming in from the bank, Albert couldn't afford to be picky. He was half-crippled from rolling the tractor six years before. He'd spent the night pinned underneath that overturned old Farmall with a cracked pelvis and a shattered leg, gritting his teeth against the pain, thinking about his health insurance deductible and co-payments, and waiting for help that might never come.

The way Albert figured it, he was lucky to be working at all.

The big boar was the one that would turn on Albert if it got loose. Knock him down and tear him up with those sharp tusks. Eat him piece by piece if it could. Hogs would eat anything, and Albert's bad leg wouldn't let him move fast enough to get ahead of it.

Usually he tried to take out the biggest boar first, but pigs didn't get that kind of size by being dumb and easy to kill.

In Albert's experience, wild hogs were pretty dang smart, and this one was smarter than most. Maybe it had been trapped before, and got away. It couldn't resist that shelled corn bait, but it knew a few tricks. Albert could see the bent wire where it had tried to root up the bottom of the corral fence. Even now it kept circling behind the sows like it knew exactly what Albert meant to do, and Albert wasn't fast enough to get a clean shot. So Albert had taken the sows as they came, making it harder for the big boar to hide.

It didn't matter how big or smart a boar was, Albert always won in the end.

"You gonna kill them hogs or just chase 'em around for fun?"

Albert turned and saw his brother, Judah Lee, coming down the dirt track from the farmer's house.

Albert was short and stumpy, thick in the arms and shoulders from a lifetime of labor, but staring hard at the far side of middle age. Most days the pain of his badly healed bones felt lodged so deep it took a handful of pills to turn down the volume. More pills every week, it seemed.

Judah Lee, Albert's little brother, was a good foot taller and ten years younger, in the prime of his life.

Big as he was now, you'd never know Judah had been a scrawny little kid, with Albert always trying to protect him from their daddy. The old man had called the boy Runt, or "that accident," as in, "Get that accident out of bed before I beat both your backsides. You know Runt's got chores before school."

Making Albert his brother's keeper, which was a long, hard road.

Judah Lee might have started out skinny and scared, but early on he turned that scared part into something mean. If he got pissed about something—sometimes real, just as often some imagined insult—he'd never come out and say it to your face. Albert would pull back the covers on his bed and find a copperhead coiled up and shaking its tail. Or open his car door and find a bobcat hissing in the footwell.

How Judah Lee managed to get a dang bobcat into that little Ford Fiesta, Albert never quite figured out. But the stink of bobcat piss never went away.

Judah Lee never went after their daddy, who'd beat them both with a belt. Just Albert, who was looking out for him, and often as not took Judah's licks for him.

Truth was, Judah Lee had never been quite right, not since the day he came out with the umbilical cord wrapped around his neck. Scared, angry, and mean, and it was always somebody else's fault. When he grew into his size at nineteen, he wasn't scared anymore. After that, he was just plain mean.

Albert was still trying to be his brother's keeper after all these years, but Judah Lee didn't make it easy. When Albert was in the Army, trying to find a way into college, Judah Lee got himself kicked out of high school, bounced from job to job and fight to fight, ending up at Parchman Farm. He came out ten years later, bulked up from pumping iron and covered with ink, even on his face.

But that wasn't the worst of it.

The worst was the smile he gave when Albert picked him up on the outside.

His teeth sharpened to points with a rat-tail file from the prison shop.

Albert told himself Judah Lee was just protecting himself in there, trying to look scary, trying to stay safe. That he hadn't really joined himself up with those people.

Albert wanted to believe it.

But in his heart he knew that Judah Lee had turned himself into a monster of his own free will.

To Albert's mind it was all their daddy's fault, the stories he told about his own daddy and his granddad before him. Stories of their vanished family wealth going all the way back to before that ancient war that felt new every time the plow blades unearthed another hand-poured musket ball, or the dirty bones of long-dead men that still ghosted up through the soil after all those years.

Even from the grave, their old man was still telling stories, and Judah Lee still believed them. Or wanted to.

Somehow, Albert had been pulled into Judah Lee's scheme, despite his own best judgment. He was still trying to look out for his little brother, that was what he told himself. Truth was, maybe he had the same hope that something long ago taken from them might be restored. Their rightful place in the world.

There had to be more to life than killing hogs.

Now Judah Lee took their daddy's long-barreled .44 from Albert's hand. "She loaded?"

Judah Lee didn't wait for an answer, just flipped the cylinder open to check the rounds like Albert wouldn't even know how many shots he had left, like Albert hadn't already reloaded with one under the hammer like their daddy had taught them both.

Then Judah Lee took a quick few steps, put a hand on the wooden frame of the trap door, and vaulted the five-foot wire fence into the corral.

The big boar ran right at him, a three-hundred-pound sharp-tusked meat torpedo, but Judah spun like a dancer, put the gun before the running boar's ear, and pulled the trigger.

The pig's heavy head exploded, a drop-kicked watermelon. Judah Lee smiled.

"Come on, Albert. We got something more important to do."

"There's a thousand pounds on the hoof yet to deal with. I leave for an hour and these pigs'll be under that fence or through it. Then I got to come back and rebuild the trap and these pigs'll just be that much harder to catch."

"Brother, you got the wrong priorities," said Judah Lee, who hadn't talked that way before all those sessions with the prison psychologist. He showed Albert his new teeth. "But I hear you. Let me help you out with that."

He stomped through the corral, using heavy knees to fend off the smaller panicking sows while he put the pistol to their heads, one by one, and pulled the trigger. Then stood planted in the mud with the splatter of pig's blood across his hands and clothes. His blue tattoos stood out on his flushed pink face. "There. Can we leave now?"

Albert sighed. "What would Daddy say about leaving

good meat to spoil? It'll be faster with you here to help. Go on, toss those carcasses over the fence. You hang 'em up and I'll skin 'em out."

They got the remaining hogs quartered and on ice, but Albert knew Judah Lee was losing patience. He'd never had much to begin with. So Albert left the stake-bed Mack with its coolers and carcasses standing beside the corral and followed his brother up the dirt track toward the road, where an old Ford Country Squire was parked on the gravel.

"Where'd you get this?" Albert peered into the back seat, seeing thick steel plate lining the seatbacks and blocking the doors, wedged in place and held together with angle iron and C-clamps. Two cases of Coors were stacked in one footwell, a rolled-up old horse blanket in the other. "What in God's name are you up to now?"

"Get in the car," said Judah Lee, climbing behind the wheel, setting the reloaded .44 on the dashboard. "And don't ask questions you don't want the answer to. When are you gonna grow up?"

Talking to him like Albert was the little brother. Albert just shook his head. He knew he was going to regret this, but he got in the car anyway. The family farm was all he had left, and even that would be gone if the bank and tax man had his way. Albert needed what their daddy had talked about as much as Judah Lee. Maybe more.

When Judah turned onto the highway, Albert realized where they were going. "Are you out of your dang mind?

We can't go back there. We have to wait. We talked about this."

Judah Lee showed his teeth. "I don't want to wait. Turns out I been waiting all my life and I didn't know it. I saw that house on the news at the bar. They said that woman's still there. Looks to me like that truck didn't do enough damage. Bitch needs a harder push." They drove the rest of the way in silence. But when Judah finally stopped in front of that ruined old house, Albert saw what he'd been talking about. The beginnings of repairs, a blue tarp nailed up to keep the rain out.

Judah Lee turned off the car and buttoned the single key into his shirt pocket. "You see what I mean? She's not moving out. She's digging in." He dropped the .44 in Albert's lap. "Feel free to shoot anybody dumb enough not to run away. You get me?"

Then he climbed into the back seat, took the rolled-up horse blanket from the footwell, and unwrapped a dang machine gun.

Not the ancient AK-47 their daddy had smuggled home from Vietnam and used for killing possums on the farm. Definitely not some bolt-action deer rifle. This was a genuine machine gun, long and ugly with a folding bipod on the barrel and a bagful of bullets hanging from its belly.

"Judah Lee, what in the name of almighty God . . ."

Then Albert saw the steel plate lining the back seat in a new way. Judah Lee had made himself a bullet-proof box.

Judah dropped the long barrel on the windowsill, set

himself on the worn fabric seat, put the butt to his shoulder and his finger to the trigger. "Better cover your ears," he said.

"Wait a minute, Judah, just—"

All hell broke loose.

The gun was louder than the crack of doom in the closed car, nothing like firing that old .44 out at the edge of the woods. Bullet casings flew everywhere, scorching hot to the touch. Albert was afraid they'd start melting the floor mats, or worse.

He crouched down in his seat, waving his arms, shouting at his brother, words he couldn't hear himself and they were coming out of his own mouth. But his eyes were glued to the house, the bricks flying off in chunks, shattered window glass dropping from broken frames, wooden porch posts splintering like kindling.

The destruction was glorious.

He didn't even know someone was shooting back until the radio exploded in the dashboard. Albert ducked farther down, hoping Judah's steel-plate box would protect him, too.

When the machine gun stopped firing, Albert heard the deliberate gunshots coming from somewhere behind them, the dull *clang* of the rounds hitting the steel. He peeked over the seatback to see Judah Lee crouched down, changing out the ammunition belt, the barrel smoking and the smell of spent powder filling the station wagon. The rear window was spiderwebbed, the tailgate and cargo area full of holes. No sirens, no lights. Just shots coming from somewhere behind them.

Albert pointed their daddy's .44 out the back window and pulled the trigger until it was empty. The other gunshots stopped for a moment, then started again from a new angle, and coming closer. Judah Lee, oblivious, snapped the cover over the new belt and hunkered down over the sight, ready to open fire at the house again.

"Give me the key," Albert shouted over the ringing in his ears. He couldn't even see who he'd been shooting at. But whoever it was, he was still shooting back, and the police were surely on their way. "Judah Lee, give me the dang car key!"

Judah Lee looked up at Albert without understanding, eyes bright with excitement, pointed teeth dimpling his lower lip. Lost in the pleasure and the noise and the violence of the moment.

Albert drew back and clouted his brother in the face with a thick fist. Judah Lee blinked, reeling away. Albert reached forward and tore open his brother's buttoned shirt pocket and fished out the key. Whoever was shooting at them wasn't likely to stop.

Albert slid into the driver's seat, fumbled the key into the slot, threw the car into drive, and got them out of there.

They were four blocks away and headed for the freeway before he realized the hot barrel of the machine gun had set the car's plastic upholstery on fire.

16

"I told you this was going to escalate," said Detective Gantry.

Peter had been shot at and emptied both magazines into the old station wagon, but mostly he was thinking about that weird blue face, maybe a mask, maybe not, staring back at him from the back seat of the station wagon. He wasn't sure what to make of it, or even what he'd seen.

After the station wagon pulled away, he'd scrambled to find Wanda in the crawl space of the ruined house, back braced against the heavy front bumper of the dump truck, with her camera bag under her raised knees and her laptop clutched hard to her chest.

She was shaking, wired to the gills, scraped and dirty from the slide down the splintery slope of the living-room floor in her bare feet. Still, she'd had enough training from her military embeds to know to shelter behind the engine block, and it had kept her alive.

Peter had wanted to get Wanda into her car and gone

before the cops arrived, but he was still trying to talk her out of the crawl space when he heard the sirens.

Now she sat blanket-wrapped and adrenaline-crashed on the back bumper of an ambulance, while Peter stood in the side yard with his ears still ringing and Gantry, the cop who sounded like Elvis, asking Peter questions he didn't want to answer.

Detective Gantry didn't look like Elvis. He was black and balding and built like a bowling pin in French cuffs and tasseled loafers. And he wasn't happy that Peter didn't have any valid ID because his wallet was gone. Peter didn't tell Gantry that his driver's license was long expired.

Peter didn't tell him about the gunner's blue mask, either. Just that he hadn't seen the man's face. He wasn't sure what he'd seen, and he didn't want to sound like a lunatic.

After the detective finished grilling him about the station wagon, which Peter was pretty sure was a 1960s Ford Country Squire, and what he thought the gunner's weapon might have been, Peter handed Gantry the flash drive Wanda had given him.

"Pictures from yesterday. Wanda got faces and license plates from people driving by. Maybe something there you can use."

Gantry looked at him sideways. "Sounds like a lot of overtime." But he slipped the little drive into his pocket.

"Where would somebody get a big machine gun like that?"

Gantry shook his head. "Military weapons are popping up all over the Mid-South," he said. "Old stuff, probably slated to be destroyed but still functional. Rumor mill says they got sold out of one of the big bases in North Carolina, but it all got hushed up. We're still paying the price."

Then Gantry brought the questions back to Peter, as he'd known the detective would.

"When we talked on the phone earlier, you said you didn't have a gun," Gantry said. "So where did this one come from? I'm just asking because it'll go through ballistics. You seem like you're trying to do the right thing here, but I don't want any surprises."

The young uniformed officer, directing traffic the day before, now stood a few steps away, listening in. Or maybe ready to step in if needed.

"I borrowed it," Peter said. "I don't know where else it's been."

"Well, who'd you borrow it from?" Gantry asked.

The Memphis detective really did sound like Elvis. The disconnect was a little disconcerting, as if the rest of Peter's day hadn't been weird enough. But he saw an opportunity in this conversation.

"You know, I never got her name," Peter said. "She was wearing a red-and-white-seersucker jacket, driving with a guy named Robert Kingston. They were giving me a ride back here after my truck got stolen."

Gantry's eyebrows shot up. He shared a glance with the officer, whose name tag said R. MCCARTER.

"You hitched a ride with King Robbie? And took this weapon off Charlene Scott?"

Peter shrugged, innocent as a baby. "Like I said, I never got her name. Who's King Robbie?"

Peter knew he wasn't fooling anyone. Gantry, for all his charm and nice clothes, had those flat cop eyes that could see down deep into your secret soul. But it was Officer McCarter who answered.

"King Robbie's the man who runs Memphis like his personal ATM," he said. "Drugs, human trafficking, extortion, armed robbery, you name it. Anything bad happens in the city, King Robbie either started it, runs it, or gets a piece. And that's just his side gig. Memphis is a transit hub, right? That's why FedEx has its headquarters here. King makes his real money, serious money, moving weight."

Gantry said, "That nobody Vinny Charles, who used to own Ms. Wyatt's house? He was almost certainly working for King. Even if he didn't know it."

"So how much is serious money?" Peter asked.

"Before King, a guy named Isaac Bell ran the show," Gantry said. "When we put him away six years ago, we found about ten million dollars in various offshore bank accounts. We rolled up as much of his operation as we could. King Robbie was a smaller fish back then, but he stepped up hard, took out anybody who might have been a competitor, then built a new organization on the foundation of the old one. He's been the man to beat ever since."

"He's not real stable," added McCarter. "There's been a lot more killing since he took over."

"Huh," said Peter. "What about this Charlene Scott?"

"She's his shooter," said McCarter. "Allegedly, because witnesses change their minds or disappear. Was there a big guy behind the wheel? Like the size of an elephant?"

Peter nodded. "Kingston called him Brody."

"He's the muscle," said McCarter. "If your legs need breaking, or maybe your arm pulled out of the socket, he's the man for the job."

Gantry looked at McCarter curiously. "You're a beat cop?"

The uniformed officer shrugged. "I came up in this neighborhood," he said. "Got some local knowledge."

Gantry nodded, filing that information away for future exploitation, then turned back to Peter. "And they just happened to be driving by. Offered you a lift."

Peter shrugged. "My truck was stolen. They were very nice. I thought it was some of that famous Southern hospitality."

"And you're just a carpenter, here to fix up the house." Gantry stared at Peter. "But that wasn't always your job, was it." He wasn't asking.

Peter smiled. "I think of myself as a problem solver."

"Solve any problems overseas?"

"Not many," Peter said. "Maybe caused more than we solved, looks like now."

Gantry shook his head. "I don't know what your game is, but you should take your ball and go home. These are serious people."

"Somebody's got to get Wanda's place fixed up," said Peter. "And keep an eye out for Wanda. I'm fairly serious about that myself."

Gantry looked at the building, the dump truck lodged

in the living room and the brick walls all shot to shit. "That house might be past saving."

Peter looked at Wanda, still sitting in the open back door of the ambulance. He thought about the man with the machine gun. Then he thought about the look on the face of the kid who'd taken his truck, and the hard people chasing him.

"I don't believe there's anything past saving, long as you put in the work."

Gantry looked at McCarter. "That's just what we need. A goddamn idealist."

Peter asked Wanda to go inside and collect as much of her work stuff as she could. He offered to help, but she just shook her head, so Peter waited in the yard and listened to the uniformed cops reporting back to Gantry from their neighborhood door-knocks.

Miraculously, no immediate neighbors had been hit, although there were a few minor injuries from exploding lamps and shattered windows as the machine-gun rounds pierced houses in the block behind Wanda's, and the block behind that. Peter knew the effective range of the weapon was a hell of a lot farther, so it was still possible someone had been hurt and the police hadn't connected the dots just yet.

Regardless, everyone was lucky that Wanda's walls were twelve inches of solid masonry, red brick three layers thick. Soft, old brick, but still brick, and they soaked up a lot of rounds. The house was a big enough target that even a lunatic asshole with a firehose weapon hadn't managed to miss it too often. Wanda's old blue Toyota Land Cruiser was parked directly behind her house and remained somehow intact.

If Peter's truck had been in the driveway, like it had the night before, it would probably look like a truck-shaped sieve. So maybe the kid who'd stolen it had actually done him a favor. If Peter ever got it back.

A man with an aluminum construction clipboard walked up the drive, staring intently at the house. He wore work boots and cargo pants and a wrinkled button-down shirt with a pair of mechanical pencils in the breast pocket. He hesitated at the cluster of cops, but Gantry waved him forward.

"I'm supposed to do a structural assessment on this property," the man said, handing Gantry and Peter business cards for a building consulting business. "I'm Mark. But maybe now isn't a good time?"

Peter looked at Gantry, who shrugged and passed the card to Peter. "Crime scene techs are done," he said. "Might as well. I hope you've got workman's comp."

"Oh, I work all over," said the engineer. "You wouldn't believe the crap I see. Although this place is pretty damn old. I went to the city and this address showed up on the tax rolls in 1894. But it looks a lot older'n that to me."

"Me too," Peter said.

"In this part of town?" Gantry asked. "Isn't it too small?"

"You'd be surprised how many historic houses are scattered around," said the engineer. "They're not all grand homes. This here was probably a farmhouse, from back when the land was taken from the Indians. It's smaller, but all brick. The farmer was probably fairly prosperous. The city just grew up around it."

"The crawl space entry's around back," Peter said. "Come find me when you're done. I'm going to need drawings for temporary structural reinforcement to get the dump truck out. And probably more drawings for the city, when we rebuild."

The engineer looked at Peter. "Are you kidding? I could tell driving up, this place should be condemned. History or not, the repair cost will be two or three times what the house is worth."

"Tell that to the woman who calls it home," Peter said. "Sometimes it's not about the money."

The engineer shook his head. "It's your money. You want drawings, I'll do drawings." He walked toward the house.

Peter turned to Gantry. "What are the chances we can get a patrol car here overnight?"

"You'll get a car," Gantry said. "If I can spare them, I'll put an unmarked at each end of the block, and a few officers in the house overnight. Maybe we'll get lucky and they'll try again. Probably use artillery or something. But you're not staying here, you know that, right? You're getting Ms. Wyatt to a hotel or a friend's house, something."

"I tried that last night," said Peter. "Maybe now she'll listen to me."

A white truck from EBOX slowed to a stop on the

street with a hiss of its air brakes, carrying the Dumpster Peter had ordered that morning. The can on the back wasn't anywhere near new, but it was six feet tall and twenty-two feet long and made of heavy steel. When the driver got out, Peter walked over and told him exactly where he wanted it.

When the driver finally unhooked his greasy cable, the big Dumpster sat parallel to the street with the back corner snugged up to the rear bumper of the dump truck. Combined, they made a steel wall in front of the house almost thirty-two feet wide.

Gantry looked at Peter. "Are you fortifying this building?"

Peter smiled. "Whatever gives you that idea?"

While the EBOX driver was dropping the can, the Eubanks Lumber truck arrived with a full unit of plywood and a stack of framing lumber. After EBOX was clear, Peter directed the lumber man into the driveway. When the hydraulic bed tipped up, the load slid down, angled along the side porch, making a wooden barrier four feet high, twenty-four feet long, and four feet thick.

Gantry shook his head. "If I see a sniper's nest, you're in trouble."

Peter changed the subject. "What was going on when we talked this morning? Seemed like a lot of sirens in the background."

"Some baby gangsters robbed a jewelry store out at the mall. It got pretty ugly." Gantry looked at Peter. "What's your interest?"

"No reason," said Peter. "Just curious. Seems like a lot of major crime in Memphis."

Gantry looked harder. Still not fooled. "It was pretty quiet until you got here. Now it's like bees in a bottle, all shook up."

Peter couldn't resist. "Anybody ever tell you that you sound like Elvis Presley?"

"Thank you," said Gantry. "Thank you very much."

"Now you're doing it on purpose."

Gantry's phone rang. He put it to his ear and walked away.

17

Peter found Wanda circling the dining room, with her 9-by-12 prints spread out on the table, all scattered from their neat stacks.

"I thought you were packing," he said. Broken window glass crackled under her sneakers.

She still had the paramedic's silvery rescue blanket wrapped around her, loose ends bunched in one fist. "Yeah, no." Her eyes drifted from one print to the next. "I still can't decide what images to use in this show. I'm running out of time."

"Wanda, you need to get your things. We're moving you to a hotel, remember? A nice quiet place where you can work."

"I can't afford a hotel." She kept circling. "This is my home."

Peter wasn't crazy about hotels himself. "What about family or friends?" he asked. "Anyone with a spare bedroom?"

She shook her head. "Those bridges got burned a long time ago."

Peter looked at the ruination of the house, at the half-empty bottle of Tito's vodka on the coffee table, the chipped cereal bowl filled with orange prescription bottles. He imagined Wanda wasn't easy to live with, especially not like this.

"The hotel's on me," he said. "We'll find you a nice place with room service. What's that big old place downtown?" She didn't answer. "Wanda?"

She just made another circuit of the table, touching the corners of the rough prints with a fingertip. All those images of bloodshed and carnage.

"Wanda." Peter spoke more quietly now. "You know we have a problem, right?"

"I know." She didn't take her eyes from the prints. "I'm on deadline. Will you just leave me be so I can work?"

Peter hoped the paramedic had given her something to calm her down. Either that or she was in worse shape than he'd thought.

Whatever challenges Wanda had carried home from her work as a conflict photographer, the dump truck and machine-gun attacks had brought them forward again. Peter was familiar with that.

Now she was trying to focus on something specific, something she could control even if it didn't make sense. Anything to keep her from reliving what she'd just gone through. Peter knew Recon Marines, warriors all, who'd lay out their gear on their rack after each brutal contact with the enemy, each item set in a particular place, cleaned and oiled and adjusted and readjusted to some millimeter-scale plan only they could see.

The back of Peter's truck was pretty goddamn organized, too. At least, the last time he saw it.

"Sure," he told Wanda. "You do what you need to do."

He went into the family room and surveyed the chaos. Wanda's obsession did not extend to housekeeping. Dirty clothes in a heap, the kitchen a mess, fruit flies circling over the trash can. Debris from her ruined home office spread out all over.

Behind him, he heard Wanda pacing around the dining table, muttering to herself.

She was so deep in the weeds she couldn't see her way out.

Peter knew how that felt, too.

So he washed and dried her dishes, put away the food that was salvageable, and threw out the rest. He filled a pair of garbage bags with her dirty laundry. He had no idea how long it would be until she could come back to the house. If she ever would.

There was no decent container for her office computer gear, so he pulled out the biggest kitchen drawer he could find, stacked its contents neatly on the countertop, then filled the drawer with a wide monitor that looked like it might still work, along with the disassembled desktop computer, and the leftover parts tucked gently into Ziploc bags.

With some regrets, he added the vodka bottle and her collection of pills.

The surprise came when he went into the bathroom. Her toiletry kit, fully stocked, hung from a nail pounded into the back of the door.

He pulled back the shower curtain. Inside the ancient bathtub, he found a compact rolling duffel, a battered black waterproof messenger bag, and a high-end camera pack.

In a conflict-area hotel, in case of a mortar or machine-gun attack, the safest place was often either under the bed or inside a cast-iron tub.

Her house was a mess, but her work gear was in perfect order. He opened the duffel and found hardworking travel clothes, so she'd be ready to get on a plane at any time. The messenger bag was her portable office, neatly stocked with a high-end laptop, spare storage drives, a stack of neatly rubber-banded reporter's notebooks, a satellite phone, and an expensive pair of noise-canceling headphones. Her camera pack carried multiple lenses and camera bodies wrapped in scraps from old flannel shirts and tucked into padded compartments. Chargers and spare batteries, memory cards snapped into plastic cases.

Either she'd known she could be ready to go at a moment's notice, or she was so far gone she'd forgotten.

Like any number of guys he'd known, including maybe himself, it was possible that Wanda was better in the fight than out of it.

He found her keys and carried everything out to her blue Land Cruiser. It only took him three trips. Then he dusted off an empty brown accordion file, went into the dining room, and walked along behind her, gathering her prints into neat stacks and tucking them into the pockets.

It wasn't until she'd made a complete circuit of the table and found it empty that she realized what he'd done.

She looked at him with utter outrage. Her short dreadlocks quivering, her sharp-featured face ran rapidly through every emotion known to humankind. She struck his chest hard with her narrow fists, and opened her mouth to howl.

He opened his arms and gathered her gently in. Held her like a sister while she screamed and moaned and stomped her shoes on the broken glass. Her tears soaked the collar of his shirt.

Finally she calmed enough to take a deep, shuddering breath, leaned into him, and became still.

After a few moments, he felt her come back to herself. He opened his arms and took her by the shoulders and looked into her face. "Better?"

A tired smile. "I wish you were a woman. Then we could do the full treatment."

He smiled back. "I'll take that as a compliment. Now can we get the hell out of here?"

In the backyard, the engineer was stepping out of his coveralls. "I was just getting ready to come look at the inside. This house is a lot older than I thought. I love that old tree stump holding up the center of the house, and those cast-off bricks in the dirt around it. If you really want to rebuild this place, we're going to have to talk."

"No problem," said Peter. "I have your card." He took the man's pencil and wrote Wanda's cell number on his pad of graph paper. "Call when you're ready."

Peter had a few things to take care of before he could start house repairs.

Figure out who was trying to destroy it, for one thing.

For another, get his truck and tools back.

What was it about that skinny kid?

18

Eli Bell sat on the three-legged couch, guitar on his lap, fingers frozen on the strings.

He'd wanted to sleep, but every time he closed his eyes he could see it in his mind, the startled look on Skinny B's face as those three red splotches showed on his white painter's suit.

Eli had long ago lost count of the number of people gone missing from his life. Some had got caught up fighting each other, young boys trying to prove to themselves and everyone else that they could stand up like a man in this world. Others had stepped into the drug trade, the only real way ahead they could see. Most of those had been taken by the police, like Eli's father, or cut down by rival sets, like his brother Baldwin. Still others, like his mother, had picked up a pipe or a needle. The needle had killed her. Others it turned into walking ghosts.

Now three more people lost, boys Eli might as well have killed himself. He'd imagined his own death, and accepted that possibility, but not theirs. The regret and shame felt like a suit of stones weighing him down, too heavy to move.

Another reason Eli played the guitar: to help him forget.

It wasn't working now.

He looked out the rear window at the old truck pulled way back out of sight from the street. With the overgrown bushes enclosing the yard, the truck was as hidden as he could make it.

Eli knew that ancient green beast couldn't stay there. Neither could he. Once the names of the dead became known, and the fact that one robber had managed to make it out with the goods, someone would put the pieces together and figure the fourth. It wouldn't take long before they came after him, King Robbie or Mad Chester or any of a half dozen others.

He didn't know what to do next.

Something, he had to do something.

But still he sat. The musty smell of the old couch was a comfort.

He'd left the trash bag full of watches and rings on the floor of the truck. Eli didn't know what to do with that, either. It was supposed to be Coyo's job, paying King Robbie his piece, then getting the stuff sold. If anyone could have made that work, it was Coyo.

If Eli tried, he'd probably lose everything. Including his own skin.

Now he was out of ideas, rooted in place like this empty house collapsing in on itself. Leaving Memphis wasn't a possibility. He was homeless, without people or place, but he'd grown up on those streets, he knew how they worked. The dangers and the sweet spots. Any world outside walking distance might as well have been the moon. But he had to do something.

At nine years old, Eli hadn't been real clear on how things fell apart.

His pops, who already worked a lot, suddenly stopped coming home. Then the police came and put Eli and his mama out of the house, letting them take only what they could carry. They moved into a smaller place, where the floor tilted at unexpected places and the pipes leaked under the kitchen sink.

Eli's mama had always been fierce, but she took the change hard. Sometimes she paced and raged, sometimes she drifted on the couch watching the silent, flickering TV. Most mornings, Eli had to get himself to school. Most nights, Eli had to find himself supper. His mama didn't seem hungry.

His big brother, Baldwin, nineteen years old, was living above the corner store where their dad had worked. *Don't worry,* he'd told Eli, *I got this. Give me a month, maybe two, to sort this out. Your job is to keep it together and take care of Mama.* That was when he'd given Eli that guitar. Because their mama loved music.

When Baldwin got shot in the face, something broke inside her. Overnight, she seemed twenty years older. She seemed to curl in on herself, and spent all her time either staring out the window or asleep. She got skinnier by the day. A week after Baldwin died, Eli came home from school and she was cold on the couch with her mouth wide open and the needle still in her arm.

Then Eli's nana took him in. Coyo came by sometimes, and his nana hugged him a lot. She was a good cook. She checked his homework. It lasted six months, until she had a stroke and died and Eli's entire family was gone. He was truly on his own.

Later on, Eli pieced it together, or some of it, anyway. Who his pops had really been, and why he went away, and how both his mama and Baldwin had protected him from the hard truth of the family business. The war that had followed. How Baldwin had tried to win it, until it killed him. None of it made any sense.

He only knew that King had ended up on top.

Now he forced himself to unlock his fingers on the guitar. To play anything. He started with the first song he'd ever learned, an old murder ballad called "Tom Dooley." That basic chord progression turned into something he'd been working on, until he got lost in the complex simplicity of the twelve-bar blues.

This was the main use of what Eli called his mathematical part. Music had a logic of its own, and the mathematical part allowed the musical possibilities to open up ahead of the actual song.

In his mind, Eli could braid melodic and harmonic lines together before his fingers ever found the notes, and in that way find the road that best suited the song.

All blues was built on the same basic framework, Eli had known that longer than he'd known anything. What made the blues your own were the choices you made along the way. The mathematical part was all about seeing the choices before he had to make them.

As the song raveled out of his calloused fingers, twelve bars at a time, Eli thought about his gig that night and the old men he was lucky enough to play with.

Maybe he could front some goods from that black trash bag to Dupree for enough cash to buy a new guitar. He loved playing the old man's 1932 National "O"-style resonator guitar, with its steel body and big sound, much bigger than Eli's old Sears acoustic. Dupree had offered it to Eli more than once, but that just felt like charity. Work was one thing, but charity was something else, and Eli had been doing for himself for a long time now.

If he bought an old National of his own, though, that bigger sound could make him more money on the street, even playing without an amp. He could polish it up, get it shiny, bring in the tourists. Maybe even get ahead, get some money put away.

But he'd still be Eli Bell, playing for tips, slipping from empty to empty, and that shiny guitar would just make him a target. Make it look like he had something worth taking.

Plus anything he gave Dupree would put a target on the old man. Dupree was a friend, no matter the fifty years of age between them. He'd shown Eli a world of kindness. Eli wasn't going to bring down a beating on him, or worse. Pain and trouble Dupree didn't deserve.

Knowing anything about that trash bag could end Dupree's life.

No, Eli had made this problem. It was up to him to solve it, too.

He swung through the turnaround, ten fingers moving, the mathematical part racing ahead. The song had started as a slow blues, but picked up speed along the way until it was at the far edge of his control, catching up with the mathematical part, then flying beyond. Like running downhill as fast as he could, lost to the pull of gravity, just trying to keep his feet under him and not plow face-first into that hard cracked concrete.

Then he knew. The mathematical part told him.

If Coyo and the others were gone, Eli had to do for himself more than ever.

Maybe he needed to step into his brother's shoes. Figure how Baldwin would have done things.

Eli walked down to the Wet Spot. It was the only way he knew to get word to King Robbie. He had ten dollars in his pocket and Coyo's shitty disposable pistol jammed into his waistband, hiding under his untucked T-shirt.

Skinny B's plan had been to give King and his people a few of those Rolexes, both pay the man his piece and get other people interested in buying. Coyo hadn't seen a problem with the idea, and Eli didn't, either.

That was back when Coyo's wild-man reputation and his history with King would work in their favor, get that deal done. Without Coyo, it meant Eli would have to make things happen. Eli had no rep at all outside of his dead brother and locked-up father and what Eli himself might do with a guitar.

In the world of King Robbie, that was less than nothing.

That was a goddamn negative rep. The opposite of respect.

Although the mathematical part thought it might give Eli an edge.

19

The Wet Spot was a two-story brick box painted the color of vanilla ice cream. Set on a corner, it had narrow buckled sidewalks and cracked streets on two sides, a green-tangled vacant lot for a neighbor, gravel parking in the back. Eli had never been inside.

Metal security grates covered the big front windows, and a heavy security door stood open at the front, held with a stone. The side windows were bricked up.

It had been a corner store ever since Eli could remember, although it had only been the Wet Spot for a half-dozen years. The name was hand-painted in bold black letters above the windows and on the side around the corner. Beside the windows, in the same dark print, were the words: COLD DRINKS, SOFT-SERVE, GROCERIES, CIGARETTES, CIGARS.

On the vacant-lot side, a wooden stairway climbed to second-floor rooms where Baldwin, ten years older than Eli, had once lived, before it was the Wet Spot. Eli had never been up there, either. His mother had forbidden it.

Now it was King Robbie's place. Everybody knew it.

The Wet Spot was King's friendly face, with cheap beer and groceries and ice cream for the kids. King's way of getting the neighborhood on his side. He'd park his big Mercedes right out front, not hiding from anybody.

It wasn't parked there now.

Eli took a deep breath, climbed three steps to the little landing, and walked through the door.

He saw a long room with a dark wooden counter along the left side and shelves of groceries along the right. One back corner was sectioned off for bathrooms or something. The other corner had a table and chairs and a couch, with a silent TV on the wall beyond it, showing police cars outside of Macy's. The words across the bottom of the screen said, "Wolfchase Galleria heist, two robbers dead, two missing."

"What you need, little brother?"

A middle-aged man sat, expressionless, on a high stool behind the metal-topped counter. His head was shaved, the skin bunched in thick wrinkles at the back of his neck. A black laptop stood open in front of him and a weird-looking walkie-talkie squawked softly by his right hand.

He looked, Eli thought with a pang, like what Anthony might have looked like in twenty years, with the same black-framed glasses slipping down his nose, the same broad shoulders, the same thick fingers. If Anthony hadn't signed on with Coyo and Skinny B. And Eli.

"I'm looking for King Robbie."

The counterman's expressionless face remained unchanged. "We got soft-serve, dollar a cone. Drinks in the cooler over there."

"I got a message," Eli said. "Man told me to come here and find King Robbie."

"Well, King's not here, little brother. Tell me your message and I'll pass it on."

"I don't know," Eli said. "Man told me to ask for King Robbie himself."

The man reached down, took a big black pistol from somewhere, and slapped it down hard on the metal countertop. The walkie-talkie jumped. "I'm close enough. And I'm done asking."

Eli let himself show his nerves and took a quick step back. "Okay," he said. "The man told me to say he knows he owes King his piece on something happened this morning. Wanted King to know."

The counterman's eyes flashed at the walkie-talkie beside him. "What something?"

"I don't know." Eli looked at the door as if he wanted to run. Which he did. "He gave me ten dollars to come here and say what I said. That's all."

The counterman put the gun away. "Who's the man?"

"I don't know, I never seen him before. I was just walking down the street. He pulled over next to me and asked if I knew where the Wet Spot was. I pointed the way, but he wanted me to go, like I said, and talk to King."

The counterman looked at him, black-framed glasses magnifying his eyes. "What was he driving?"

Eli shook his head. "I don't know. Janky old car. It was red."

"Who you with? Pershing Park Boys?"

"Not with nobody," said Eli. "Tried being a trap-house lookout a few years back, but I was no good at it."

The counterman nodded, recognition dawning. "I thought there was something. You're Eli Bell, right? Win Bell's baby brother. You're starting to look like him."

Eli's stomach dropped, a pit opening up. He'd hoped to be just a kid walking in off the street, but the neighborhood carried too much history for that.

The counterman didn't seem to care. "Okay, Eli Bell, you delivered your message, earned your ten dollars. But I got a new job for you. Easy money. King's people are out looking for an old green pickup truck with some kind of box on the back, like work trucks have, you know? But made out of wood."

He pulled a twenty and a cheap flip-phone from under the counter and held them out together. Eli didn't move. How'd they know about the truck?

"Come on, take it. Talk to your friends, put the word out. There's a reward, a lot more than twenty dollars. Old green pickup with a wood box on the back. You see something like that, you call me, tell me where it is. My number's already programmed in."

Eli kept his face still. "What's King want it for?"

The counterman slowly shook his head. "Not your business. Just know he wants it."

That's when Eli knew he was in bigger trouble than he'd thought. King Robbie was already digging into this thing. Paying him off wasn't going to be near enough.

The mathematical part began to run the odds, to consider what he knew of King Robbie's reach and power.

What King might already know, what he might learn, and when he'd learn it.

Eli was barely fifteen.

In his world, more than old enough to know he was likely already dead.

The question was, what was he going to do about it?

He'd thought he was making a move by walking into the Wet Spot. His only choice now was to brazen it out, work his negative rep, and play the fool. Everyone knew Eli Bell wasn't in that life. Leave the truck on the street with the trash bag still in it. Take his guitar and find someplace new to stay.

Maybe Dupree could help. They were playing tonight, no way Eli was going to miss that gig. He could talk to the old man then.

Skipping that gig would be as good as telling the world he'd robbed that store himself.

First things first.

He stepped forward, picked up the phone and the money, then nodded at the counterman and walked out the door.

Twenty dollars was twenty dollars.

He was tempted to get an ice cream cone, thinking it might be his last, but thought better of it.

20

When you're a big guy, and quiet, most folks figure you're not that smart.

Dennis Brody kept his mouth shut and let them think what they wanted.

He watched and listened and learned.

Now he drove King's armored Mercedes like a cruising shark, riding the currents down North Memphis and Frayser side streets, eyes out for that green truck.

They were all looking. King in the back seat, tapping his damn toes, practically vibrating in his seat from the habit he'd been working on for the last six years. Charlene up front with Brody, smoke coming out of her ears at the fact that the white workingman had taken her gun. Made even angrier that he'd touched her.

Everybody knew Charlene Scott was real particular about who she allowed to touch her.

By the time she'd come of age, she'd killed everyone who knew why, everyone but Brody, and he wasn't telling. Because he'd helped her do it. Because the dead men, her uncles, had deserved worse, every last one of them.

Girl had one shitty-ass childhood, leave it at that.

It's why Brody and Charlene got along, as much as she got along with anyone. Together, they'd learned how to survive, even thrive, in that furnace of violence and poverty. Brody had his mind and his size. Charlene picked up a gun and got good with it. You learned to be ruthless, to make your own chances, or you died. Some died fast, some died slow. But everybody died.

That lean, ropy character in his work-worn clothes had some big brass ones, Brody had to admit. Not just for taking on Charlene, either. He hadn't known what she was, and anybody could get lucky once. Brody would make sure it didn't happen again.

No, it was the way that workingman, Peter, had sprinted off toward the sound of the machine gun, carrying only Charlene's pistol, when everybody else, including most police, would have turned tail the other way. Dennis Brody had never seen anything like it.

Only Brody's mom still called him Dennis. He'd moved her into a nice little house near Overton Park, with a big backyard and a high, strong fence that gave her some privacy and helped her feel safe. He'd told her he ran a bar off Beale Street, which accounted for the cash money and his busy hours. If she believed any different, she didn't say anything. As far as Brody knew, she'd never been to the bar. She was grateful to be out of the little apartment in South Memphis.

"Turn this bus around, Brody," said Charlene. "I

want to find that white boy and hurt him some. Get my damn gun back."

"Not now, Charlene." King's voice had a crooked edge after all that product he'd been putting up his nose. "We got work to do. That place will be crawling with police, and I'm not getting stuck there. We'll catch him up later."

Brody knew King wouldn't shut down Charlene entirely. He had to let her off the leash sometimes, especially if King didn't want her to turn around and bite him. The next time Charlene saw that Peter, she'd take him apart, and wasn't nobody going to stop her. Not when she took something personally.

Charlene liked to start with the ankles and work her way up from there. A few years back, she'd shown Brody a medical book she'd bought, just to learn all the places to shoot a man that wouldn't kill him. She already knew the spots to kill a man with a single bullet, and was good enough to do it. She'd been practicing for years, on targets and people. Charlene could shoot the legs off a fly from a block away.

She was who she was, nothing less, nothing more. She'd turned her negatives into a positive, did her job without complaint. She wasn't particularly ambitious, and her personal life never interfered with her work. Not often, anyway.

King took another hit from that little silver spoon. "Either of you ever hear anything like that big gun? Damn, where do you think I could find one of those?"

King Robbie didn't carry anymore, at least not

day-to-day. Brody and Charlene did most of the heavy work, although King still had an active interest. When King was making his big move after Isaac Bell got sent up, he'd kept an Uzi or an AK close to hose down a rival crew or house or car, and he still let loose once in a while. Held out a hand for Brody's gun just for the pleasure of doing the deed himself.

Even when the guy getting put down was making them money. Had overstepped, sure, deserved a beating, maybe a fine. Some reminder of the rules he'd broken.

Not every problem, in Brody's opinion, had to be solved with a bullet.

But King was as wild as he'd ever been, and more than a little crazy. Brody thought hard about doing business, running people, making money, keeping order. He could see all the ways King's reckless behavior had cost them.

Being King's muscle was a job. It paid well, and Brody was good at it. Not like he had many choices, growing up where he did. But it gave him no pleasure to hurt somebody, not like King. No, what Brody liked was seeing how the pieces came together, watching it grow.

He'd been the muscle for six years.

Now he was starting to think about what else he might be.

Reckless or not, King was still the boss. Brody kept his opinions to himself. But he didn't like how King was getting more and more unpredictable. He wasn't making good decisions. It was bad for business.

A big machine gun? Man, that'd only make things worse.

. . .

King's phone rang. Besides Brody and Charlene, the only other person with the number was Chris, working the scanner back at the storefront.

They all cycled through cheap work phones every week, to keep their business private. Brody also had a loaded new cell he kept for personal use. Pictures, social media, his mom. He kept it on airplane mode when he was working.

King answered on speaker. It wasn't how Brody would have done it, but as always, he kept his mouth shut. "Anything?"

"Not from the scanner," said Chris. "But one of our friends in blue called, says there were four of them wearing some kind of white coveralls. Two dead at the mall, one shot and gone missing, one just plain gone. Young niggas, not grown men."

"Young don't mean shit, you know that," King said. "Just means they ain't had much practice yet."

Brody had watched King Robbie beat a grown man to death on his fourteenth birthday. Almost like a present to himself. Seeing it had made Brody sick to his stomach. He'd thought about it for months, trying to put it out of his head. All these years later, it wasn't the worst thing he'd seen—or done himself—but it still came back sometimes, if he wasn't paying attention. It took him years to learn to shut down enough to do the job he was paid for.

King bragged about that killing to this day.

He was just plain Robbie Kingston back then, and the

killing let him take ownership of a corner. It was the first of many moves like it. A corner, then a house, then a captain's position. The captain had misjudged Robbie, as they all did, despite everything Robbie had already shown himself to be.

At the time, in awe of King's ability to take what he wanted, and to talk his way out of the problems he caused himself with the bosses, Brody had thought King was some kind of genius. Even when King had schemed to bring down Isaac Bell and take the whole town for his territory, Brody had gone along and got Charlene to come with him.

Not like there was much choice. Brody had learned that, too. Sometimes standing still wasn't an option. Sometimes you had to move up or get cut down.

When Bell's operation fell, it was a free-for-all, but King, Brody, and Charlene moved fast to consolidate. In less than a month, King and Charlene took out any serious contenders while Brody hand-picked the new house captains and reached out to the suppliers.

Eventually, though, Brody realized that King wasn't a genius. He'd kept jumping up the food chain because he didn't know how to run what he'd already taken. That's why he started shoving that shit up his nose, faster and faster. Which didn't help anything.

Now King said, "Get any names?"

"No official ID yet, but our friend in blue says he knows the two got dropped. Skinny B and Anthony Wilkinson."

"Doesn't ring a bell." King's voice turned threatening. "Tell me you asked around."

Chris didn't let it ruffle him, kept his voice nice and even.

"'Course I did, boss. Skinny B used to work outside one of your houses. He wanted to move inside, but the house captain told me the boy wasn't ready, probably never would be. Kid didn't like hearing it. He up and quit about three months ago."

"Maybe trying to go on his own?" asked King. "Serves him right. Police saved me a bullet. I keep telling you, Chris, you gotta stay on these young niggas all the damn time."

Even on a fresh phone, King wasn't talking about the real reason he was pissed. The jewelry store was a money laundry, a good one, turning drug cash into legitimate profits. So those were King Robbie's goods that got stolen, and King Robbie's single best laundry wrecked in the process.

"I know, boss, I know," Chris said, his voice tinny over the cheap phone. "But you can't kill everybody, right?"

"What about this Anthony Wilkinson?"

"Part-timer, lived with his mama. Smart kid, ran a lookout crew at that same house, still going to school. You and I talked about him a while ago, how maybe we should take him off the street, send him to U-Memphis. Get him working the clean side."

Brody thought about the description that workingman Peter had given King about the guy who'd jacked his truck. It didn't fit with these young men, unless someone older was running them as a crew without getting King's okay. That would turn into serious trouble.

King was obviously thinking the same thing. "Somebody forgot who runs this damn town. Maybe they didn't believe the price they'd pay. We're gonna make it clear, set a damn example. Write it out in blood."

King didn't want his people to get any big ideas. Least of all Chris, Charlene, or Brody. Maybe that was why he put the phone on speaker, thought Brody, so he could deliver the message to everybody at once. King was half-crazy, but he wasn't stupid.

To Chris, King said, "Tell me you know who these niggas run with."

"No crew to speak of. Anthony Wilkinson was doing the work, but he didn't hang around. He wasn't all in, you know? Skinny B was on the outside. But the house captain talked with some of the lookouts who saw them with Isaac Bell's youngest boy. The guitar player. Shows up at the Lucky every once in a while."

"Yeah, I remember. Goes by Eli, right?"

At the time, King hadn't considered nine-year-old Eli worth killing. He hadn't wanted to draw the heat. But Brody had made a point to keep track of young Eli as he grew. With Isaac Bell for his father and Win Bell for his brother, you never knew who that boy might turn into. Could decide to put down that guitar and pick up a gun. Brody knew the boy paid his piece to King's man like everyone else. It wasn't much, the kid was scraping bottom, but it was a positive sign that the boy knew how things stood.

"That's him," said Chris. "But he's got this homeboy from way back. Put out the word a few years ago, Eli Bell gets left alone on the street. He's protected."

King was getting impatient. "Homeboy got a name?"

"You know him. Name's Coyo."

Brody took the next turn faster than he'd planned, the heavy Mercedes dipping on its springs. Charlene put out an automatic hand to steady herself, but kept on staring out the windshield, thinking whatever she was thinking inside that head of hers.

King was trying to keep himself calm, but Brody could hear the effort. "You think Coyo could have put this thing together?"

"Coyo's got talent, we both know that. Cooler than ice cream when things get hot. But he's not the kind to plan things out. More like he makes it up as he goes, just shows up and gets it done."

Brody thought about Isaac Bell, the organization he'd made before he got sent up. Isaac had been a planner. He'd built something so tight nobody could touch him, especially not the police. King himself had only managed to bring the man down by turning snitch, throwing anonymous tips to the feds. Nobody else knew but Brody.

No, King's heavy street rep was built entirely on what he'd done before, and his ruthless cleanup afterward. There were more than a few young guns who'd made King work for it. Young Baldwin Bell was the strongest contender. Almost made it, too.

Eli had that same strong blood running through him. And he was tight with Coyo?

But neither boy linked up with that workingman Peter's description of the carjacker.

It was a puzzle.

Brody liked puzzles.

"One last thing," said Chris. "I'll tell you right now, you're not gonna like it."

King's voice turned threatening again. "You know I don't like bad news, Chris."

"Yeah, but sometimes you got to hear it. Right before our friend in blue called, before I made my own calls, Eli Bell walked in here looking for you. Said he had a message from some stranger in a red car who told Eli to come tell you he knew he owed you for something this morning."

King gave a half-strangled scream and kicked at the back of the seat with his pointed boots. Brody heard the thick leather tear. "Tell me you got him stashed away someplace."

Chris coughed nervously. "Wish I could, boss, but it didn't come together until after he walked away. I sent him out with a phone and twenty bucks, told him to watch for that same green pickup truck. Now I got people out looking for him."

"Hey, Chris." Charlene spoke without looking back at King. "You hear anything about that big shooting in North Memphis today?"

"Charlene, there's only two things on the news today, and that shooting is the other one. It's the same house somebody drove a dump truck into yesterday." He paused. "You know whose place that is, right?"

"No, who?"

"Wanda Wyatt," Chris said. "That's Wanda's new place."

Charlene whipped her head around to glare at King.

Brody made a point to be quiet, think before he spoke, and be careful what he said. Charlene, on the other hand, usually said what was on her mind.

"Wanda's." Her voice was a flat crack, like a gunshot on the river. "That's how I'll find him."

Brody watched King in the rearview, staring hard at Charlene. Reminding her who was in charge.

"Once we find those young niggas and what they took," King finally said, "you're free for a few days. Do what you need to do."

21

Downtown Memphis made Peter nervous.

It was an old city, but once he got past the highway the streets weren't particularly narrow. Wanda's Land Cruiser was in good shape, and traffic wasn't bad at all. Still, it was a dense urban area, and Peter's sight lines were clogged up with parked cars and tall buildings. Every alley, intersection, and red light was a possible ambush. His head was on a swivel and the white static was sparking up high.

He told himself he wouldn't feel this way if he hadn't taken a pistol from a gangster's gunny just that morning. Right before he'd taken a run at a lunatic with an armored station wagon and a machine gun intent on blowing the shit out of Wanda's house.

Maybe he was telling the truth.

What really made him uncomfortable was the fact that he didn't truly mind the white static. The blast of adrenaline, the hyper-awareness.

In fact, he liked it.

June knew it, too. The year before, when they'd only

known each other a few days, she'd told him to come
back when he'd gotten it out of his system. He wondered
now if he ever would. If he even wanted to.

Wanda looked at him from the passenger seat. She sat
in a boneless slump, her eyes at half-mast. Her knees were
drawn up to her chest, Chuck Taylors propped on the
dusty dashboard, the accordion folder with her photo
proofs clutched in both hands.

"You never told me what happened to your truck."

Peter turned left into the driveway of The Peabody
hotel, an ornate thirteen-story building in the heart of
downtown, and pulled under the covered entrance area.
"Long story," he said. "I'll tell you later."

A uniformed bellman opened Peter's door. "Welcome
to The Peabody, sir. Do you have any luggage?"

"We do," said Peter. "We had some problems at the
house, so we're not very stylish, I'm afraid."

"Not a problem, sir." The gray-haired bellman had an
easy smile under a crisply tailored mustache. "We all have
days like that once in a while."

The Peabody was a Memphis monument to old white
money. Built in 1925, everyone from U.S. presidents to
Elvis Presley had stayed there. Aside from the fact that
the online photos were gorgeous, Peter had picked The
Peabody because he knew, with its high-end clientele,
the hotel would have a lot of practice taking care of difficult guests.

Wanda wasn't going to be easy.

The bellman brought over a cart and began to load
the black, professional go-bags that Peter had found

stashed in Wanda's bathtub, the big kitchen drawer full of office gear, and the pair of white trash bags full of dirty laundry. His face betrayed no evidence that their baggage was in any way unusual. Wanda watched anxiously, the accordion folder in a two-fisted death grip, her purse slung across her chest.

Peter figured she was ready to crash. He kept the Land Cruiser running. He still had her phone.

He touched her shoulder. "So, this is a little awkward," he said. "I misplaced my wallet. I had to put the hotel reservation on your credit card. It's a nice room, and it's not cheap, but don't worry about the money. I'll transfer everything to a new card tomorrow."

She looked at him plaintively. "You're not coming in?"

"I need to get my truck back."

She blinked at him. "Where exactly is your truck?"

"Somebody took it this morning," he said. "While I was getting gas."

"Wait." A sleepy smile blossomed across her face. "You got jacked?"

Peter didn't want to explain it, how he'd felt sorry for the kid. How desperate the kid had seemed, but also how profoundly capable and dangerous. How Peter might have stopped him from taking the truck, but didn't.

He just nodded. "Yes."

"I should go with you." She screwed her knuckles into her eyes, trying to wake up. "I know most of these bangers. I've been taking their pictures for years. Tell me about the guy who jacked you."

There was no way Peter was going to allow her to come along.

"Sure," he said. "But let's check you in and get your stuff up to the room first. You go ahead, I'm going to make a quick call." He still had Wanda's phone.

Faster than he thought she could move in her impaired condition, Wanda reached past him into the Land Cruiser and took the keys from the ignition.

"You're not fooling me one bit," she said. "I've learned my lesson. I've been screwed out of too many stories."

"What about choosing the prints for your show?"

"I'll do that later," she said. "I'd rather go shoot gangsters any day."

Again, it took Peter a moment to realize she was talking about shooting pictures.

The bellman closed the Toyota's rear hatch and pointed his cart toward the hotel entrance. "You're welcome to leave your vehicle there for a few minutes, sir. If you like, I can get started on your check-in. What's the name on the reservation?"

Peter sighed. "Wanda Wyatt."

The hotel lobby was vast, with a high, elegant ceiling coffered in dark wood. The open second floor hallway wrapped around the lobby in a balcony halfway up. On the main floor, a bar stood at one end, a grand player piano at the other, and a wide fountain occupied the middle, along with couches and chairs and table seating.

The static sparked higher up Peter's brainstem. Maybe it was the dim, cavernous space. Maybe it was the piano's version of "Hound Dog," which sounded like it was recorded by a hyperactive middle-school kid from Nebraska. Maybe it was the aggressive air-conditioning, or all the Elvis memorabilia.

But Peter knew deep down that the static was rising because his truck was gone, maybe for good. That truck was the closest thing to a home he'd had since moving out of his parents' house at eighteen. Even more than June's valley compound, which he liked, and with all the repairs he'd done, he felt some sense of ownership there. But it was still June's place, not his.

Wanda signed at the check-in desk, then handed Peter her spare key card. She waved a tired hand at the fountain. "See the famous Peabody ducks?"

Peter watched the birds paddling serenely in the water. "I read about this on the hotel website. They live in a little palace on the roof and take the elevator down for a swim every day, right? With a red carpet and an escort?"

"Since the thirties." Wanda clutched her car keys in her fist. "Guess they figure a plush prison is better than living free and watching for shotguns." She glared at Peter, swaying slightly. "Don't think I don't know what you're doing."

She was right, of course. Peter was definitely hoping she'd be so comfortable she'd just crash in her room. One less person for him to worry about. The bellman waited by the desk to escort Wanda to her suite.

"You go ahead," said Peter. "I really do have to make a phone call."

Wanda leaned close. The smell of alcohol came off her like a wave. "Let me guess, you don't have any cash, either. So I have to tip this nice man, too?" She shook her head. "You are one lousy damn date."

She took the bellman's arm, leaning on him as they walked toward the elevator.

It was a relief to step outside into the heat and call Lewis.

The phone rang on the other end, but nobody picked up. Peter left a message. "I'm on a borrowed phone. Call me back."

Wanda's phone rang again thirty seconds later.

Before Peter could say anything, Lewis said, "Did you lose another goddamned phone?"

"I loaned it to someone," Peter said. "I'll get it back soon enough."

"Uh-huh. Is this June's friend's place all over the news again? Some kind of major automatic weapon? Military grade?"

"I might be a little outgunned here," Peter admitted.

"No shit, Jarhead." Peter could hear that tilted smile. "But I'll hook you up. See you tomorrow, early."

Peter was slightly scared to think what artillery Lewis might show up with. When they'd first met, he'd favored a sawed-off 10-gauge shotgun, which would put a serious hole in a person.

"Listen, Lewis."

"Yeah?"

"I'm sorry about this."

Lewis gave his low, rumbling chuckle. "No, you're not. You're just trying to pretend you ain't having fun. 'Sides, things are a little boring around here anyway."

"What about Dinah and the boys?"

Peter heard the smile again. "You got a shrink, right? For your post-traumatic shit? Well, Dinah says running with you is my therapy."

"Lord help us all."

Lewis's chuckle deepened. "I'll be in touch." The phone went silent.

A moment later, the screen lit up with a text. *BTW, June saw the shooting online, can't reach you, called me twice already. Don't be that asshole.*

Now Peter was getting relationship advice from a career criminal.

On the other hand, Lewis and Dinah seemed to be doing pretty well.

Peter called June.

You sonofabitch, what the fucking fuck is going on?"

One of the things Peter loved about June was that she swore like the carpenters he'd grown up working with. Not quite like a Marine drill instructor, but that was the pinnacle of the art, a high bar for a civilian.

"June, I'm sorry. I misplaced my phone and haven't had time to call. Things are a little busy here."

"I saw the footage of Wanda's house after that thing with the machine gun." He heard her breathing hard on the other end of the line. "Tell me you're wearing that vest I bought you."

"Absolutely," he said. "It's a great fit, super comfortable. Safe as houses."

Although maybe that last expression wasn't the best choice given the circumstances.

"Don't fucking lie to me." Her voice broke a little. "It's bad, isn't it?"

"It's definitely gotten interesting," he said. Understatement of the year. "Lewis will be here in the morning."

"I can't believe I asked you to go."

"Actually, I think you *told* me to go," he said. "Because I was driving you nuts."

"*Completely* nuts," she said. "You were like a crackhead hamster running a squeaky wheel, all day every day."

"But now you miss me. Can't live without me." He smiled. "Mission accomplished."

"Don't push it, Marine, I'm still pissed," she said. "Have you figured out why someone is trying to kill Wanda?"

"I'm not convinced that's what they're trying to do. If they are, there are certainly easier ways to go about it. Whoever they are, they mostly seem to want to beat the shit out of her house. I've got her checked into a nice hotel, trying to keep her out of sight for a while. But I don't think she's going to stay in her room."

June laughed. "No, I'd guess not. How's she holding up?"

"Not so well," Peter said. "She seems wound pretty tight. Was she always like this?"

"Wanda's a handful. She sleeps with her camera under her pillow and her finger on the shutter. Is it worse than that?"

"Seems like it. Vodka for breakfast, all kinds of pills."

"Shit," June said. "She's been shooting war zones and refugee camps for the last fifteen years. Her last assignment was four weeks in fucking Syria. She won't talk about any of it, at least not with me. Maybe she'll talk with you?"

"I'll try. Thing is, she's got this gallery show scheduled in New York. She hasn't really said anything, but it seems like kind of a big deal. The gallery owner, Garry somebody, he keeps calling. She still hasn't made her selections for the show, and I guess she's running out of time to get the big prints made. Her house is a wreck, she's kind of a mess emotionally, I just don't want her to ruin her professional life, too."

"So maybe you need a hand wrangling Wanda?"

"Jesus, do I ever." Peter had no idea how to cope with Wanda's intensity.

"This isn't going to be like last time, is it?"

The last time, June had gotten locked in the trunk of a car. Neither of them had been happy about it.

"The last time, I asked you *not* to come, remember?" The phone gave back an icy silence. "But this time I'm asking. You can stay at The Peabody with Wanda. You'll be in stealth mode. I got her a suite, it's pretty plush. Please, will you come help?"

"Well," she said. "I guess. But only because I already bought my fucking ticket."

22

It was after four. Peter was ready to go upstairs, hoping Wanda had fallen asleep and left the car keys somewhere he could find them, when she bounced through the double doors. She had a wide smile on her face. "Okay, homeboy. Let's roll!"

She'd showered and changed into what Peter assumed were her working clothes: dark-blue ripstop pants that would hide all manner of dirt, a plaid short-sleeved button-down shirt made of some sweat-wicking miracle fabric, and running shoes. She carried her Nikon with a fat lens in a padded open tote bag.

Wanda seemed to have only two speeds, wired to the gills and off like a light. Now she walked toward Peter with a swagger he hadn't seen since Camp Pendleton.

Her pupils were enormous.

She'd obviously taken something uplifting from her vast collection of pills.

Peter walked around and opened the passenger door for her, but she jumped into the driver's seat and fired up the engine.

He said, "Maybe I should drive."

"I know this town a lot better than you do. Plus my reflexes are like *lightning*." She threw the car into gear. "You coming or not?"

Peter had to hop in while she was already moving. She made a hole in the one-way traffic and cranked the Toyota through the turn. "Your truck's already long gone," she said. "You know that, right?"

"I have to look." He shrugged. "I put a lot of hours into restoring that rig. Plus it's got all my tools in the cargo box, everything I need to fix up your house."

Not to mention the armored vest June had bought him.

For his own personal safety, he wanted to be wearing it when June showed up in town.

Wanda pulled around the block to B.B. King Boulevard, a one-way street headed north, and Peter got a chance to take a closer look at downtown Memphis. For every two restaurants or shops, he saw a vacant storefront that looked like it had been empty for a long time.

It was hot and humid, and Peter's clothes were sticking to his skin, but Wanda drove with all the windows down, pointing out the highlights of the municipal center.

"The streetcar runs down Main two blocks over, but they're renovating, so for now it's just fancy buses. Court Square is a block that way." Peter looked left and saw shade trees and a fountain, on the right a gorgeous stone church.

"County courthouse here, county jail up to the right." Big buildings designed to be impressive and intimidating, demonstrating the power of the government. Another beautiful church, this time in red brick, then parking lots mostly empty, then yet another church.

"Yeah, we do a lot of church in Memphis," Wanda said. "I'm a sinner because, you know, I dig chicks, so I'm not much for church myself." She pointed right. "That's the Lauderdale Courts, used to be apartments, now a hotel. Elvis lived there for a while." She frowned. "We do a lot of Elvis, too."

Then under the freeway and into Uptown, where things changed. Wanda zigged and zagged, taking Peter on a tour of wide vacant lots and shuttered businesses, two blocks of newer multistory apartments or condos across from two churches and a park, then a store selling African crafts across from a small barbershop. An auto-repair shop and junkyard surrounded by a sheet-metal fence. A print shop, boarded-up apartment buildings, vacant lots neatly mowed. Battered old houses and small businesses surrounded by tall, ancient trees providing shade. A few blocks of small, newer homes, clearly some kind of modest development.

"Where'd you get jacked?"

"Up Watkins past the freeway," said Peter. "At a Texaco station."

"In Frayser?" She turned right on Chelsea. "Good thing I'm here, 'cause you clearly don't have the sense God gave a goose. You're lucky you walked away at all."

The thick heat was a tangible thing, even with the breeze through the open windows. Peter felt like he was swimming through invisible mud.

They passed a newer four-story apartment building across from more overgrown vacant lots, then a little convenience store with security grates across the windows and doors, then a big painted-brick former church that looked abandoned for decades. It was surrounded by a high chain-link fence.

"What happened to Memphis?" Peter asked.

"White flight, forty and fifty years ago, same as a lot of other places. Now most of the money's in the suburbs. Uptown, where we are, was starting to pick up speed until the crash hit in '08, when everything stalled." She shrugged. "Downtown has a little arts district, the Orpheum Theatre, the National Civil Rights Museum. Beale Street, Graceland, the Stax Museum, and Sun Studio bring in the music pilgrims. There are a few other pockets of recovery in the city, but big chunks of Memphis proper haven't even come back from the *seventies*."

She turned left onto Watkins, the route Peter had taken earlier in the day. On the long bridge, she pointed out the window at the brown water below. "The Wolf River," she said. "Flows to the Big Muddy. This whole area, along with the freeway, is what segregates Frayser from the rest of the city."

She drove past the Texaco without slowing. The kid's red car was still parked down the street.

"Where are we going?" Peter asked.

"Around." She turned into a residential area. "Keep your eyes open for your truck. If you're lucky, your new friend just drove it to his mom's house. Or we might find it wrapped around a tree."

Inside Frayser, the street grid devolved into loops and alleys and dead ends, contained by the contours of the land. Enormous oaks and chestnuts gave steady shade. The low frame houses were small, but the front porches were wide and deep. The lots were big, too, with plenty of space between the buildings.

Wanda made her way through section after section, slowly but methodically, working her way out from the Texaco. Frayser varied widely from block to block, from house to house. Some homes were neat and clean. Others were sturdy but needed paint and basic repairs. Still others looked like they were being eaten alive by the landscape growing wild around them. Board-ups were frequent, and on many streets remnant foundations of demolished homes lay cracked and bare amid high grass, cooking in the hot sun. Some vacant lots had been untended for so long, they'd turned into quarter-acre wilderness, trees towering over dense tangled scrub and weeds gone to seed.

Wanda drove with her left arm hanging out the window while she palmed the wheel with her right. She seemed calmer on the move, or maybe whatever combination of pills she'd taken at the hotel had kicked in and created some kind of equilibrium.

She seemed to know almost everyone in the neighborhood. She called out to the older men and women on their porches and the young mothers with strollers, and waved to the boys on the corners, who waved back. She raised a low-key hand to the young men collected in the yards of certain vacant houses, who gave her slow nods of recognition.

Peter looked at the vehicles parked on the asphalt verge, up the long gravel driveways, and in front yards, looking for the familiar silhouette of his 1968 Chevy. There was a pattern to Wanda's driving, but he wasn't quite sure what it was.

He thought of the cereal bowl full of pill bottles and the vodka on the coffee table.

"I'm guessing you saw some serious shit in Iraq."

"Sure," she said, voice flat, face blank. "Who didn't?"

Peter thought about his own veterans' group. How talking helped. "You want to tell me about it?"

"No," she said. "I don't."

"Might help."

She stared furiously out the windshield, a vein throbbing in her temple. "What makes you think I need your fucking help?"

"No reason." He kept his voice calm. "Except for the vodka for breakfast and pills for lunch. Listen, war can really mess with you. I, ah . . ."

He'd gotten more practice talking about it, but it still made him uncomfortable. Acknowledging that weakness. But maybe this was another way he could help Wanda. He cleared his throat.

"I was eight years a Recon Marine," he said. "An elite unit, even for Recon. Command told us we had indispensable skills. I stopped counting my deployments. I was fine in the fight, all eight years. But I got off the plane for the last time, three days from mustering out, and suddenly I had this insane claustrophobia. I could barely go inside, even for a few minutes. The shrinks told me it was post-traumatic stress. I get these panic attacks. Sometimes I can hardly breathe."

"You went into *my* house." Her dreadlocks quivered with her intensity. "I saw you go into that crawl space."

"I've been working at it. I'm not saying it's easy, but it gets better. Facing it helps. Talking about it helps."

She shook her head. "You don't know what I've been through."

"I would if you told me. You told anyone?"

For a long minute, she didn't answer. "No," she finally said. "Not really."

23

After an hour's driving with no sign of Peter's truck, Wanda came to a corner where a boy, maybe ten years old, stood surveying the streets in cheap sunglasses, a baggy white T-shirt, sagging jeans, and disintegrating sneakers. She slowed and waved, and the boy's cultivated cool fell away when he recognized the blue Land Cruiser.

"Miss Wanda! Miss Wanda!"

She pulled over, and the boy ran up to her window. He was thin as a reed, maybe malnourished, his hair shaggy, his skin a dusty brown.

"Are you taking pictures? Will you take mine?"

"Maybe," she said. "What's your name?"

"Stevie." He made a face. "They call me Stinky, but I don't like it."

"I like Stevie better, too," she said. "I'll make you a deal. Tell me where the trap house is and I'll take your picture."

The boy glanced past her at Peter, just for a moment. "Who's Casper?"

"He's with me," Wanda said. "A friend. His name's Peter."

Peter raised a hand. "Hi, Stevie."

The boy ignored him. "I gotta get permission." His tone was matter of fact. "Boss'll beat my ass if I don't."

"I hear you," said Wanda. "Who's the boss there?"

"Chester." Stevie looked a little nervous.

"Mad Chester? With the lightning bolt tattoos?"

"Yeah, but, uh, you know he don't like to be called Mad Chester, right?"

"I know. Tell him Wanda says hi. We'll wait right here."

Stevie stepped into the shade of a huge chestnut tree, half-hidden by the untrimmed low-hanging branches. He pulled a cheap walkie-talkie from his back pocket and brought it to his mouth.

Wanda turned to Peter. "Chester's a local power, on his way up," she said quietly. "If he likes you, he could put the word out about your truck. He's got a temper, but he's vain as hell. He'll want his picture taken."

"What's the trap house?"

"A place to score and a place to use," said Wanda. "Usually crack, meth, or heroin, sometimes all three. Lately there's a whole lot of heroin. We've passed a few already, the boarded-up places with the kids standing in the yard."

"I noticed those. Why is it called a trap house?"

"There's one way in and one way out, like a trap. Heavy security inside the house, with the guys in the yard to weed out the crazies and keep things moving along. Stevie's just a lookout, watching for police or cars loaded up with a rival clique. They'll have young boys like him posted two or three blocks out, all the way around, some-where between six to ten kids at a time, depending on the streets. Usually four shifts, six hours each."

"He's young."

"Yeah, younger than most for that job. Especially for this shift. He's either somebody's relation or he's pretty smart. This is entry-level, pays a couple dollars an hour. Maybe he's helping feed his family, maybe he's on his own and he's feeding himself. The first step on the ladder."

Peter watched Stevie standing under the tree, tuned in to the walkie-talkie. "There's no other ladder to climb?"

Wanda shook her head. "There are other ladders, but they're steep, and that first rung is damn hard to reach," she said. "I know these folks. Schools are lousy, families are fractured, most people are dirt-poor. A lot of these corner boys, they don't have anybody who really cares about them. They find their community on the streets. If they can earn money in that community, it seems like a good decision. The fact that they might die doing the work, well, that's part of the deal. They might die anyway."

Stevie shot a glance back at the Toyota, kept talking. Maybe working his way up the food chain. Wanda the gangster photographer would be easy. Casper the Un-known Ghost was the problem.

"You got out," he said.

"As much as anybody does," she said. "I came back, too. Taking people's pictures is pretty intimate, you know? You're looking at them, and they're showing you who they are. You see their humanity, even these gangsters. Sometimes especially. Most of them are just kids anyway."

"How'd you end up photographing war zones?"

"I grew up in one," she said. "Half a mile from here. Back then it was crack, now it's also meth and heroin. You could get beat up or shot just walking home from school, no reason at all."

"Sounds rough."

"I got lucky," she said. "I found something I liked, and I had people who encouraged me to chase it. My uncle would loan me his Polaroid if I'd watch his kids. At Frayser High, a teacher saw my pictures and gave me an old Nikon. She had a darkroom in her closet at home, made me a deal. We traded good grades for film and paper and darkroom time." She gave Peter an odd little smile. "I was her project. She was tough on me, but she found me a scholarship at DePaul in Chicago. She was also the first lesbian I ever met."

Peter looked at her. Wanda shrugged. "It's not like she forced me. Serena was only ten years older than me, and kinda cute." She looked away into the past. "Lot of worse things could have happened. And did."

Peter watched her hand tremble as she took it from the steering wheel. She reached down, lifted the camera from her bag, and took a few shots of Stevie on his walkie-talkie under the low-hanging branches.

Holding the camera, her hand was steady.

Stevie turned and walked toward them, all smiles. "Chester says okay."

He gave Wanda directions, and she got out of the car

and took a dozen or more pictures. Stevie grinning and happy, then flexing his muscles in a strong-man pose, then with his hands formed into pistols and crossed over his chest, dead-faced as any hardened gangster.

Ten years old.

She wrote the boy's Instagram tag in her notebook, leaned in to kiss him lightly on the cheek, and they drove away.

Peter said, "That house is in the only part of Frayser we haven't seen. You already knew where it was."

"And who runs it," she said. "I was hoping we'd find your truck someplace else first. And it's better if they know we're coming."

24

The house was two blocks away, a small, narrow, shotgun-style structure in dire need of a new roof and everything else. The windows were still covered, but someone had taken the plywood down from the front door and laid it over the rotten planks of the leaning front porch.

Three teenagers were ranged out across the small dirt yard, one of them with a broken-off branch the size of a baseball bat, the bark peeled away, a heavy knot at one end. A shirtless man stood in the doorway, mid-twenties and heavy with muscle. He had a pair of black lightning bolts tattooed across his wide brown chest.

"Wanda," he called out. "How you doin', girl?"

"I'm good, Chester, how 'bout you?" She got out of the car. "I was hoping to take some pictures today, if that's okay."

"Long as you start with me." Chester gave her a wide toothy smile. "We're light on customers right now anyway. Just keep the house out of the pictures."

Peter opened his door and stepped out. He had Wanda's notebook in one hand and a pencil behind his ear.

"Who's that you got with you," Chester asked.

"My name's Peter, I'm a friend of Wanda's. How's your day going?"

Mad Chester's smile dropped like a stone. "I didn't ask you."

"He's my helper," Wanda said. "Taking down your tags so you can find your pictures on my feed. I know all you gangsters follow my ass online." She raised her camera. "Now give me that handsome smile again." Her finger flickered on the shutter.

She spent fifteen minutes taking pictures of Mad Chester and three other men from inside the house, portraits and group shots. The men were solid and capable, sure of themselves, their brown skin dense with tattoos. They brought out pistols and long guns to pose with, empty faces and hardware on display.

Peter had met enough warlords to know who these men were. They lived in a world where there was no safe place, no refuge, and it changed them. Like an occupying militia, they would be hard and unpredictable and violent, killers when necessary. Some of them might have learned to like it. The youngest were a kind of cannon fodder, and each year of survival both marked them and moved them further up the food chain.

Peter wasn't one of them. He was tolerated only because he was sponsored by Wanda, under a kind of cease-fire.

But he'd worked and served with men from every background and every major religion, with every skin tone under the sun. His best friends from the Corps were two sergeants, one black, one Hispanic. One was dead, one ran a roofing company in Seattle. Lewis was his closest friend and a career criminal. Each of those men had put their lives on the line for Peter, without hesitation, more times than he cared to think about. And they'd killed for him, too.

So he had no problem talking with these rough men as he wrote their tags in Wanda's notebook.

They were guarded, not quite sure how to react, because he clearly wasn't afraid of them. But he didn't act like a hard-ass, either. To Peter, they were serious men with real responsibilities, facing significant threats, and he treated them with respect. By the end of the session, they'd each looked him over and given him the slow nod, which was pretty good for fifteen minutes.

Wanda took less time with the yard crew, who were younger and goofier and maybe hadn't lost as many friends as Chester and his group. Peter noticed she took a lot more pictures, though, most of them candid shots while the boys weren't looking.

As she worked, a few men and women began to linger on the sidewalks, ragged and twitchy, customers looking to buy but unwilling to interrupt and maybe risk a beating. When Wanda asked if she could take their pictures, too, their faces lit up like fireflies, even though their smiles were full of holes, their clothing thin as old lace.

Chester let her shoot until seven or eight customers were waiting and two got into a shoving match. Then he sent his men back inside and the yard crew formed the customers into some kind of order, the boy with the stick breaking up the argument without having to hit anybody, sending the muttering main offender to the back of the line.

When everything was running smoothly, Chester came over to Peter and stood a little too close. He still had a flat black pistol hanging loosely from his right hand.

"Okay, white boy. Now tell me what you're really doing here."

"Honestly? I'm looking for my truck," Peter said. "Somebody held me up this morning."

Mad Chester threw back his head and laughed.

Peter said, "I don't care about my phone or my wallet. I don't even care who did it. But I want my goddamn truck back."

"Well, what's in it for me, white boy?"

"A thousand for you and five hundred for the kid who finds it."

Chester stopped laughing and looked at Peter thoughtfully.

"What kind of truck?"

"A clean green 1968 Chevy with a nice wood cargo box on the back. You'll know it when you see it."

Mad Chester's fingers slowly gathered the pistol into a tighter grip. It was a banged-up Colt 1911, a weapon Peter knew well. It was one of the options for Marine officers when he'd signed up. He also was pretty sure he knew what was coming. He tasted copper in his mouth.

Chester said, "What if you're not the only one looking for this truck?"

Peter figured he might as well get this over with. "I know I'm not. I caught a ride with King Robbie this morning."

"That was you?" Chester's voice was quiet. The gun still hung down, but it twitched in his hand. "I don't know what you did, but you're in some serious shit. Charlene Scott wants you bad."

"Chester, come on." Wanda kept her voice light, but she was taking slow, deep breaths, suppressing her nerves. "Peter's with me. He gets a pass today."

"Nobody gets a pass from the King."

Mad Chester stood close, staring Peter in the face. Chester would be strong and used to fighting. There would be no warning.

Peter smiled. The adrenaline sang in his blood. He was ready. He was always ready. He said, "Why do they call you Mad Chester?"

Chester raised the pistol and Peter grabbed it with both hands. He pushed the barrel down and away, with a finger jammed behind the trigger to keep it from firing, then twisted the gun butt inside, hard and fast. Chester was thick with muscle, but he was too close. He tried to head-butt Peter, but Peter turtled back to avoid the blow and twisted harder, pulling the other man off-balance.

Chester had no other move. His hand released its grip automatically to keep his wrist from breaking, then Peter had the gun.

If it had taken another half second, Peter thought

Chester might have let his own wrist break to keep hold of the pistol.

Not that it would have made any difference.

Peter stepped back to put some space between them, the heavy automatic now reversed toward Mad Chester. The man took a deep inward breath, the lightning bolt tattoos rising with his chest, shoulders back, arms hanging heavy at his sides. As if finally facing something he'd long known would eventually arrive.

"Go on, do what you're gonna do. My boys will come out shooting."

Peter shook his head. "I don't want to kill you, Chester. I just want my truck back."

Mad Chester's mouth bunched up like a fist. "You some kind of pussy, afraid to kill a man? Never done it before?"

Peter locked eyes with Mad Chester. The white static crackled between them, a living thing. "You have no fucking idea what I've done," Peter said. "What I'm capable of. If I leave you standing, it's a gift. You hear me?"

Peter watched Chester's face change, just a little, as he saw something surface in Peter. Something Peter didn't allow to show very often. Something he wasn't always proud of, but something that had been an inseparable part of him since the war. Sometimes it was useful. Sometimes it was necessary.

Then Chester dipped his chin, a minimal nod. "All right."

"I'll ask again. Have you seen my truck?"

Chester shook his head, again the smallest possible

gesture. As if each concession hurt, no matter the risk. "No."

Peter believed him. "Okay. You got anything else to say?"

"You the one holding the gun."

Peter tripped the release and dropped the mag into his right hand, then cycled the action to pop out the extra round. He tucked the empty gun into the back of his pants, the mag into his pocket, then held his hands out, palms up. The whole thing in under three seconds.

"Now I'm not." He gave Mad Chester his werewolf smile. "You got anything else?"

Chester's muscles popped and twitched under his bare skin. The man's barely contained violence like a shimmering wave of heat and rage. His weight shifted forward onto his toes.

Peter's balance was perfect. He felt his chest fill with oxygen. A breeze stirred the leaves in the trees. This whole thing a bad idea, but a welcome chance to burn off this surge of aggression, vent his frustration. Do some damage and damn the consequences.

The boys in the yard, the men in the house. Wanda behind him.

He wanted Chester to come. He longed for it.

Then Chester stepped back, shaking his head. He'd seen it, too. "White folks are fucking weird."

Peter nodded once. "Not all white folks," he said. "Just me. Are we done?"

"Call it a truce." Mad Chester looked steadily at Peter.

"Get out of here before my boys get itchy and somebody end up dead."

Wanda had backed away to avoid catching a stray bullet. She had good instincts, thought Peter. Now she stepped carefully to her Toyota and fired up the engine.

Peter slapped the magazine back into the pistol, scooped up the fallen round, and hopped into the passenger seat.

The yard crew stood there wondering what exactly had happened.

Peter wasn't quite sure himself.

But now he had a half-decent weapon again.

25

Wanda was breathing hard, her entire body shaking as she found her way back to Watkins and headed south. Driving with her knees, she fumbled a pill bottle out of her purse, shook a few out into her hand, and swallowed them dry. "What the fuck was that?"

"Sorry," Peter said. He was checking out the 1911, mostly to give his own hands something to do. He chambered a fresh round and thumbed the extra into the magazine. The action was smooth and the weapon smelled faintly of oil. "Is that going to come back on you?"

She waved it away. "When were you planning to tell me about King Robbie?"

When would he have mentioned it, Peter wondered. While she was in shock? Or nearly comatose? Or wired to the gills, driving around King Robbie's business district?

"There's not much to tell," said Peter. "He gave me a ride after my truck got stolen. He was pretty interested in the truck and the kid who took it. I guess that trickled down the food chain to Chester."

Wanda looked at him, the Land Cruiser drifting from its lane. "You say this like it's nothing."

Peter shrugged. "It is what it is. Anyway, I asked King to drop me off a block from your place. But that lunatic with the machine gun was there, so I took a pistol from a woman named Charlene Scott to try and chase him off."

"I know who Charlene Scott is." Wanda still stared at Peter, the Land Cruiser still drifting. "We went to Frayser High together. She kills people for King Robbie."

Now she was crossing the yellow line into oncoming traffic. The other cars honked and swerved but she didn't seem to notice. Peter reached out and put his hand on the wheel to ease her back into her lane. "Is Chester's house part of King Robbie's operation?"

"That house is like the farthest tip of the longest tentacle. Chester runs four houses total, I think. King might not even know about that particular house. But yeah, it's his, it's all his. And now he's after you?"

"I guess so." Peter smiled. "But maybe I'm after him, too."

"Sweet Jesus." Wanda shuddered. "You're as bad as Chester. You are in *way* over your head. Does June know how crazy you are?"

"Pretty sure," he admitted. "But she puts up with it because I've got mad skills in the sack."

"Oh, no," she said. "You are *not* going there."

"Horizontal mambo? The beast with two backs?"

"Ugh!" Wanda groaned. "Like I wanted *that* picture in my head. Straight people!"

But she was smiling again, and focused on the road. Her pills had kicked in. Peter took his hand off the wheel.

She made it under the freeway and across the Wolf River before she spoke again.

"You weren't afraid of those guys at the house. I mean, before Chester tried to shoot you. Why not?"

"I was afraid, and for the same reasons as you. They're gangsters with guns and drugs and anger management problems. They're unpredictable. But they've got no reason to hurt you unless you give them one. They're just people. They've got friends and grandmothers like everyone else."

"They're not like everyone else," Wanda said. "They're dangerous. They kill people."

"I've spent a lot of time with dangerous people. We have a lot in common." Peter didn't mention that he was a killer, too.

"And the guys with the machine gun? The guy with the dump truck? What about them?"

"I'll work on that tomorrow. At least King's motives are clear. I have no idea what those other assholes want."

"So now we've got two groups of people after us."

"This is why I wanted you to stay in your hotel room," Peter said.

"Yeah, I'm not so good at that."

"No, really?" He bumped her shoulder with his elbow. "Me neither."

"I thought you were supposed to help, not make things worse."

"I've got a friend coming down in the morning. He's pretty good."

"He better be." She shook her head. "I need a god-damn drink."

26

"What were you thinking?" Albert shouted, lost in central Memphis and trying to find his way back to a freeway.

"Bitch was still there," Judah Lee said. "The dump truck didn't do its job. So I stepped it up a notch."

The hot barrel of Judah Lee's machine gun had set off the vinyl seats of that old Country Squire like they were soaked in gasoline. Driving fast with the windows gone only made them burn hotter. Albert had felt his hair scorching like the Devil himself was riding their bumper.

He was so busy getting their sorry backsides out of there, he never did get more than a glance at the man who was shooting at them. He was tall and white and rough-looking, that's about all Albert could swear to. Although the wolfish grin showing behind the pistol was caught pretty good in his mind.

Albert had to admit, Judah Lee had handled the fire pretty well. He tied the seat belt to that big machine gun and hung it out the window to cool off, put the extra ammunition in the way back, then started shaking up cans of Adolph Coors's finest and spraying down the upholstery.

Albert was pretty sure Judah Lee hadn't planned it that way. There were cheaper ways to put out a fire than with two cases of pisswater beer. Mostly he was glad his brother hadn't brought a half gallon of cheap whiskey. The plastic bottle would have caught fire in the flames and made things a whole lot worse.

Trailing the stink of burnt vinyl and hot beer at a high rate of speed down some wide boulevard, Albert said, "Whose dang car is this?"

Judah Lee climbed over the seatback into the front. "Got it from Carruthers."

"Are you serious? He is not going to be happy."

Judah Lee put a pointy-toothed smile on his tattooed face. "Let me worry about Carruthers," he said. "This boat will get us home."

"Not home yet," said Albert. "We got a hog trap to take down and hog meat on ice worth six hundred dollars."

"You need to stop thinking small," said Judah Lee. "We got our family fortune to reclaim."

Albert just shook his head and kept driving. He was so dang tired of this conversation.

He didn't even want to think about where that machine gun had come from.

He was pretty sure Carruthers had something to do with it.

. . .

Back at the steel-sided butchering house, Albert put fresh ice in the coolers and opened the bottom stoppers so the bloody meltwater could run down the sloped concrete floor into the drain.

The smell of raw hog mixed with the chemical odor of disinfectant wasn't Albert's favorite. The only part of Albert's life that didn't stink was the farm itself. The clean tang of freshly turned earth, the young plants after a spring rain. The home place was everything to Albert. He'd spent most of his lifetime caring for it.

He was afraid of what he'd have to do to keep it.

In the butchering house, he tried to keep the smell of the farm in his mind, but he couldn't. He'd missed lunch and his bad leg ached like the tractor was still sitting on it. He was getting jittery without his pain pills, but none of it mattered because there was knife work to do, and that didn't go well with the soft edges those pills brought on.

When he was done, he thought, he'd give himself a few extra. Seemed like they didn't do what they used to do, anyway. He had three different doctors now writing him prescriptions. Maybe it was time to find a fourth.

He worked quickly, his hands strong and sure. He used a heavy knife to separate the joints, and a thin boning blade to harvest the best cuts. The rest would go into the grinder or out the back door to the burial trench.

It was better working in the new steel prefab than the old barn, the way they'd done it when his daddy was alive and they were just putting up meat for the winter. Now he had good light and stainless-steel sinks and hot and cold running water.

You got to spend money to make money, that's what they say. After the tractor accident, when Albert had lost his job at the Blue Springs Toyota plant, he'd emptied his savings and borrowed on the farm to put up the building and buy the equipment. The big walk-in freezer, the band saw, the smoker, the grinder, and the sausage stuffer. He'd sell in bulk to restaurants. Heck, he could sell chops on the dang Internet. Call it wild organic pork and charge a bundle. That was the plan.

Albert hadn't counted on the medical bills, which kept coming, or the state inspector. The man held up Albert's papers on some technical crap Albert hadn't seen coming, demanding changes Albert couldn't afford to make. He'd been butchering for his family and friends for years. He was clean and careful and never had any complaints. When had it all gotten so dang complicated?

He didn't want to admit that, with all the pain pills, maybe he hadn't paid close enough attention.

Bottom line was, without papers and a stamp, restaurants wouldn't buy the meat. The bank wouldn't loan him the money for the inspector's changes until Albert paid back the first note. Selling cheap illegal meat to his neighbors didn't earn enough to make loan payments and taxes both. Beset on all sides, he'd made payments as he could, but not enough, and not on time. Now everybody wanted their piece or they were taking the farm.

That's why Albert was running around with his idiot

brother, chasing their daddy's crackpot dream. Why he'd been willing to use the farm's seed money to bid on that house at auction.

It hadn't been enough to outbid that woman.

Maybe he shouldn't have taken the leap for the slaughterhouse. The farm had been theirs, free and clear, for generations, unless you counted the tax man's pound of flesh. The corn and hay had always been enough to buy seed for the next planting, pay the taxes, and keep the equipment running, never much more than that.

Albert still thought the hog business was a good idea, even now, up to his eyeballs in debt. Get paid to trap them, and paid again for the meat. If he could get Judah Lee to do his dang part, they might get caught up. There was no shortage of hogs in Mississippi and Tennessee, nor barbecue joints looking for pork.

After ten years in prison, though, Judah Lee had other ideas stuck in his head.

Like porcupine quills, their barbed ends went so deep, they might never come out.

Long past suppertime, dog-tired and hurting, the fresh meat in the cooler all wrapped in clean white paper, Albert carried a pair of thick chops up to the farmhouse. Judah Lee had left the old Country Squire wagon parked in the yard where anybody could see it, windows shot out, bullet holes in the sheet metal, still stinking of burnt vinyl and beer.

"Judah." Albert stepped into the kitchen and let the

screen door slap shut behind him. "Get that Carruthers car off the property before somebody sees it."

He found Judah at the dining room table, surrounded by empty beer cans and piles of the old family papers. Those faded ledger books and sheaves of handwritten letters went back 170 years and more. Precious history.

"I've already been through all that a dozen times." Albert walked back into the kitchen.

"You missed something," said Judah Lee. "I know you did."

Despite the size of him, there was something childlike about the way Judah Lee turned the papers over and over in his hands. Especially when he was looking down and you couldn't see the big tattoo on his face, or the teeth he'd filed to a point.

"Suit yourself. I'm too hungry to argue. But you better not spill beer on those papers, you hear me?" Albert lit the burner under the big cast-iron skillet with a kitchen match and laid the chops down with butter and slices from last fall's wrinkly, half-sprouted potatoes. Between the farm and the hogs, at least they weren't going hungry.

Cash money was another matter entirely.

Their daddy had gone over those papers more times than Albert could count. As the meat sizzled in the pan, Albert looked up at the family tree framed on the wall, drawn up in their daddy's strong, confident hand. Not the whole tree, more like a side branch, going from Albert and Judah Lee back seven generations to a woman named Rose Marie Burkitts.

Connected by a dotted line to Nathan Bedford Forrest.

Forrest was a man who'd come from poor beginnings and made a fortune in cotton plantations and the Memphis slave market. During the Civil War, Forrest became a general, commanded a cavalry brigade known for its ferocity, and was considered a tactical genius and a hero of the Confederacy. He was also accused of allowing a massacre at Fort Pillow, and was rumored to have been the Grand Wizard of the Ku Klux Klan. But Albert also read that Forrest had later rejected the Klan, and given a speech about how blacks and whites should live together in peace.

Albert didn't quite know how he felt about any of that.

He guessed Forrest was probably a complicated man.

On Albert's daddy's family tree, the dotted line meant a relationship out of wedlock. Rose Marie Burkitts, their great-great-great-great-grandmother, had been Forrest's mistress. Taken all together, the letters told the story.

Forrest had loved her enough to build her and their son that sturdy little brick house in what would become North Memphis.

They hadn't known the house's address until after their daddy had died. It was in his last will and testament, along with the records of all the times he'd tried, without success, to buy it back.

Somewhere in that ancient, damaged house was their legacy.

No matter that Albert and Judah Lee had done most of the damage.

. . .

Albert dished out the chops and potatoes onto a pair of chipped china plates, took tarnished knives and forks from the drawer with paper napkins, and brought them out to the table. Carefully, making sure his hands were clean and dry, he picked up the family papers and moved them to the far side of the table. Next to the file of papers from the bank, serving notice on the farm's foreclosure.

"Tell me about it again," said Judah Lee. The old wooden chair creaked under his weight. "I can't hardly read any of that old handwriting."

It wasn't just the handwriting. Judah Lee had never been much of a reader, or one to take time to learn things for their own sake. Albert had tried to get him involved in the workings of the home place, but Judah had quickly lost interest in the long cycle of planting and harvest, especially when he learned how little money there was to be made. He only truly paid attention when there was something right in front of him. Judah Lee had always been one to take what he wanted, when he wanted it, and ignore the accounting. Another way he was like a child.

Some, like their famous ancestor, got rich that way.

Judah Lee had gotten ten years in prison, and lucky he didn't get more.

"It's mentioned in one of his letters," said Albert. He reached out and plucked a paper from the piles, squinting down at the faded ink. "June fifth, 1862. The day before the First Battle of Memphis."

The First Battle of Memphis was a great naval

engagement on the Mississippi. It had taken only two hours and, contrary to Confederate expectations, had been a complete disaster for the Confederate's river fleet. By winning the battle in such a decisive way, the North gained control of the city and its lines of supply. That battle helped turn the tide of the war.

"Forrest writes, 'My dearest Rose Marie.'" Albert could have quoted the passage from memory, but he liked to see the letters on the page, the man's actual handwriting. It felt more real that way. "'The Bearer of this Letter is a man I trust. I send him ahead of the Northern Army to store Goods of Real Value in your house. Do as he directs and stay at your Sister's for a time as I would not wish you to be burdened with the Knowledge of what he will leave, or where he will leave it. Tell no one of this, not even your Sister. I will come to claim my things in due time.'"

"He says it plain as day, 'In your house.'" Judah Lee tore into his pork chop, those pointed teeth shaped for tearing flesh. "There's a letter from her sister in there, too. Daddy showed me before, but I couldn't find it."

Albert sorted through the papers and found the letter. "The sister talks about how nice it was to visit with Rose Marie and her son. Then she says, 'Perhaps I might visit you in turn and we could make a Game of it, to search the house and see if we are as clever as that young Sergeant.'"

"So we know Forrest's man came, and he put something there."

"They think he did," said Albert. "But nowhere in all these papers is written what he left, or where he put it.

For all we know, it's ten thousand dollars in Confederate notes turned to dust in a tobacco tin buried in the yard."

"Daddy said it was most likely silver or gold." Judah Lee forked potatoes into his mouth. "I asked him once if it didn't get spent over all those years, little by little until it was gone. But he always said there was nothing like that in the ledgers. They always balanced out. No sign of anything extra."

Albert had been through those ledgers, too. Year after year, they'd shown every penny spent on flour or salt, each dollar earned with each harvest. The farmland being sold off, piece by piece, a few acres at a time, until only the house remained.

"They wouldn't have sold the acreage if they didn't have to," Albert said. "Wasn't until Great-granddad's mule-trading took off that they finally sold that house and bought this farm."

"You know Daddy always thought nobody came to claim that prize," said Judah Lee. "He said there was no mention of Forrest even visiting Rose Marie after that in any of his letters, in all the letters from her sister. Maybe Forrest's man got killed on the way back, and nobody ever knew where it was hidden. Not even Forrest himself."

Albert had gone to the Memphis library and looked through the old newspaper archives. He couldn't find any record of a windfall at that house, or any of the newer houses that had grown up around it. No wealth, not even anything with some history to it. After Elvis and the fifties, Memphis had gone right down the tubes.

Forrest's fortunes had fallen after the war, too. His

plantations in ruins, his slave market gone, Forrest had turned to the railroad business, but the company ended in bankruptcy. Once among the wealthiest men in the Mid-South, with monuments built to remember his achievements, his name on streets and schools and parks, Nathan Bedford Forrest had died in near-poverty in a small log cabin.

There was no evidence he'd gone back to Rose Marie's little brick house for what he'd left there.

Maybe it still remained, whatever it was. Somewhere inside that house.

Albert's dinner had grown cold, uneaten. Despite himself, Albert found that he was caught up in the idea. Like Judah Lee, he wanted to believe.

Their family legacy, just waiting for them to claim it.

Judah Lee was right about one thing. The house would be empty soon enough.

Only a crazy person would stay.

Before long, Albert and Judah Lee could get inside and start looking.

Judah Lee had already finished his own meal. Now he put his hand on the lip of Albert's plate and began to pull it across the table. "What about that guy at the house today, the one shooting at us? I didn't get much of a look at him. Did you?"

Albert stabbed Judah's hand with a fork and reclaimed his plate. "Not really."

"You think he was police?"

Albert shook his head. "He was all shaggy. Looked kinda wild, you ask me. I think it was personal." He took a bite of pork chop. "Felt pretty dang personal to me, too, the way he came after us."

"And he was white," said Judah Lee. "So he's a race traitor."

"Don't start with that crap," said Albert. "You got all the worst parts of Daddy."

"That reminds me. What'd you do with that stuff he had in the barn?"

"What stuff?"

"You know what stuff," said Judah Lee.

Albert shook his head and took a bite of potato. "Long gone," he said. "It was old. It went bad in the humidity. I threw it away."

Judah gave him a look. "Come on, big brother. You never threw away anything in your whole goddamn life. Where is it?"

"I already told you."

Judah pushed back his chair and got to his feet. "I'm gonna get that station wagon out of sight."

"We got to think about this thing," Albert called after him. "Don't go doing something stupid."

27

The daylight was fading as Wanda made her way toward Uptown and stopped at a bright blue cinder-block rectangle with palm trees painted along the sides. The blue was mismatched where the building had been repainted in sections over many years. It stood on a corner with two vacant lots beside it and three more behind. A long row of cars sat parked on the unmown grass. Wanda pulled into a space under a tree and turned off the engine.

"They have food here?"

"Best burgers in town." Wanda shot him a sideways look. "It's a neighborhood joint," she said. "Nothing fancy."

"Great burgers beats fancy every time."

The two wide front windows were covered with plywood painted like a pair of desert islands, with tan sandy beaches and more palm trees, but the paint was faded and peeling. At the bottom were the words COLD BEER and LIVE MUSIC. A plank over the door had once perhaps told the name, but the lettering had become illegible with time.

Peter got out of the car and tucked Mad Chester's 1911 into his pants at the small of his back, where his shirt would cover it. Wanda shook her head. "You'll have to give that up at the door," she said. "They have lockers. You'll get it back when we leave."

The weight of the gun was comforting given Peter's recent experiences. "I'm not sure that's a good idea."

"You'll be fine," she said. "This place is a kind of neutral ground, like a church but with better security. Plus I have a friend who might be playing here tonight. He's also a brickmason. I want to see if he's got time to work on my house."

"Okay," said Peter. "Give me a second."

He walked around the side looking for another entrance, and found a back door sheltered under a tin-roofed overhang. The trio of cheap folding chairs and an oil-drum barbecue told Peter this area was part loading dock, part employee lounge.

The overhang was supported by a pair of rusted triangular iron brackets bolted to the wall, probably there since the fifties. They were tilted out at the top, the years slowly separating them from the building. The stubbornness of inertia resisting the relentless pull of gravity.

Peter eyeballed the gaps behind the tops of the brackets. The space on the right side was slightly wider. He took the 1911 from his waist and tucked it between the metal and the cement block wall. The weapon fit, but just barely. He hooked a finger around the barrel and the gun fell into his hand without protest.

He put the pistol back in place and walked around front to meet Wanda.

Inside, the light was low and the air-conditioning was high. The static flared, but Peter damped it down with promises of a burger and a beer. A dark, narrow man blocked the entryway.

"Wanda Wyatt." The narrow man's mouth formed a smile but his eyes were on Peter.

"Saint James." Wanda held open her camera bag so he could see inside. "The man playing tonight?"

"Due any minute. Get a seat while you can."

James had a boxer's scar tissue around his eyes, a well-worn nylon shoulder holster carrying a big pearl-handled automatic, and a cylindrical snap-top case on his belt that probably held an expandable spring-steel baton. Everything a bouncer needs for crowd control.

He still hadn't looked away from Peter when he touched Wanda's bag with a finger. "You're good, honey. Who's this?"

"This is Peter, a friend." She closed her bag and stepped forward. "He's with me."

"Don't know him," said James. "Arms up, turn around."

The frisk was quick, impersonal, and utterly thorough, evidence of years of practice and learning from past mistakes. When James was done Peter was pretty sure the other man knew his shoe size, the number of fillings in his teeth, and whether he wore boxers or briefs.

James put his eyes back on Peter. "Wanda tell you the rules?"

"Play nice and get along?"

"Don't be an asshole and keep your hands off the waitresses. If you get drunk, be a happy drunk."

Peter looked past James at the big room. A bar ran down one long wall, rows of tables down the other, with a small raised stage at the far end. The back hallway would lead to the kitchen, bathrooms, and the rear door where he'd left Chester's 1911.

The ceiling was high and had been patched so many times the pattern had begun to look deliberate. The dark paneling was decorated with framed photos and newspaper clippings and old tour posters. Ella Fitzgerald was playing on the sound system, but not so loud you couldn't hear the chatter of customers and the friendly clatter of glasses and silverware.

The bartenders were huge, all three of them, and their hands poured drinks while their eyes watched the crowd. Peter figured they had a couple of shotguns behind the bar, and baseball bats cut down to be useful in a tight space.

"When was the last time you had real trouble?"

Saint James gave Peter a tight smile. "Not since I been here, and tonight won't be the first. Go on, sit down. Relax and have a drink. The band is something special."

Wanda had found a table by the wall. The place was filling up fast, everyone from men in work-stained Dickies to couples dressed in flashy suits and flowery dresses. The waitress had just taken their order—Ghost River Gold for Peter, a double vodka on the rocks for Wanda—when the musicians emerged from the back hall, carrying their gear.

Wanda pointed at the two older men. "That's my friend Dupree, with the standup double bass in the tall brown case. The guy in the hat is Romeo, the drummer."

But Peter's eyes were glued to the skinny kid with the guitar.

28

He was still dressed in the same black Fender T-shirt and baggy jean shorts and sneakers he'd been wearing that morning. He carried the guitar on his back, neck down without a case, with the wide cloth strap across his narrow chest like a gunslinger's bandolier. He didn't carry it off like Johnny Cash, but nobody else did, either.

Stepping onstage, the kid unslung the guitar and leaned it carefully in a corner as he surveyed the crowd. The lights were in his face and Peter had already turned away.

While the older men began to unpack what they'd carried, the kid went back down the hallway and returned with a hand truck loaded with round drum cases stacked like a wedding cake. He was small and thin, but he didn't have any trouble moving the equipment. Two more trips for amplifiers and stands and milk crates packed with cords and microphones and other gear, and a final trip without the hand truck for another guitar in a heavy-duty black plastic case. He carried it with both hands, as if the contents were made of some rare, precious material.

Part of Peter wanted to get up and brace the kid, find out where his truck had gone, what he'd done to get those gangbangers all worked up. But that wasn't an option, not with Saint James at the door and those nimble giants behind the bar.

Not unless Peter wanted to kill somebody, and he didn't.

Not over a 1968 Chevy.

He wondered if his truck was parked right outside the club. He was pretty sure the kid was too smart for that, but he wanted to go see for himself. Then he looked around and realized that if he stood up to leave his pale Wisconsin skin would stand out like a spotlight in this brown Memphis crowd. The kid would see him and spook, and Peter would be no better off.

Besides, he'd just ordered a beer. Wanda'd said the burgers were the best in town, and Peter was hungry. He didn't want to be rude.

He also wanted to know if the kid was any good on that beat-up guitar.

The drinks came while the musicians were still setting up. The beer on tap was excellent. Wanda's double vodka went down in a hurry and she held up her hand for another. She was on the down slope of a long and difficult day, and the pills wouldn't hold her up forever. Another reason for Peter to stay put and see how things played out.

Her friend Dupree perched one cheek on a tall stool,

positioned a microphone, then draped himself around that upright double bass like a man ready to dance the tango with his wife of many years. He was somewhere in his sixties, iron-gray hair cut short, face creased by the sun, solidly built in jeans and a black suit jacket over a crisp white button-down shirt. Ella Fitzgerald faded out on the sound system and the microphone came up. Dupree spent a few seconds tuning, then began to play a tight-walking blues line, his long fingers effortless on the strings. The crowd noise began to soften.

The kid helped the drummer put his kit together. It wasn't much, just a bass, a snare, a tom-tom, and a hi-hat, and it didn't take long. The drummer, Romeo, was about the same age as Dupree, thick but compact in blue work pants, a white short-sleeved shirt, a red vest, and a pale straw fedora. He nodded the kid away, pushed the hat to the back of his head, and sat behind the kit. After a few tiny adjustments that only he would notice, he picked up a pair of brushes and began to do something soft and slippery behind the bass, which was gaining momentum. The crowd got quieter.

The kid arranged a pair of microphones and two control pedals in front of a wooden ladder-back chair. He went to the rear corner of the little stage and laid the heavy-duty black case gently on the floor. He knelt before it, unfastened the clasps, and lifted out a metal-bodied National guitar that flashed silver under the lights.

He sat in the chair and set the guitar on his lap with a green glass bottleneck slide on the little finger of his left hand. He fished a flat pick out of his back pocket, and struck the open chord. Even with his microphones off, the bright metallic sound of that steel resonator filled the nearly silent room.

He was a small, skinny kid, dressed in unwashed clothes, but he seemed somehow bigger up there. He played a quick shimmering series of notes, barely touching the tuning pegs before nodding to himself. After a sideways glance at Dupree, he adjusted one mike to the guitar and the other to his face, tapped the control pedals to turn them on, then launched into what Peter quickly recognized as a version of the classic "Good Morning, Little School Girl."

The sound was tremendous.

The kid played a rich open tuning, punctuated by liquid licks with the slide, some kind of oddball style of his own invention. He made altogether more music than had ever been intended to come out of even that magnificent guitar. He wasn't showing off, not playing too fast, but every note and every space was in the exact right place. The amplified bass kept steady time at the bottom, and the drummer fooled around the edges, the brushes slapping, the hi-hat a syncopated *snap*.

Then the kid began to sing. His voice, coming out of that narrow chest and boyish face, was stronger and deeper than it should have been. His eyes were closed.

Can I go home, can I go home, with you.

Tell your mama and your papa, I once was a schoolboy, too.

It was a haunting song, filled with longing for something that would never come to be.

Peter thought of June. He wondered if he'd ever be able to stay with her, if she needed more than he could give. What each would have to give up to be together. If it would ruin them to try.

He looked at Wanda.

She was staring at the stage, camera forgotten in her hand, tears running down her face.

This music had *power*.

Jesus Christ, this kid was good.

When he finished, everyone in the room stood up and shouted and whistled and stomped their feet.

And that was just the first song.

The band picked up the pace with some blues classics. "Wang Dang Doodle" followed by "Got My Mojo Working," then "Seventh Son," "She Caught the Katy," and the dirtiest version of "Little Red Rooster" Peter had ever heard. Dupree sang some, the kid sang others. Couples abandoned their meals half-eaten to dance between the tables. Some songs got a different tuning on the shining National guitar, which the kid seemed to do without conscious thought. The band didn't sound rehearsed, but spontaneous, like water welling up from a spring. Peter couldn't see a set list anywhere. One of the musicians started playing and the others joined in.

A pair of Louis Armstrong numbers, "West End Blues" and "St. James Infirmary."

"That's where Saint James got his name," Wanda called through the music. "When he was police, he put a lot of people in the hospital. Nobody wanted to go to the Saint James Infirmary."

When the kid switched to the battered old acoustic guitar for "Walkin' Blues," the drummer took up the harmonica and Dupree kept time by thumping on the body of the double bass. It was a sad song played faster than flight, a joyful racket. The kid sang this one, too.

Time to clear on out of my lonesome home
Got up this morning and all I had was gone.

Singing with his eyes closed, the kid's face looked shining and clean, entirely different from that desperation he'd been carrying when he took Peter's truck.

Peter knew how he felt. He was unarmed in a dark, crowded club with only two exits. He should have been jumping out of his skin from his claustrophobia, but the music had reduced the white static to the faintest whisper. Or maybe the static had been raised up into something new.

Wanda had her camera up, taking pictures of the dancers while the band raced through a few crowd-friendly soul classics. Without that Memphis horn sound, the songs felt stripped bare, taking on a new, more elemental life. The kid's rich, greasy guitar licks filled in the gaps while women raised their arms and shook their hips.

Dupree mopped his face with a white handkerchief and said, "This ain't Beale Street, but we still work for tips, so we appreciate anything you can give." He launched into Tom Waits's "Jesus Gonna Be Here," done the way the Blind Boys of Alabama played it, while Saint James locked the front door and walked around with a tin bucket, stopping at every table and every seat at the bar. He didn't say much, but the bucket filled quickly.

After a few more songs, Dupree laid down his big bass and mopped his forehead again. "We're gonna take a little break, but we'll be back in twenty minutes."

When the kid looked up, he saw Peter staring right at him.

29

Peter had to give the kid some credit. He didn't just run for the door.

He let his eyes slide past Peter as if just scanning the room. He went to place that shining National guitar back in its heavy-duty case, snapped the clasps, and stuck something in his back pocket.

Then he picked up the old acoustic by the neck and wandered over to the far end of the packed bar, where a young waitress handed him a tall glass of something fizzy, maybe Coke or Dr Pepper. The kid put his elbow on the curved wood and took his time with his drink, watching the room and talking with the waitress, who couldn't have been any older than he was.

Oddly, she appeared to be wearing gloves.

Wanda was watching, too. She was on her third double vodka with her camera in her hand, starting to unwind. "You see how that girl leans toward him? She likes him. He's really good, isn't he?"

"Yes, he is."

The kid made a casual gesture toward the tables.

When the young waitress's head turned to search the crowd, Peter got to his feet. "Be right back."

He left Wanda at the table staring after him as he slipped into the crowd.

It was a happy tangle of people, mostly well-dressed and half-drunk and visiting from table to table. Peter was tall enough to see Saint James with his pearl-handled automatic back on station at the front door. The bartenders were hustling hard, trying to keep up with demand from people standing two deep and waving money. The kid was talking earnestly into the young waitress's ear.

Peter closed in through the mass of people, sweating now despite the air-conditioning. He lost sight of the kid twice, but put eyes on him again within seconds, still talking with the waitress.

Then a fat guy in a maroon three-piece suit stood up and stretched, blocking Peter's view for a third time. When he got clear, the kid was gone, so was the waitress.

Peter felt the static stir and rise.

This wasn't going to go well.

Still, the kid couldn't have gone far. Peter turned his head, searching, but the kid was too short to be seen. Peter saw only the swirl of someone passing through the crowd in the back hall. He followed at speed, his hand cleaving the crowd like a blade.

The hallway had a swinging door to the kitchen on one side, a pair of restroom doors on the other, and the rear exit at the end. Over the heads of the women waiting for both restrooms, Peter saw the back door swinging shut.

Then the same young waitress stepped in front of him

holding a large oval serving tray in both hands as a sort of shield. She was, in fact, wearing thin leather gloves.

"Oh, 'scuse me," she said, but she didn't move.

She stood barely five feet tall, and couldn't have been older than fifteen. The tray was almost as big as she was.

When Peter stepped left, she mirrored him with a smile.

When he stepped right, she mirrored him again, like the accidental hallway dance where each person moves where the other person is trying to go.

"I'm so sorry." Her grip tightened on the tray.

She was doing it on purpose, and not nervous about it, either. Earning the kid a few valuable seconds. It was just one more reason to like him, that, for his sake, this bright-eyed girl was willing to put herself in Peter's path.

Saint James had only two rules, and one of them was to keep your hands off the waitresses. All she'd have to do was scream for the bartenders and Peter would be up to his eyeballs in baseball bats.

So Peter took hold of her serving tray with both hands and swung her around like a dance partner, trading places in the hallway. "Your friend with the guitar has much bigger problems than me," he told her, then re-leased the tray and banged through the back door.

Where he found Brody, thick-necked driver and leg-breaker, up to his knees in the tall night grass with a shattered guitar hanging from one hand and the skinny kid dangling from the other.

30

Night had fallen. The streets were dark. The kitchen exhaust rattled and carried the smell of grease and meat. The single yellow bulb under the rusty tin-roofed overhang didn't cast much light, but Peter could see the scene clearly enough.

Brody's big hand wrapped securely around the kid's narrow bicep, holding him off the ground. The kid's anguished face, his feet scrabbling for purchase in thin air, his free hand rooting frantically in his back pocket. The guitar smashed shapeless, held together by strings.

Brody's track jacket hung open, showing his gun in its shoulder holster.

"You let this boy take your truck?"

Peter shrugged. "He had a gun, and I didn't."

"Young man's not quite how you described him." Brody's face was utterly unreadable.

Peter couldn't tell if Brody was making a joke or stating a fact. "I didn't see the point in making it easier for you," he said. "I know you want him, but I saw him first."

"I already got him," said Brody. "And it's King who wants him. Wants you, too, truth be told."

He opened his hand to drop the guitar. As it began to fall, Peter stepped left with his arm extended and hooked a finger behind the rusted metal bracket. Chester's automatic dropped into his hand, a round already in the chamber. Peter had the muzzle aimed at Brody's chest before the guitar hit the grass. Brody's hand was deep inside his jacket.

"Stop." Peter's voice held the crack of command.

The big man stopped. The kid still kicked and swung like some kind of toy, his weight seemingly irrelevant. The kid's free hand was frozen in his back pocket, too.

"Nice and easy, Brody. Two fingers, please."

Brody's hand opened slowly inside his jacket and he brought out his weapon with just his thumb and forefinger on the grip. His other three fingers curled upward like he was taking afternoon tea. Brody's big mitt made the gun look like a toy. But it wasn't.

"Now throw it into the grass."

"King owns this boy for what he's done," Brody said. "I can't just give him up."

"If I shoot you in the chest, you'll give him up for sure."

Brody nodded, a grudging acknowledgment of that basic fact. But he didn't throw away the gun.

"I could always shoot you in the leg," Peter said pleasantly. "Or let the kid shoot you a few times wherever he feels like it. I'm pretty sure he's got a crappy little revolver in his pocket."

Brody snapped his head over to look at the kid, who pulled out the rusty little snub-nose and pointed it awkwardly across his body at the big man. Not an easy move when you were hanging by one arm.

"Kid's better than he looks," Peter said. He was very aware of the clock ticking. Of Saint James, and the bartenders, and Wanda inside. "Both of you, throw away the damn guns and we'll figure this out."

The kid set his jaw. "I ain't giving up my gun."

He was scared and sweating, a boy caught up in a deadly game, and in no position to bargain. But still hanging tough and thinking furiously. This kid was something else.

Which kid was he, Peter wondered. The smart, desperate kid who'd stolen Peter's truck at gunpoint? The guitar player who made such rich and haunting music? The cool cucumber who'd managed that oh-so-casual escape from the club? The boy now hanging, helpless but defiant, from the big leg-breaker's grip? All of the above? Or someone else entirely?

"Just put it back in your pocket," said Peter. "Don't shoot anybody, either."

The kid put the revolver back in his pocket.

"Brody," Peter said. "Your turn."

The big man flicked his hand and the gun flew away into the darkness. "I'm not putting him down. He's just gonna run."

"No, he won't," Peter said. "He'll come with me."

The kid's shirt was damp with sweat. "Why would I go with you, Saltine?"

"If you go with Brody, they'll hurt you. Break all your fingers, wreck your hands, smash your elbows. Set some kind of example. You'll never play guitar again, and that's if they don't just kill you outright."

Brody's face showed nothing.

But the kid's eyes were lit with fear and desperation now. He'd carried that thought as a secret in his head, but hearing it spoken aloud made it real. He struggled harder, the tips of his tattered sneakers barely brushing against the blades of the tall grass. Brody didn't seem to notice or care.

"On the other hand," said Peter, "if you come with me, all I want is my truck back. You keep your gun and whatever else you've got. Live to fight another day."

Wanda came out the back door, her camera bag in one hand and a fresh drink in the other. Her eyelids drooped. "I thought you went to the bathroom."

Then she saw Brody holding the kid, and Peter holding the gun. "Aw, hell."

"Hey, Wanda."

"Brody. I hope you know I'm not a part of this."

"King ain't gonna care," Brody said. "You know how he is."

Peter said, "Wanda, please go get the car." She was in no condition to drive, but Peter was in no position to complain.

Wanda tightened her lips. "You are just a goddamn shit magnet, aren't you, Peter Ash?"

Then she walked behind him, out of the line of fire,

trying hard not to spill her drink as she rounded the corner of the building. Heading, Peter hoped, for the Land Cruiser.

He wondered if she'd come back for him, or just drive away.

31

"Where's King Robbie?" Peter asked.

Brody considered for a moment before answering. Peter got the impression Brody considered everything.

"At his place on the river," said the big man finally. "With an ounce of uncut product and a couple of girls."

"And you're here, doing the heavy lifting. How'd you know the kid would be at this place?"

"Educated guess. Plus King owns the club." Brody looked at the young man still dangling by one arm. "King owns a lot of things."

The big man was thick, but he also had to be extremely strong to hold the struggling kid up in the air for so long. Even that skinny string bean had to weigh 120 pounds or more, especially wriggling like a freshly caught fish. Brody held the kid with no visible strain.

Although he probably wouldn't show the effort, no matter how much it took.

"How about you," said Peter. "He own you, too?"

"I take his money, I do what he says."

Peter nodded. It was a good answer. "What if he were dead?"

"What are you asking?"

"I'm trying to get this kid out of trouble."

"This kid who stole your truck."

"Yeah, I know," Peter said. "But what if King were dead?"

"He's not. I do what he says."

Peter nodded again. "Where's Charlene?"

"Around."

"If she were here, I'd be dead already."

Now Brody nodded.

"She's watching the house?"

Brody didn't answer.

Peter heard an engine start up. He hoped it was the Land Cruiser. "Better give me your phone, too. I don't want you calling for help."

Brody shook his head.

"You'd give up your gun but not your phone?"

Brody gave the hint of a shrug. "It's my phone."

"You'd let me shoot you over your phone?"

"I like the pictures," Brody said. "Besides, if you were gonna shoot me, you'd have done it already."

It was the problem with not shooting someone right off the bat, Peter thought. They stopped believing you'd shoot them at all.

This was often Lewis's argument for killing people right away.

Peter saw a large rectangular outline in Brody's right-front pocket, and a smaller outline in his left-front pocket. "Looks like you've got two phones." He pointed the gun at the larger rectangle. "I'll shoot the big one first," he said. "That's probably your personal phone. Lose your pictures, and you'll never walk right again. All with one bullet."

Brody just looked at him.

Peter raised the 1911 and snapped a shot past Brody's ear.

Brody didn't even twitch. His face was empty. He looked again at the kid still dangling by one arm.

"I'll toss them into the grass," he finally said. "Not far enough to break them. But it'll take me a while to find them."

"Just shoot him," the kid said. "I'll give you your damn truck back. I've still got it."

"Shut up." Brody gave the kid a shake, a Rottweiler with a kitten. Peter heard the kid's teeth clack together like castanets. "The grown-ups are talking."

The Land Cruiser lurched around the corner, Wanda behind the wheel. She leaned out of her seat to open the back door.

"Your phones," said Peter.

Brody fished them out of his pockets and skimmed them into the night.

Peter held out his hand. "Now the kid."

The big man lowered the boy to the ground, but kept him close with that heavy hand on the boy's bicep. Peter wasn't going to make Mad Chester's mistake. He wasn't going to get anywhere near Brody's powerful arms.

"I can still shoot either one of you," said Peter. "Or

both. Come on, Brody, lengthen the leash. Kid, reach out your hand."

Brody extended his arm and the kid put his free arm out. Peter was almost eight feet from the big man when he clamped his fingers around the kid's thin wrist. Far enough.

Brody let him go.

As Peter pulled the kid past him, the gun still on Brody, the boy scooped up the ruined remains of his guitar one-handed. Peter crab-walked to the Land Cruiser, the gun still on Brody, moving the kid ahead of him. The kid didn't resist. He climbed into the car with Peter's grip tight on his wrist. "Put the window down," said Peter. "Then scoot over."

The kid put the shattered guitar on the seat, turned the crank with his free hand, then slid over to make room, gathering the guitar up on his lap.

Peter got in after him, then put his gun through the open window of the open door.

"Let's go," he said.

Wanda hit the gas. The acceleration closed the door, but Peter kept the gun on Brody through the open window the whole time.

The Toyota bounced through the tall grass, then over the curb. Through the back window, Peter saw Brody staring after them.

As Wanda turned down the road and away, Brody bent down and began to search for his phones and his gun.

32

The skinny kid looked at Peter, his eyes wide. "You should've killed him. You know he'd have killed you."

Peter hated that the logic of gangster Memphis was the same as the logic of the Middle East. "I'd rather not kill anybody if I can help it."

"They're coming after us all now. I hope you know what you're doing, Saltine."

"I'm saving your life, kid. If you behave."

The young man's face was hollow in the darkness of the back seat. "I'm dead no matter what. You're just drawing out my time."

"It doesn't have to be like that," Peter said. "Where's my truck?"

The kid looked out the window at the passing streets. "Not far. Not a scratch on it, neither."

"Good." Peter still had one big knuckly hand wrapped around the boy's thin wrist. "Now give me the gun. Slowly, please."

The kid frowned. Peter could see the gears turning behind his eyes. "Thought I was keeping the gun."

"I lied." Peter smiled. "I might reconsider if you aren't a pain in the ass."

The kid wasn't happy about it, but he leaned slowly sideways, the ruined guitar staying on his tilted lap as if of its own volition. When he extracted the little snub-nose from his back pocket, he used his thumb and fore-finger, just like Brody had done, and held it out. A fast learner.

"On the floor, by my feet." The kid gave the gun a little flip and it dropped into Peter's footwell.

Wanda glanced over her shoulder. She wasn't driving fast, but she wasn't all over the road, either. Her double vodka rocks sloshed slightly in an aftermarket cup holder that hung from a heat vent. "Where am I going?"

"This way's good," said the kid. "Left on Thomas."

"How old are you?" Peter was curious.

"None of your damn business."

"What's your name?"

For some reason, this was even more outrageous. "Man, why the fuck you want to know my name?"

"I can't keep calling you Kid. You do have a name, right?"

The kid rolled his eyes in an eloquent statement. "El-lison," he said. "Ellison Bell." Then his face went still, as if he'd suddenly walked across a fresh grave. He turned back to the window. "But nobody calls me Ellison no more. You call me Eli."

"Okay, Eli. I'm Peter. What'd you do to get yourself in this kind of trouble?"

Eli shook his head, the sheen of sorrow and

desperation worse now than ever. He seemed to be shrinking into himself. He pulled the shattered remnants of his guitar close to his chest. His voice seemed to come from far away.

"I don't know."

"You did something. What was it?"

"Robbed a jewelry store up at the mall."

"That was you?" Wanda's voice came sharp from the front seat. "People died."

Eli nodded. "I didn't start it, and I didn't kill nobody. But I did what I did." He took in a long breath, then let it out. "When it went bad, I was the only one walked away. But I don't know why King wants me so bad. We were way outside his turf."

"That's what's in the garbage bag," said Peter. "The stuff from the jewelry store."

Eli nodded again. He seemed even smaller now. "My friend was going to help us sell it. The news says only two dead, but I'm pretty sure he's dead, too. I thought I could sell it to King Robbie, but he's got every crew out looking for me. He's just gonna take it, then probably kill me." To Wanda, he said, "This is Thomas up here."

She turned left onto a four-lane street. Nameless gas stations and untended apartment buildings and vacant lots with cracked cement steps leading from the sidewalk up to unmown grass.

"You could give yourself up to the police," Peter said.

Eli shook his head. "It's manslaughter, what I did. Looked it up on my phone. Armed robbery resulting in a death. They try me as an adult, I get ten years in state prison. King Robbie can have me killed there just as easy. Maybe easier, 'cause he'd know where to find me. But he'll prob'ly just get it done while I'm sitting in the county jail. He's got people everywhere."

Peter didn't want to think about how this young kid knew so much. How he could foresee his own death with such clarity.

He released Eli's arm. "You got any people to take you in?"

Eli shook his head again. "All my people are dead or gone." He rubbed his wrist, then massaged the bicep where Brody had held him. There would be broken blood vessels, a dark band of bruises forming under his blue-black skin, although it was too dim in the car to see. The muscle would hurt for days.

If Eli lived that long.

They passed a chicken joint, a church, a funeral parlor. Boarded-up businesses. The night air through the open windows was thick with humidity, and the same temperature as skin.

Wanda said, "You any relation to Isaac Bell?"

Eli blinked. "That's my pops. He's up at Henning, got three life sentences. But he can't protect me in there, not from King Robbie."

Peter pointed at the ruined guitar. "Where'd you learn to play like that?"

Eli took in a deep, shuddering breath. "Seems like I always knew, like I was born with it in my hands or something. My mom and pops always had music playing when

I was little. I practically grew up at that joint, the Lucky Lounge. My pops used to own it."

Over her shoulder, Wanda said, "You know who Eli's father is? Isaac Bell ran the Memphis drug trade before King Robbie. Everything from trap houses to local distribution to moving bulk from New Orleans to Chicago. Total vertical integration. Only reason he got caught is a series of anonymous calls to the police tip line. There was supposed to be a big payout if a tip led to a conviction, but nobody ever claimed the reward."

The kid leaned forward. "Is that what happened?" he asked. "Somebody tipped off the police? And didn't even claim the reward? You know who that was?"

"I don't know anything," said Wanda. "I just ask myself that old reporter's question. Who benefits? I know it wasn't your brother Baldwin. He got killed in the war that came afterward."

Peter saw the kid's gears turning again, watched the revelation arrive like a freight train. "King's the one who came out on top. Was it King who set up my pops? King who killed my brother?"

Neither was really a question. Peter could see that Eli already knew the answers.

Wanda looked uncomfortable and turned back to the road. "I really don't know, Eli. It was a bad time. But I knew your dad, he was an okay guy. He tried to keep the peace when he could. Things have gotten a lot worse since he went away."

"Is that what you're after?" asked Peter. "You want revenge for your dad and brother?"

"No," said Eli. "I tried that life and was no damn good at it. All I ever wanted was to play music. I only ended up in that jewelry store because my boys were gonna fuck up my guitar if I didn't." He looked at the broken thing in his arms. "I guess it don't matter now."

The street was getting more industrial, but no more prosperous. Low rows of long metal and cement-block buildings, tall fences with barbed wire. It wasn't clear how many of these places were still in operation. Peter saw a lot of signs saying FOR SALE OR LEASE. Stuff was made here, once. Cracked slabs of concrete where workers had parked, back when there were jobs. Not many cars now.

"So what do we do with him?" asked Wanda.

Peter looked at Eli. "What would it take to get you out of this mess?"

"Why in hell would I trust you? Far as I know, once I take you to your truck, you'll shoot me in the head with my own damn gun."

"Eli, I let you take that truck to begin with," said Peter. "I could have just left you with Brody just now, let him beat the location out of you." He laid Chester's 1911 on his leg, now pointed away from Eli. "Besides, what other offers do you have? Talk to me. What would it take?"

Wanda looked at Peter in the rearview mirror. "Are you fucking serious?"

"He's fourteen or fifteen, Wanda. You never made a mistake?"

"Is that what you call robbing a jewelry store? A mistake? Which he followed up by stealing your truck at gunpoint, by the way."

"We've all done things we're not proud of."

Peter had a long list himself. War tended to do that to people.

And Ellison Bell had surely played the hell out of that guitar.

"Let me ask you something, Wanda. How old were you when you started taking pictures?"

He watched her face in the rearview. "Eleven. My uncle's Polaroid. He'd let me borrow it for the day if I looked after my little cousin."

"When did you know you wanted to be a photographer?"

She screwed up her mouth. "The first time I looked through the damn viewfinder."

"And what did you give up to get where you are now?"

That uncomfortable look again. "Just about everything."

"Anybody help you along the way?"

She sighed. "Okay, but." The muscles flexed in her jaw. "You remember those other people are trying to kill me, right?"

Peter smiled. "I can walk and chew gum at the same time."

Wanda's voice got loud. "This is my life here, not some fucking game. Bad men with guns."

Peter reminded himself that Wanda was tough and experienced, but under major stress. Suffering from some kind of major traumatic event. And she was a civilian, no matter where she'd been.

"I know, Wanda." His voice was gentle. "But it's Eli's life, too. What's the next turn, Eli? Where are we going?"

"Let me look at my phone." He showed Peter his hands, then dipped three fingers gently into his front pocket without disturbing the guitar fragments. He pulled out a cheap phone and brought up a map. "Three more blocks, then take a right at the pizza place."

The turn took them through a sprawling industrial plant that took up both sides of the street. One well-lit storage yard held hundreds of pallets, pink-packaged bundles of what looked to Peter like roofing shingles. Cars and trucks were parked behind a high steel fence, even at this evening hour.

Peter looked around. "Where the hell are you taking us?"

"This place is busy, there's always cars parked in these lots. I figured the truck would be safe here."

Ahead, the road thinned down and split into a Y. The roofing plant abruptly ended in sawgrass and high brush, a rough, tangled no-man's-land behind a four-foot chain-link fence. There were no visible streetlights past the Y. Both narrow roads disappeared into the overgrown darkness.

"I don't like this," said Wanda, letting up on the gas.

"Stay to the right," said Eli. "It's not far." He tucked his phone back into his pocket, gathered his broken guitar up in his hands.

Wanda steered to the right, slowing further. Twenty miles an hour, then ten. The fence on both sides of them now. "Peter."

The road curved away into the night. Behind them, Peter saw nothing but the dimming lights of the roofing plant. Nothing ahead but road and fence and power lines and Tennessee bottomland grown weedy and wild.

He pointed Chester's gun at Eli again. "Don't piss me off, here."

"Hey, Saltine, you want me to trust you? Well, you gotta trust me." Eli glanced out the window. A long section of fence covered with vines. "Your truck is this way."

Wanda let the Land Cruiser coast to a fast walking pace. "I really don't like this."

Eli pitched the wreckage of the guitar at Peter's face and jumped out the door, already running when his feet hit the pavement.

"Shit." Peter untangled himself from the strings and splinters and went after him, Chester's 1911 in his hand.

33

The skinny kid was fast.

By the time Peter got his feet under him, Eli was down the embankment and into the sawgrass. The vine-covered fence was up to the kid's chest. It didn't even slow him down. He bounced over it like his legs were made out of springs.

Peter had been a distance runner since high school. His time in the Marines had made him lean and strong, and he hadn't let up since, especially not in the last six months, running the loop around June's little pocket valley. He'd have no problem catching this kid.

He jammed the big pistol into his front pocket to free his hand as he ran down into the grass to the chain-link. He'd lost a good ten seconds untangling himself, and Wanda had coasted forward another twenty or thirty yards, so there were no vines here. It'd be easier to climb.

He put both hands on the fence top and felt the bloody bite of sharp-cut tips. Instead of the usual bent-wire top, this was a security fence. The top rail on the far side set three inches below spikes, nothing decent to grab. This was going to hurt.

Too late now. He ignored the pain, still moving, carried by his own momentum. He reached over the spikes to the crossbar, tearing up his wrists and forearms as he dug his boot-tips into the links and swung himself over the top. He'd get a tetanus shot later, he thought, then felt Chester's 1911 slip from his pocket.

Landing on both feet, he looked for Eli. The kid had angled away and stretched his lead, up to his waist in the grass running toward the power lines, just another nighttime shadow with his dark skin and black T-shirt, headed for the trees.

He'd lose Eli if he stopped to search for the gun, so he left it behind and pushed himself into a sprint, running blind into dark, unknown territory without a weapon. Horrible tactics. Did Eli have friends in those woods? Some crew of feral street kids?

Peter would find out soon enough.

His hands were blood-slick from the fence-top but his legs were fine. He felt the sweat begin to pop through his skin. His breath came easily, but the ground was uneven, the sawgrass lumpy underfoot. Sprinting headlong was a bad idea. His old combat boots helped keep his ankles steady, but he had to slow his pace or risk a fall.

Ahead of him, the kid was practically invisible in the night, running for the power lines and getting farther ahead with every stride.

How was Eli moving so fast over this rough terrain in his ratty old sneakers?

Maybe Eli hadn't jumped from the car at random. Maybe he'd picked his spot by the vine-covered fence, where the security spikes were covered by thick vegetation. With those few extra car-lengths Peter had needed to untangle himself from that damn guitar, he'd ended up jumping the fence farther along, where those spikes were exposed.

Had Eli known that might happen?

What else did Eli know that Peter didn't?

He angled left to find the route the kid had taken.

After less than a minute, he stumbled at a narrow flattened section, then saw a faint line heading away, slightly brighter in the night than the tall grass around it.

A path, or something like it. The lumps beaten down by foot traffic. An old shortcut headed somewhere.

Eli hadn't just jumped when he saw the chance. Eli had known exactly what he was doing. And where he was going.

Peter's truck was nowhere near here. And Eli was more than halfway gone.

Hands throbbing, Peter ran faster. His boots felt better underfoot now, his legs strong, his chest and shoulders lubricated with sweat. The power lines were closer. Was that Eli in his black Fender T-shirt running ahead of him, or some tall, dense-leafed shrub blowing in the wind?

Peter passed the shrub.

He pushed harder.

To find his truck, yes, but for Eli, too.

Because the kid had been right, back in the car.

King Robbie's men were after all of them, now.

Peter wasn't even going to think about the blue-faced dump-truck driver with the machine gun. One problem at a time.

Under the power lines on their crooked creosoted poles, the path met a gravel utility track for service vehicles. The gravel pointed toward a brighter patch of sky, some well-lit place. The path picked up again on the far side and headed into the trees, and Peter knew it was where Eli had gone. The utility track would lead to a closed gate, a parking lot, a paved road. The trees would be better cover, and the Wolf River was over there somewhere.

A million places to hide, for a while. Until Eli got hungry.

What safe place did he have, then?

Peter could see ahead to where the path slid between overgrown weed trees and into the woods. Maples and oaks and chestnuts. If Peter was laying an ambush, this is where he'd do it. Stand to the side with a tree branch and knock down the chaser as he came in blind.

But Eli was far out in front and in familiar territory. Peter was much stronger and would have the advantage in any direct confrontation. Eli was smart, thinking ahead a half dozen moves or more. He wouldn't stop running. He had a plan.

If Peter couldn't catch him, he hoped to hell Eli had a plan.

He felt the white static flare as he approached the dark trees. He raised an arm to keep the branches out of his eyes and ran headlong into the forest.

. . .

In the sawgrass, there had been some ambient light from the city, and a brighter glow to the east from that lit-up place down the gravel utility track. Under the canopy, it was far darker. He could barely see his hand in front of his face, let alone any trail through the underbrush and years of fallen leaves.

He stopped.

Tried to quiet his panting breath. Listened hard.

He heard the quick, light crunch of running footsteps in the distance. Peter turned his head to one side, then the other, letting his ears find the direction. Waiting for his eyes to adjust.

There it was. The crooked line of the path, but much fainter in the darkness.

He was off again, pushing even faster now, weaving through the trees. As he got deeper inside, they got bigger and far older. Tall, gnarled trunks. In the middle of industrial Memphis, this odd little piece of ancient forest. Running, he imagined Union scouts under cover here, or a band of Confederate raiders planning their next attack. Or a rest stop on the Underground Railroad.

And here was Peter, a white man, chasing this black kid through the woods.

Thinking he knew what was best.

Hoping like hell he was right.

His lungs burned, his hands sticky-slick with blood. He wanted to stop and listen again, but was breathing too hard to hear anything but the pounding of his own heart.

So he followed the meager path where it led him, running harder than ever, pushing past his limits. Branches slapped his arms and face. Eli wouldn't have this problem. Slimmer and smaller, he was a rabbit ahead of the hounds, running for his life.

Then Peter came around a low thicketed rise and the forest was brighter, light shining in through the trees, the path clear before him. Eli out there somewhere.

With a final blast of speed, Peter pushed through the last thick stand of branches and into a field of waist-high grass around a high-fenced enclosure topped with a coil of razor wire. A big bright electrical substation with towers and transformers and a windowless brick control building.

No sign of young Eli Bell anywhere.

The path led through the grass to a dead-end asphalt turnaround, then disappeared into the grass again. More trees beyond, and the wild land along the river.

The Land Cruiser stood silent on the road.

Wanda leaned her angular frame against the fender, shaking her head.

Peter came to a stop at the car, chest heaving, legs wobbly, nauseated from the long hard sprint. He bent at the waist and put his bloody hands on his knees. He was fairly certain he wasn't going to puke.

Eli Bell had beat him like a rented mule.

"You're not very good at this, Peter." Wanda's short dreadlocks bounced with her laughter. "You can't even keep hold of one baby gangster."

When Peter could breathe again, he said, "Why does he call me Saltine?"

"Baby, don't you know what a saltine is?" Her smile was luminous in the floodlights. "It's a white cracker."

She dissolved into hysteria and fell giggling into the high rough grass.

Peter dropped beside her. She looked over at him, eyes half-closed again.

"I finished my drink," she said sleepily. "And took another pill. Maybe you'd drive?"

34

Peter stopped to collect Chester's 1911 on their way back to the Peabody.

He found the remains of the guitar on the road to mark the place he'd run from the car, then used the flashlight on Wanda's phone to follow his own trampled path. The pistol lay beneath a clump of sawgrass not far from where he'd gone over the fence.

The tubular crossbar was stained with his blood.

The thighs of his pants were imprinted in red with the shape of his hands.

He used the melted ice from Wanda's drink to rinse his hands, then wiped them on his pants to blur the marks. He'd hoped it would make him appear less like an ax murderer. Now he just looked as though he'd been splashed by thinned red paint.

He'd done this whole thing very badly.

Eli and Wanda might well pay the price.

In the hotel's parking circle, Peter touched Wanda's shoulder to wake her, then offered to help her up to the suite. She shook her head without a word and assembled herself in the seat of the Toyota. With a tight grip on her camera bag, she walked through the entrance with her head held high.

After a moment, he followed her inside, checking to see that she got on the elevator.

In the high-ceilinged lobby, with its elegant fountain and dark-stained woodwork and grand player piano tinkling out "Don't Be Cruel," he was acutely aware of himself. He stank of the sweat from his confrontation with King Robbie and Brody and his sprint through the woods. His pants were filthy, but without his truck, they were his only pair.

The young clerk at the front desk eyed him nervously, her hand on the phone, even after he showed her his key card. "Just making sure my friend made it upstairs," he said. "We had a little too much fun on Beale Street." Hoping that might explain how he looked.

He asked for an envelope, put his key card inside, wrote June's name on the front, then handed it to the clerk. "She'll pick it up tomorrow afternoon," he said. Then asked for directions to the bathroom off the lobby.

Avoiding his own face in the mirror, he scrubbed his hands and arms with soap and hot water.

It would be easy to think Wanda was just a woman having a little too much fun.

Her collection of pills told a different story.

Something terrible had happened, and she was trying to push it down deep. But it wouldn't stay down, not forever. Not even with all the booze and pills in the world.

Peter had some experience with that.

He'd help her with the hidden part of her life if he could. If she'd let him.

It wasn't exactly his area of expertise.

Between the white static and Peter's restless need for motion, his own mental health wasn't exactly stellar. To deal with it, Peter's default was to go kinetic. It was fun.

Of course, most people would run screaming from the things Peter found fun. The kind of action that damped down his own static, or put it to use.

Peter wasn't most people.

And he was pretty sure he had at least one more thing to do that night.

He smiled wolfishly as he hit the gas, steering the Toyota out of the parking lot and into the street.

Driving from The Peabody toward Wanda's house, he kept his eyes on the rearview mirrors. The hour was late and the roads were mostly empty. If someone was following him, they were very good.

He was fairly certain there was no tracking device on Wanda's car. He'd checked the underside after collecting Chester's gun, not that it was any kind of guarantee. The technology was getting better and cheaper all the time.

If anyone was tracking the car remotely, they could have moved on Peter and Wanda many times in the last few hours.

King Robbie's operation probably had that level of sophistication, but what they lacked was the opportunity. This whole thing was unfolding too quickly. King Robbie and Brody and Charlene had only gotten involved that morning, after Peter's truck was stolen.

The guys with the machine gun had been harassing Wanda for weeks, but they hadn't crashed the dump truck into her house until early yesterday. Peter couldn't discern much of a plan there besides reducing the house to rubble.

It would help if he knew what they wanted. He wondered if they knew themselves. Maybe they just wanted to ruin something.

He drove a slow, lights-out surveillance route around Wanda's house at a four-block radius, saw nothing, and didn't attract any followers. He drove another circuit, three blocks out. Still nothing. He left the Toyota tucked behind an elementary school and crossed Vollintine on foot.

Just another saltine out for a walk on a warm May night in North Memphis.

With Chester's 1911 tucked into the back of his bloody pants.

If the cops picked him up, he'd be in serious trouble.

Now two blocks out from Wanda's.

Some streets had homes with fresh paint and tidy yards. Others had more vacant lots than houses. He walked on the sidewalk or into the vacant lots, trying to stay invisible. Most houses had security lights outside, but the interiors were dimly lit or dark. He could hear the murmur of televisions through open windows, and the occasional hum of air conditioners. There was no traffic. Most newer cars were parked in driveways, behind gates. The cars on the street were usually old beaters.

He spiraled closer, now just a block out. He'd have liked to slip through people's backyards, but most were enclosed by tall fences. Some houses had dogs, too, he could hear them barking as he made his way along. He wasn't going to hurt somebody's dog, no matter how big or mean. He wasn't in the mood to climb any more damn fences, either.

He was definitely in the mood for what he thought was coming, though.

He could feel it, filling him up as he walked.

The smell of the dense, living greenery in the warm night air was intoxicating.

Finally he stood in the shadows on the far corner of the block behind Wanda's house. He pictured how it lay, with the Dumpster in front and the lumber pile angled toward the driveway. Her leaning garage in the back. A wood-sided bungalow on one side of her, a flat, grassy vacant lot on the other.

Peter wondered if Gantry had delivered on the police cruiser.

He hoped not.

He looked down the street. Behind Wanda's neighboring vacant lot, he saw a small brick Cape Cod with a neat white fence in front and a yard bursting with flowerbeds. Flanking it were two wide lots filled with tall, spreading trees and low bushes. Not cleared, exactly, but tended, like small parks. The farthest one was directly behind Wanda's house.

Peter thought he'd like the people in the brick Cape.

Maybe they'd be good for Wanda, too.

In front of the farthest tended lot, silent at the curb, sat a long, low sedan. It was a newer model, all angles and planes, and painted matte black, even the rims and trim.

It reminded Peter of a stealth bomber.

He knew it didn't belong to the neat little Cape with the colorful flowerbeds. Style aside, the Cape had a big old Buick in the driveway with plenty of room behind it.

Across the street, a leaning trio of small frame houses crouched, hunkering into their weedy dirt yards, with two cars on cinder blocks out front. He was pretty sure the stealth-bomber sedan didn't belong to one of them, either.

Its engine was off. He couldn't see anyone inside, although his sightline was poor.

He crossed the street at the closest parklike lot. He saw no silhouette through the sedan's rear windshield.

If it were Peter, he wouldn't be waiting in the car.

She wouldn't be, either.

She'd be closer to her target.

He continued into the trees and slipped slowly and silently toward the back, allowing his eyes to adjust. He kept off the gravel path, grateful for the noise of the Cape Cod's air conditioner.

The house behind, on the far side of Wanda's neighboring mown lot, had no fence, but it was surrounded by a dense wall of high thorny bushes. He walked down the line of bushes, Chester's 1911 in his hand.

He wished for the vest June had given him. And a helmet. And an M4 carbine with a thirty-round mag racked and ready, with spares in his pocket. Hell, as long as he was wishing, he'd take a micro-drone with an infrared camera flying above, and a voice in his ear feeding him directions.

And no nice neighbors who might end up as collateral damage.

He wondered where she'd be set up. Inside the house? In the shadow of the Dumpster?

How would Peter do it?

Then he knew.

There was a narrow space where someone had pruned back the thorny bushes to make room for the brick Cape's tall plank fence. He could smell the preservative in the new wood.

As he slipped through the gap into the grassy vacant lot beside Wanda's house, a soft rain began to fall. He stood there in the corner for a moment, silent and invisible, and listened to the patter of the raindrops on the trees behind him. It was a welcome sound.

It would hide the noise of his passage.

It would make her restless, uncomfortable, more likely to show herself.

Still, he didn't like coming out of the trees. The mown lot was like Kansas. Too open, too exposed. If he was wrong, he'd make an easy target.

There was no helping it. He dropped into a belly

crawl, working his slow way forward on his forearms and toes. Down low, it wasn't so bad. Untrimmed weeds grew knee-high at the base of the fence, creating rounded shadows he could blend into. The grass hadn't been cut recently, and was at least eight inches tall. The rain was cool as it soaked into his clothes.

It was better than bare, sandy desert. Almost anything was.

Soon he could see past the lumber pile to a police cruiser parked at the curb. Detective Gantry had come through, but Peter didn't think it would make a difference. Not to her, not if he'd read her right.

It didn't make a difference to Peter, either.

He found her in the backyard, out of sight from the cruiser with good visibility and multiple escape routes. The grassy vacant lot Peter had just crossed to her left, the neighbor's yard to the right, and the stealth-bomber sedan a quick sprint through the tended trees behind her.

She was very good.

He watched for at least twenty minutes as she sat on the edge of a wooden chair in the deep shadow surrounding Wanda's leaning, vine-strangled garage. She was hidden from the police car by the lumber pile. If she felt the rain, she didn't show it. Every minute or so, she turned her head to scan her surroundings, from Wanda's yard and house on her right to the vacant lot on her left where Peter lay flat beside the untrimmed weeds along the fence. Then she turned to face the street again, where the police car sat. She had an opinion where he'd come from, but she wasn't taking chances.

Behind Peter, the brick Cape's air conditioner rattled and hummed. It had an odd rhythm, cycling louder and softer, either low on coolant or the compressor starting to go. He used that rhythm and her shifting gaze to get closer, bit by bit. Behind her on his belly by the weeds in the thick wet grass, the taste of copper in his mouth. The rain fell harder.

Forty feet away, then twenty. Then ten. He slowly gathered his feet under him, dug his toes into the dirt.

Then launched himself at her and knocked her off balance against the side of the garage into the tangled vines, Chester's 1911 jammed into the soft flesh beneath her jaw.

He said, "Hello, Charlene."

She still wore her red seersucker jacket.

In that final rush, she'd felt him coming and had made it halfway off the chair. She held a new gun in her fist, some utilitarian automatic. She tried to bring it up but Peter pushed Chester's 1911 hard into her neck with one hand while he wrapped the other around her pistol.

Unyielding, heedless of the gun to her skin, she fought him hard for her weapon until he finally twisted it away. She was surprisingly strong, but Peter outweighed her by at least sixty pounds. Not exactly a fair fight.

He'd have felt bad about it if she hadn't been waiting to kill him.

"I owe you a gun. This isn't it." He kept his voice calm and quiet as he shoved her deeper into the vines. "I behaved disrespectfully in King Robbie's car this morning, and I apologize for that. A friend of mine was in trouble, and I didn't have time to ask nicely. I don't know if you'll understand that or not."

She was shaking, but not with fear. To survive in the life she'd made, she'd likely have drained her fear away, and replaced it with something cold and hard. Contained until she needed it. An anger so deeply embedded she wouldn't know it as something separate from herself. If any fear remained, it would come in the dark of night while she slept.

"If you're going to kill me, shut the fuck up and do it already."

"I'm not going to kill you unless I have to. I told you I'd replace that pistol, and I will. But right now I'm going to walk you back to your car and let you drive away. That's my trade for the disrespect this morning. Your life."

She jammed an elbow into his ribs. "Then get your fucking body off me." Her voice was sharp. He thought she might bite him.

He pitched her gun into the weeds and pushed himself off the garage. He stepped back to a safer distance with Chester's 1911 still trained at her chest while she extracted herself from the vines and resettled the damp jacket on her shoulders. Her hair remained twisted into spikes, even with the rain.

"Maybe you don't consider it a fair trade," he said. "That's up to you. But if I see you again, I'll believe you mean me harm and kill you without a second thought."

Even in the shadow of the garage, he could see her scowl, her hands still shaking with fury. He hadn't convinced this hard woman. He'd beaten her twice and hurt only her pride. It was an insult. A challenge.

At that moment, he knew that she wanted to kill Peter more than she wanted anything else in the world.

But he couldn't shoot her in cold blood. Maybe, like Chester, she thought that made him weak. He knew Lewis would say that Peter was dumb to live by these rules of engagement. Unwilling to put a bullet into her, just because he'd disarmed her.

Charlene seemed to agree. Her scowl turned into a sneer.

"You'd have died young in this town," she said. "We'd have eaten you as a child."

"Let's go." He nodded toward the parklike lot behind Wanda's. "Hands where I can see them. I'm right behind you."

He followed her through the trees to the stealth-bomber sedan. In the street, she caught his eye and waggled the fingers of her raised right hand. "Keys."

He nodded. She dipped two fingers into the front pocket of her jeans, extracted an electronic fob, and did something to it. The windows slid down silently and the engine began to purr.

Peter glanced inside and saw no weapon on the seats or the floor. If there was something under the seat or in the center console, he'd know soon enough. She looked at him and he nodded again. She opened the door and slipped into the black leather seat.

She put both hands on the wheel where he could see

them. "That's twice you got the jump on me," she said through the open window. "You know this ain't over."

Peter smiled pleasantly. "You want to try a duel, like fine Southern gentlemen? Pistols by the river at dawn?"

She showed him her teeth. "Fuck no."

He dropped the smile. "If I see you again, I'll put two in your chest and one in your head."

She put the car into drive. "Not if I see you first."

As she ghosted down the street, he told himself he'd made the right choice, not killing her.

He tried to believe it.

35

After supper, Albert washed down a handful of pain pills with a beer and sat on the porch rocker, waiting for the ache in his leg to fade away. But it never did. Not enough to give him rest. Seemed like he hurt all the time, now.

So he made a pot of coffee, poured it into his thermos, and climbed into his old Ford Fiesta.

Past midnight and Albert was back on the road.

The trip from Benton County into Memphis took him about an hour and a half. Driving felt like he was doing something.

He wasn't sure what.

He told himself that he hadn't gotten a good look at it, before. After that machine gun, he wanted to see it. He wanted to know if what Judah Lee had done—what Albert helped him do—had done the job. Gotten that woman out of their house.

When he got off the freeway, even in the middle of the night, the city was loud. He could hear the racket of people all around him, on the street and seeping through open doors and windows, noise from radios and televisions, kids crying. People yelling.

He could never live like this. Just driving through it made all his muscles go tight. If it were up to Albert, he'd never leave the farm, deep in the peace of the woods.

He came to the street. Not too fast, not too slow, he went down the block like he belonged there, although he didn't. He was glad he'd replaced the noisy exhaust on the Fiesta.

He saw a police car parked at the curb, engine running, a black elbow angled out the open window. The cop's black face lit up in Albert's headlights, looking at him. Albert didn't make eye contact, just raised a casual hand to the man and took his foot off the gas to take a look at the place, like anyone might have done.

At first he didn't even recognize the house. He'd seen it in the daylight with the dump truck stuck in the living room because he'd driven past later that day, one of a hundred sightseers trying to catch a glimpse of someone else's disaster. He'd seen the woman standing on the porch. She'd stared back like she was memorizing each face in the long line of cars. It was unnerving, that stare.

He'd seen the house again from the Country Squire while Judah Lee pounded it with that big gun. It looked different with a blue tarp hanging down to keep the rain out. Albert hadn't liked that tarp, so neatly placed. Only one reason to put in the time for that.

Now the house had changed again. Somebody had parked a Dumpster right beside the truck's rear end.

That wall of steel looked like some kind of fortress, protecting the place. Beside the Dumpster was a tall stack of lumber.

It didn't look like the woman was leaving.

To Albert, it looked like she was getting ready to rebuild.

Back home, he drove directly to the new barn, the one their granddad built back in the late forties, flush with money from the mule-trading business. It was framed with timbers that came out of their woodlot, and walled with stones from their fields.

The new barn was where the Farmall tractor lived, along with the harrow and plow and harvester and all the other equipment needed to run the place. Each piece was old enough to belong in a museum somewhere, but they still did the job, if Albert put in the time to keep them working. It seemed like he was always trying to break the rust on some bolts so he could sharpen the blades or replace a broken drive chain. He flipped on the light and saw the heavy workbench and the welder and the pegboard with his daddy's tools. The man door stood open to the night. Judah Lee's red pickup stood silently by, its crumpled-up passenger side a reminder of Judah's ruthlessness.

But there was no sign of Judah Lee or the station wagon.

He limped across the grass-grown gravel and down the hill past the clump of oaks to the old barn.

It might have been older than the farmhouse. Albert didn't store anything of value there. Moss grew thick on the windblown roof. Rain and sun and starlight came through in equal measures. The siding planks were falling away, and the whole building had a sort of diagonal lean, like Albert's daddy when he was drunk, at the exact moment before he'd either fall over or lash out with a fist hard as a pine knot. Even at eighty, the old man had still hit plenty hard.

Could a man be sorry his daddy was dead, but glad at the same time?

Albert had reinforced or repaired the old barn's log frame more than a few times. When he was a younger man, before the accident, he'd even rigged a tow chain around the top of the building and tried to pull it back upright with the Farmall. But the barn hadn't stopped at upright. It had just kept going, and now it sagged in the other direction, farther than ever. The best Albert could do now was prop it up with timbers.

After his daddy died, Albert had thought he might take that barn apart piece by piece. He knew rich people would buy old wood to make their houses look rustic. Maybe he could pay the taxes, or even some of the note on the farm. But he couldn't bring himself to do it.

The old barn would never be right again, but it was his dang barn.

Now he saw light seeping through the cracks.

The heavy sliding door was as hard to open as ever, its rollers still needing to be cleaned and greased. He'd rather things worked the way they should, but they rarely did. Not without a whole lot more time and effort than Albert had to give.

The Country Squire sat just inside, still stinking of scorched plastic and beer. On the far side of it, Judah Lee stood at some kind of table under the cone of a single light. He was looking at Albert.

"Stop right there, big brother."

Albert stopped in the doorway. "What are you up to?"

Judah walked toward him, a massive shadow lit from behind.

"You sure you want to know? Otherwise you best turn around and walk right out of here."

"I just come from Memphis," Albert said. "I took a look at the house."

That caught Judah's interest. "Yeah? What'd you see?"

"A Dumpster set like a rampart right in front. And a stack of lumber. She's fixing to rebuild. There was a cop parked out front. We're not getting in there anytime soon."

Judah shrugged. In one hand, he held a half-empty liquor bottle, glass cloudy with age, label long gone, and stoppered with an ill-fitting cork. His voice was soft but it carried in the humid night air.

"So we kill the bitch. What's one more dead nigger? Won't be my first." He unstoppered the bottle and held it out. "Drink?"

Albert stared at his brother. "What is wrong with you? When did you get like this?"

"Which part," said Judah. "The killing part or the nigger part?"

"The whole thing," said Albert.

Judah Lee flashed that pointed smile, the tattoo on his face just a deeper shadow in the darkness.

"You know Daddy and Granddad never tolerated anybody wasn't like us," he said. "But it was prison made everything clear to me. We're a minority in there. Get yourself murdered in the yard just for being white. It's only natural to look after your own kind. I met some men who helped me understand. Great men. They asked me to kill a nigger to prove myself."

Albert took a step back. "Tell me you didn't." But Albert found that he knew already. He'd known for a long time. He wasn't sure what was worse, the knowing, or the not being surprised.

Judah Lee shrugged. "It didn't mean nothing to me. Less than nothing, like killing a hog. But it was important. It made me part of something."

"Is this about Carruthers and his group? The New Dixie Knights? The new Klan is what they are."

"Could be we see things more clearly than you." Judah's tone was mild. "The way things really are. Us against them."

Albert shook his head. "Carruthers and his crowd are a bunch of ignorant no-account inbred white-trash peckerwoods."

Judah Lee took another taste from the bottle, then held it out to Albert. His voice was soft and low. "Let me ask you something. You see our lives getting better, year to year? Or getting worse? There's more of them out there every day. They breed like rats. Most of our taxes go to pay for their damn kids. They take our jobs, our money, our women."

"I don't know what on earth you're complaining about." Albert took the bottle, but didn't raise it to his lips. The glass was thick and strong, still in use from some bygone time. "You never paid taxes in your life. Or had a real job, neither, unless you count working for cash as a bouncer at that biker bar."

Judah Lee shook his head. "You fail to understand. You haven't seen what I've seen. We're coming down to it, now. It's us or them, brother. Us or them. Who do you want to inherit this earth?"

Albert had never seen Judah Lee like this before. Even at a whisper, he was passionate. Dang, he was persuasive, even if they were Carruthers's words coming out of his brother's mouth.

Maybe this was what old man Carruthers had seen in Judah Lee. This potential for riling up ugly feelings.

Albert could see right through the words, though. Race was only part of it. Mostly it was about loss. Watching the old covenants disappear, seeing the world change faster and faster while you got left farther and farther behind. Feeling poor and powerless and afraid, and wanting someone to blame.

Race was the excuse, the reason to set loose your freefloating worry and fear and anger onto the world.

To make someone else hurt the way you did.

To make the world fear you back.

For Albert, that part of Judah Lee's argument carried some weight. Not the race part, but the part about their lives getting worse. Except for a lucky few, everyone's lives were getting worse. Time was, if a man could make it through high school, he could get a job, buy a house, support a family. Build a life. Now those jobs were gone. There wasn't much left in the world for a man Albert's age.

Nothing left but what you could take for yourself.

Albert was going to have to do just that.

Otherwise he'd lose the farm that had been in his family for generations. In the end, there was no choice to be made, no choice at all. Just action.

It surprised him, how easily it came. How natural it felt.

Like taking off one suit of clothes and putting on another.

Albert still held the antique bottle in his hand. Some of their daddy's high-test, he could tell by the color, even through that cloudy glass. He raised it to his mouth and took a drink. It tasted like liquid gold, and it burned going down. He felt it fill his chest and rise into his head.

He took a step through the open doorway and pushed the bottle back into Judah Lee's hand. "All right," he said. "Show me what you're doing in here."

"No turning back," said Judah.

"Like I could before?"

Albert pushed past his brother and stumped toward the lighted table.

Under a battery-powered lantern, he saw an improvised workbench, planks laid over sawhorses.

Daddy's old .44 revolver stood by a roll of duct tape, an old coffee can full of rusty roofing nails, and short sections of threaded black pipe in a neat row. A pile of black caps for the ends. A cordless drill. A long coil of slender rope that Albert knew was fuse. A gallon plastic container of Goex Black Powder. A dirty white funnel. A tube of pipe dope to make the caps go on easy.

You surely wouldn't want an accidental spark.

Their daddy had used the powder for his muzzleloaders. He'd been a Civil War reenactor. He'd also used it to blow stumps and boulders from the fields. It was always the high point of the winter, when you got to blow stuff up with Daddy.

Black powder wasn't near as powerful as dynamite, but you didn't need a government license. You could buy as much as you wanted. And you could make the blast more powerful with tools even a child could use.

Judah Lee stepped close to the table, their daddy's old revolver within reach. From a cardboard box, he picked up and held out a piece of black pipe, capped at both ends. One end had a hole drilled in it, with a six-inch piece of fuse coming out. Albert didn't take it. He was staring past the workbench to a half-rotted brown canvas tarp peeled back from a pair of long rectangular boxes. One box was open. The light showed Albert twelve long rifles, looking worn-down but deadly in their angularity.

"Those are M16s," he said. "Where'd you get those? What are these dang pipe bombs for, Judah Lee?"

His little brother, now grown so much bigger and taller, gave Albert a fearsome smile. "You're in it now," he said. "It's a war. Us or them, remember? These are the kind of weapons we'll need to win. Guns and grenades."

"What in God's name does this have to do with that house in Memphis?"

"We need more weapons. Bigger bombs, bigger guns. Whatever prize Forrest left in that house, that's what I mean to use it for."

"Your half, you mean."

"Well, yeah," said Judah Lee. "My half."

Albert thought about how Judah had tried to pull Albert's full dinner plate across the table just a few hours earlier.

How he'd had to jab a fork into his brother's hand to keep him from taking it.

He wondered what he might have to do next.

Judah Lee held out the pipe bomb again. "Come on, big brother, take it. We need to test a couple, so we know they're gonna work. Don't you want to blow some shit up?"

Thing was, Albert did. He really did.

PART 4

36

Wrapped in his ground cloth under the back of the dump truck, Peter woke, just after first light, to the smell of coffee.

He turned his head to the right and saw a white cardboard cup standing on the grass an arm's length away. Steam wafted gently from the hole in the lid.

Part of Peter had slept like the dead. Another part, not entirely conscious, had monitored the night noises of the city as they changed into the early-morning sounds of neighbors rising before dawn, readying themselves for work. He'd heard a child, crying. He'd heard part of a radio sermon from a passing car.

He hadn't heard anyone approach the house.

No arriving vehicle, no footsteps in the yard.

No soft sound, three feet from his head, as the cup was pressed into the grass so it wouldn't tip over.

Peter peeked out at the street.

No police car at the curb, either.

In a single movement, Peter scooped up Chester's 1911 and rolled out from under the dump truck.

On Wanda's front porch, Lewis sat on a wooden folding chair, feet in the air, balanced on the chair's rear legs without any evidence of effort. He held his 10-gauge sawed-off shotgun across his lap and a white cardboard cup in his hand. A box of shotgun shells stood on the porch floor beside a grease-stained paper bag.

He gave Peter a tilted grin and raised his cup in salute. His voice was deep and liquid and full of humor.

"Rise and shine, Jarhead. The motherfucking cavalry has arrived."

Lewis wore creased black jeans, polished black combat boots, and a crisp white button-down shirt with the cuffs rolled up exactly twice. The fine cotton of the shirt was bright against his dark skin. He'd been driving all night, but he looked like he'd just woken from eight hours' sleep.

He was the most dangerous man Peter had ever met.

Peter put the 1911 on safe. "You're not the cavalry." He stepped onto the porch. "You're a band of goddamn Comanchero raiders. Hell, you're fucking Geronimo."

The tilted grin got wider. "Now you're just sweet-talking. Why I take these little trips."

Peter held out his palm. Lewis gave him a slow low five, still maintaining his effortless balance on the chair's back legs, but ready for anything.

Like Peter, Lewis was always ready.

"You practice that chair trick at home?"

"It's my natural talent, motherfucker. Like you getting your ass in trouble."

"I'm going to get my coffee." Peter stepped down into

the grass, then spun without warning and pitched the pistol at Lewis in a fast, flat arc.

He caught it in the air one-handed. Without spilling his quadruple mocha, or letting the shotgun slide from his lap, or allowing the chair to waver in any way.

Peter shook his head. "You totally practice that at home."

His coffee was still hot.

As it turned out, the grease-stained bag held barbecue breakfast sliders and peach Danishes. Peter's coffee was thickened with an extra espresso shot.

"Geronimo wouldn't have brought Danishes," Peter said. "I withdraw the comparison."

While they ate and drank, he brought Lewis up to speed.

He talked about the brick through Wanda's window and the burning cross video, how Peter had come to Memphis to help. He talked about how things had escalated with the dump truck crashed into her living room, then the machine-gun attack. He told Lewis how much progress he'd made on Wanda's problem—exactly none.

Instead, Peter had been chasing a talented street kid all over Memphis trying to get his truck back and maybe somehow insert himself between the kid and the group that controlled most of the crime in the city.

Lewis gave a deep rumbling chuckle. "Let me guess. You want to help this boy."

Peter shrugged. "I kind of like him. His name's Eli. He's in real trouble. And you should hear him play."

When he told Lewis about King Robbie, Brody, and Charlene Scott, Lewis perked up. "I call dibs on the gangsters."

"The thing is, I've actually made things worse for Wanda," Peter said. "Because now King Robbie knows she's connected to me."

Lewis gestured at the huge Dumpster and the lumber pile protecting the house. "Well, you sure fortified the place. You got no line on the machine-gun guys?"

"I might have something, but I've been too busy scrambling to follow up. I need to make a phone call, maybe go see somebody."

Lewis wiped his fingertips with a paper napkin. "I'm up for whatever. You want me to come?"

"I'm trying to visit the West Tennessee State Penitentiary."

Lewis raised his eyebrows. He knew about the white static. "You up for that?"

"It'll be good practice," said Peter. "You should come. Maybe you'll be scared straight."

"I think I'll stay here," said Lewis. "Stand watch. Maybe take a nap."

"It might be a little loud for a nap. Wanda's got some people coming to stabilize the house. The towing company wants to pull the dump truck out without bringing the house down with it."

Lewis cast a critical eye at the house. Between the dump truck and the machine gun, the damage was considerable. "Why're you bothering? Looks like a tear-down to me."

"The engineer seems to think it has some historical value," said Peter. "Plus Wanda's pretty attached."

"It's just a house." Lewis stuck his thumb into one of the bullet holes in the brick. "A 240 Bravo is serious hardware. Where'd they get a gun like that? You think these guys are ex-military?"

Peter shook his head. "This whole thing is too goofy for that. They're making it up as they go. I don't think they even know what the hell they're after."

The tilted grin again. "Sounds like a jarhead I know."

"Fuck you," Peter said. "Can I borrow your ride for a few hours?"

"You gonna get it stolen? Or just hand it over to the first threatening preteen you meet?"

"Probably not. I'll get lunch, though."

Lewis handed over his keys. "Tan Yukon, parked on the next block. Don't get pulled over, though. Hardware in the back." He meant weapons.

"Good to know," said Peter. "One more thing. You got any money? And maybe a credit card?" Eli Bell had picked Peter clean.

Lewis looked at him. "Who the fuck am I, your dad?"

"I'll be home by midnight, I promise."

Lewis flipped open his wallet, thick with bills. "How many phones have you lost now?"

"I had a backup package this time. Five grand in cash, a spare credit card, and my passport."

"So where is it?"

"Secret hiding place." Peter smiled and plucked Lewis's wallet from his hand. "Under my truck."

"You can't use my driver's license," said Lewis. "Not until you get a better tan."

Peter pulled out five hundreds and handed them to Lewis, pocketing the rest. "In case I don't come back."

Lewis gave Peter a stern look right out of the Brady Bunch. He put on a white suburban voice. "If you're not home for supper, your mother and I will be very upset."

Before Peter could leave, they heard the rumble of a big engine with a perforated muffler coming up the street. Lewis stepped off the porch, the shotgun held down along his leg. The 1911 was tucked into the back of Peter's belt.

An antique one-ton Ford with dual rear wheels rolled into Wanda's driveway. The hood and side panels were all different colors, parts from multiple different vehicles. The cargo box had been replaced with a wide wooden dump bed with high steel toolboxes for sides, topped with a custom-welded ladder rack.

Dupree, Wanda's friend and the bass player from the night before, opened the driver's door and hopped down. "Put that gun up, sonny boy. I'm invited."

He wore crusty brown-duck Carhartts and a clean white T-shirt. He was twice Peter's age, his face deeply lined, but the T-shirt showed cannonballs for biceps and forearms like carved mahogany.

Romeo, the drummer, jumped down from the passenger side. He was short, shirtless, and thick with muscle. He wore a ratty straw hat at a rakish angle. Like Dupree, he was over sixty.

"This is your demo crew?" Lewis looked at Peter. "They don't get enough from Social Security?"

Romeo stared up at the house, already taking mental inventory of the damage. He didn't look at Lewis. "Work yo' ass into the ground any day of the week, pretty boy." He had a deep-South marble-mouth accent.

Lewis smiled. "I do believe you might."

Dupree shook Peter's hand. "We didn't get introduced last night, but I saw you with Wanda. You running this show?"

"Nice to meet you. I'm Peter, this is Lewis. And I'd rather you run the job, so we can chase the bad guys. Did Wanda tell you what's been going on?"

"Yep. But even if she didn't, you can see it plain as day." Dupree waved a hand at the house, the dump truck, the machine-gun damage.

"You know those people are still out there, right? You're okay with maybe getting shot at?"

"Wouldn't be the first time," said Dupree. "I like where you got the Dumpster dropped. That'll help some."

"Okay," said Peter. "The engineer's due with reinforcement plans this morning."

"Don't need 'em," said Romeo, now hauling scaffold sections from the back of the old Ford. "This ain' 'zackly rocket science. Just gotta get in there, see what's what."

"Wanda wants to save the house," Peter said. "I'd appreciate your opinion on that."

Dupree looked skeptical. "I always tell people, we can fix anything," he said. "Just depends how much you want to spend."

"Least the truck didn't knock her off the foundation." Romeo hauled coiled extension cords and a heavy-duty Bosch masonry drill kit. "That's somethin'."

Peter thought of Wanda the night before, barely able to walk into the hotel lobby under her own power.

She'd been knocked pretty hard, too.

He hoped June would be able to get her back on her feet.

Romeo set down his load and walked back to the truck, eyeballing Lewis. "You gonna help carry or what?"

Lewis snorted, but leaned the shotgun against the lumber pile and followed Romeo back to the Ford.

To Dupree, Peter said, "How do you know your guitar player?"

The older man's face split with a smile. "He's pretty goddamn slick, ain't he? He hears things I don't and I been playing for fifty years. That boy's an old soul. I met him because he's friendly with my granddaughter. I try to get him to work construction with Romeo and me, give the boy some trade skills, but he'll only show up for a day or two at a time. He learns quick, he'd be real good if he wanted. But I think he only does it when he's real hungry."

"Do you know where he stays?"

Dupree shook his head. "I don't know that he stays anywhere long. He's living wild, got a hard family history. He won't talk about it."

"You ever ask him to stay with you?"

"More than once, but he doesn't want anything to do with it. Like charity, you know? He's proud. Wants to make his own way."

"How do you get hold of him when you want to rehearse?"

Dupree laughed. "We don't rehearse, son, we just play. The kid's a natural. I don't think anybody taught him, he just kinda hears it, like he pulls it out of the air, you know? Like he was born with Louis Armstrong's ears. The first time we sat down was like we'd been playing together for years."

"But how do you reach him?"

Dupree looked at Peter for a moment, then turned away. "Enough about that guitar-playing fool. I got work to do."

"His name is Eli," said Peter. "You know he's in trouble, right?"

Dupree turned back quickly, very serious. "I talked to Wanda. I know he took your truck. But I'm not giving him to you, not for no repair job. Not even for Wanda Wyatt."

"That's not what this is about," said Peter. "Not the job, not the truck. Eli robbed that jewelry store at the mall. King Robbie wants him very badly. I'm trying to help before he winds up dead."

Dupree closed his eyes. The lines on his face deepened.

Peter said, "I'm sure Wanda talked to you about me, too."

"She did." Dupree opened his eyes again. At that moment he looked a thousand years old. "Why would you want to help young Eli Bell?"

"Selfish reasons," Peter said. "I get restless. I like to be useful. Plus he's got my truck."

"That ain't all. What else?"

Peter smiled. He wouldn't tell Dupree everything. But he'd tell him enough. "Eli's a pain in the ass, but I like him. And I've heard him play, remember? I'd like to hear him play again. I don't want that sound gone from this world."

Dupree looked out across the Dumpster at the wrecked house.

"That 1932 National he was playing last night, that's my guitar. He sure makes it sing, don't he?" He shook his head. "I tried to give it to him, but the boy won't take it. Says he's got no safe place to keep it." Dupree sighed. "I haul that guitar to every gig, just hoping he'll show up."

Softly, Peter said, "How do you reach him?"

Dupree looked back to Peter. "I text my granddaughter, Nadine."

"He can choose the place and time. I just want to talk."

"Nadine's gonna need to meet you."

Peter smiled. He was pretty sure he'd already met Nadine. "Why don't you invite her for lunch? I'll pick up some sandwiches. We'll sit on the porch and talk."

"Nadine might like that," Dupree said. "Or maybe not. With Nadine, there's no telling."

37

When Peter had first met Lewis, he'd been driving an old sheriff's department Yukon that had been retired and sold at auction. It had been badly damaged in Milwaukee, and Lewis had replaced it with another retired law enforcement SUV, but a newer model. This one had the same law enforcement performance package, with the big motor and the upgraded suspension and the heavy tubular front bumper. It didn't look like anything special, just a basic SUV with a few dents and dings.

You'd never know it was built to be a hunter-killer on the highway.

From the driver's seat, Peter called Detective Gantry.

"Can you get me in to see the guy who used to own Wanda Wyatt's house?"

"Vinny Charles, who drove his car into a bridge abutment? Are you on that again?" Gantry still sounded like Vegas-era Elvis.

"There was something weird about what you said, before. The guy was a drug mule, right? Who didn't know what he was carrying, where it was in the car, or who he was carrying for."

"Uh-huh."

"But he knew the job he was doing. He'd done it before."

"He didn't confess, if that's what you're asking. I went through his file. He told the investigating officers that a man he'd never met had asked if he wanted to drive the car from New Orleans to Chicago. The whole thing was done by text, including where to pick up the car and the keys. Cash payment in an envelope under the seat. That's all he knew. Turns out, the car was stolen in Houston, the license plates came from the New Orleans airport, and the texts came from a burner phone. Zero contact and total deniability, which is how King moves his product. Plus your friend Vinny had no visible means of support. The taxes on that house? He paid them in cash. So my guess is yes, he'd done it before."

"More than that," said Peter. "It sounds like he made a living at it. But with all that in mind, does he sound like the kind of guy who'd be driving ninety on the expressway, high as a kite, seeing visions of the devil with a death warrant?"

"You don't know what goes on with these guys," said Gantry. "They don't exactly operate using the rules of logic. Vinny was carrying a whole pharmacy in that car. Maybe he found the stash and took a taste, I don't know. Maybe the stash was uncut and Vinny got more than he bargained for. What's your point?"

"I want to talk to him. I want to know what happened."

"Wait. You think this is about the house?" Gantry asked. "Not Ms. Wyatt?"

"That place has the living shit beat out of it. If they wanted to kill her, there are a lot easier ways. Wanda didn't even lock her door. Whoever it is, I think they want her out of there."

Gantry sighed. "I'll have somebody dig up the name of Vinny's PD. You'll have to see if she can get you in."

Two hours later, Peter had bought some clean clothes and a cheap, anonymous phone with some of Lewis's cash. He'd sent a text to June with his new number and put Wanda's hotel room on Lewis's credit card.

After a quick stop at Donald's Donuts on Union Avenue, he was fighting the white static on the second floor of the Criminal Justice Center on Poplar Avenue.

Breathe, he told himself as he carried the box of a dozen frosted with sprinkles through a glass entryway past a sign that read, JUSTICE FOR A NEW GENERATION, LAW OFFICE, SHELBY COUNTY PUBLIC DEFENDER.

Martine Hopkins waved a hand at her guest chair and glanced at her watch. She was young, in a bright blue blouse, her jacket on a hanger on the back of the door. Discreet diamond studs in her ears, her hair in a short natural style that showed off her elegant neck.

"Thanks for your time," Peter said.

"Thanks for the donuts," she replied, "but you didn't have to come down here for this."

The office was small but as organized as an overworked public defender could make it. Her desk held just a computer and a photo of a handsome black man with a puppy in his arms. Her Emory University School of Law diploma hung on the wall. Manila folders were stacked neatly on tall file cabinets along the wall, beside a potted plant that was somehow thriving in the fluorescent light.

The plant was doing better than Peter. At least he wasn't sweating yet.

She said, "I understand that you don't have any official status, correct?" Peter nodded. "So I can't just walk you into a state prison without prior authorization. The Department of Correction has an application process that requires identification, fingerprints, and a background check. It takes thirty days, sometimes longer."

"I don't have thirty days." Eli Bell had taken Peter's wallet, so he didn't have ID, either. "Do you remember the case?"

"It would be hard to forget Mr. Charles," she said. "He's lucky he didn't die in that accident. As it is, he'll never walk again." She leaned back in her chair and steepled her fingers. "Detective Gantry told me what's happened to the woman who bought Mr. Charles's house. I'm truly sorry for her troubles, but what exactly are you hoping to learn from my client?"

"I'm not sure," said Peter. "Gantry said that your client drove off the road and into a bridge abutment. But he also said your client had a somewhat different version of the story?"

"Mr. Charles had an *entirely* different version." She glanced at her watch again, then at the computer, then back at Peter. Her eyes were deep brown, very large, and very serious. "Do you believe Mr. Charles is responsible for what's happened to your friend?"

"No. The police don't think so, either. But something about it keeps banging around in my head. I thought if I could talk to him, I might figure out what that is."

"The police didn't follow up on his statement," she said. "They found the drugs in his car and heard his crazy story and that was that. They couldn't imagine that he might be a victim, too."

"What kind of guy was he? Somebody you'd have coffee with?"

She gave Peter a sharp look. "I'm a defender. He was my client." Then her face softened. "He was a nice man. He didn't deserve what happened to him. Regardless, nobody else was looking out for him. Just me."

Peter found himself liking Public Defender Martine Hopkins. "Was he high during the accident? Anything in his system?"

"The blood test showed only marijuana," she said. "He admitted to being a habitual user. But so is half the city. And for a habitual user, smoking marijuana wouldn't account for his behavior, or what he says he saw."

"Would it be possible for me to see a copy of his statement?"

She pulled in a breath, then let it out. "I can do better than that," she said. "The detectives who interviewed him in the hospital made a video recording. It was part of his trial, so now it's in the public record. Would you like to see it?"

38

Martine Hopkins brought up a video window on her computer.

The screen showed a soft brown face half-covered in white bandages. One arm was in a bent fiberglass cast up to the shoulder, and both legs were in casts that disappeared under his gown. Steel rods extended from the casts to points on a metal immobilization cage, the modern version of traction.

His free wrist was cuffed to the bed rail.

"This is Vinson Charles, two days after the accident," she said. "He's on pain medication, but the doctor said he wouldn't be cognitively impaired, and he wanted to talk to the police quite badly. He was worried about the medical bills. I think he just wanted it to be over."

She ran the cursor over the time bar at the bottom of the window.

"This early part won't interest you," she said. "They read him his rights, they asked about the drugs in the car. He didn't know there were any drugs. He never met the guy who hired him, didn't have any information to trade. They had him on a Class B felony, possession with intent to distribute. Eight to thirty years, and up to a hundred thousand dollars in fines. I suggested he plead guilty and hope for a light sentence based on his injuries. He'll be an expensive inmate, which helps."

"You were there?"

"I was his defender, of course I was there." She kept scrolling forward until the figure on the screen lurched in the bed. She stopped the video and backed it up just a bit. "Here we go."

A soft drawling voice said, "Do you have anything else to add, Mr. Charles?"

"I do," said Vinny Charles in a wet rasp. "Y'all keep calling this an accident. I'm telling you, it wasn't no accident. It was the Devil himself run me off that road."

"How do you know it was the Devil?" The drawling voice didn't laugh, but Peter could hear the amusement in it.

"I saw him." Vinny Charles tried to lift himself up in his bed, the casts rising, the immobilization cage flexing. "He drove a shiny red pickup truck, and he came up behind me like he was flying. He sat on my tail and I tried to outrun him, but I couldn't. Can't nobody outrun they sins. He pulled up beside me and I saw him, clear as day. A grinning blue skull with pointed teeth."

"Was it some kind of mask?"

It was the same question Peter had asked himself about what he'd seen in the station wagon at Wanda's house. That blue shadow across a pale face. With pointed teeth.

"Y'all must not go to church," said Vinny. "I may have

lost my way, but I know the Devil when I see him. When he pointed to the road ahead, I looked and saw the bridge coming up. When I looked back, the Devil laughed and turned the wheel of his big red truck and pushed me off the highway. I was going way too fast to stop."

"I see," said the voice offscreen. "The Devil made you do it."

Vinny eased himself back down, his face a grimace of pain. "I'm laying here in this bed, all broken up and bound for prison, but I know what I saw. The Devil driving his road to hell. Only the Lord God knows why, but He saw fit to spare my life. From now on, I will be His servant on the righteous path."

Martine Hopkins paused the video and looked at Peter. She saw something in his face. "What?"

"I don't know." He nodded at the screen, Vinny Charles and his injuries frozen in time. "Do you believe him?"

She sighed. "I believe he saw *something*," she said. "But I don't need to believe in some blue-faced devil to know there's evil in the world. I see it in my work every week."

"Has Vinny Charles followed a righteous path in prison?"

That earned Peter a wry smile. "The prison medical system isn't the best," she said. "I'm told he'll be in a wheelchair for the rest of his life. Burn scars cover half his face. But he's become a lay preacher. He assists the chaplain, ministers to the sick in the infirmary. Maybe seeing the Devil was good for him."

"Maybe so," Peter said absently.

Thinking that the only thing Vinny Charles and

Wanda Wyatt had in common was the house they were living in.

Peter thought again about what he thought he'd seen in the back of that old station wagon.

What would a blue-faced devil want with that broken-down old house?

Back in Lewis's Yukon, Peter checked Wanda's phone, which he'd put on mute during his meeting with the public defender.

There was a text from Dupree, telling Peter that his granddaughter, Nadine, would come at noon, and she'd bring lunch for all of them. Peter liked her already.

The caller ID also showed that a Garry from the Bedrosian Gallery in New York had called. Peter listened to the message.

"Wanda, it's Garry. We are running out of time. I understand that your life is in turmoil right now, and I'm sorry to have to say this, but if I don't have the images ready for production in the next two days, I'll be forced to cancel your show."

Peter made a face.

He checked his new anonymous phone, which he'd left in the car, and saw a recent text from June. *Layover in Denver. Will call when I get in.*

He pressed the call button. When June answered, she was chewing.

"What's up?"

"Oh, not much," he said. "How was your flight?"

"Fine." She was still chewing. "I left Seattle at seven a.m. I get to Memphis at two thirty. I'll call you when I get to the hotel."

"I left a key at the desk," he said. "Um, is everything okay?"

"Oh, I'm fucking great." Her voice rose. "I talked to Wanda this morning, and got an earful about some Memphis gangsters you pissed off. You took a gun off some guy named Mad Chester?"

"Wanda might be exaggerating a little," he said. "And I was going to call you about that. I've been busy."

"Uh-huh."

He heard her take another bite of whatever she was eating. It sounded crunchy.

"June, I'm sorry. Things have gotten complicated."

More chewing, even louder now. "Uh-huh. It's always fucking complicated with you."

"This one's more complicated than usual." He put a smile in his voice. "On the upside, Lewis got here this morning."

"Oh, things always calm the fuck down when Lewis shows up." Chomp, chomp, chomp.

"So, I'm thinking maybe you're angry?"

"You," she said, "are a fucking genius." She swallowed, slurped something through a straw, then sighed. "I'll call after I get in, okay? It'll be better when I can kick your ass in person."

"I look forward to it," he said. "Listen, while you're all worked up? Wanda's gallery guy left a voice mail. They're going to cancel her show if she doesn't get her shit together. She's got two days. Any chance you could call them?"

He heard a different sound on the other end of the line. Maybe a growl.

"Those fuckers. Forward me that voice mail and any contact information you have."

"Yes, ma'am," he said, but she'd already cut the connection.

He sent the voice mail and contacts as quickly as he could.

He was eight years a Marine, boots on the ground in two ugly wars. Hand grenades for breakfast, mortar shells for lunch.

Sometimes he was a little afraid of June Cassidy.

39

Coming down the block toward Wanda's house, Peter saw that the lumber pile was half-gone, and the swing door on the Dumpster was open. He could hear the *pop pop* of a framer's nailgun coming from inside.

When he pulled the Yukon into the driveway, Lewis stepped out of the Dumpster, shotgun at his shoulder. He lowered it when he saw Peter.

Lewis was shirtless and shining with sweat, stacked slabs of muscle on his torso, veins standing out on his arms and shoulders. His skin was smeared with red brick dust and the ancient black patina of centuries-old wood, but he was smiling broadly. Behind him, the container was filling with broken bricks and shattered lumber. A wheelbarrow stood waiting.

"You've found your true calling," said Peter. "Demolition man."

"Been doing that for years," said Lewis. "Just not with houses."

"Are you ever going to tell me how you used to make a living?"

"Prob'ly not." Lewis twirled the shotgun like a majorette with a baton as he glanced up and down the block. "Learn anything useful?"

"I don't know," said Peter. He told Lewis about his faint glimpse of blue on the face in the old station wagon. "The guy who owned this house before Wanda, he swears up and down that the Devil ran him off the road. Not a guy in a mask, but the actual Devil, with a blue skull and pointed teeth."

"I thought the Devil was bright red, with horns and a forked tail."

"I'm told the Devil comes in many forms," said Peter.

"You think someone was trying to kill him?"

"I don't know," said Peter. "Easier just to shoot him, right? But maybe better if it looked like an accident. He ended up in jail and lost the house because he had drugs in the car. But if he was too hurt to work, or went broke because of his medical bills, he'd have lost the house that way, too."

"This is the South," said Lewis.

"I'm aware of that," said Peter. "Although I believe Memphis considers itself the Mid-South."

"There are white supremacist groups in the South."

"Not just the South, they're all over," said Peter. "Spreading like a disease."

Lewis gave him a look. "The really hard-core white-power assholes, sometimes they get facial tattoos. They don't want to blend in, they want to scare people. Some of them get radicalized in prison gangs, and that's where they get their tattoos. The equipment is pretty primitive, maybe just a sharpened paper clip dipped in ink, or a modified electric stapler. They don't have many colors to choose from, either. The ink usually comes from ballpoint pens. Black or blue."

Peter felt stupid. He was used to that, talking with Lewis, but it had been happening a lot more these last few days. "You think the blue is a facial tattoo. A jailhouse tattoo of a blue skull."

"If our guy's been in the criminal justice system, identifying marks will be in that database. That Memphis police detective should be able to narrow the search."

"If I tell the cops," said Peter, "that takes us out of the loop."

"All depends," said Lewis. "Sometimes law enforcement needs somebody to do what they can't do themselves."

Peter had noticed that Lewis's street accent often fell away when he was talking about something that interested him. Which was almost everything.

"Where do you learn this stuff?"

Lewis gave an elaborate shrug, and put the street back in his voice. "You know the most dangerous man in America."

Peter finished the reference to the Malcolm X quote, something he'd heard from Lewis many times. "A black man with a library card."

More than anyone Peter had ever met, Lewis was the product of his own creation. He'd grown up on the streets of Milwaukee and, as far as Peter knew, had never finished high school. But he was smart and curious, a voracious reader, and very good with money. He'd taken the financial windfall from their little Milwaukee adventure and grown it into a large and diversified fortune.

Lewis continued to insist that half of that fortune belonged to Peter. He'd gotten hold of Peter's Social Security number somehow, and signed Peter's name on a bunch of incorporation paperwork. He'd even issued Peter a no-limit credit card, paid automatically each month from a corporate account.

But Peter was uncomfortable with how they'd acquired that money in the first place. Aside from the occasional emergency purchase, he was still living off the remains of his savings from the Marines. It wasn't difficult. The things Peter spent money on were groceries, gas for his truck, and backpacking gear.

At the end of the block, a slim figure on a bicycle turned the corner and pedaled steadily toward them. The bike had a big wire basket on the front with a brown paper package sticking out of the top.

"I think that's lunch," Peter said. "Better go wash up. We're trying to make a good impression."

He stepped past the dump truck in its newly widened brick hole to see the shattered planks and timbers of the living room cut away and scaffolding built up around it. The dirt-floored foundation crawl space was open to the air, along with one side of that ancient tree stump that had held the center beam of the original structure.

The floor structure of the bedroom above, crumpled

like an accordion by the high leading edge of the dump bed, had also been removed. Dupree and Romeo were up on the scaffolding over the truck body, busy reinforcing the rafters to hold the walls together when the truck came out.

"Dupree," Peter called. "I think Nadine's here."

40

The girl rode an old blue Schwinn with wide handle-bars, rusty blue fenders, and a big paper grocery bag in the front basket. She stood on the pedals for the climb up the sloped gravel drive, and made it with ease. She swung one leg over the back wheel while the bike was still rolling, then stepped off and walked the bike to a stop.

Peter had seen her before.

She was the young waitress from the club, who had blocked Peter's way with a serving tray in the hall, buying time for Eli to run out the back.

This time, she wasn't wearing her thin black leather gloves. But he could see them poking out of her pocket.

In the club, she'd seemed very young and brave. Out in the daylight, she was different. With her light step and slender figure, she still looked like a schoolgirl, but she had a strange air of self-possession, as if some invisible part of her was deeply rooted in the world. A young woman who'd come into her own while nobody was pay-ing attention.

Her face was clean and pure in a way Peter couldn't quite define. Her hair was in a modest Afro pushed up toward the top of her head with a pink elastic band. Her threadbare blue men's dress shirt was too big for her, tucked into shorts made of men's khaki pants roughly hacked off at midthigh and cinched tight with a too-long leather belt. The extra length of the belt was looped over itself and tucked back through. The faded pink flip-flops on her feet were dressed up with bright pink toenail polish.

Dupree slipped around the dump truck and walked toward them. "Nadine," he called. "Thank you so much for getting lunch. This is Peter, the man I was telling you about."

She looked Peter carefully up and down. "We've met."

Peter put out his hand. "It's nice to see you again."

She looked at Peter's extended palm as if it might explode.

"Nadine doesn't shake hands," Dupree said. "What did you bring us, child? And how much do I owe you?"

"I went by Central Barbecue," she said. "Twenty dollars will do."

"For five sandwiches?"

"I can buy my own lunch."

"Still, it must have been more than that. And you delivered them, too." He pulled out his wallet and extended three twenties folded lengthwise. "For your trouble, child."

She dipped her head in thanks, took the money without touching her grandfather, and held out the paper bag by one corner of the folded top.

Romeo walked from the back door carrying two more chairs. He set them on the porch and gave Nadine a small, polite bow from several steps away. "Miz Nadine."

She gave him a radiant smile. "Mr. Romeo. Thank you." She put a pink flip-flop on the bottom porch step. She began to grasp the porch post in her hand, but jerked it away as if it were electrified.

Blinking, she cleared her throat. She put her foot carefully back on the ground.

"I believe I'll sit in the yard."

Romeo hurried for the chairs, but she waved him away and sat on the lumber pile with her foil-wrapped sandwich and a Dr Pepper. Dupree brought his chair down from the porch, and Romeo arranged the others in a semicircle by the lumber pile. Peter sat beside Romeo, across from Nadine.

Lewis came from the parked Yukon, glancing up and down the street. He wore a clean black T-shirt and carried the shotgun in one hand. He'd washed his face and arms and dusted off his black jeans, although they were still stained with red brick dust. He sat on the lumber pile where he could see the street, leaned the shotgun against his leg, and gave Nadine a gentle smile. "Thank you for lunch, Miss."

Staring at him, she dipped her head in hello, but didn't say a word.

They unwrapped their sandwiches—pulled pork on soft buns, rich and flavorful—and ate in a strange silence.

Finally, Dupree wiped his fingers on a paper napkin

and said, "Nadine, I hope you can do something for me. Your friend Eli is in trouble."

She opened her mouth to speak, but Dupree put up a hand to stop her.

"I know you're sweet on him. I think the world of that boy. But King Robbie and his people are after him. I want to help." He gestured at Peter and Lewis. "We all want to help. But first we got to find him. You're the only way I know to reach him."

She was so young, but already smart and composed enough to make her way anywhere she wanted to go.

She ignored Peter entirely.

She kept her eyes on Dupree, her face calm and focused. She knew what was at stake. Peter figured she'd seen more at fifteen than most people had at forty.

"He's safe enough for now," she said.

Her degree of self-possession was almost eerie.

"But for how long?" asked Dupree. "This is King's town, you know that as well as I do."

"He doesn't trust your friend," she said, somehow indicating Peter without a single gesture. "Says he's no different from the rest."

"You've known Miss Wanda since you were a baby," said Dupree. "Well, she's got some serious troubles, and this man Peter drove halfway across the country to help. Nobody's paying him a dime. Not for his time, not for gas, not for all this lumber you see here. Certainly not to get shot at. So he's all right by me. I don't know if that's good enough for you, but I hope it is."

Now she turned to look at Peter for a long slow moment without blinking. Her eyes were a vivid golden color, with a startling depth.

"Is that true?"

Peter found himself answering almost without volition. "Yes."

"Where does the money come from?"

Had she still not blinked? Her eyes were hypnotizing. He had to remind himself she was only fourteen or fifteen.

"My friend and I." He lifted a finger toward Lewis, still sitting on the lumber pile with the sawed-off leaning against his thigh. "We took it from some pretty bad people, a few years back. They're gone now. But money's no good if you don't use it for something bigger than yourself. When Wanda needed help, we came. As it turns out, your friend Eli needs help, too."

She raised her eyebrows in rebuke. "There are a lot of people need help around here."

"I'm sure there are," said Peter. "But I don't know them. I do know Wanda. Maybe I know Eli a little now, too. Eli's not just anybody. He's special. I'm sure you see that better than I do."

She regarded him with that eerie calm. "Give me your left hand."

He stood and walked to her and held out his hand.

She studied it without touching it. Then she took it,

palm up and open, in her right hand. With a single feathery left-handed fingertip, she traced the paths of the hard lines etched there.

A deep shiver ran through Peter's body.

As though someone had lifted his worn, crumpled soul from its shadowy hiding place and shook it out into the light, where it shone gossamer and translucent.

He felt utterly naked.

Hot and cold at the same time.

It was spooky as hell.

Nadine shuddered, then closed her eyes and abruptly curled Peter's fingers back into his palm and let him go.

When she opened her eyes again, they were different, he thought. Were they lighter or darker? Or was it in the way she looked at him? It was hard to tell.

She stood with fluid grace and turned to go without another word.

"Nadine?" Dupree called after her.

She didn't look back as she swung her leg over the seat of the old blue Schwinn. "I'll text you later."

Then she rode down the slope of the driveway to the street, once again just a pretty young girl in hand-me-down clothes and pink flip-flops.

Peter looked at his palm. His whole body hummed with a faint electric tremor. He looked at Dupree. "What just happened?"

"You felt it?" Dupree raised his eyebrows. "Nadine's got some of that old-time gypsy woman in her. The family come up from New Orleans after Katrina. Her grandmother had it, too."

"But what happened?"

Dupree gave him a kind smile. "I believe you passed the audition."

Lewis squeezed his empty sandwich wrapper into a ball and tossed it into the Dumpster. He stood with the shotgun in his hand and glanced up and down the street.

Then he looked at Dupree. "Does your gypsy granddaughter just do people, or she do things, too?"

Dupree didn't answer.

Romeo spoke softly. "She found my sister's four-y'-old grandbaby by holding his teddy bear. Lost in the woods by the river, a mile away. She walked right to him."

Lewis nodded. "Okay," he said. "So what do you suppose she felt when she touched that porch post? When she jerked away like it was a dog trying to bite?"

41

Dupree said, "I don't understand."

"Peter thinks Wanda's troubles might not really be about Wanda," said Lewis. "Might be more about this house she was staying in. Somebody wants something pretty damn bad. Be nice to know what the hell it is."

Dupree nodded, took out his phone and talked into the texting app. "I'm sorry to ask you for something more. Did you notice anything about the house?"

He pressed Send, but before he could put the phone back in his pocket, it chimed. He looked at the screen, then at Peter.

"What did she say?"

"She said there's something evil down in the dirt."

"What? Where?"

Dupree shook his head. "That's all she said."

Peter took in a breath, then let it out. "Huh," he said. "I wonder."

They followed him past the dump truck and into the house.

With the floor structure cut away around it, the big Kenworth looked smaller now in the area that had been Wanda's living room. The scaffolding around it went from the dirt floor of the foundation crawl space to the exposed rafters of the second floor above. The space still smelled of hydraulic fluid and coolant and exhaust, but it also smelled like sawdust and plaster dust and fertile bottomland soil left covered for a century and a half.

"I wish Wanda were here," said Peter. "She'd be taking pictures like crazy."

The Kenworth's front bumper had plowed the dirt right up to the huge, ancient stump at the edge of the living room. The stump had carried the center beam of the original house, and it looked as firmly rooted as the day the tree was cut down, despite the impact of twelve tons of dump truck.

Peter ducked under the remaining floor joists and scrambled around the stump to the far side. The clearance was still very low. He was on his forearms and toes. The static wasn't happy, either, although it didn't mind as much this time, because he was only a few feet from open space. Light trickled in from the work lamps set up in the living room.

When he'd gone into this crawl space on his first day in Memphis, the same day the truck had crashed into the house, he'd approached it from the root cellar under the rear addition as Wanda took pictures of his bootsoles vanishing into the dark.

The engineer had gone into the crawl space, too, for his structural evaluation.

They'd both noticed the odd, misshapen bricks around the base of the stump.

At the time, Peter had thought the bricks had been foundation leftovers, broken or badly made, laid down like cobblestones to make it easier to work in the spring mud of West Tennessee, or to block the exit to an animal's den under the stump.

But what if they'd been laid down to pave over something?

Something down in the dirt.

His fingers couldn't move the cobbles. They were firmly set in the packed earth.

"Would somebody toss me a hammer? Something with a straight claw." It would make a half-decent excavation tool in the tight space.

Dupree wriggled up behind him and laid the handle of a framing hammer into Peter's waiting palm.

The static rose, sparking up his brainstem, as he used the claw to lever up the first dirt-crusted bricks. He thought about the long tradition of frontier families hiding their modest savings under a loose hearthstone or floorboard.

Part of Peter expected to find a small pouch of silver coins, or silver tableware saved for a dowry, or just a few copper pennies wrapped in oilskin, money kept away from the tax collector or thieves or some wrongheaded relative. Planning for a better future.

Nobody would have gone to this much trouble to hide a few copper pennies.

Another part of Peter, a much bigger part, was expecting bones. Someone long dead and buried, the crime hidden away. Maybe multiple bodies. Flesh and blood long ago reduced to soil.

As he pulled up the loosened bricks, he pushed them back to Dupree, who pitched them out of the darkness and into the light. Soon he'd get to what lay beneath.

The bricks were small and uneven, roughly two inches by two inches by four, flat on top and slightly rounded on the bottom. No good for building a wall. They were heavier than he expected. He figured some kind of local clay with lead in it. There were maybe forty of them.

When the bricks were gone, he attacked the packed dirt with the claw hammer.

He went down six inches, then a foot.

There was nothing beneath the bricks.

No bones, no silver spoons or coins.

Just ordinary soil.

Then he stopped.

"Lewis," he called out. "Take one of those bricks and wash it under the hose. Use a scrub brush if you have to."

"Hang on," Romeo said. "My water bottle's right here."

"Let me see." Dupree squirmed backward out of the crawl space.

Peter lay on his belly in the dark for a moment as the static sparked up around him. Feeling the measureless weight of that ancient, damaged house pressing down from above. Then he turned himself around and scrambled toward the light.

Lewis knelt in the dirt, the tipped water bottle in one hand, a small, misshapen brick in the other.

With his calloused thumb, he rubbed mud from the surface, then dropped it abruptly in the dirt.

The brick wasn't made of clay.

Under the work lights, the exposed surface glowed a soft, buttery yellow.

Gold.

Forty bricks of it.

Evil, down in the dirt.

Dupree's eyes were round as saucers. Romeo looked a little queasy.

Lewis wasn't smiling. "I guess now we know what the bad guys are after."

42

They didn't wash any more bricks.

Better that they looked like ordinary rubble.

Lewis backed his Yukon behind the Dumpster to get it closer. When Peter began to drop the bricks into the wheelbarrow, Dupree picked up a long crowbar, his biceps swelling his shirtsleeve. "Where are you taking these?"

"Someplace away from here," said Peter. "Someplace secure." He looked at Lewis. "Safety deposit box?"

Lewis leaned his shotgun against the dump truck, then picked up a dirty brick and weighed it in his hand. "Ten pounds, more or less," he said. "Forty bricks would be four hundred pounds. I don't know the weight limit on a deposit box, even a big one. Forty pounds? So ten boxes, ten different banks? That'll take all damn day."

"This stuff is Wanda's," said Dupree, the crowbar easy in his hand. Behind him, Romeo had picked up a shovel. "We clear on that?"

"Absolutely." Peter raised his hands. "It's Wanda's. And I'm not married to the safety deposit box, either. If you've got a better idea, let's hear it."

"They ain't that big," Lewis said. "But they're heavy. Can't just go under your mattress."

"I got a safe in my shop," Dupree said. "For long guns. It's a good strong safe, and it's bolted to the floor."

Peter looked at Lewis. "What do you think?"

"Fine by me. The faster we get this shit out of here, the better." Then Lewis had the shotgun back in his hands. He stared hard at Dupree, then Romeo. "Long as we still clear. This is Wanda's."

Peter had felt the weight of that stare before. It was almost physical in its force, like a hot desert wind. Romeo nodded quickly, eyes wide, lowering his shovel.

Dupree still held the crowbar in one capable hand. He met Lewis's stare with his own. "Absolutely," he said. "I've known Wanda most of her life. But I don't know why you're in this. You ever even met her?"

"Don't need to," Lewis said. "Friend of Peter is a friend of mine."

Whatever passed between them, Peter couldn't see it. Dupree just nodded and turned to hang the crowbar on the scaffold again.

Lewis shouldered the shotgun and reached for his keys. "I'll move my ride. Let's get your old hooptie back here for a shorter carry."

"Hooptie?" Dupree followed Lewis out. "Boy, you got no idea what you're talking about. She may be old but she gets the job done."

"Just like your mama," said Lewis. "That's the word at the barbershop."

Dupree's voice drifted around the corner. "Boy, I ain't too old to whup your ass."

"Keep talking, old man."

Romeo looked at Peter. "Would he have pulled the trigger?"

Peter took out Wanda's phone. "You don't want to know."

Detective Gantry answered on the fourth ring.

"I want to ask a favor." Peter heard a clamor in the background, a crowded room full of people. "You in the middle of something?"

"Aside from the mayor's press conference, and the armed robbery at the jewelry store? No, I have nothing better to do."

But he'd answered Peter's call.

"You making any progress on the jewelry store?"

"No comment," said Gantry. "What's the favor?"

Peter said, "I couldn't get in to see Vinny Charles, but I did talk with his public defender. She showed me the footage from the hospital bed, where Vinny talked about seeing the Devil, remember? Running him off the road? He seemed pretty convinced."

"How could I forget?"

"Well, the Devil he described was a blue face with sharp teeth."

"Get to the point."

"When I went after that station wagon, before the

driver peeled out, I got a glimpse of the machine gunner's face. Not much, just a glimpse. There was something blue there, too. What if it's the same guy? And what if the blue is a tattoo?"

"You didn't tell me about the blue on the shooter's face." Gantry sounded annoyed.

"To be honest, it was fairly weird. I didn't know if I was seeing things or not. But maybe you could run a search. Isn't there a national database?"

"Yeah, the FBI runs the NCIC and the Triple-I, that's the National Crime Information Center and the Interstate Identification Index. The information mostly comes from self-reporting by a zillion different jurisdictions. It's not always accurate, but it's the best we've got."

"How long will that take?"

"I can't search by identifying marks, I need names or aliases. But the records returned will have physical characteristics, and I can narrow from there. Get me some names and I'll run them. Now it's my turn for a favor. We finally got results back on that station wagon you shot up. The plate you gave us didn't go anywhere, it was from a Toyota was supposedly totaled in an accident six months ago. But the car itself, you thought it was a yellow 1960s Ford Country Squire, right?"

"I'm sure of it," said Peter. "My grandfather had one just like it."

"Well, there aren't many left. Only a couple in Tennessee, and they're show cars with antique plates. Rebuilt or restored, and worth tens of thousands of dollars. Same goes for Missouri and Arkansas and Mississippi. All accounted for except for one located in rural Mississippi. Canary yellow. Its registration expired four years ago, and there's no record of a sale."

"It could be parts for collectors. Or just in the crusher."

"Well, it was last registered to one Archibald Carruthers, now incarcerated at the Mississippi State Penitentiary, also known as Parchman Farm."

"Like the Mose Allison song?" asked Peter.

"That's the one. Carruthers is sixty-eight years old. I looked him up. He's been at Parchman for fifteen years, and he'll be there the rest of his natural life. He's not your guy, but the man's record reads like he ain't no friend of mine. He set fire to a black church after nailing the doors shut. Ten people burned to death inside."

"Jesus." Someone had sent Wanda a video of a burning cross. "Sounds like there's something there. What's the favor?"

"I asked the locals to go ask Carruthers's wife about the car, but they can't be bothered. I could ask harder, but I'd have to get someone involved at the state level. That juice just ain't worth the squeeze." Gantry's voice was sour. "And my boss won't spare me from this jewelry robbery for half a day to run to another state."

"You want me to go."

"Oh, no," said Gantry. "I'd never ask that. It would be entirely inappropriate. For one thing, you're not a sworn peace officer. For another, Bird Hill, Mississippi, is way outside my jurisdiction."

"Of course," said Peter. "You better tell me where she lives, so I don't end up there by accident."

"See, that's the favor I wanted to ask," said Gantry. "I want you to write it down somewhere safe. If I lose my notebook, I wouldn't want to forget."

Peter didn't need to write it down.

He wasn't going to forget.

43

They tossed the small, dirt-crusted bricks from man to man and stacked them in the toolboxes on the sides of Dupree's truck.

The heavy bricks didn't look like much.

They didn't even take up much room, for all that they weighed.

Lewis and Peter followed Dupree back to his workshop on the other side of Chelsea, less than a mile away. It was an unpainted cinder-block building that might have been a service station long ago. Now it had a new roof and a heavy-duty roll-up door in front and tall green pecan trees all around.

The door went up and Dupree drove inside. Lewis parked the Yukon out front and they walked past the wide array of woodworking and metalworking tools to look at the safe in the back corner.

It was big and black and almost certainly older than Dupree, a combination model that looked like it belonged in Al Capone's office. It came up to Peter's shoulder, with walls thick enough to be lined with cement.

"Came with the building thirty years ago," said Dupree. "Works like new. Guy told me it was fireproof, so I use it to store flammables, varnish and paint thinner and such. Plus my deer rifle."

"How many people know the combination?" Peter asked.

"Just me," Dupree said. "But I never lock it."

"You're locking it today," Lewis said.

Dupree shook his head. "I'm starting to wish we'd taken all this to a bank."

Peter put a hand on his shoulder. "It won't be here long. Once we deal with these assholes, we'll find a better home for it."

They passed the bricks from hand to hand and stacked them neatly in the bottom of the safe. When the door was closed and the long lever thrown and the combination dial spun, Peter said, "Maybe you guys shouldn't go back to work. Take the rest of the day off. Go fishing or something."

Then he looked at a five-gallon bucket loaded with cylindrical cast-iron sash weights, used to counterbalance windows in old houses. "Actually, I have a better idea."

He explained.

Dupree nodded. "We can do that. What are you going to do?"

"We're heading to Mississippi to see a woman about a car."

Peter's phone map app had the address about a hundred and ten miles from Dupree's shop. They took I-55 south past Graceland and the Memphis airport, past Southaven and Hernando and Coldwater toward the Batesville turnoff for Oxford, home of the University of Mississippi. Bird Hill was some distance past that.

Lewis was going ninety, the Yukon solid as he moved from lane to lane, smoothly passing other cars, tires humming on the road. The radar detector on the windshield didn't seem to care one way or the other.

Outside, past the drainage ditches, there were few buildings. The landscape was lush and flat, trees and fields in a hundred shades of green. Peter could feel the afternoon heat through the window glass, and he was grateful for the air-conditioning. In the distance, a high wall of black clouds dropped curtains of rain that never touched the ground.

"I know you've done the math," said Peter.

"What math?" Lewis gave Peter his tilted smile.

"You know what math."

"Forty-two gold bricks at ten pounds apiece multiplied by today's spot price in troy ounces? That math?"

"Did you even have to look up the price of gold? Or the conversion from pounds to troy ounces?"

"Well, the spot price comes up on my phone every

morning. And there are approximately 14.58 troy ounces per pound. So, round number? About eight million bucks."

Peter whistled. "I guess Wanda can afford to rebuild. Or move anywhere she wants."

Lewis looked at Peter for a long moment. The Yukon didn't waver from its lane. Then he said, "You feel anything when you touched those bricks?"

"Like when Nadine touched my hand? No. You?"

"I don't know. Maybe. Hard to say."

"What was it like?"

Lewis shook his head. Either he didn't know or he wasn't saying.

Peter said, "Where would that gold have come from?"

"Depends when it got put there," said Lewis. "Did you take a look at those little bricks? They're lumpy and uneven, each one a little different. Definitely not uniform weight. They weren't made in any kind of modern smelting plant. They were probably made in a hurry, using basic sand molds. A long time ago."

Peter didn't ask how Lewis knew about the various methods for making gold bars. Lewis read the way everyone else breathed, and he remembered everything.

"The engineer who looked at the house," said Peter. "He thought it was built around the time of the Civil War."

"That war ruined the Southern economy," Lewis said. "In some places for decades. Parts of it, like rural Mississippi, have never really recovered. I'm guessing those bricks probably don't date from after the war. But before the war? This area was wealthy, with only two ways to make that money. King cotton and the slave trade."

"And cotton was farmed with slaves," Peter said. "Almost entirely. So it was slavery all the way down."

Lewis nodded. A few miles passed.

"You know I ain't one of those touchy-feely guys," he finally said.

Peter kept silent.

"But I sure as hell felt something when I got the dirt off that chunk of gold."

The Mississippi countryside flew by. Green and hot and seemingly endless.

"Something cold and heavy and tight around my neck." Lewis looked sideways at Peter again. "Kinda freaky, right?"

Peter thought about Nadine, how she'd traced the lines on his palm, and a shiver passed through him.

"No," he said. "Not at all."

Then pointed at the sign for the exit. "This is our turn."

Down 278 through Oxford and beyond. The fields got smaller and the trees got larger. They turned onto a two-lane state highway, then another. Lewis had the Yukon down to seventy.

The 10-gauge lay in the rear footwell, out of sight but within easy reach. Mad Chester's 1911 sat in the passenger-side door pocket, easy to grab.

When they stopped for gas, Peter had bought a

DeLorme atlas for Mississippi, and he held it open on his lap now. The large-format maps showed everything from major cities and interstate highways to gravel roads and trailheads and boat ramps. In the back of Peter's truck was a box with similar atlases for nineteen states. He wondered if he'd see them again.

The countryside became more rugged, with still more trees and fewer signs of people. The highway twisted through low hills. Lewis slowed to sixty, then fifty.

Past Tula they were on county roads, the blacktop sunken and cracked in places, or humped with roots. Oaks and elms and maples growing tall and crooked alongside. The only sign of modernity was a single thick power line on plain wooden poles gone dry and cracked from the heat. Narrow gravel trails diverged, seemingly at random, into the dense, impenetrable woods.

On the map, Peter followed the curves of the road with his finger. "Coming up on the right," he said.

Lewis turned onto a thin unnamed gravel road, barely wide enough for the car. Weeds between the wheel ruts thumped on the Yukon's underbody. The road curved around rising hills covered by ancient unidentifiable trees strangled by kudzu vines grown wild.

"We're looking for a driveway on the left," Peter said. "Five or six miles up."

"You got an address?"

"More like directions. There's probably not even a mailbox. Gantry said look for the cars."

"And listen for banjos." Lewis shook his head. "Good thing we're heavily armed."

. . .

They crested a low rise, and on the far side they saw an ancient round-fendered car cracked open like an egg by some prior cataclysm. The ragged-edged metal had turned to flaking rust, and a forty-foot box elder grew through the hole where the windshield had been.

Past the car was a faint dirt track. On the far side of the track was a seventies-era luxury sedan that stood vertically on its front bumper, its undercarriage leaning only slightly against an enormous elm, like a toy left behind by a giant child. Someone had cut the kudzu back so the scene remained relatively untouched.

"Oh, look," said Lewis. "Cars."

"Maybe we should stop here," Peter said. "Check out your inventory."

"I didn't bring a bazooka," Lewis said. "Mighta been a mistake."

They got out of the Yukon and walked around to the back.

The heat was thick and stifling. Peter felt himself begin to sweat almost instantly.

Lewis popped the rear cargo hatch, where a pair of leather duffels sat on a striped wool blanket. "Nothing to see here." Then he slung the duffels over the seatback and threw the blanket after them, revealing the top of a low, carpeted compartment contoured to fit the space.

The carpet matched the nap and color of the rest of the interior, and the contour was seamless. The compartment was less than five inches tall. Even without the striped blanket, most people would have to look at the carpet three or four times to realize it wasn't the actual floor of the cargo area.

"Aren't you Mister Fancy Pants," Peter said.

"Dinah wanted some bookshelves made for the living room," Lewis said. "Cabinetmaker was pretty good. I asked him for a little something extra. Did a nice job, too."

He lifted the compartment lid.

Inside, laid out on old white bath towels turning gray with gun oil, were a matched pair of Heckler & Koch assault rifles with scopes and lights and retractable stocks, a very nice scoped Winchester deer rifle, a pair of 12-gauge combat shotguns with five-round tubes, a half-dozen pistols with holsters, and assorted spare magazines and boxes of ammunition.

"Dude, this is so lame," Peter said. "Is that all you've got?"

"Oh, no." Lewis smiled cheerfully. "I bought an old industrial building not far from Dinah's house. I keep the rest there."

Peter pointed at an unvarnished hickory ax handle that lay beside the shotguns. "What's this for?"

"I figgered it was traditional down South," said Lewis, sounding now like purebred grits and gravy. He picked up the ax handle and took an experimental swing. "Fer whuppin' ass. I'm jes' trying to fit in. Ain't you never seen *Walking Tall?*"

Peter looked at Lewis in his black silk T-shirt, black jeans, and combat boots, the ax handle in his hand. "Of course," he said. "How could I have missed the similarity? Sheriff Buford Pusser, in the flesh."

They heard hounds baying. Lewis looked down the dirt track, which vanished in the trees. "The guy's a convict and a white supremacist. What do you suppose his wife's like?"

"We'll find out," said Peter. "I'm more concerned about who else might be there."

44

Peter kept the ax handle and took a Beretta M9 with a low holster he threaded onto his belt and strapped to his thigh. He stuck two extra magazines into his back pocket and climbed behind the wheel of the Yukon.

Lewis sat in the passenger seat with a gigantic chrome-plated automatic in a shoulder holster and the Winchester butt-down in the foot well.

The faint dirt track wound through a green tunnel of trees for almost a half mile, branches scraping the car as they passed.

At the top of a rise, they saw the trees open up ahead of them and the low roof of a house came into view. When Peter slowed, Lewis opened his door, stepped out, and vanished into the woods.

Peter drove forward into the clearing.

The house was old and sagging, with a deep front porch to keep the heat out. It sat beside a modest pole barn in the middle of a vast sea of automobiles. Hundreds of them, with weeds grown up thick and tall in the narrow aisles between them. From newer models to vehicles from the middle of the last century, including a number of heavy trucks and what looked like an old Blue Bird school bus with a stovepipe coming out of the roof.

Some looked like you could hop in and drive away. Others were up on blocks or had their hoods open, parts removed or laid out for repair. A few were upside-down. Many were visible only as long lumpy mounds of kudzu vines.

As Peter continued toward the house, a group of leggy, long-eared, flop-jowled hounds bounded out of the pole barn, howling as they churned around the Yukon. The biggest one stood its ground on the dirt track.

Peter rolled closer, slowing, but the big dog didn't move. Either brave or very territorial or just not that bright. Peter slowed further still, inching closer, until the dog stared the Yukon right in the grille, baying like it had cornered the world's biggest raccoon.

Peter shook his head, then lifted his foot off the brake for a count of three. The Yukon gave the big hound a bump. It responded by trying to bite the steel tubular bumper.

Definitely not that bright.

Peter sighed. He liked dogs, but he wasn't going to be dog food.

He opened his door and the main pack darted away so the big dumb hound could come around to meet him, teeth bared. Peter bopped it lightly on the nose with the butt of the ax handle. The hound jumped back, long ears flopping, but came directly for Peter again. He gave it another bop, slightly harder, followed by a tap on the hindquarters, and the hound yelped and shook its head and sat down. After that, the other dogs backed off, circled the Yukon, sniffing, then lay on the dirt in the shade, tongues out and panting.

The heat of the afternoon sun was thick and oppressive. The door to the pole barn stood open, showing pale fluorescent light and the back end of a big sedan. Peter could hear the sound of a hammer pounding on sheet metal, but saw nobody inside. He told himself he'd worry when the pounding stopped.

A woman came out of the house and stood on the broad front porch. She was built like a weathered old fence post, with irregular iron-gray hair she might have cut herself with garden shears. She wore a faded print dress and a flowery red apron that hung around her neck and tied at the waist.

Poking out of the apron pocket was a thick-bodied revolver with a long barrel. Something powerful and expensive. Her right hand on the grip.

No wonder the mechanic kept working in the pole barn.

Peter leaned the ax handle against the Yukon and walked closer.

"Stand right there. Y'all's on private property." She had a face like an albino crow, sharp-nosed with bright darting eyes. "Y'all's armed and I ain't seen no badge, so I'm in my rights to shoot you dead where you stand."

The hammer stopped beating, but nobody emerged from the pole barn. Peter reminded himself that Lewis was somewhere behind him with the scoped Winchester.

Then came the metallic whine of a grinder on steel. Peter put on his most winning smile.

"Are you Mrs. Carruthers?"

She shifted impatiently. "You going to show me a badge or not?"

"I'm not with the police, ma'am. I'm not here to harm you in any way. I'm here about a car you own, or maybe used to own."

She took the pistol from her apron pocket and gestured at the vast collection of vehicles arrayed around her. "Y'all can see we got a few," she said. "They ain't all ours, neither. So I can already say I don't got the faintest idea what y'all's talking about."

"The one I'm interested in," Peter said, "is a late 1960s canary-yellow Country Squire station wagon, long and low."

She looked at him with her bright crow's eyes. "That one's gone."

"Who's got it now?"

She shook her head slowly from side to side, just slightly. As if examining him first with one eye, then the other, down the long beak of her nose. "It's my husband's. I don't meddle in his affairs."

"I know who's got it," Peter said. "A man with a blue skull tattooed on his face."

She didn't quite react, but even from twenty feet away, he could see the tension humming through her body. "I'm done talkin'." She flapped her free hand at him. "Y'all best get gone, and I mean right now."

"What's his name? Did he know your husband at Parchman?"

She raised the big revolver and thumbed back the hammer and held it out at arm's length with both hands. "I'm a real good shot," she said. "I got a practice range behind the house. Y'all want to see how good I am? Get buried in the hill out back?"

Peter held his hands out and shook his head, hoping Lewis got the message not to shoot.

"No, ma'am. I'll take your word for it. I'll just be on my way."

He felt a tingle between his shoulder blades all the way back to the Yukon.

Lewis was waiting beside the dirt track outside the clearing, the Winchester at port arms. Peter was already on Wanda's phone to Gantry. Cell reception was spotty, but Peter made himself understood.

"Call the warden or whoever at Parchman Farm. I'm pretty sure our guy was an inmate there. He has a blue skull tattooed on his face, and he knows Carruthers. Someone in that prison sure as hell knows who he is."

45

When they got off the dirt track at the gravel road, Peter pulled over so they could return the artillery to the Yukon's secret compartment. Lewis got behind the wheel for the ninety-minute drive back to Memphis.

As the road wound back through the low wooded hills, Peter told Lewis about his conversation with Mrs. Carruthers.

"I don't care who her husband is, or how much of an asshole he might be. I can't imagine that woman being intimidated by anybody. Whoever was in that pole barn had been so confident she could handle any visitor, they didn't even bother to stop work to check on her. She didn't care about me at all, not until I brought up the guy with the blue skull tattoo. Whoever he is, that mean, tough woman with a pistol in her apron is scared to death of him."

"Maybe he's why she's got the pistol in her apron."

Peter nodded. "Fair point."

Wanda's phone buzzed in Peter's pocket. It was Dupree. "I got a text from Nadine," he said. "She'll meet us with Eli tonight after dark. She'll send the address right before."

"Sounds good. Anything else?"

"She told me she's going to see Wanda. Wants to help."

"How does Nadine know where Wanda's staying?" Peter hadn't told anyone.

"You've met the girl," Dupree said. "Some things she just knows."

"She better not tell anyone. This thing is getting ugly."

"She knows that, too. She wouldn't tell me a damn thing and I'm her grandfather."

"Okay. I'll call when we get closer. You making progress over there?"

"Paint's only so thick," Dupree said. "It's not gonna fool anybody for long."

"It won't have to, I hope. Do as many coats as you can."

After he hung up, Lewis said, "You have any clue what you're doing?"

"I thought you were supposed to be the brains of the outfit."

"I'm serious, motherfucker."

"I'm working on a few ideas."

"Is that supposed to be reassuring?"

The burner phone buzzed in his lap.

"You got a lot going on," Lewis said.

"Tell me about it."

It was a text from June. *I'm at the hotel. Call when you can.*

He had two bars. He hit the call button. She answered

by saying, "This hotel is fucking awesome. How long until you get here?"

"Well, I'm in Mississippi with Lewis right now, but we're on our way back to Memphis. How's Wanda?"

"She's asleep. You know how many prescriptions she has?"

"A lot, and from a couple of different doctors, too. I don't even know if I found them all."

"I've been online looking up her meds. I found a couple of pretty gnarly drug interactions, and instructions on three of these bottles say to avoid alcohol entirely."

"She's definitely not doing that. She's caught in a pretty bad spiral. It's why I wanted you to come. But don't leave the hotel, okay?"

"I'm not leaving Wanda, period. I talked to that gallery owner. He's not fucking around. Wanda's blown off three deadlines already. I did some research on his gallery, it's a very big deal. Wanda really shouldn't screw this up."

"Can't the gallery owner just pick the photos for the show?"

"He wants between twenty and twenty-five images to print in large format, but he's only seen a dozen, and he wants at least fifty to choose from. He also wants Wanda to be part of the decision. I think he's actually a pretty decent guy. They made this deal over drinks, basically on a handshake, before her last overseas trip to Syria. He told me she's a different person since she came back."

Peter knew how that felt. "Did she talk to you about that trip?"

"We've barely talked since our last project together.

She's been passed out since I got here. I practically had to stick a mirror under her nose to make sure she was breathing."

"I could tell when I showed up that something was wrong, but I thought it was just the dump truck in her living room. I didn't realize how bad it was until the next day. I tried to get her to talk about it, but she wouldn't. Plus she was always wired to the gills."

"We'll figure it out," June said. "The concierge put me in touch with a doctor who'll come to the hotel." She sighed. "I feel like it's my fault. We used to talk every few weeks, but she started returning my calls with texts. I should have known. I should have come sooner."

Peter knew how that felt, too.

"Listen, you're probably going to get a visitor, a young woman named Nadine. I, ah . . . I don't really know how to describe her."

June must have heard it in his voice, some echo of that feeling when Nadine had touched his hand. "Peter?"

"She's just a schoolgirl. Fourteen or fifteen years old. But there's something about her. You'll see what I mean."

Wanda's phone buzzed on the center console. It was Gantry again.

"Hey, I gotta go," Peter told June. "Talk to you later."

"No, I'll *see* you later," she said. "Don't make me come after you. And you better be wearing that goddamn vest I bought you." She hung up.

Lewis laughed. The last part had been loud enough for Lewis to hear, even though she wasn't on speaker. "Woman's got your number, Jarhead."

"Don't even start." Peter picked up Gantry's call, this time on speaker. "What's up?"

"Where are you now?"

"Almost back to Oxford. You find him?"

"My boss called an old friend in Jackson, who talked to Parchman's superintendent. You were right on the money with the tattoo. Our guy's name is Judah Lee Burkitts. His parole officer says he's staying with his older brother, name of Albert Burkitts, at the family farm near a tiny place called New Canaan, Mississippi. Albert's on some kind of disability. Highway 7 north from Oxford, the farm's off Highway 72. I'll text you directions and a photo. Mississippi DMV shows Albert owning a 1986 red Ford Fiesta and a 1954 Mack Model B, some kind of big farm truck."

Gantry still sounded like Elvis, but now in a movie as a tough cop. Peter didn't think Gantry was going to break into song anytime soon. He figured Gantry was a pretty capable detective.

"By the way," Gantry added, "tell Ms. Wyatt she did good with those pictures. The Fiesta showed up on that flash drive you gave me. Maybe Judah Lee borrowed his brother's car. He's got no current vehicle in his name."

"She'll be glad to hear that," Peter said. "What did your boss tell his friend in Jackson to get such quick results?"

A short laugh. "As little as possible. His friend has a lot of pull, but there might be some leakage, if you know what I mean. Law enforcement in Mississippi has a long history of not always being on the right side of things. You better haul ass if you want to get there first."

"Tell me about Burkitts."

"He's the number-two guy in the biggest white-power faction at Parchman. Six foot seven. The skull tattoo is full-face. He's filed his teeth to fucking points. He obviously couldn't care less what anybody in the straight world thinks of him. The superintendent was fairly certain Burkitts had killed seven men during his time at Parchman, all of them black, one of them a guard. All of them with a knife. But nothing caught on video, and nobody would testify."

"So he's big and scary and probably a little crazy. But not stupid."

"Right on the money. So drive fast and watch your ass."

"How in hell did Burkitts manage to get probation?"

"His father died. Either some idiot felt sorry for him or somebody else got paid off." Gantry paused a moment. "You got anybody with you on this?"

"You don't want to know." Peter looked at Lewis. "You have any questions for Detective Gantry?"

"Just one," Lewis said. "Anybody gonna get officially upset if this guy ends up dead?"

"I'm sorry," Gantry said. "You're breaking up. I didn't hear the question." They were in the outskirts of Oxford by then, and the reception was perfect. "Call me back when you get to the farm."

Lewis put the pedal down.

The big engine roared and the Yukon leaped forward.

46

They drove north through long stretches of good two-lane highway with nothing but trees crowding close alongside. Every few miles they passed a prosperous farm or a small house or a ragged trailer. The hot Southern sun cooked through the window glass.

Gantry's text came through with directions to the Burkitts farm and an institutional photo of a square-headed man with cropped pale hair like a field's winter stubble. A ballpoint-blue skull tattoo accented his brow, his jawline, his cheekbones, and around his eyes, turning them into deep hollow caves. The jailhouse artist was pretty good, Peter thought. Tombstone-shaped teeth were tattooed directly on his upper and lower lips, which were clean-shaven and drawn closed.

There was another picture where Burkitts opened his lips, showing rough, pointed teeth turning black at their roots. His face devoid of expression.

The result was unnerving.

Peter wasn't sure he truly believed in evil, but that picture put a heavy thumb on the scale.

Traffic was thin and Lewis slid through it like a blade, driving so fast that cars he passed seemed to be standing still. Past I-22, through Holly Springs, angling northeast until they hit US-72, a four-lane, then due east for a few more miles to a turnoff on the right.

They passed a big church standing in the center of an empty cracked asphalt parking lot, long narrow driveways that disappeared into the trees, and cultivated fields growing low green crops Peter couldn't name.

After a mile, the asphalt stopped with a bump and the road turned to gravel. Lewis checked his mirror and pulled over. "Time to suit up." He popped the rear hatch.

From one of his leather duffels, he removed a pair of thick tactical vests and tossed one to Peter.

It was a desert-camo plate carrier, just like he'd worn in Iraq. The weight of it was comforting.

"You couldn't have given me this when I went to talk to Mrs. Carruthers?"

"I didn't think she'd have Dirty Harry's Magnum in her apron," Lewis said. "Anyway, wearing that vest, she wouldn't have said a thing to you. What we're up against now, this is different."

"Plus June will beat your ass if I get shot."

"Like a redheaded stepchild. I do not want that woman mad at me."

They put sidearm holsters on their belts, then pulled the vests over their T-shirts and checked each other. Peter snapped mag pouches in the same old places and loaded two extras for both the Beretta and the HK. He adjusted the sling on the assault rifle. His T-shirt was already soaked through in the dense afternoon sun.

It was all so fucking familiar. He found himself smiling.

"You think a hundred thirty-five rounds is enough?"

"If it ain't, we're screwed, blued, and tattooed. Although I admit I wouldn't mind a grenade launcher."

"You know this is a bad idea, right? Just the two of us?"

"Yep," Lewis said. "You want to wait for the county mounties?"

"Hell, no. I want to get this done."

Lewis closed the hatch and they took their places in the Yukon.

Slower now, they looked at the addresses on the mailboxes posted like sentries at the ends of weedy dirt driveways. Windows down, the heat so thick it was almost liquid. The fields were calm and utterly still, the only wind that of their passing. A dust plume followed behind and settled slowly like a fungus on the green growing leaves.

They found the address on a dented red mailbox beside a modest new building on the road. Metal roof and siding, a small loading dock, a massive air conditioner, and a small sign, red letters on a white background. FERAL HOG ERADICATION AND MEAT PROCESSING.

There were no cars in the gravel lot. Lewis looked at Peter, who shook his head. Lewis turned up the driveway that threaded past the building. They drove up a low hill and into the trees.

Lewis stopped at the crest in the deep lingering shadow of towering oaks and elms and walnuts. Fifty meters on, a clapboard farmhouse stood tall and narrow across a broad weed-and-gravel patch from a fieldstone barn with its big door partway open. Past the farmyard the trees opened up, showing small, neatly tended fields just beyond.

Lewis turned off the Yukon. The sound of the natural world returned. Insects, bird calls.

They heard no radio, or engine, or machine noise of any kind.

Peter looked through binoculars he'd taken from the glove compartment. The house windows were open, but there was no visible movement. Beside the house was a red Ford Fiesta with rusted-out door panels. An old round-fendered stake-side flatbed truck sat parked by the barn, probably the Mack that Gantry had mentioned. A steel hand-crank crane was bolted to the back bumper, and the rear planks were dark and layered with the unmistakable stains of old blood.

"Both the vehicles we know about are here," Peter said.

Lewis held out his hand for the binoculars. "We should have gotten out at the road."

"If we had a platoon," said Peter. "Or even a squad." He looked at his friend. "Last chance before we do something stupid."

Lewis put the binoculars on the dash and opened his door. "You want to start with the house or the barn?"

Peter walked down the drive and into the open, rifle at low ready, head on a swivel, the taste of copper in his mouth. Sweat trickled through his hair, but he wouldn't have minded a helmet. This was no way to die. Any asshole with a decent .22 varmint gun could put a round through his head from thirty meters. Now twenty. Ten.

He could feel Lewis to his right, just outside his peripheral vision. Both moving steadily forward.

They went up the outer edges of the porch steps to minimize the creaks. The front door stood wide open. The static climbed up his brainstem like a friendly parasite.

Inside, the heat was like a sauna.

Three rooms on the main floor, three bedrooms upstairs.

A few clean dishes stacked on the kitchen counter. Furniture with flowered cushions from a bygone era. Narrow beds with wrinkled sheets, clothes folded neatly on a dresser. Flies circled frantically in the golden rays of sun through the windows.

Nobody home.

They sprinted across the yard to the barn.

A vintage tractor stood in the main bay, with an antique plow rig and hay baler lined up behind it. Not painted up for show, but good old working machinery. To the side was a workroom with tools left out on a bench and a welder standing by a half-open man door, power cord still plugged in to the wall. Tire ruts deep in the mud outside. Baled hay stacked in the loft. Otherwise empty.

Peter looked out the open loft door toward the fields. A faint track ran down the far side of the hill, past an odd round wire fence enclosure to a modest stand of enormous trees. Through their leaves he could see the angled line of a roof gable.

He climbed down, caught Lewis's eye, and ran down the track, his boots soft in the weeds, his gear creaking with every step. Lewis circled behind.

It was an ancient barn, mossy roof sunken in, the structure leaning like a drunken uncle. The big door was rolled aside revealing the canary-yellow Country Squire parked in the main bay. It reeked of burnt plastic and cheap beer.

Eyes scanning, Peter side-stepped around the car, but nothing was moving. He glanced down into the car, looking for the steel-plate firing box built into the back seat to protect the gunner, but it was gone. He saw only shattered glass and melted vinyl seats and the holes punched into the side panels by the pistol he'd taken from Charlene.

Where was the steel plate?

He stopped thinking about it when he looked past the car and saw a makeshift table cluttered with tools, metal plumbing parts, snips of thin blue rope, a plastic funnel. A scattering of dark granules. Not what he wanted to see.

Even worse, past the table stood a pair of scraped-up rectangular composite cases. Peter had seen Hardigg cases just like them many times before, in loading bays and armorer's shops at Marine Corps bases across the world. Cases the military used to ship and store automatic weapons.

They were unlocked but heavy. He flipped the latches and lifted the lid.

M16 carbines, dusty and old, probably slated for disposal like Gantry had said. With the plastic insert, the crate capacity was twelve to a box, but he saw only ten weapons. He tipped back another lid. Beat-up M4s. Again, only ten in a crate meant for twelve.

Thankfully, he didn't see another big machine gun like the 240, nor did he see any ammo boxes. But you could buy rounds and magazines to fit those carbines at any gun store across the country.

He was searching through the rusty old junk accumulated in the rest of the barn, finding nothing worth worrying about, when Lewis stuck his head through the doorway.

"You better come see this."

Peter smelled it before he saw it. The acrid spent-powder smell of an afternoon at the gun range, but different. With the lack of wind and rain, the odor lingered in the dust and unmown grass.

He passed a heavy homemade picnic table turned on its side like a barricade. The top was scarred and chipped, with black metal shards stuck deep into the thick wood.

"Over here." Beyond the table, at the edge of the clump of enormous trees, Lewis stood beside a giant tree stump. It was four feet across, or it had been once. Now it had overlapping circular chunks taken out of it, like giant bites from an angry rodent, and it was scorched dark along with the ground around it. More black metal shards were embedded in the remains.

"Shit," said Peter. Now he knew the smell. Modern smokeless powder had a cleaner tang than the old black powder used by antique firearm enthusiasts and reenactors. Black powder smelled more sulfury, like brimstone.

With its faster combustion rate, black powder had other uses, too.

Lewis saw the look on his face. "What'd you find inside?"

"The makings for pipe bombs."

"Remote detonation?"

"I don't think so. I didn't see any wiring or anything electronic, just cut-off bits of fuse. I think what we see here was a kind of rehearsal. This guy likes to get close."

Lewis let out a long slow breath. "Then you know where we'll find them."

"Yes." As they ran back to the Yukon, Peter told Lewis about the automatic weapons, the missing steel plate, the welder, and the deep tire tracks. "I don't know what they're driving, but we'll know it when we see it."

"Jesus." Lewis reversed at high speed down the long driveway. "What we need is a fucking tank."

Peter scratched his stubble. "Funny you should bring that up."

PART 5

47

Skin still sweat-slick from dodging that saltine whose old green truck he'd taken, Eli had slipped through the midnight woods and crossed the river into Frayser on the old railroad bridge.

There were only so many ways across. When you were a skinny black boy without a crew, the tracks could be a good way to travel without people taking notice. He'd gone back and forth to the Lucky Lounge on that rusty bridge many times.

After a long afternoon and night playing for tips on the street, heading back to the empty with a pocketful of singles and his guitar slung over his shoulder, or wrapped in a big plastic garbage bag as protection from the rain, he liked to imagine that he was walking the path of Muddy Waters or John Lee Hooker, or one of those other great old bluesmen, taking the train to seek their fortune in Chicago or Detroit.

Sometimes, after a night with Dupree and Romeo at the Lucky, with the music they'd made still resounding inside him, he felt like he was one of those bluesmen himself, walking his own path. Wherever it might lead. Maybe even with Nadine at his side.

Not anymore. Now, with his boys dead and gone, and King Robbie and this saltine after him, and his guitar smashed to splinters, walking the tracks felt like the end of everything good and the start of something bad.

He couldn't stop thinking about what Miss Wanda had said, something that had flipped a switch for Eli. Who benefits?

Now he knew.

King Robbie had somehow got Eli's daddy put in prison so King could take over.

King had killed Eli's big brother Baldwin to get him out of the way.

And Baldwin's dying pushed Eli's mother into overdose.

Which had killed her.

Now, despite what he'd told that saltine about not wanting any part of that other life, Eli felt the anger rise up in him. He wanted to hurt somebody the way they'd hurt him.

He'd thought wrecking that guitar had mattered, but it didn't. Not anymore. The guitar was the only thing Eli had left in the world because King had already taken away his family. Taken away everything that had really mattered. Turned it all to hell and ruination.

Looked like Eli was going to have to step into his brother Baldwin's shoes for real.

Do a man's job. Settle the score.

The only question was how to go about it.

And whether Eli had it in him to do what had to be done.

It was hard to walk on the railroad timbers. The spacing was off, he couldn't take a decent stride. The rounded stones were soft between them, and gave way with dull notes under his sneakers. So he put both feet onto a single steel rail as he sometimes did late at night when nobody was near.

While his conscious mind was focused on managing his balance on that narrow rail, shifting his weight to keep him moving forward, the mathematical part made its deeper calculations. What to do, how to do it.

That little gun Coyo had given him was gone.

First thing, he needed a new one.

The tracks were down low, under bridges, running through a gap in the trees. He ghosted under the busy four-lane, under Whitney Avenue and Frayser Boulevard and behind the houses along Madewell Street. Once he slipped by the Corning Village Apartments and made it past the Steele Street crossing and the Pershing Park Apartments, he was almost back at the empty.

He hoped he'd be safe there. Could still spend the night. Make his plans.

While he walked, the mathematical part kept getting stuck on Miss Wanda, the picture taker. All the gangsters knew Miss Wanda. Her rep was major. She was fearless.

Nobody messed with her. With that camera, anywhere Wanda stood was safe ground. What's more, the gangsters all bragged that you weren't nobody in the hood until she'd tagged you on her feed.

Even the dead. Wanda didn't care how they got killed, or what they'd done to end up that way. Wanda knew that the worst bangers still had brothers and sisters, mothers and fathers. And most of them hadn't done nothing near wrong enough to deserve that cold, dark, lonely grave.

She used her feed to keep those dead alive.

So what was Wanda Wyatt doing with that saltine, Peter?

The only answer the mathematical part could find was, maybe that Peter wasn't such a damn saltine after all.

Eli walked silent up the familiar street and slipped around back of the empty. No sign of King Robbie's big Mercedes. No sign of Charlene in her low, dark ride. No light peeping through the boarded-up windows. The chairs still stood in a circle in the high grass, where he and Skinny B and Anthony and Coyo had started this damn stupid thing.

They'd ambushed him, sure, and threatened to break his guitar. Not that it mattered now. He should have let them break it, because it was gone anyway, like everything else. At least those boys would still be alive and walking, talking shit like always. Except for Coyo, who never said a thing unless he meant it.

Had it all happened just in the last few days? His shitty idea for a robbery, then taking the man's truck because Coyo's crappy car gave out? There it sat, the old green pickup, half-hidden in the overgrown tangle, reminding him of his failure.

The death of his friends.

He knew Skinny B and Anthony were dead. The news had told him as much at the Wet Spot earlier. With all the gunshots and all the cops, he was sure Coyo had to be dead, too. It was the only thing that could have happened.

Now the house would be truly empty.

He wondered if Wanda had ever taken their pictures.

He'd see them in his sleep, he knew. Like he saw his brother, his mother, his father, everyone else who'd been taken away. Damn nightmares, sure, but somehow welcome for all that.

Just to see their faces.

He had a foot on the back stoop when he heard the sound coming through the partly open door. A slow rasp, back and forth, like Dupree with his sandpaper, making rough things smooth. But Eli knew there wasn't nobody looking to smooth out this rough old house. It was just waiting for the wrecking claw.

Back and forth. Slow and low and unsteady.

Eli put his fingertip on the door and pushed it open.

The rasp came from the living room, darker inside than out. Eli turned on his run-down phone to get some light from the screen.

It was Coyo, laid out flat on the three-legged couch. The slow rasp was his shallow breathing.

In the faint light of the screen, Eli saw the old, plaid couch fabric stained dark.

Coyo was alive. Maybe just barely. But alive.

Eli wanted to cry, but the mathematical part shut it down and shifted gears.

"Coyo."

There was a hitch in the breathing, then it went back to how it was before. Maybe the breaths took a little longer. That rasp a little deeper.

"It's Eli. Don't pretend."

Coyo didn't sit up, but his eyes opened, lit like lamps. His whisper was just another rasp. "I'm sorry, Eli. Didn't have no place else to go."

Like it was a damn inconvenience. Eli stood over him. Raised the phone so he could see better. Coyo wore the same old cut-off jeans and a white T-shirt turned red and black with blood, wet and dry. His pistol was tucked by his leg where he could reach it.

"You dying?"

"Prob'ly. Shot me three times."

Maybe a little proud of it, too. As if getting cop-shot was some kind of accomplishment. Damn this neighborhood.

Coyo's eyes blinked slow. "Anthony make it?"

"Just you and me. We all that's left."

His mouth tightened. "You still got the bag?"

"Yeah."

"Good, good."

"How'd you get here? I didn't see a car."

A faint smile. "I walked. Slid out through that Macy store. Hid in some bushes. Walked some. Hid some, rested. Drank some Cokes. Walked some more."

"All that way? It's got to be fifteen or twenty miles."

Coyo just shrugged with his tired eyes.

It came as no surprise to Eli that a young black man could walk across Memphis, clothes red with blood, and nobody stopped to help or called the police. They probably didn't even look up from their phones. People like Eli and Coyo were invisible, disposable. Except to each other.

"Whyn't you go to the emergency room? You must've passed three or four on the way."

Coyo shook his head. "Hospitals report gunshot wounds, you know that. Next thing, I'm talking to the cops, after that I'm in jail. I ain't going to jail."

Eli didn't see how jail could be worse than dying. But he'd heard plenty of jailhouse stories, and he didn't want to go, either.

"You always was stubborn." He rubbed his chin. "I'm going to the Walgreens, get some supplies. Get you fixed up."

Coyo reached out a hand, surprisingly strong, and grabbed hold of Eli's wrist. "No, Ellison. Stay here with me. You got any water?"

"Sure. Be right back." Eli detached Coyo's hand, then went out back. He rinsed an old Coke can with water from the bucket set under the gutter overflow, then filled the can up again, nice and clean.

He brought in a cracked vinyl chair from the yard and sat beside Coyo, raised the can to his lips. "You need help. Let me find that old doc does fix-up for the neighborhood."

Old Doc Schweigart had lost his license before Eli was

born. His pale hands were shaky and his brain was wet, but he knew things and he'd help, and you could pay him in liquor. He could even be kind, when he'd had enough to drink. "Call me Bill," he'd say, swaying on the street corner, and tell unlikely lies about his years in the Coast Guard. Eli had stood in the old doc's kitchen more than once while he patched up some half-dead boy laid out on the tarnished chrome-legged table.

Coyo's breath rasped louder. "You can't go out. It ain't safe. King's got riders out everywhere. And you know Doc Schweigart works on King's people, too. You can't trust him."

"We can pay him to keep quiet," said Eli. "We got something to trade now."

"That won't help. He'll just smell more money."

Even shot full of holes, Coyo knew all those angles.

"All right." Eli got to his feet. "Let me go out and look through that truck. Maybe I can find something to help."

"I saw that old thing. Where'd it come from?"

"I took it," said Eli. "At the Texaco on Watkins." He felt neither pride nor shame at the telling. It was what he'd had to do at the time.

Coyo made a face. "That ain't you." He pushed himself up on one shaking elbow, straining toward Eli. "Not s'posed to be, anyway. I wanted you to keep making music. I wanted to keep you out of this. I wanted you to be better than me." His face twisted up with the effort and pain, and he sank back down into the couch. "But here you are, up to your neck, and it's all my doing."

"I made a choice," said Eli. Which was the truth. Nobody stuck a gun in his ribs. "We all gotta eat. 'Sides, that red car crapped out. I had to get back here, is all."

Coyo's eyes closed again, worn out from the conversation.

Eli put a hand on his friend's chest, and saw again the gun tucked beside Coyo's leg.

He took the gun in his hand and found the release for the magazine. Coyo had reloaded.

Whatever happened, Eli could move forward on the next part of his plan.

This time, alone.

Eli went out to the old green truck, took the keys from under the floor mat, and used the last of his cell phone battery to find the odd-shaped key that fit the funny round padlock on the wood cargo box.

He found a short flashlight set in a kind of holster fastened to the back of the hatch. He turned on the light and saw slender darkwood shelves built inside like fine furniture, nicer than Eli had ever seen before. Set into the spaces were all kinds of wooden boxes, sized to fit just right, gleaming with polish, each made of some different kind of wood. Simple curved handholds called out for fingers.

He pulled out one box and saw power tools he recognized from his time with Dupree, laid out neat and clean with their cords wrapped around them. He pulled out another, smaller box and saw hand tools set in padded cloth pockets. Their grips were worn smooth by use, but Eli didn't need to test the chisel edges to know they were sharp.

He wondered at the kind of person that would take such care to build something this beautiful into the back of an old pickup truck.

Seemed like he was reconsidering that saltine Peter over and over again.

He found a bright red box with a white cross and took it down from its place. This one had a lid with a latch, but Eli knew a first-aid kit when he saw it. He turned to go, but his eye caught on a piece of black clothing sitting alone on a shelf. Eli was chilled by the night, by his constant teenage hunger, so he took it down, thinking to warm himself or Coyo.

He didn't understand why the coat was so heavy until he unfolded it and realized it was some kind of armored vest like the police wore. He tucked it under his arm, backed out of the cargo box, and locked up, while the mathematical part made changes to his plan's earlier equations.

He took another hurried minute to search through the cab of the truck. In the ashtray, he found a phone charger for the cigarette lighter and a couple of different power cords. One fit Eli's phone, so he fired up the engine, set his phone to charge, then left the truck rumbling low and carried the red box and the flashlight and the vest back to Coyo.

Inside the red box, he found a prescription bottle with a label that said, Take two every twelve hours for pain.

He shook out four and got them into Coyo with some water. He sorted through the kit, finding the supplies listed on the plastic instruction card while he waited for the pills to kick in and his own courage to arrive.

It never did. But there was nothing else to do but start. "This is gonna hurt."

Coyo grunted. "Do it."

He cut Coyo's shirt open with scissors from the kit and wiped away the blood with a square of wet gauze from a foil packet. He found two small, neat holes, one down low in the torso and another through the meat of the shoulder. He put his forearm hard across Coyo's chest and trickled alcohol from the kit into the wounds while Coyo bucked beneath him, an anguished growl burbling up from deep inside that Eli knew he'd hear in his dreams for the rest of his life.

Following the instructions from the card, he covered the small holes with gauze and taped bandages over them. Then he rolled Coyo onto his side to see the exit wounds, which were larger and uglier. Again with the cleaning and the alcohol and gauze packed deep into the raw meat, then bigger bandages covering his friend's ruined body. Coyo was silent now, panting short shallow breaths.

Eli's vision got blurry. He realized he was crying.

Then he remembered Coyo saying he'd been shot three times. Eli looked him over and realized Coyo's jean shorts were soaked red at the hip. He closed his eyes.

"Come on." Coyo's voice was ragged, nearly unrecognizable. "One more."

Eli wiped his eyes and cut away the shorts and saw the exit wound in the front this time. Coyo had been shot in the ass, probably as he was running away.

That's how they do, he said to himself. That's how they goddamn do.

He cleaned and rinsed and packed and bandaged as Coyo panted and hurt like some car-hit dog left to die in the street. He knew Coyo wasn't good. Coyo had done way more than his share of bad. But he was Eli's friend, had always been his friend. And nobody should be left to die alone.

He laid Coyo flat on the couch again, with Eli's own blanket over the bloody cushions and Skinny B's sleeping bag over Coyo's shivering body. He didn't know what else to do. "More water?"

Coyo opened his mouth a little and Eli poured in a slow stream until the can was empty.

"Goddamn I'm tired," Coyo said when he was done. "You'll watch out for me? While I sleep? I'll be better in the morning, I promise. We'll get in that old truck and get the hell out of Memphis. Find someplace new."

He pulled in a deep, raspy breath, then let it out. His eyes were already closed. "If I don't wake up, don't tell nobody." A faint smile played on his cracked, dry lips. "Tell 'em I went to Chicago. Then you go instead. Use those watches to buy a new life."

Eli sat on that cracked vinyl chair beside his oldest friend in the world, maybe the only one left. Besides Nadine, who sometimes scared the living hell out of him, Coyo was the only person left who really knew him.

Everyone else was gone. His pops in prison for the rest of his life, his mama dead by her own hand. His brother murdered by ambition, his own and King Robbie's.

Before that moment, Eli had always been able to sit with his guitar and let his fingers turn that pain to music. That's what the blues was for, wasn't it?

But his guitar was history. Now, with Coyo lying on that three-legged couch, steeped in his own blood, Eli tried a new mechanism. He built a small fire with his pain, and turned that fire into anger. For his mother, his father, his brother, his friends.

He sat beside Coyo through the long, dark night, stoking the frozen flames into an ice-cold fury. His hand on Coyo's chest as it rose and fell, listening to that shallow, raspy breath, while his mathematical mind made its deadly calculations.

In the faint morning light, he left Coyo just long enough to collect his charged phone from the green truck, turn off the engine, and search the cargo box for something to eat. He found a cooler with a pair of apples and a quarter-jar of peanut butter and a few stale slices of brown bread.

It was enough for what he had to do.

While he ate, he listened to Coyo's breathing grow ever more shallow.

He went over his plans again.

48

It was well after noon and Coyo had not yet woken. He was bleeding through his bandages. Eli was waiting for something, but he didn't know what.

He heard a noise at the back door and jumped up with Coyo's gun in his hand.

"Eli?" Nadine peeked around the door.

She'd found him, of course. Nadine always knew where to find him. She got all over town on that old bike, covered miles like they were nothing.

"Put that down." She flicked her hand at Coyo's gun like it was something filthy and not Eli's tool for revenge. "That's not you."

"Somebody's gotta pay." He looked at her, suddenly full of icy rage. "You know what King did? To my father? My brother?"

She nodded. "I know what King Robbie is. But you didn't need to know everything. You could have left it be. Made a different life. Instead, you brought it all back with

that robbery. You need to own that, Eli, what you did."
She gave him that calm, steady stare. "You don't need to
make things worse."

"I need to be a man, Nadine. I need to stand up for what
happened to me and mine. To my whole damn family."

She stepped forward until they were almost touching.
He knew better than to touch her first, no matter how
much he wanted to. It was part of Nadine. Her gift also
carried a curse, the steep price she paid. She couldn't
turn it off. He waited.

Finally, she leaned in and let her full, soft lips gently
brush his, just for a moment.

He felt that miraculous flash like touching a live wire,
that direct line between them he'd never get tired of.

They'd only ever touched for a few seconds at a time,
never done anything more than that brief brush of the
lips. It scared him, how exposed he felt, how deeply she
could see inside him. But it also made him hope hard for
what might come next. Between nightmares about his
mother, his brother, his father, his friends, he dreamed
about Nadine, that deeper way of knowing, what might
be possible.

Now that spark carried a message, because sometimes
the current flowed two ways.

She was terrified that he might die.

For all the power of Nadine's gift, she didn't know the
future.

But she knew something about what he planned.

"Please wait," she said. "Wait for that Peter and his

friend. They want to help you, I know it. They're good at this."

"I can't wait. I got to do this myself. I got to be a man and stand up."

"What you've been through, you're already a man," she said. "But you're waiting on something." She looked at Coyo, who stirred restlessly on the three-legged couch. Maybe awake and listening, maybe not. "You waiting on him?"

Eli knew then it was true. "Gotta get him good enough to travel. I'll do what I need to do, then drive him into Arkansas. Find a hospital somewhere nobody knows him."

"What about you and me? What's that worth to you?"

"Almost everything," he said. "You know that. But I can't let this be. I gotta stand up or it's gonna eat me from the inside."

"It doesn't have to be like that," she said. "Make your peace and walk away."

The frosty anger turned his heart to ice. "My brother didn't walk away. Coyo wouldn't walk away, neither."

She looked down at Coyo, laid out on the couch. "You know I never liked that boy. He brought you back into this. What's he ever done but bring grief and harm to the world? Let him die. You and I can move on to something new."

Coyo's eyes were still closed, but a faint smile ghosted across his lips. "Always knew you was tough, Nadine." His voice was no longer sandpaper, but something rougher, wetter. "Had no idea you was so damn hard."

"He's my friend," Eli said simply. "I don't have so many left I can just let one go."

Nadine looked down at Coyo for a long moment, considering. Then, with that effortless grace, she seated herself on the edge of the cracked vinyl chair, wrapped one arm tight around her chest, planted her flip-flops firmly on the floor, and laid the palm of her free hand on Coyo's forehead.

He spasmed on the couch.

Nadine's face and neck and arms and legs showed every muscle and tendon, but she kept hold of Coyo. He convulsed like a rag doll shaken by a heedless child. Something unknowable passing between them.

When, finally, Coyo sank back into the cushions, his face was smooth and empty of lines for the first time Eli could remember.

Nadine slumped into the chair, exhausted. She took Coyo fondly by the hand, like a little brother. "See, you're not so bad." Her voice was soft. "Now you can choose. To hold on or let go. Live or die as you will."

Coyo gave her the gentlest smile Eli had ever seen. Then he took in a deep, shuddering breath.

He held it for a long moment, as if poised at the edge of some great precipice.

When he let it all out again, it was altogether more air than seemed possible for one gunshot black boy to ever hold inside.

After that, he never took another breath.

Nadine stood, unsteady on her feet, and walked carefully toward the door. She didn't touch Eli. She didn't even look at him. Swaying slightly, she stood in the doorway and stared out at the weedy, overgrown yard, at the old green truck parked there.

When she spoke, her voice was distant.

"Time to decide, Ellison Bell. Time to decide who you want to be."

She stepped outside and climbed on her bike and rode away.

49

It was nearing nightfall when Albert and Judah Lee had parked on the street behind their ancestor's battered house, and walked silently through a wooded vacant lot to their ancestor's weedy, neglected backyard. What with the dump truck and machine-gun fire, the house itself was mostly open to the air, but empty-feeling inside, and dark.

Judah Lee had brought flashlights.

Albert wished he'd brought his pain pills. He was starting to ache.

They'd walked through the kitchen and dining room, Albert wide-eyed at how much damage Judah Lee had caused—no, how much damage Albert and Judah Lee both had caused. It was one thing to catch sight of it driving past, but another entirely to get close up. This was their ancestor's house, yes, but stepping inside and seeing that woman's personal things, no matter how scattered and broken, Albert could feel that it could be her house, too.

Judah had argued that, whatever they were looking

for, it had to be hidden somewhere in the structure. Otherwise it would have been discovered long ago. Which left the spaces inside the walls, or else the attic or root cellar or crawl space. Albert had agreed, hoping that it would get them out of the house faster, before the inevitable police patrol saw their lights.

He was starting to wonder how much of this whole deal was actual hope in finding their ancestor's legacy and how much was just Judah Lee's free-floating anger looking for a place to land.

It turned out that the walls were solid brick, three layers thick, and there was no attic to speak of, unless they were willing to tear into every rafter bay. Doing that would be real noisy, take most of the night, and probably bring the police.

So they went around back to the root cellar. Judah Lee searched behind the shelves and in the joist bays, then began to probe and pry at the loose brick pavers, hoping to find a soft place where a buried strongbox had rotted away.

He gave Albert the job of stuffing himself into the narrow crawl space, bad leg and all.

Albert made his way to the big stump holding up the center of the house without finding anything but cobwebs and old wood and a deep and abiding ache in his hip. Judah Lee met him on the other side of the stump, where the dump truck's bumper met the ground. Judah pointed his flashlight at the ground.

"You see this, big brother?"

At first, Albert didn't see anything but dirt. Bringing

his face closer, he began to make out rectangular impressions in the packed soil around the stump. The imprints were scuffed around their edges by loose soil and dig marks made with some kind of two-pronged tool.

He put his fingers into the tool marks.

The dirt inside was tightly packed and still slightly damp.

"They found it," said Judah Lee. The flashlight in the crawl space lit his face from beneath. The blue skull tattoo and the pointed teeth going dark at their rotten roots were truly terrifying. "Those goddamn people took our family legacy."

They walked back through the vacant lot to the street behind, where they'd left Judah's red pickup. It was parked across from a neatly kept little house with a picket fence out front and flower beds blooming like crazy.

Albert put his powerful hand on his brother's thick arm. "Let's go home, Judah."

That morning, before they left the farm, he'd set up the corral trap where the south field met the trees. Hogs had been rooting up the sweet potatoes again, looking for the tender shoots. Now he had a bad feeling. A stone in his belly. He wanted to go check the corral. Anything to get out of there.

Judah shook off Albert's hand and strode toward the little house.

"Let's find another way, Judah. Let's just go home."

Albert never could keep up when Judah Lee was in

full stride. He was afraid of what his brother had in mind. But arguing with Judah Lee had never done any good. Usually it made things worse. Gave him ideas.

The house had a good steel security door facing the street. Without a word, Judah Lee turned and walked up the driveway, past an old Buick, to the high wooden fence that wrapped the backyard. There was no dog, and Judah shouldered through the gate before Albert got close enough to put a hand on him.

There was no security grate at the back porch. Just a thick wooden door with a pair of heavy-duty deadbolts.

Judah Lee leaned back and kicked it in.

An elderly man at the kitchen sink reached for a cast-iron fry pan, but Judah brushed it aside and smashed the old man to the floor with a single heavy fist. An old woman screamed and dropped beside him, covering him with her body. Albert had to shush her with the back of his hand to keep Judah from taking up the fry pan and beating them both to death.

"It's for your own good," Albert told them as he tied their skinny wrists with clothesline. He stuffed dishrags into their mouths, then left them together on the living room sofa amid lace doilies and dried flowers, like his own grandmother had kept. While Albert turned out the house lights, Judah took their keys and moved the Buick across the street, then drove the modified pickup into the small garage with the sound of rending wood. The beefed-up truck was too big for the door.

When Judah came back, he loomed over the couple.

No mask over his face, not even a handkerchief tied bandit-style.

They shrank away from him, and Judah smiled.

Albert knew then that his brother had lost the desire for disguise, had stopped caring for any consequence that might bring. The stone in his belly got heavier.

"We don't need to do any of this," he said. "We can still go home."

Judah gave Albert a look as empty as the eyes of the skull tattooed on his face.

"That race traitor will come by soon enough. Tonight or tomorrow, we can wait. I'm guessing he's careful. He'll check these streets. We'll follow behind, and he'll lead us to what he stole. Or we take it out of his hide, then go after the woman who lives there."

Judah turned to stare out the wide front window at the falling darkness while Albert stood uneasily in the unlit living room, shifting his weight from one foot to the other, looking at the elderly couple huddled together on the couch.

"Here's how it is," he told them. "When we see who we're waiting for, we're gone. But you never saw us, all right? We weren't never here. If we find out different, we'll be back. And we won't be so nice."

The tied-up old couple nodded their heads with solemn dignity undercut only slightly by the dishrag ends hanging from their open mouths. The old man's brown face was turning dark where Judah had hit him.

Time passed with painful slowness. The tick of the

grandfather clock filled the room. Then Judah pointed at a big SUV driving past. "We see them before?"

"I don't know." Albert was tired. He'd been up most of the night before with Judah, and spent most of the morning setting up that corral trap. He didn't know why he'd thought catching hogs still mattered.

"Losing your nerve, big brother? Afraid of your true self?"

Albert didn't know who his true self was anymore.

Maybe it didn't matter. He was in this now. He couldn't think of a way out of any of it. Losing the farm. Going to prison. Or dying along the way.

Maybe that last one was the best.

"Here it comes again. Look. You recognize that guy?"

"No, I don't." Albert didn't want to look. He just wanted to go home. But his head turned, and his eyes followed the SUV. And he *did* recognize the man in the passenger seat. That shaggy dark hair, that bony, long-muscled arm hanging out the window, those searching eyes like a wolf on the hunt.

"Dang," said Albert. "It's him."

"Okay." Judah rubbed his hands together. "Get the truck. You're driving. I'll be right behind you."

Albert limped to the garage and climbed into the driver's seat. It was hard to maneuver, even harder to see where he was going with the changes they'd made to the truck. He took out a corner of the garage with the big new fender, then a section of fence.

That wasn't who Albert thought he was, someone who wrecked things. But that's who he'd become.

He sat waiting in the driveway, but he couldn't see Judah Lee through the tiny space he'd left in the window. Afraid they were going to lose the shaggy wolf-eyed man, he opened his door to call out but saw Judah Lee walking down the front steps.

He wore a wide pointy grin as he wiped the blade of his knife on the leg of his pants.

Then Albert knew Judah had killed the elderly couple.

The stone in his belly got heavier still. There truly was no way out. Albert might as well have killed those folks himself.

Judah hopped on the back bumper and into the sheltered bed of the pickup. He thumped the roof of the cab. "Time to go, big brother. Hit the gas."

And, God help him, Albert did what Judah Lee told him to do. Again.

The problem was, now Albert was too far behind the big SUV to follow. He'd watched them take a right turn a few blocks up, but by the time he got there, the SUV was nowhere to be found. The narrow view ports only made it harder to see.

"Goddamn it," howled Judah Lee from the back. He slammed his heavy hands on the cab roof, denting it in his rage. "You are fucking useless."

"Screw you," muttered Albert. But he kept driving, head craned forward as he peered through the little opening in the windshield. The SUV he'd seen was boxy and newer, which made it different from everything else in this neighborhood of beaters. He'd gotten a good look. It didn't have much traffic to hide in, either. He knew which way it was headed.

Albert had been hunting almost since he could walk. He had a good eye. He could spot a deer silhouette in the thickest brush.

He'd drive until he found that SUV, and the shaggy, wolf-eyed man in it.

While the stone in his belly grew heavier by the minute.

50

Peter and Lewis spiraled in toward Wanda's house from a long way out, looking for the Burkitts brothers. Windows down in the thick evening heat, their pistols within easy reach, the long guns under a blanket on the back seat. They cruised the busy avenues and side roads and the parking lots in the gathering dark, not knowing what vehicle they were trying to find, but fairly sure they'd know it when they saw it. As they circled closer, Peter peered into the tangled depths of the vacant lots, finding nothing.

Finally Lewis drove down Wanda's street. Her house was still standing, with no sign of new damage, and no watchers in sight.

He didn't stop. "Either we beat 'em here, or they're laying up somewhere, waiting."

"It doesn't matter," Peter said. "We might have gotten lucky if we'd caught them by surprise, but we can't compete head-on, not with what I think they've got. We need a serious upgrade."

Lewis circled around and drove across the Wolf River

into Frayser as the last of the daylight winked out behind the high granite clouds to the west.

Peter knew where they were going. Starting from the Texaco where Eli had taken Peter's truck, they followed Fat Rudy's original directions to find a phone.

The Wet Spot stood on the corner, a rectangular white brick building with a storefront below and sagging wooden exterior steps climbing to apartments above. Metal grates over the front first-floor windows, steel security doors at the front and rear, the storefront's side windows bricked up years ago.

There was a vacant lot to one side and another behind the alley. The parking area at the rear had two cars, Charlene Scott's long, low, matte-black stealth ride and a plain blue four-door Ford pickup. King Robbie's big Mercedes SUV sat right out front.

Lewis cruised past without slowing. "See all the cameras?"

Peter had counted sixteen. Eight mounted at the building corners above the first floor, for overlapping views of the immediate area, and eight more at the parapet wall above the second floor, to look down the surrounding streets. "Reminds me of your old place in Milwaukee."

"Only better. These people aren't messing. Plus it's a damn ice cream shop and grocery store. You don't know what kind of civilians gonna be in there. Women and children. And we can't just hang out and wait until it's empty, because they'll see us on the monitors."

"What I want is a conversation."

Lewis snorted. "Jarhead, you humiliated these people. Took that girl shooter's pistol, then held up his muscle at gunpoint. Made even more of an insult because you didn't respect them enough to kill them." He shook his head. "Better to just put on a ski mask and walk inside and shoot them dead."

Peter looked at his friend. "Sounds like you're speaking from experience."

Lewis looked right back. "You keep asking what I used to do for a living? Well, this is how I got started, back in the day."

At the corner, he turned and pulled to the curb, out of sight of the cameras.

"I used to stick up the corner boys for food money when I was a kid. Moved fast and beat 'em down and got it done. Didn't get rich, but I didn't starve to death, either. After Uncle Sam taught me to kill people and not give a shit, I moved up the food chain to the big boys."

Peter had collected enough snippets of conversation from his friend that he'd already guessed this much. "I'm disappointed," he said. "I thought you sold encyclopedias door to door."

Lewis faced forward, the cords standing out in his neck. "Man, I *hate* dope dealers. They poison their neighborhood six ways from Sunday. We should go in there and kill them all."

"Power hates a vacuum," said Peter. "Remember what Iraq was like after the ruling party got dismantled? The Baathists all kicked out of office with nothing to replace them? The army sent home without pay? That's when the civil war started, and everything went to hell."

Lewis snorted. "This is no fucking joke. People at this level, they made it there because they're smart and fast and half-crazy. They're heeled and ready and they will not hesitate to kill you dead without a second thought. Your only advantage is surprise."

Peter smiled. "No, our advantage is that we're smarter, faster, and completely crazy. So we'll suit up, park right in front, and go in hard. But no killing unless we have to."

Lewis shook his head. "Jarhead, why you always got to make things so damn difficult?"

"I have a feeling," said Peter. "Maybe a way to stabilize things."

"It's a mistake to think they'll stick to any deal you make at gunpoint. I hope you know what the fuck you're doing."

"We'll adjust to whatever comes. Don't worry, I won't hesitate."

"Tell me again why I hang out with you?"

Peter clapped Lewis on the shoulder. "Because I make your life so goddamn interesting."

They still wore the tactical vests from their approach to the Burkitts brothers' farm. They'd put on thin windbreakers to be less conspicuous on the road, but now they peeled off the jackets and checked their gear in silence.

Peter's last task was to set his phones to airplane

mode, but when he pulled out the burner, he saw a text from June. *Don't mean to cramp your style but where the fuck are you?*

Peter showed the text to Lewis. "I think I need a minute."

"Yeah you do."

They sat in the Yukon, pistols snug in holsters and the angular HK rifles butt-down in the footwell while June's phone rang in Peter's ear.

She answered. "What the fuck?"

"Hi, honey. Lewis and I are just getting ready for a meeting."

"Don't bullshit me. I am not happy with you."

Peter had never been able to fool June for a single minute.

"I know. I'm sorry."

"When will you be here?"

"I don't know. There are too many hairy assholes still out there, but we're working on it. Can I get back to you later?"

"As long as you come back to me," she said. "You hearing me, Marine?"

"Yes, ma'am. How's Wanda?"

"The doctor came and took a look. She told me that Wanda's malnourished and probably addicted to half these goddamn pills. I got a referral to a therapist and a plan to taper Wanda off those meds. I also made an appointment for a full physical next week."

"Did that young woman Nadine show up?"

"Less than an hour ago. She barely said hello, just

went into Wanda's room and closed the door. I thought I heard somebody crying. They're still in there now." He heard the concern in her voice.

"I'm sure they're just talking."

He was fairly certain it was more than that. He changed the subject.

"I'm still thinking about Wanda's gallery show. You think there's any way she'll make her deadline?"

"Oh, I'll make it happen, even if I have to choose the images myself. Actually," June said, "I was looking at Wanda's laptop. She has these other photos, they look like they were taken in a nightclub. Very different from her other stuff. A lot of life there, dancers and musicians, people all dressed up. They're really good, I think. I called the gallery owner and he said to include as many as we like."

"That's great," Peter said. "Maybe she can find something new to focus on."

"Maybe so." Then she said, "Is that him, the kid onstage with the silvery guitar?"

"Yes."

"I can see who he reminds you of, and why you want to save him. They don't look anything alike, but they have the same kind of presence. Even in the photo, you can see it."

Peter didn't glance at Lewis. "Let's talk about this later."

"Wait." A muffled sound, maybe her hand over the phone. Then, "Nadine just came out. She says she's worried Eli's going to get himself into worse trouble." June read off an address. "She said that's where Eli's been staying. She said get there soon. And bring a shovel. Maybe two."

"What?"

"That's all she said." June pushed out a breath. "We need to have a serious fucking conversation, Marine."

"I know," he said. "We will. But not yet. I need to finish this thing, and I need to know you're safe while I'm doing it."

"I'm safe here," she said. "You stay safe, too."

"Lewis brought vests. We'll be fine."

"Put him on."

"What?"

"Put Lewis on the fucking phone."

He handed it to Lewis. June did all the talking.

Peter couldn't hear her words, but he could hear the tone. Loud. Insistent.

Lewis just listened with his small, tilted smile. It didn't take long. Finally, he said, "Yes ma'am. Loud and clear."

Then ended the call.

Peter looked at Lewis. "What was that about?"

Lewis shook his head. He looked down the darkened street. The night clouds were lit from the city below, looming closer with their hanging curtains of rain. "Your girlfriend is something else."

"What'd she say?"

Lewis shook his head again. "That woman is a keeper, Jarhead. I hope you understand that, what you got with her."

"Lewis, what the fuck did she say?"

He turned to face Peter. The intensity of his stare was almost physical.

"She said kill anybody I have to. Long as I bring you back in one piece."

Peter blinked. "Jesus Christ."

"Uh-huh." Lewis drummed his fingers on one leg. The Yukon's engine growled almost below the range of hearing. "You still looking to do this?"

Peter wanted to feel regret, but he didn't. He took a deep breath and felt the familiar lift of adrenaline, the best high in the world. The taste of copper filled his mouth.

"Oh, hell yes," he said. "Let's roll."

51

They left the Yukon a car length behind the big Mercedes and went through the door without discussion, as if they'd done it a hundred times before. Peter first with his rifle up and ready, Lewis a half-step behind, then fanning to Peter's right with the sawed-off 10-gauge snug at his shoulder and a big smile on his face.

"Hands up," Peter shouted. "Hands up, hands up, or you're all gonna die."

"Jarhead's a goddamn natural," Lewis murmured softly, as if to himself.

The white static kept Peter crisp and tight. He saw grocery shelves to the right and a long counter to the left with a bald man standing behind it. He had black-framed glasses slipping down his nose and hands sliding out of sight.

The white static sizzled and Peter fired a three-round burst past the bald man's ear. His hands flew empty into the air as the soft-serve machine bled chocolate ice cream slowly down its polished chrome front.

Behind a big gleaming table in the back, King Robbie jumped to his feet. The abrupt movement rocked the table, knocking over beer bottles and dumping a big pistol sideways to the floor as his chair toppled behind him. King's eyes bulged and he reached for the gun that was no longer there.

On the near side of the table, Charlene Scott had already stood and turned toward Peter with her right hand inside her seersucker jacket, hand closing on the butt of her pistol, face empty as a headstone waiting for the carver.

Beside her, Brody reached his arm out across her chest, blocking her draw. His other hand hung at his side. He'd evidently found his gun in the grass, and wore it in the same shoulder holster over a black T-shirt. The size of him was startling in the open room.

"That's a ten-gauge," he said to Lewis. "Am I right?"

Two professionals, recognizing each other at the point of a gun.

"Barrel's cut down." Lewis stepped forward and glanced around, making sure nobody else was in the room. "Loaded with double-aught pellets like .38 slugs. This range, me to you, pattern's about the size of a beach ball." The tilted smile got even wider. "Way you're standing all clumped up, I can hit all three of you with one pull of the trigger."

Brody and Charlene flicked their eyes briefly at each other, but otherwise didn't move. The bald counterman stood like a statue. On the back wall, a giant flat-screen television flashed on mute.

King Robbie tilted his chin up, indicating the surveillance cameras in the high corners of the room. "All the footage is stored remotely, outside and in. Anything happens, your faces are caught on a server outside of Salt

Lake City. My people will hunt you down." He began to work his way around the table.

"Stored for how long," Lewis asked. "A day? A week? A month?" He smiled wide. "We can drop your ass so deep underground, won't nobody find you, not ever. 'Cause the four of you the only ones with keys to this place, right? We mop the floor, wash the walls, lock the doors, and nobody'll think twice. The whole damn neighborhood'll be happy as hell to see you gone."

King paused and gave a long sniff, either a reflex or a runny nose. Peter watched the man's fingers twitch like spider legs and knew King was wired like a motor.

Peter glanced at Brody, thought he saw something in Brody's flat gaze.

"Think about it this way," Peter told King. "I could have killed you several times over. All three of you in the car, when I took Charlene's gun. Brody, I spared you again behind that nightclub. Charlene, I let you live outside of Wanda's house. And again just walking in here, when we could have painted the walls red. So you know we didn't come here to kill you, not if we don't have to. We came to talk. To come to an agreement."

"Fucking kill them," said King Robbie, wiping his nose on his shirtsleeve, spider-leg fingers still walking in air. "Kill them now."

"We try, we're all dead." Brody slowly raised his free hand. He kept the other held out across Charlene's chest without touching her. "Ain't nobody pulling triggers, King. Man wants to talk, we let him talk."

"I am not negotiating," said King, stepping again

around the big table toward Brody's side. "You come into my place of business—"

"Who's got the account numbers and passwords?" Lewis adjusted his aim toward the moving target. "Just King? How about you, big fella? Or the man behind the counter? 'Cause if King ain't gonna deal, we taking everything, and I only need one of you to get the money." The bald guy by the bleeding soft-serve machine was frozen in place. There was a faint scent of chocolate ice cream under the smell of spent powder.

"No, brother, hold up," Brody said. "We can talk."

"Here's the deal," Peter said. "I'll give you what was taken in that robbery. I don't know why you want it, and I don't care. Maybe you're just greedy."

"My guess, it was a laundry," Lewis said. "Washing your money. You can run a lot of cash through a jewelry store. Where else you do your laundry, I wonder?"

"I don't care," said Peter. "I'll give you what Eli took. We'll go on our way. But it stops here. Everybody lives, including Wanda Wyatt. Eli Bell gets a free pass. Forever."

"I am not giving you Eli Bell," said King Robbie, now fully out from behind the table, two long steps from Brody. King's gun lay where it had fallen, on the plank floor beside the big man.

Brody was solid and strong. Charlene's hands were drifting, one fast move away from pulling her pistol. But King had a wild energy that filled the room as his voice rose.

"He fucked with me and he fucked with my business.

Nobody does that and gets away. Matter of respect. The kid dies." King's whole body taut as a rubber band about to break.

"Eli walks." Peter kept his voice calm. "You get what he took. We'll deliver it tomorrow. That's the deal."

Lewis said, "You think these people gonna keep their word once we're gone? Let's just kill 'em now and be done."

Before King could start shouting, Brody spoke up. "Maybe you sweeten the pot a little."

Big Brody, the voice of reason.

King brightened. "You got one of those big machine guns?"

"No." Peter fished in his pocket and brought out a slender golden disk. "I have this." He flipped it into the air toward King. It flashed in the light, then fell to the floor where it bounced and rolled under the table.

It didn't make that pure clear ringing sound. The sash weights were junk metal, whatever was left molten in the foundry hopper at the end of the day, a hundred years ago. But when Dupree had sliced them up and painted them gold, he'd cut them just the right thickness to chime a little bit.

"Nineteen more just like it," said Peter. "Worth at least forty thousand."

He could feel Lewis looking at him. Wondering what the fuck Peter was planning.

King said, "Where in hell'd that come from? And how many more you got?"

Brody looked at Peter and shook his head, just slightly.

Peter saw Charlene catch the movement. Her drifting hands stilled.

Peter thought it might work.

Until the front door slammed open behind them and everything went to hell.

Eli Bell flew through the opening, a pistol in one hand, June's armored vest hanging oversized on his skinny frame. His face shining with fury and desperation.

52

Peter glanced sideways at the kid with the gun and the vest, then opened his mouth to speak.

Before he could say or do anything, Lewis backpedaled fast with some kind of low spin kick that knocked Eli's legs out from under him, skidded the kid's pistol away, and brought himself back to vertical. The shotgun was locked into his shoulder like he'd never moved, only now he stood over the boy like a mama lion over a cub.

Peter saw enough to know it was under control, then turned back to the group at the table.

The bald counterman was dropping down behind the bar.

King had a hand on the butt of the big automatic in Brody's shoulder holster.

Brody moved his arm away from Charlene, and reached out toward King with both hands.

Charlene's fingers wrapped tight around the butt of her own pistol and began to pull.

Brody put one huge mitt on each side of King

Robbie's head, pulled it toward his massive chest, and gave it a quick hard counterclockwise twist.

He held King there for a moment, gone limp but still twitching.

Then let King fall, neck broken, brain-dead before he hit the floorboards.

The stink of the man's voiding bowels overpowered the smell of leaking chocolate soft-serve.

"Wait, now," Brody said. "Everybody just wait."

Peter stood ready, finger tight on the trigger, eyes on Charlene. Lewis behind him, shotgun up. Eli silent and still, crouched on the floor.

Charlene had her own pistol almost up, but her eyes stuck down on King Robbie's body.

Brody put his hand out across her arm without touching her. "Charlene, I need you to let this go."

She jerked her eyes up to Brody's face. Blinked twice, then again, then gave him a single nod. Her pistol vanished back into its holster.

Brody turned to the bald counterman, now peering over the top of the bar, the barrel of a gun just visible. "Chris. We cool?"

The counterman straightened up. He looked at Peter and Lewis and Eli, then looked back to Brody, thick-rimmed glasses sliding down his nose, pistol ready in his fist. "How's it gonna work?"

"We'll figure it out," Brody said. "You and me. First

thing, better splits. King was taking way more than his share."

Chris nodded. "Okay."

The world's most efficient transfer of power, thought Peter. The king is dead, long live the king.

"I hate to break up your board meeting," he said, "but who am I dealing with here?"

Brody's enormous head swiveled to bear on Peter. "Me."

"Good," said Peter. "Let's recap. You get whatever came from the jewelry store. Wanda's out of trouble. Eli gets a free pass. But I should tell you, that gold coin? It's not real gold."

"I knew by the sound," said Brody. "It's all right. Deal's good. Cutting out King is worth a lot more." He looked steadily at Peter. "I ain't no soft touch, though. Don't mistake me for nice."

"Wouldn't dream of it," said Peter, dropping the HK to low ready. He glanced back at Lewis, who nodded. Peter looked next at Eli, climbing to his feet, flexing his elbow. "You okay with this?"

Eli looked at King Robbie, cooling on the planks. "Okay enough." He raised his head to Brody. "Long as we're good, you and me. For real."

Brody nodded. "I always liked your brother. You stay right, we'll do fine, you and me."

Peter turned back to Brody. "You know I'm going to hold you to that."

The big man raised his eyebrows. "I ain't King Robbie."

"I know," said Peter. "It's why you're still standing. But I need one more thing."

"Now what."

"I want the armored Mercedes."

Brody's face remained expressionless. "Don't push your damn luck."

"It's not likely to come back in one piece, either. I just want to be clear on that."

Brody frowned. "You know how much that car cost?"

"With King gone, you'll make it back in a month."

Chris looked down at something behind the bar. "Hey." He put down the pistol, brought up a laptop, and tapped a few keys. The big television on the back wall changed from the muted news to a grid of sixteen boxes. Video feed from the outside security cameras.

"These guys with you?"

53

Chris clicked a few more times and the grid of sixteen changed to a split screen, larger images from two cameras. He did something else and one of the cameras zoomed in.

It showed a red pickup truck, or a vehicle that had once been a red pickup.

Now it was something else. It resembled a pickup truck the way an ankylosaurus resembled a chameleon.

Rusted steel plate was spot-welded together into a kind of pillbox inside the cargo bed, extending up to the top of the cab. Scorch marks from an acetylene torch highlighted narrow firing slots cut roughly into each side.

Strips of steel plate protected the rear tires on the sides and the back bumper, and steel boxes had been built out around the front wheels so the rusty beast could still turn. More steel plate was welded over the doors and windows and windshield with only small viewing ports to allow the driver to navigate.

Brody peered at the screen. "What the hell is that?"

"They're not with us." Peter sighed. "But we know

who they are. This won't be pretty. They're heavily armed and deeply disturbed."

"I can tell just looking at that thing." Brody sighed. "Wanda Wyatt was right about you, white boy. You are a shit magnet." He pulled a set of keys from his pocket and tossed them to Peter. "Go on, get the fuck out of here. Take the back door."

"What about you? These are the assholes with the machine gun."

Brody shook his head. "This place is a fortress. King was paranoid as hell. That front glass is inch-thick and bulletproof, the doors are reinforced steel. The bar is poured concrete on three sides. We tip that table over, the underside is laminated with three layers of Kevlar."

Eli blinked, no doubt realizing now that he'd never had a chance against somebody like King Robbie.

Chris picked up his phone. "I'll call Mad Chester and get some people here."

Brody shook his head. "Not our fight. Those folks not after us. They after these two troublemakers."

"Plus your people will just get killed," Peter said. "You're not set up for these guys. Better if we draw them out of here. Get on the highway and out of town where fewer people will get hurt."

Lewis watched Eli, standing still and silent. "The kid walks out with us. Goes his own way."

"King's people still out looking for him," Brody said. "Better he stays until Chris gets the word out."

Lewis gave Brody that hard stare. "I'm giving you notice. Anything happens to him, it's on you."

The look would have made anyone else flinch. Brody's face remained still. "No offense, brother, but who the fuck are you?"

Lewis showed Brody his teeth. "Remember that bit of business in Atlanta, couple years back? Some major entrepreneurs wound up dead? Police found garbage cans full of product, bleach dumped all over it, but no money?"

Peter glanced sideways at his friend. Would Lewis ever stop surprising him?

Brody just blinked thoughtfully. "I remember a couple of those," he said. "Miami, Houston."

"More than you know." Lewis angled his head at Peter without taking his eyes off Brody. "This motherfucker's the only reason Memphis ain't seeing the same thing right now. So I'll say it again. Anything happens to young Eli Bell, it's your head on a stick. Theirs, too."

Brody nodded. "Like I said before, I got no beef with Eli. He's under my protection now. We'll even break out the Hot Pockets and ice cream. 'Course, somebody shot out the chocolate side, so we're stuck with damn vanilla." He looked at Eli. "You okay with vanilla?"

Peter turned to Chris. "Are they still in their truck?"

"Far as I can tell. They probably can't see for shit inside that goofy thing. Might not even know they're on camera."

"Show me the rest of the screens again?"

Chris clicked back to the grid of sixteen. "Nothing else I can see out there."

"Okay. Thanks."

Peter glanced back at the screen. No movement

outside, not yet. Something was going to happen soon. They needed to get out while they still could.

He turned to Charlene. "Are we evened up, you and me?"

"You still owe me a pistol." She twirled the spikes of her hair into sharper tips. "I ain't the type to forgive and forget."

He nodded. "I know. Me neither. But aside from that."

She gave him a fluid shrug. "I'll let you know."

"Fair enough." Peter stepped carefully around her and opened the back door.

The deep rumble of the red pickup, with its rough, rusty armor, came all the way around the corner and into the room with them. He felt Lewis at his back, heard his voice cutting through the noise.

"Time to go to work, Jarhead."

Peter stepped outside, Lewis right behind him, sawed-off 10-gauge up and ready.

The steel door closed behind them.

The garbage cans stank in the hot alley.

54

In front of the Wet Spot, Peter's truck was parked at the hydrant behind the Yukon, then the Mercedes, with plenty of space between them. The red behemoth was across the street and up a few car lengths. If the Burkitts brothers planned to use the big machine gun, they'd certainly given themselves a clear line of fire at the storefront windows. Not to mention the entire line of cars.

Peter assumed they were waiting until he and Lewis came out the front door.

He crouched with Lewis at the corner of the building, still mostly hidden behind Peter's Chevy. They could see the front end of the red pickup through the gap between the vehicles.

"Can we get inside the Yukon's weapons compartment?" Peter whispered. "Something tells me we're going to need all the help we can get. Ammo especially."

Lewis nodded. "I made some electrical modifications. I can unlock remotely without flashing the lights. I'll go in through the back door on their blind side. Maybe they won't see me, maybe they will. Those thin body panels won't be much use against that 240."

Peter noticed again that the street in Lewis's voice, which was almost exaggerated inside the Wet Spot, had fallen away outside as they looked at the red truck. As usual, when his focus tightened, Lewis became very crisp and precise. He must have gone through those Atlanta drug lords like a .50 cal through tin foil.

"Get what you can," Peter said. "If they start shooting, get the hell out. I'll distract them."

"If you can get a round through one of those firing slots, it'll bounce around pretty good. Maybe do some harm."

"Sure," said Peter. "But let's not fuck around too much. This is a residential neighborhood, and these assholes have homemade pipe bombs. Better to let them chase us the hell out of Memphis before anyone else gets hurt."

Lewis gave Peter his wide, tilted grin. "A little less conversation, a little more action."

Then he slipped away like a shadow across the sidewalk. He was in good cover behind the Chevy, but exposed briefly in the brightly lit space before the Yukon. He opened the Yukon's rear passenger door and floated inside.

As Peter watched, an oblong gray lump the size of a loaf of bread with a sizzling red tail flew in a low arc over the top of the firing box.

It hit the asphalt, bounced once, and rolled toward the Yukon.

Peter felt his heart in his throat as he ran toward it, shouting, "Lewis, incoming."

55

Peter was still in motion beside his Chevy when he heard a *crump* and the heavy Yukon rose on its springs.

It didn't fly tumbling into the air, consumed with fire, like it would have with an IED made from the kind of big repurposed artillery round that the insurgents had been so fond of. Still, the big SUV gave a good hop, the rear tires just leaving the ground.

Peter felt the heat and push of the blast, but most of the force was deflected by the steel undercarriage of the Yukon and the front of his Chevy, so he kept his feet. The Chevy's front end dropped as its tires blew out.

The world had turned momentarily silent, so he didn't hear the sound of the shrapnel, but he felt it slither through the air beside him, whatever they'd packed inside that gray wrap to turn a basic pipe bomb into a true antipersonnel device. The high curb, the steel rims, and the density of the Chevy's engine compartment were the only things that had kept the shrapnel from slicing Peter's flesh into ribbons.

He didn't know if he'd been hit and he didn't care. He

was still mobile. His ears rang. He smelled gas. He pressed his boots into the concrete and leaped toward the Yukon.

Its back hatch rose, and the plywood cover for the hidden weapons compartment flew out and crashed against the Chevy's front bumper. Inside, Peter saw Lewis crouched in the cargo area, jamming pistols and spare magazines and boxed ammunition two-handed into an open leather duffel.

Peter knelt at the back of the Yukon and fired three-round covering bursts at the rust-red beast, alternating from the view ports in the cab to the firing slots in the steel pillbox on the back. His heart racketed in his chest. His rounds kept missing the gaps in the armor, the ricochets sparking orange in the night. The stink of gasoline was stronger, the punctured tank leaking nicely now. Gas pooled at the curb.

"Lewis," he shouted. "Time to move." He could barely hear the sound of his own voice. Another pipe bomb would ignite the gas for sure. He peeked over his shoulder. Lewis was still stuffing the duffel. Peter couldn't see any sign he was hurt. "Lewis, move your ass."

"Take these." Lewis tossed Peter a pair of combat shotguns and hopped out into a crouch, his 10-gauge in one hand, the duffel in the other. "I think the rear differential saved my ass." He was shouting but Peter could barely hear him, his ears still ringing.

A gun barrel poked through the pillbox's firing slot. "Go go go," Peter shouted as he shoved Lewis around the Yukon. The shooter pulled the trigger on full auto, clearly not worried about running out of ammunition.

Peter and Lewis dropped flat on the sidewalk, hoping the high curb and the chassis of the Yukon, sunken now on four flat tires, would protect them. From the sound, Peter could tell the weapon was an M16 or M4, not the big M240. He was grateful for that, even as the Yukon's glass spiderwebbed and fell, and loud high-velocity rounds turned the door panels to Swiss cheese. Peter wanted to check Lewis for injuries but now was not the time. The smell of spent powder and gasoline was intoxicating.

Lewis shook his head as he tightened his grip on the duffel. "Man, I *liked* that car."

Peter got the shotguns in one hand and the HK slung on his back, ready to travel. "Hate to break it to you, but that's not a car anymore."

There was a short pause as the resident asshole racked a fresh mag.

Without discussion, Peter and Lewis launched themselves to their feet and sprinted through the gap toward the big armored Mercedes, fresh rounds stitching the concrete at their heels as Peter hit the locks and the remote start on the fob.

"Who's driving?" He was still talking too loud.

"Why you bother asking when you already know the answer?" Lewis ducked inside, over the center hump, and into the driver's seat, towing the duffel behind him. Peter followed him in with two shotguns and his HK. He heard rounds hitting the driver's-side glass as he saw the back of Lewis's white shirtsleeve turning red. The oversized head of a roofing nail stuck out of Lewis's right tricep.

"Lewis, you're hit. Hey."

"Leave it." Lewis threw the Mercedes into gear and put the hammer down.

The heavy SUV accelerated away from the curb and down the street.

Peter turned to look behind them and saw the rust-red behemoth making a labored U-turn in the intersection, a man standing up in the armored bed. "Any bets on who's driving?"

"The older brother, the one on disability." He shook his head. "You trust that Brody? I really don't like leaving that kid back there."

"We didn't have much choice," said Peter. "I think Brody's okay, for what he is." He stared out the back window, watching the red truck finish its turn. "Here they come."

"I liked this idea better when we were on offense," said Lewis. "What's the shortest route to the damn freeway?"

56

"Left here." Peter had a map up on his phone.

"This thing has some juice." Lewis eased up on the gas to keep the red pickup behind them.

"Once you hit Watkins, head south toward Memphis proper. There'll be an on-ramp to the right. We want I-40 West, that'll put us on the big bridge over the Mississippi." Peter looked over his shoulder again. The rust-red pickup turned the corner behind them, lurching under the burden of its heavy protective steel.

"Sounds good. Lot of open space, no houses." Lewis grinned. "We need to, we can always jump over the side and swim for it."

Peter reached over and plucked the roofing nail out of Lewis's arm.

"Ow, shit. You asshole." Lewis clapped his free hand over the injury.

"That's right, honey, apply pressure," Peter said. "It'd only hurt more if we waited." He tore the sleeve from his T-shirt and tied it around Lewis's arm. "That'll have to do for now."

"Florence fucking Nightingale," Lewis muttered.

South on Watkins, the road mostly empty, Lewis flew through a green light, slowed for a red to let the rusty beast gain ground behind them, then picked up speed again. "Here," Peter said, pointing.

Lewis hit the long on-ramp that would take them through a wide sweeping curve to join the freeway. The speedometer was steady at eighty, slow enough to keep the red pickup in sight behind them, although it was gaining.

Lewis eyeballed the rearview. "So what kind of armor we got on this thing?"

Peter's platoon had spent a short period assigned to diplomatic protection, so he'd ridden in armored civilian vehicles before. Uncle Sam had favored Suburbans over Mercedes, but the technologies were the same. "Depends what King was willing to spend."

"Brody called him paranoid. So I'd imagine King bought on the higher end, given how he fortified that little ice cream shop."

"Agreed," Peter said. "So we're probably looking at high-hardened steel outside, with ballistic fabric inside the doors, under the carpet, and above the head-liner. Laminated bulletproof glass for all windows. The gas tank and underbody will be armored, too, because none of the other stuff does you much good if the vehicle won't drive."

"Tires?"

"Run-flats, probably with Kevlar protection. You get fifty miles or so once they're punctured. They feel all right? Anything off with the steering?"

Lewis swerved back and forth in the lane. The freeway merge was coming up fast. "Seems fine," he said. "The car is heavy, you can feel it, but it's not a boat."

"Well, it's not a tank, either. It's designed to let the occupants survive an initial attack, then get the hell out. The glass is the weakest point."

"We could outrun 'em, easy." Lewis glanced at the rearview again. "That's a decent newer truck, plenty of power, but it's still a pickup carrying at least a thousand pounds of steel, maybe twice that, depending on the thickness."

"I don't want to lose them."

Lewis grinned. "I know you don't. So how we gonna do this?"

The interstate was busy but fast, three lanes of traffic moving at or above the speed limit. Not surprisingly for a major freight hub, there were a lot of long-haul tractor-trailers.

They had about a mile to the next freeway merge. Peter could see the giant glass Bass Pro pyramid to their right, and the iconic curved trusses of the Hernando de Soto Bridge lit up beyond it, an elegant giant M across the Mississippi.

Lewis eased the Mercedes forward, weaving through the other vehicles, trying not to show its power or acceleration too dramatically. They'd need that to come as a surprise.

"Stay in the left two lanes, that's our route." Looking

behind them, Peter saw the red truck picking up speed in their wake, faster on the freeway than it had been cutting corners on city streets.

A man's massive head and shoulders rose up from the armored bed to crouch over the top of the cab. From a hundred yards away, Peter couldn't see what he lifted onto the roof. A long gun of some kind. Then Peter saw the figure flip down the bipod barrel support.

"That 240's coming out," he said. "Get something between us, fast."

Lewis goosed it to cut right in front of a big Peterbilt, but not before the machine gun began to fire with a heavy *thump thump thump*. They took four hard rounds to the armored tailgate and two more starred the back glass before Lewis got out of the way. The gunner was undisciplined, having fun with his toy, no surprise. Tracer rounds flew past, glowing electric pink in the half-light of the nighttime highway.

It wasn't easy to aim effectively from one fast-moving vehicle to another, especially when the target was taking evasive action, even on a good road with a rapid-fire weapon. Unlike some of the talented turret gunners Peter had known in Iraq, who'd seemed to float above their bucking Humvees like Muhammad Ali, this asshole thankfully didn't seem to have a lot of practice.

His wild rounds found targets anyway. To their left, a sedan's rear window exploded into shards and the driver slammed on the brakes. Tracers flew like angry, turbo-charged fireflies across the barrier into oncoming traffic, but the Mercedes was moving too fast for Peter to see the damage. The gunner corrected as the Peterbilt dropped back and a work van's rounded rear took on holes like an industrial-sized colander before a tire blew out and it slewed sideways, colliding with a little tin-foil hatchback.

Peter imagined the wrecks piling up behind them. Civilians, drivers and passengers, injured or dead.

Peter wasn't pulling that trigger, he was the target.

But it still felt like Peter's fault.

Then he saw holes stitched across the long silver box of the semi-trailer ahead of them, marching backward toward the armored Mercedes.

"Get us out of here," he said. "This isn't working. They're willing to kill anyone just to put a few rounds into us."

The interstate had forked for the merge, and their section narrowed to two lanes. Lewis slid to the right again, this time into the narrow breakdown lane and out of sight. The speedometer was at ninety, then ninety-five, the rumble strip howling. They flew down a long line of semis, red brake lights coming on as the other drivers noticed the headlights coming up fast on the wrong side. The freeway began the long curve toward the river.

Then the rust-armored pickup swerved into the breakdown lane behind them with a clear field of fire. The rear window starred twice more and they felt the hard impact of yet more rounds on the rear hatch. It was getting difficult to see anything out of the back.

"Shit." Lewis hit the brakes and slid left, tucking the Mercedes between two big trucks.

"Stay here," said Peter. Lewis matched speeds with

the semis. Peter put the 10-gauge on his lap and hit the button to roll down the window.

Nothing happened.

Of course, he thought. The laminated glass was too thick, and there was too much soft armor in the door panels, for the windows to go down. Obviously, there was no skylight.

So much for his attack plan. How the fuck was he going to fire back?

"Slide over half a lane, make us a little harder to see. Then grab my belt."

"Fucking jarhead." Lewis rolled his eyes, but did as Peter asked.

When he felt Lewis take hold, Peter opened his door six inches with the shotgun in his hand and waited. Wishing for a helmet or a firing port or a grenade launcher as the hot stink of the roadway washed through the car.

He remembered that Lewis's right tricep was the one that'd had the roofing nail in it.

The red truck came up fast. Peter leaned out, trusting his weight to Lewis's punctured arm, and fired at the gunner's head and shoulders still hunched above the cab. The buckshot sparked off the steel, but Peter had no idea if he'd hit anything vulnerable. The gunner dropped down behind the thick, rusty steel. Peter had time to rack the slide and fire twice more at the driver's small view port before the red truck dropped back out of sight. He'd managed to obliterate the other pickup's side mirror, but didn't think he'd done any other damage.

Still, he'd returned fire, which felt better than it had

any right to feel. And the red truck's ruined rearview would help when the time came.

Lewis went left, escaping the slowing convoy of semis. A merging highway added another lane to work with.

Peter pulled up his map again. He found something that might work. He peered out the starry but still intact rear windshield to see the red pickup coming up behind them again.

Then they were on the Hernando de Soto Bridge, the view ahead framed by the complex geometry of steel girders studded with bolts. The Mississippi River a dark void to each side.

"Coming up," he said. "Three miles."

57

Albert had the A/C cranked up high but it was still warm as hell inside the pickup.

Between all that heavy quarter-inch steel plate they'd tack-welded in place, and the speed they needed to keep up with that rich man's car, the pickup's engine was running hot. Albert could feel it cooking through the firewall.

Part of the problem was the sliding window open to the armored bed of the truck, which let the air-conditioning escape. Judah Lee used the window to shout orders, like a general from his horse.

Which made Albert what, exactly?

He leaned forward to peer through the narrow viewing slot they'd cut in the steel tacked across the windshield, watching the sleek black Mercedes SUV cut through the traffic ahead of them. Albert was keeping up with it, somehow, because of the thick traffic or the big V8 engine in the pickup. Sometimes he could even gain on it, although the pickup didn't handle how Albert would have liked at that speed. It was slow to brake with the heavy load they were carrying, and it leaned and lurched with each lane change.

Something else to make Albert sweat.

He kept thinking about the hog corral, set up back at the farm. It had seemed so simple. Borrow some money, start a business.

He'd never imagined it would come to this.

When Judah Lee opened up with that big gun, the bipod perched on the cab roof, the whole driver's compartment thumped like a drum beaten by a wild man. Albert felt his excitement at the speed turn to fear.

When Judah's stray rounds hit the wrong vehicles, shattering glass and puncturing their thin skins like so much paper, the other drivers slammed on their brakes or slewed sideways. Albert had to slip and slide like a demolition derby driver to make it through the crash course of cars too damaged to run.

He wondered for a moment, as he frantically worked the pedals and spun the wheel, if the other drivers were okay. But just for a moment.

Albert was too busy trying to survive to worry much about anyone else.

That black Mercedes didn't seem to feel a thing. Judah had hit it at least a dozen times that Albert could see, but aside from some white splash marks on the glass, the big gun hadn't seemed to make a dent. It made Albert want to catch up, to make that big expensive car hurt the way Albert was hurting now. His hip, his leg, his head.

When the big shaggy guy leaned out of his open door with that shotgun and fired three blasts from twenty feet away, Albert slammed on the brakes and just about shit himself. It took him a minute to realize that none of the pellets had made it past the steel plate or found their way through the viewing slots in the windows. The windshield and side window were still in one piece.

Then he looked out the small square left-side viewing slot and realized his side mirror was gone. He was blind on the left. And the center rearview was blocked by the high armor plate at the tailgate. And he was still going eighty miles an hour.

"I'm losing visibility," Albert called through the sliding rear window.

Judah Lee didn't seem to hear. He was laughing, long and loud. "They can't touch us, brother." He thumped on the top of the cab with his meaty fists. "Faster," he roared. "Come on, faster. Catch up and we'll take them down."

Albert wasn't sure they'd ever catch up to that fancy car. Why it wasn't already farther ahead, he had no idea.

The viewing slots were smaller than Albert had wanted. He'd known he was going to be the driver, he should have been the one to make the decision. He'd let Judah Lee's louder voice shout him down. Now it was harder to see than ever.

Only one of too many mistakes, Albert was starting to see.

That heavy armor worked both directions. What had seemed like a way to keep the family farm had become something else.

Something he was both trapped inside and part of. And responsible for.

Judah Lee's murder spree.

Sweet Jesus.

Then Judah's enormous head was at the rear window. "What the fuck're you doing? We need to catch up. Put the hammer down."

"I can't barely see." Albert had to shout over the noise of the engine and wind.

"You ain't runnin this show. Just do what you're told."

Maybe there was another way, Albert thought. He'd given up too many decisions. He'd just gone along with Judah.

But the pickup wasn't registered to Albert. Judah Lee had gotten it from somewhere, the same as that old Country Squire. If Albert could get rid of them, get both vehicles clean of any sign he'd been in them, he might keep his life. Might somehow find a way through this mess. Make some kind of amends.

He could still see forward. He could see the right rearview through the viewing port. There was no telling what his brother would do, no matter that they might all die in the doing of it.

Maybe that was all that remained of Judah Lee's plan. His own last explosion of rage, taking as many other people with him as he could.

Albert didn't want to be one of them. No, he thought, the only way out was through.

So he leaned forward to find the black car through the narrow viewing port, then stepped hard on the gas.

Ninety miles an hour on the long bridge across the river. Ninety-five as they passed the rest stop on the

Arkansas side, Albert sweating like a pig in the hot pickup. Then the Mercedes was slowing for an exit, Martin Luther King Jr. Drive into West Memphis, Arkansas.

Albert followed. Cars were bunched up at the bottom.

On the cab roof, the big machine gun began its deafening *thump thump thump* again.

The light was red at the bottom of the ramp, but the dark Mercedes swerved around the waiting vehicles and made a wide left through moving traffic, a half-dozen truckers blasting air horns loud and angry behind it. Judah's gun punched holes through cars and semi-trailers, tracers chasing the black car and catching it low on the side with glowing red splashes that faded in the bright-lit intersection.

Albert took the same path behind his quarry, using the stunned stillness of the other cars to speed his route, barely slowing as his armored fender caught the front corner of some tiny car and slammed it away.

Under the freeway, Albert saw the black car's brake lights flash, then it turned again, this time onto some kind of service road. Albert was a hundred yards back and cornered hard. Felt the top-heavy pickup lurch to the side, not quite on two wheels but close.

Through the open back window, he heard a curse and the clatter of metal sliding across the bare cargo bed. Albert glanced at the center rearview and saw Judah braced in the corner with both hands, pointed teeth bared, his skull tattoo glowing blue under the pale, unearthly glow of the streetlights.

Albert peered out the front viewing slot again.

They were in truck-stop land, with tall signs and high flat covers over lines of diesel pumps and rows of rigs parked in giant lots for an easy exit. The service road curved around in a long loop, but it was empty ahead of them.

The black car's taillights were gone.

58

Here." Peter pointed.

Lewis slung the Mercedes over a low curb to avoid a wide-turning Mayflower moving van, then coasted at speed down the wide aisle through the Wingfoot Truck Care Center, lights out, foot off the brake.

Peter turned in his seat to look behind them. The SUV was tiny compared to the rows of parked tractor-trailers, but still visible from the service road under the bright sodium lamps. He couldn't tell whether the red pickup had passed them. He didn't see any movement or headlights on their tail.

Now Lewis slipped to the right, this time around the far side of the blue-and-white steel Wingfoot service building, cutting a wide curve to shed some velocity.

"We clear?"

Peter peered through the white-spalled windows, looking behind them for the rust-red beast and not seeing it. "I don't know."

Ahead of them stood a broad row of tractor-trailers seen from the ass end, their drivers filling up at a wide bank of gas pumps under a tall sheltering canopy with LOVE'S TRAVEL STOP written across it in large letters. Beside the pumps was yet another parking area filled with heavy trucks. Lewis rolled across a yellow-striped section of pavement between the pumps and the parking area, headed toward the far exit, but stopped short beside a cinder-block structure, sheltered from the return loop of the service road.

A classic speed-trap waiting spot.

But instead of radar guns, they had the other kind.

Lewis's leather duffel sat wedged onto the transmission hump between the rear footwells. Peter reached into the bag and dug out boxes of ammunition, 10- and 12-gauge shells and rifle rounds for the HK.

"I'm gonna say fifteen seconds," said Lewis.

"One," said Peter. "Two." He set the boxes in a row on the floor behind his feet, pulled out three shells, and thumbed them into Lewis's shotgun.

As he said, "Thirteen," the red pickup roared past them down the service road.

Lewis hit the gas and the Mercedes leaped forward to the road, then slewed in behind the pickup, coming to a halt on the passenger side as it idled at the intersection. Part of a blue face peered through the burnt-edged slit in the rusty armor plate. Peter opened his door and stepped onto the blacktop, raised the shotgun into the V formed by the open door and the windshield pillar, fitted the buttstock into his shoulder, and fired.

The blue face disappeared. Peter racked the slide and fired again. He saw the marks in the steel. The red truck lurched forward and turned to the right into traffic. Peter racked the slide and fired again, this time at the driver's now-visible passenger-side viewing port. The side mirror blew forward on its mount and the pickup was away.

Peter dropped back inside, pulling his legs behind him, and Lewis had the hammer down before Peter was fully back in his seat. The acceleration closed the heavy armored door on its own. Peter saw the nose of a big FedEx semi getting larger and larger in Lewis's side window. Then Lewis was through the corner and in pursuit.

"Get him?"

"No fucking idea. But the driver's got no more side mirrors, so he's pretty much blind behind."

Ahead of them, the red pickup roared around a pair of fat sedans and across the overpass for a different highway, I-55, then blared through oncoming traffic toward the on-ramp, where it turned east. Headed back across the Mississippi toward Memphis.

The black Mercedes was right behind them.

Peter reloaded the 10-gauge.

59

The bombs started coming before they got to the river.

The highway was tight, two lanes on each side with a chest-high concrete divider between them. A hundred yards ahead, the red truck was swerving through traffic, occasionally jammed up behind a slower car until the other driver looked in the mirror and saw the rust-clad monster on its rear bumper and got out of the way as quickly as possible.

Peter had the map up on his phone again, thinking of the directions this might go, when he saw a pipe section with a sizzling red-tipped tail come over the top of the rusty pillbox, then bounce down the roadway toward them.

Lewis slid into the next lane and slowed down. The bomb took a side hop into their lane and went off with a half-round of orange-black flame maybe eight car-lengths ahead of them, followed quickly by a heavy *BOOOM*. The sound of it was deep and throaty, the roar of some-thing ancient and terrible.

They felt the pressure wave buffet the car and heard the clatter of shrapnel against the armored glass and hardened steel as they drove through the blast. The car's ventilation system carried the sulfury chemical smell of spent black powder and melted asphalt. Beside them, a white hatchback's windshield turned to spiderwebs and its driver slammed on the brakes. Peter felt sick to his stomach. No armor on a Volkswagen.

He didn't even want to think about all those big semis behind them, too heavy to slow in time. At best it would be a huge traffic jam. At worst a massacre. His fault. He should have found them sooner, gotten to their farm a day earlier, or stayed there, waiting.

Kept all this violence far away from innocent people.

The white static roared in his head.

"Step on it. We need to end this."

Lewis hit the gas and the Mercedes surged forward. Ninety, a hundred.

A blue tattooed face popped up above the rusty steel plate.

Two objects in one meaty fist, some kind of windproof lighter in the other.

Two sizzling red tips soared toward them, then danced randomly on the asphalt.

Lewis slalomed past. *BOOOM BOOOM*, the bombs blew in their wake. "How do we fight this?"

"Get closer."

At twenty yards, they could see the pointed teeth in the grinning blue face now, standing at the rear holding three pipes in one hand, thumb clicking the windproof lighter in the other. "That's definitely him," said Lewis.

"Judah Lee Burkitts. Same ugly face as that prison picture."

"Get me up there." Peter was on his knees on the seat, wishing he was right-handed. "The shotgun or the HK?"

"What, you're going to surf the roof? Don't be stupid." Lewis eased away. "We need to wait until the traffic thins out. There are too many people."

"He doesn't care about that," Peter said. "Better to stop him fast. Get me close and I'll put some rounds inside that pillbox."

Three bright tips flared, but didn't fly. Burkitts stared at the flames. The red flickering was captivating.

"He's timing the fuses." Lewis took his foot off the gas.

"Hopefully he forgets he's holding them." It was one of the odd things about war, that the pyrotechnics could be beautiful, even magnificent. It could lull you into a trance, if you weren't careful.

Then Burkitts let one bomb drop, watching with the curiosity of a child.

Lewis stood on the brakes. The bomb went off four car-lengths ahead of them, *BOOOOM*, the loudest one yet. The flame and pressure wave and shrapnel were more intense.

"Incoming." The other two bombs soared toward them in a long high arc. "Punch it."

Lewis put the pedal down again, no longer any reason to hide the speed and acceleration of the armored Mercedes. Peter heard *thump*s as the metal bounced off the

roof, then the hard double punch of the blasts right behind them. *BABOOOOM*.

Behind was better than ahead. Behind, their speed reduced the relative power of the pressure wave and the
speed of the shrapnel. Blowing ahead of them, their speed
magnified that power.

Behind, though, were other cars without armor. Cars
full of citizens who hadn't asked for this fight, or any fight.
Folks who just wanted to get home to see their kids, get
something to eat, relax in front of the TV.

They reached the long bridge over the Mississippi. Angular steel trusses, less elegant than the curves of the
M-shaped bridge, flying past overhead. A pair of rusty railroad bridges barely visible on the left. "What's coming
up?" Lewis asked.

Peter took his phone from the center console. "City
streets straight ahead or a right-lane curve to stay on the
highway."

"I'm betting on the highway." Lewis dropped back to
give them room to react.

Then they were off the bridge, traffic slowing. The
curve right was a single lane. Ahead of them, the red
pickup swerved hard into the breakdown lane and passed
the line of merging cars at eighty or better, bouncing on
the rough roadway.

Lewis followed the pickup down the curve, maintaining speed and distance. Nowhere to hide now, both of
them waiting for the next bomb. The bucketing car was
too rough for Peter to make any kind of move. He felt
the urgency for action deep in his bones, a magnetic pull.

Lewis said, "You think this car can take a direct hit?"

"Probably," said Peter, still kneeling on the seat but braced between the ceiling and the oh-shit handle. "But if we take one on the windshield, we'll be blind."

They were both glad when the curve merged into three lanes of good pavement and the pickup sped up again. Eighty, ninety. Room to move.

"Come on, get up there." Peter took up the HK and pulled the charging lever to put a round into the chamber.

"Stay in the fucking car." Lewis looked at him and kept the Mercedes well back. "If you're hanging out that door when something goes off, you're dead, either from the blast or the shrapnel. Or you just plain lose your grip and hit the road at ninety miles an hour with traffic coming up behind you. Or all of the above. Hell, if that door's open, it might get me, too."

Peter grinned, a wild heat blooming behind his eyes. "Then we better do this right."

Ahead of them, the blue head and shoulders appeared. One thick hand filled with pipes, the other hand holding the lighter. Bright red spots sizzled and flared.

Peter didn't stop to count how many.

Instead he popped open his door with his right knee on the armrest, his left knee on the seat, his right elbow over the top of the door. He balanced there in the ninety-mile-an-hour wind, strong legs holding the door open as he brought the compact assault rifle to his shoulder and fired short, steady bursts. He felt that familiar staccato punch as he watched the impact marks on the rusty steel and adjusted his aim accordingly.

God, he'd missed this. The feeling of righteous rage.

The blue head disappeared. The cluster of bombs all fell at once, the red tips spreading apart as the pipes bounced across all three lanes.

Peter fired until the magazine was empty.

Then he felt himself being hauled flailing back inside, Lewis's hand hard on his belt, their speed slamming the door against the barrel of the HK still slung around Peter's shoulder, holding the door partway ajar.

"Close that fucking door." Lewis stepped hard on the accelerator and the car leaped forward toward the sizzling red lights. Peter pushed the door slightly to free the weapon, then pulled it shut.

Five bombs went off in quick succession, *BABOOOBA-BABOOOOOOM.*

Two to each side, slightly behind them, one directly in front of them.

The nose of the speeding Mercedes floated free on the pressure wave for a fraction of a second before the heavy car dropped back down.

Their side mirrors had vanished. The Kevlar run-flats seemed to be holding. Most of the windows had gone white from shrapnel impacts. Lewis held the wheel tight with both hands.

"What the fuck's the matter with you? Do you have a fucking death wish?"

"I want to kill those assholes. Put them in the ground."

Both men were shouting.

Lewis let the car drop back until it was a quarter mile behind the red pickup, then kept it there, following the other vehicle in long sweeping arcs through thinning traffic at a hundred miles an hour.

"You didn't want to kill those gangbangers," Lewis said. "You said it yourself. You had multiple chances to kill each one of them and you didn't. Even Charlene, who'd put an ice pick through your eyeball as soon as look at you. You didn't want *me* to kill 'em, either. And I *wanted* to, bad."

While he wove the heavy Mercedes effortlessly through slower cars, Lewis looked at Peter.

"So why's this any different?"

Peter didn't know.

He was angrier than he'd been in a long time. No kind of cool tactical calm, but a hot fury, barely at the edge of his control, or maybe outside of it now. The kind of reckless, blood-boiling battle rage that came in combat. Usually after the injury or death of a friend.

Breathe in, he told himself. Breathe out. He looked through the damaged windshield at the cars slipping past like they were standing still, at the vine-covered chain-link that kept the highway from the city. Breath by breath, he brought himself back.

"When you touched that gold," Peter finally said, "you felt something. Something horrible. Nadine felt it, too. But I didn't feel anything."

Lewis gave him that small, tilted smile.

"Oh, you're feeling something," he said. "Guilty. After four hundred years of slavery, plus a hundred-fifty years of Jim Crow and lynchings and red-lining and endless fucking discrimination of all kinds, you come to darktown Memphis to do some good and you're feeling guilty."

"Yes," said Peter. The landscape flying past them now, the city lit up on both sides of the highway. Suddenly conscious of Lewis in the seat beside him. "I guess I am."

"Well, you don't have to apologize to me, Jarhead. You're not oppressing me or nothing. Shit, we're friends, right?" Lewis reached out and slapped Peter on the back of the head, and not gently. "Just don't get me killed being stupid, you dumb-ass white-bread mayonnaise-eating cracker motherfucker."

A choked laugh forced its way out of Peter. "Sorry. I just—" he said. "I want to *do* something."

"You are," Lewis said. "*We* are, we're doing *this*. Ebony and ivory, brother." He gave his long, low, bubbling chuckle. "'Course, you know ivory's illegal because elephants are endangered, right?"

"That's very inspirational."

"I'm gonna get a talk show."

Lewis stayed a steady quarter mile behind the pickup. They followed it from I-55 to the 240 bypass, then to 385. Traffic faded as they got farther outside the city.

They'd seen no new bombs for almost ten minutes.

"How the fuck are we going to do this?" asked Peter.

"Outlast 'em," said Lewis. "We wait long enough, they'll run out of gas, or their engine will overheat, or the police will show up."

"He's got to be thinking the same thing," said Peter. "He's not going to wait."

"No."

"Why haven't we seen the police? With a running gun battle and bombs on the freeway, you'd think we'd have their attention."

Lewis leaned over to peer at the night sky. "I don't see any air support," he said. "We went from Tennessee to Arkansas, then back to Tennessee on a different highway, now we're almost to Mississippi. My guess is we've outrun the cops. Anyway, it's better without them." He made a face. "Less chance of getting shot by mistake."

Ahead of them, the head and shoulders popped up again, dim in the advancing headlights. They couldn't see what Burkitts was doing until they heard the heavy *thump thump thump* and saw the electric pink tracers flying toward them.

"That goddamn 240 again," said Peter. "You had to talk about getting shot by mistake."

Lewis hit the brake and dropped back, skating from side to side, but the rounds still found them, skipping off the hood and windshield. The good road had improved the gunner's aim.

Then the tracers started skipping off the pavement.

"He's going for the tires," said Peter. "That Kevlar didn't mind the bombs, but it might not like a direct hit from one of those big rounds."

"Wish he hadn't thought of that."

"I'm glad he didn't think of it sooner. There'd be a lot more dead bodies behind us."

The tracers flew beneath them. They felt a *thunk* like running over a stone in the road and heard a polite Teutonic chime.

The car veered left. Lewis pulled it back and peered at the dash. "Low-pressure sensor. He got one. Now who's bad luck, motherfucker?"

The tracers sprayed across the roadside. Another *thunk*, a second chime, and the car stopped pulling left.

"Uh-oh," said Lewis. "Steering's gotten a little sloppy."

"That'd be the run-flats," said Peter. "Specs say fifty-mile range at fifty miles an hour before the rubber shreds completely and we're down to the composite insert, which means we'll be fucked."

"What about driving a hundred?"

"Now who's the one with a death wish?"

Lewis eased his foot off the gas and the car began to slow. Burkitts must have guessed what had happened, because he concentrated his fire on the windshield.

It was weird, seeing the tracers lodge in the glass before them, glowing like pink fireflies. Knowing how much power was behind the tip of each round.

The white-splashed sections of damaged glass spread until Lewis and Peter were leaned over at odd angles to peer through the few remaining clear sections.

There was an odd whistling noise inside the previously near-silent Mercedes.

Maybe the wind against the compromised glass.

The heavy firing stopped.

Peter heard a brief, faint clatter through that odd whistling sound.

Then something bounced hard up the hood and crashed into their windshield.

The big machine gun stuck firmly in the glass. The pistol grip had punched all the way through. Only the sticky anti-spall film on the inside of the windshield saved their faces from a thousand splintered shards.

"Shit." Lewis turned off his headlights, hit the brake hard, and eased the Mercedes down into the ditch. "You all right?"

"I'm fine. We should get out of this car. They'll want to come back and finish us off."

"At least they're out of rounds for the 240."

"Your glass is always half-full, isn't it?"

Neither of them had forgotten about the M16s.

They scooped up weapons and ammunition and slipped over the low cable barrier into a hay field, where they ran along the edge of the scrub to put some distance between them and the Mercedes.

The highway was long and straight and flat as a board. They could see headlights for miles. Hunkered down with their weapons, sweating in the evening heat, they watched and waited for the red pickup to return.

60

Albert heard Judah Lee's elbows thump into the sliding glass window between the pickup's cab and bed. "I got 'em," he crowed. "Slow up and take the next turnaround, we'll go back and get what they took. If they put it somewhere else, we'll beat that out of 'em."

Albert didn't turn to look at his brother. He was hunched forward, trying to see the dark road ahead through the narrow slot cut in the armor. Sweat streamed down his face. The air conditioner might as well be broken. The temperature gauge told him that the engine was at the edge of overheating. His right side burned, his shirt sticking to the skin in a way he didn't like to think about.

Something had made it through the slot on the passenger side. Punched through the side window and showered the cab with glass, then went through the windshield, bounced off the inside of that armor, and came back through the glass again to hit him low in the rib cage.

It ground against the bone every time he shifted on the seat.

He could use a handful of those pain pills.

He was so dang thirsty. His head was killing him.

He'd listened to the noise of those homemade bombs and that heavy gun for way too long.

He was glad he had no working rearview mirrors. He didn't want to see what carnage his brother had wrought behind them. What Albert had helped him do. What Albert had done himself. The wrecked lives strewn across a hundred miles of highway.

He felt it anyway. A permanent stain, down deep. The bloody wound in his side was nothing in comparison.

Judah reached in to rap Albert on the skull with his knuckles like knocking on a door. "I said, slow up and turn around. We won, son. Aren't you listening to me?"

"No," Albert said. "I'm done. I'm going home."

Judah pulled away from the sliding window, then came back with their daddy's old .44 revolver in his hand. Albert heard the *click* as Judah Lee cocked the pistol with his big thumb. "You ain't the boss. We got a job to finish. Do what you're told, son."

Albert felt something cool wash over him, just for a moment. "We're going dang near a hundred miles an hour," he said. "We're overweight and top-heavy with all that steel plate. You want to shoot me, fine. But when I go, this truck will roll and tumble like nothing you've ever seen, if it don't plain slam into something first. Either way, you'll be nothing but strawberry Jell-O."

"You do what I say," Judah said, then pulled the trigger and fired their daddy's .44 down into the center of the floor. The noise of it was deafening inside the small cab of the pickup.

Albert swerved hard into the next lane. Judah Lee slipped back and grabbed at the window frame with the three little fingers of his gun hand, trying to keep hold of both, but his own weight was too much for him. The force of the swerve took him sideways to bounce hard off the armored sidewall. The gun fell forward onto the passenger seat. Albert swept it onto the floor.

"Goddamn it," Judah roared. Even with his ears ringing, Albert heard the clatter of the sliding M16s and Judah's boots scrabbling for purchase on the bare metal pickup bed.

He did have a rearview mirror, Albert realized, still mounted on the windshield. Because of the high steel plate, it wouldn't let him see the road behind him. But it would let him see inside the armored cargo bed.

Albert yanked the wheel the other way. Judah flew across the cargo bed again, swearing a blue streak.

The temperature gauge was running in the red.

61

Aside from the few lights of passing cars, it was very dark. Peter couldn't see any lights from houses or farms anywhere. It began to rain. They sheltered under a wide, spreading oak, but still got soaked.

After fifteen minutes, Lewis said, "They're not coming back."

Peter nodded and patted his pockets. "We need a ride." He'd lost Wanda's phone somewhere along the way. Maybe it was still in the Mercedes, or maybe it had fallen somewhere on the highway during one of his moments of stupidity.

But he had his burner, and he knew June's number.

"Hi, honey," he said. "How's your night going?"

"I got a news alert on my phone." Her voice had an odd echo, like she was on speaker. He could hear tinny music playing behind her. She also sounded pissed. "Some asshole shooting and throwing bombs on the freeway."

"I have no idea what you're talking about," Peter said. "We just had a little car trouble. Listen, can you ask Wanda for Dupree's number? We could use a lift."

"I'll call him," she said. "Where are you?"

He read her the GPS coordinates from his phone. "Tell him to top off his gas tank. And pick up a couple of cans of starter fluid and some road flares."

But it wasn't Dupree's multicolored truck Peter saw twenty minutes later, pulling over to the side of the highway.

It was Wanda's boxy blue Toyota Land Cruiser.

With June Cassidy behind the wheel, and all the windows rolled down. Ray Charles blared from the speakers. *Hit the road, Jack, and don't you come back no more.*

He wondered if she'd picked the song deliberately.

Her freckled face glowed in the dashboard light. She looked Peter up and down, checking for injuries or maybe weak spots. "I am so gonna kick your ass."

He didn't like seeing her there. "You were supposed to stay in the hotel. You should have called Dupree."

"I was already on the road." She smiled sweetly. "Wanda's phone has a tracking app."

That explained how she'd gotten there so fast. "You're spying on me?"

"You obviously need a fucking babysitter." She turned to Lewis. "Hello, handsome."

"Hey." He leaned in to kiss her cheek. "I thought babysitting was my job."

"Dude. You obviously suck at it." She touched the bloody wrap over his roofing-nail puncture. "How bad?"

Lewis put on a plummy British accent. "A mere flesh wound."

"Your boys discovered Monty Python?"

"*The Holy Grail* and pizza every Saturday night. Best part of my week." He put his hand on her arm. "You really shouldn't be here."

"Fucking somebody had to be," she said.

"Somebody else," Peter said.

She stared right at him. "Well, I'm here now. You want me to leave?"

She was quite possibly the toughest person Peter had ever met. Sometimes that made her a colossal pain in the ass.

But she was also right, most of the time.

Peter hated it when she was both things at once.

It seemed to happen a lot with June.

Peter was starting to get used to it.

They climbed into the back seat with the guns and the wet duffel of ammunition.

Peter had wanted to drive, but June shook her head. When he reached for her door handle, she'd taken her foot off the brake and coasted forward a few feet. "Don't fuck with me, Marine."

She drove them the quarter mile to the black Mercedes, where they recovered the rest of their gear, including Wanda's phone, which had slipped between the passenger seat and the center console.

The Mercedes was not in showroom condition. It was dimpled and dented and cracked, with a large machine gun embedded in its crushed windshield.

June's lips got thin. "If I was seeing that thing in daylight, I'd *really* be pissed."

"It was a good ride," said Lewis. "Took care of us as best it could."

There was something they were carefully not talking about. The running fight on the freeway, the damage they'd caused just by being there. Collateral damage was a shitty term, designed to hide the wartime reality of civilian casualties, but Peter knew well what it meant. He felt it. There was no getting around it. The undeserving dead.

He told himself that he hadn't started it. He hadn't stolen the guns or made the bombs.

He hadn't started killing strangers on the fucking freeway.

No. Peter was just trying to clean up the mess. Even if he might have to live it again in his dreams.

He pulled the 240 free, flipped open the cover to see if the gun was clear, then checked to make sure the ammo bag was truly empty before he tossed the gun onto the front seat. He opened the rest of the car doors and sprayed the interior with the starter fluid, then stepped back, sparked the road flares, and tossed them inside. The Mercedes went up with a satisfying *whomp*.

"What is it with you and burning cars?" asked June. "I know, you're getting rid of DNA and fingerprints. But why do you have to set them on fire?"

"It's fast and easy and it works." Peter climbed back inside the Toyota. "Plus it's a good send-off for a trusty steed. Like a Viking funeral."

She shook her head. "There is something seriously wrong with you people."

"Hey." Peter leaned across the seatback and put his lips to the back of her neck. The burning car flared bright as the synthetic materials caught. "Thanks for coming. I mean it."

She shivered and twined her fingers in his hair. "I'm still fucking pissed."

"I know," he said. "It didn't seem like we had a choice."

"Clock's ticking," said Lewis. "We're twenty minutes out. If you lovebirds want to get naked back here, I can drive. But I'm gonna have to turn up the music real loud."

"Really, Lewis," June said. "Have you no sense of decency?" She grinned at Peter in the rearview. "I'm going to need a helluva lot more than twenty minutes."

She threw the Toyota into gear and hit the gas.

62

June pulled into the church parking lot, a half mile from the slaughterhouse. It was well after midnight. They were less than an hour behind the Burkitts brothers.

Peter and Lewis still hadn't taken off their armored vests. The blacktop radiated the heat of the day. Peter could feel it through the soles of his boots. They drank the water June had brought and double-checked their equipment while she watched from the driver's seat of the Toyota.

"Don't wait here," Peter told her. "Turn back and park behind that Citgo we passed a few miles back. Stay out of sight from the road, they probably know what this car looks like. We'll call or we'll meet you there."

"Is this what it's always going to be like, with you? Me just waiting to see if you come home? Wondering what kind of shape you'll be in when you get there?"

"That's what it is right now," Peter said. "Unless you want us to leave those guys out there to make more bombs and work out their next move."

"No," she said. "I just don't like waiting. Or worrying."

"Me neither." He leaned in, gently brushed his lips against hers, then stood and thumped the roof of the car with the flat of his hand. "Go on. I'll see you soon."

She nodded and faced forward and drove away.

Flanked by dense scrub forest, they trotted wordlessly down the road, Peter on one side, Lewis on the other. Their boots scuffed softly on the rough asphalt, their gear locked down and quiet. Clouds thick and low. Not a light to be seen.

The vests were heavy, loaded with spare magazines for their weapons. Despite that weight, despite pistols strapped to their sides and long guns held one-handed and balanced, the two men ran easily, as if they could run forever. The way marauding night-fighters had run for millennia, with bone clubs or fire-hardened spears or long swords or flintlocks or Kalashnikovs in the vast and varied wastes of the world. Peter knew what he'd been training for all winter in the little teardrop-shaped valley. To be right here, right now, with Lewis.

To be of use. To attack and defend. To do whatever needed to be done.

Regardless of the cost.

The road turned to gravel as the trees fell away and the land opened up. It was different on foot, at night, than it had been in the car that afternoon. The wind rose, warm and thick and carrying the smell of wet soil and wild, verdant things. As they ran, the night felt measureless around them, immense beyond any reckoning.

The steel-sided slaughterhouse stood dark, the gravel lot empty of cars. Past it, the long driveway disappeared into the ancient woods.

Lewis sniffed. "You smell that?"

Peter nodded. Something was burning, or had burned. Something vaguely chemical.

They slowed as they climbed the long dirt track into the trees, long guns now held at port arms, unsure of what they'd find. Of what might find them.

They came to a walk while they were still in the deeper shadows of the ancient forest, but they could see the clearing of the farmyard ahead. The house and the newer barn were dark and still, but the chemical smell was stronger. Overheated transmission fluid, Peter thought. Maybe some melted rubber, and something else. Something burnt. Maybe just the sulfur smell of all that black powder, released by the evening's rain.

On the far side of the yard, a faint light seeped uphill from the drop toward the old leaning barn with the moss-eaten roof where the Country Squire wagon had been hidden. Where the bombs had been made and tested against the wood of the giant stump.

Peter stepped forward, his rifle up and ready. He felt something bubble up in him, rising like bile. The burning need to do some damage, to ruin something beyond repair, to set the whole goddamned farmstead on fire. As if the rage in this place was contagious.

Lewis held up a fist. Peter froze. Lewis stepped closer.

"Do me a favor," Lewis said softly. "Don't kill anybody if you can help it."

Peter looked at his friend, nearly invisible in the darkness. "Are you fucking serious?"

"Hey, if you can ask me not to kill some gangsters, I can ask you not to kill these assholes."

"Not even the guy who's filed his teeth to a point? Who murdered seven people in prison? And God knows how many more on the road today?"

Lewis raised a shoulder. "Maybe him you can kill. But the brother, the one on disability, we wait and see."

At the bottom of the hill, the hulking pickup with its improvised armor stood silent at the edge of the field like something prehistoric. Its headlights shone on the round wire-fence enclosure they'd seen earlier. Now it was filled with low shapes that flowed in darkness and light in endless circles around the perimeter of their corral.

Two men stood illuminated there. A short man with thick shoulders and arms, but with a sideways tilt to his posture and one leg gone too thin. He held his elbow tight to one side and a pistol in his hand, pointed at the other man, a giant. Broad and tall and powerful, with the overmuscled build of a gym rat.

The two men were talking.

Peter and Lewis slipped silently closer.

63

Albert could tell that Judah Lee had hit something important when he fired their daddy's old .44 into the floor. Likely some part of the automatic transmission.

Not only was the pickup running way too hot, with smoke starting to seep from under the hood, it had stopped shifting right. Albert could smell the tranny fluid overheating. All the weight of that heavy steel plate wasn't helping.

They were down to twenty miles an hour.

Soon enough they might have to get out and push. Or just start walking.

Albert's side still hurt. Nowhere near as bad as having a tractor roll on him, break his leg, and crack his pelvis, but it didn't feel good. That big double-aught shotgun pellet ground against bone with every bump in the road. He thought about what it would cost him to see a doctor. Surgery? That was money he plain didn't have.

This is where he'd found himself. Where Judah Lee had put him. Making plans to drop his sharpest knife in boiling water, swallow a few gulps of their daddy's high-test, and take the pellet out himself. Now there was a fun idea.

He wasn't going to let Judah Lee near him with a pointy stick, let alone a knife.

Turning off 72, Albert looked again at his brother in the rearview. He kept waiting for Judah Lee to pick up one of those stolen M16s and blow Albert's brains out, or come through the sliding window and twist Albert's head off his neck.

Instead, Judah Lee just sat braced into the far corner of the cargo bed, biding his time. Probably thinking that Albert could fix what was wrong with the pickup. Albert still had his uses.

They labored up the long dark driveway into the farmyard. Instead of stopping at the house, Albert let the truck coast down the hill to the old barn, where he'd set up the hog trap at the edge of the south field. Rolling up to it, he could see them in the headlights, eight or ten feral hogs roiling around inside the wire corral. Meat on the hoof.

Albert was used to working hurt.

Killing feral hogs was the least of his chores, now.

Those pigs might get a reprieve yet.

It all hung on what was gonna happen between him and Judah Lee.

He parked the truck and turned off the engine and slid out of the driver's seat with their daddy's old .44 revolver in his hand. He moved as fast as he could, but he hadn't been anywhere near fast since the accident, let alone when every motion made his blood-wet shirt pull where it was stuck to the mangled flesh over his ribs.

Albert clenched his jaw when his feet hit the ground, thinking again that a few pain pills would go down real good right now.

Soon enough, he thought. Or never again.

By the time Albert straightened up, Judah Lee had jumped over the high side of the pickup and landed easily, like Albert hadn't bounced him off the armor a half-dozen times an hour before.

Judah's hands were empty.

Albert pointed their daddy's .44 at him. "What the heck am I gonna do with you, Judah Lee?"

"You don't look so good, brother. Let me help."

"I've seen your help." Albert's side throbbed. His head hurt. "I don't want it."

"I'm family." Judah Lee smiled. "You want help, I'm all you got."

Judah's teeth, filed to points, had turned black at the roots. His breath smelled like rot. The blue skull tattoo seemed to float in front of his face, like it wasn't a tattoo at all, Albert thought, but some kind of apparition. Or manifestation.

Judah Lee kept talking, his voice a velvet purr in the warm, liquid night. "You want to save this farm, don't you? I'm your only way out of this mess you've made. But you and me, working together?" The pointed smile grew wider. "Just imagine what we can do. Carruthers won't live forever. Somebody's gotta step up to take his place."

The trapped hogs ran in frantic grunting circles

around the corral, tusks gleaming bright in the head-lights. Albert wanted to look to see how many there were, how big they might be. But he couldn't take his eyes off Judah Lee.

"What do you want to do, Albert? Run this farm? Buy more acreage? You follow my lead, we can make that happen."

Judah's voice rose and fell with a preacher's cadence.

"You used to build cars, but what about restoring old ones? We'll set you up with a shop, brand-new tools. You can rebuild those old beauties folks used to drive when we were kids. You know how many broken-down cars Car-ruthers has laying around at his place, just rusting away, waiting to get back on the road?"

Albert hadn't gone to church in years, but he remem-bered the stories. How the Devil would promise you anything you wanted. All he'd ask in return was your immortal soul, given of your own free will.

Albert was afraid his soul was already long gone.

Judah's voice was mesmerizing. "First thing we do, though, before any of that, is go back to town and find what those people took out from under that house. Our ancestor's house. Take back what was ours."

Then another voice came out of the darkness. Strong and low in the humid night air.

"Why do you think anything in that house was ever yours to take?"

64

Peter held his rifle on the big man with the blue skull tattoo, who bared his pointed teeth like he wanted to take a bite out of somebody.

Lewis kept talking, his voice calm but carrying. "Whatever might have been in that house, once upon a time, it was earned on the backs of those men and women and children whose lives were stolen from them. Human beings bought and sold, beaten and raped, worked to death. For four hundred years. For profit. So you boys have no claim to lay. You're stuck with the mess you've made."

Lewis gave them his tilted smile, the 10-gauge up and comfortable at his shoulder, as if he could stand there all day making conversation. Totally in command.

The shorter man with the pistol blinked, like he was coming out of a trance.

"Put down the gun," Lewis said, not unkindly. The shorter man—who must have been the older brother, Albert—opened his hand and the gun fell. The side of his shirt was dark with blood. "Kick it away. Go on now." Albert scuffed with his bad leg and the pistol slid a few feet.

Peter kept his eye on the monster. "That knife clipped to your pocket," he said. "Toss it."

Judah Lee flipped the folding knife away, sneering at Peter. "So you're the race traitor. The nigger lover. Hiding behind a gun."

In the wire-fence corral, feral hogs raced grunting in frantic circles, bright in the headlights then dark in the shadows. Churning up the ground with their hooves, rooting at the fence with their snouts and tusks.

The white static rose up Peter's brainstem, all sparks and lightning. Anger and frustration, trying to get out. He glanced sideways at Lewis. "You sure you don't want this one?"

Lewis shook his head. "I don't want any part of it. He's all yours."

"Okay." Peter held out the rifle and Lewis slung it over his own shoulder. Peter loosened the straps on his armored vest, pulled it over his head, and dropped it on the hot hood of the red pickup. He slipped off the leg holster and pistol and tossed them away into the night.

Without their weight, he felt light. Almost as if he were floating.

Almost.

"I don't have a gun now," he said. "I'm definitely not hiding."

Judah Lee straightened up and stared at him.

Peter tasted copper in his mouth and felt the familiar lift of adrenaline.

Knowing the man was six feet seven was one thing, but to see him standing there with his hands balled into fists, his teeth filed into points, his face tattooed into a blue skull?

That was something else.

Judah Lee smiled wider. He enjoyed the intimidation. It gave him pleasure, that feeling of power that came even before the beating or killing.

Peter had fought big men before. Big men without real training were no harder to beat than normal men. Often, they were easier, because most big men didn't really know how to fight. They were used to their size doing all the work for them. A single punch, with that much weight and power behind it, could end a conflict very quickly, so most big men rarely had to fight at all. They were used to other people backing off before the fight even got started.

But Judah Lee Burkitts had fought in prison and won, again and again. Peter could see by the loose way he stood, feet apart, knees bent slightly, weight forward on his toes, that he'd had a lot of practice.

And he liked it.

Peter didn't much mind, either.

The white static sang its song of rage and destruction.

Sometimes a Marine needs a good fight to set free his demons.

Judah Lee looked a little banged-up, but he didn't move like a man who was hurt. One moment he was standing, ready, and the next he came in way faster than Peter had expected, with a long hard left that Peter deflected with his right forearm as he slipped away.

His forearm went numb, like he'd been hit with a piece of cordwood.

Peter backpedaled and they circled in the red pickup's headlights, feinting, trading and blocking blows, taking each other's measure. He couldn't let the big man get close, or that would end it.

Judah was fast, but Peter was faster.

Peter's arms were long, but Judah's were longer.

Peter was in better shape, but all the cardio in the world wouldn't help if Peter got smashed in the face by a fist the size of a cantaloupe. And this fight wouldn't last long.

It would end fast and ugly, when Judah knocked Peter down, then stomped him into the dirt. Or when Peter landed a punch to the big man's throat, strangling him on his own crushed trachea.

Or any of a hundred other ways that Peter wasn't thinking about on any conscious level.

He wasn't going to win going toe to toe, that's for sure.

He'd known that going in.

The other man was just too big, too mean.

Peter would have to come up with something else.

Judah led with his left again and Peter pushed it away with his dead forearm, then spun inside, snapping the hard outer edge of his right elbow into the big man's temple.

It should have been more than enough to put anyone down, no matter their size, but Judah just shook his head and bared his teeth and, before Peter could get fully clear again, Judah threw out his right hand and got hold of Peter's T-shirt and reeled him back in for a heavy left to the stomach.

Peter's ribs might have cracked or broken at that moment, which could have made the next blow a killing one, but he took most of it on his arm as he rolled away from the punch, lessening the impact as he danced sideways again, making Judah pivot on his toes, chasing him without an angle.

Still, Peter's side and arm hurt like hell, and the big man had kept hold of his T-shirt. He smelled like rot and fermented sweat. The punches kept coming, to the stomach and lower back. They were glancing blows, but they kept landing. Peter would be sore as hell tomorrow.

If he lived that long.

He reversed again, using the pivot and the full force of the muscles of his leg and back and shoulder and arm to drive his left fist toward the big man's vulnerable neck.

Judah dropped his chin out of some animal instinct. Peter's bare knuckles hit hard bone instead. A bright burst of pain exploded in his hand.

Judah blinked and Peter knew the big man had felt something, because he loosened his grip on Peter's T-shirt.

Peter tore free and kicked the big man in the side of the knee on his way out, hoping to slow him down a little and keep some space between them.

They circled again, Peter's feet in a loose, easy shuffle, watching Judah's eyes and thinking without thinking.

His right forearm had lost feeling, his left hand throbbed with pain. Something broken in there, and pretty much useless as a weapon. It shouldn't have lasted this long. If Judah got too close again and started pounding him, Lewis wouldn't be able to step in without risking Peter, without risking everything.

If Judah disabled Peter badly, he was plenty strong enough to catch him up and use him as a shield. He'd rush Lewis, who might have to shoot Peter to kill Judah.

Peter still had his legs, two good elbows, both knees, and his feet. He let the white static rise higher and kept moving.

After all their circling, the wire fence of the corral was behind Peter now. The feral hogs had gone almost still, waiting like an audience before the curtain went up. He could smell the stink of their shit, the swamp mud caked on their bristles.

Judah Lee limped toward him. He was hurt, but not badly enough. The knee held his weight.

"Peter," Lewis said.

Peter barely heard him.

The world had narrowed down.

Just Peter and Judah and the hogs in the trap behind him.

He was letting Judah define the terms of the fight. It was not a winning strategy. He needed something big to hit the man with. He shouldn't have put down his weapon. The man was too big, too strong.

Peter started to feel afraid.

He let Judah Lee see it.

He kept his right elbow down, protecting his ribs. His weak spot.

He circled right, as if in a panic, but Judah countered, barely slowed by the kicked knee, keeping Peter by the fence. Peter went left, and Judah countered again, maneuvering Peter into place.

Backing him against the hog fence where the hogs gathered expectantly.

Where Judah could hold him against the strong, flexible wire and pound him until Peter was broken badly enough to fall. Then Judah would pick him up and throw him at Lewis, and use his boots on both of them until they were dead. It wouldn't take long.

"Peter," Lewis said again.

Peter ignored him.

Instead, he watched the big man's eyes, the blue skull tattoo, the sharpened teeth, and allowed himself to feel his fear.

Allowed the panic and dread to blossom and grow like a poison flower.

He knew the big man saw it. Could almost taste it. Ten feet away, he leaned forward and licked his lips.

The white static rose up higher, taking over. Fight or flight. The adrenaline surged in his blood.

Judah Lee launched himself toward Peter in an inevitable, overpowering rush.

Peter didn't allow himself to smile.

Instead he planted his boots in the fertile Mississippi soil and bent his knees.

His legs were strong from carrying that heavy pack up and down mountains, and around the steep walls of June's little pocket valley. His arms and chest and back were powerful from working on the valley's buildings and fields and gardens and trails. He could see that little valley somewhere faintly behind his eyes, the teardrop shape of it, the high waterfall at the head and the calm river wandering down through the center.

Judah Lee rushed in, committed, at full speed. Peter dipped his head. Bent his knees, down, down. The two bodies met, but not how Judah had planned.

Peter wrapped his arms around the bigger man's legs and lifted him smoothly into the air.

Used the man's own power and momentum.

Threw him clear over Peter's back, over the wire fence, and into the corral.

Which seemed to be the event the feral hogs had been waiting for.

They bore the big man down under their combined weight, ten animals, many generations undomesticated, with a ferocious, ever-hungry cunning behind their porky little eyes. It was a family group. Two big males with sharp, upcurved tusks, four slightly smaller females with equally sharp teeth, and four juveniles that the adults would defend with their lives.

The first boar's initial pass tore up the length of Judah Lee's right leg, slipping under the skin like a seam ripper through a badly sewn garment. The second boar came along his left side, opening Judah from the ribs to the armpit.

The mud turned red under the truck headlights.

Judah Lee fought to his feet, his tattooed face a rigid blue mask.

A sow slammed into him from behind, knocking him forward into a fence post, which leaned outward with the impact. He got his hand on the wire and his good leg under him and levered himself back up. The fence bent under his weight.

Albert limped forward, scooped up the black revolver, and shot his brother twice in the chest. Judah Lee dropped into the mud.

After that, things got very ugly inside the fence.

Albert stood and watched, muscles standing out in his jaw, pistol hanging down, until Peter stepped up and took it from his hand.

Peter searched the man's face. "Why on earth did you two start this thing?"

Albert just dropped his eyes to the ground.

65

The next day, Peter stood in front of the vacant house with Detective Gantry and Officer McCarter.

The detective had a hand on his holstered pistol.

The uniformed officer twirled a set of handcuffs on one finger.

"This investigation is going to be a giant shit-storm," Gantry said. "That running fight took place across three states and on federal highways. Nine people dead, three more in critical condition, more than forty injured. The FBI is involved. They're not pulling any punches."

Peter nodded, remembering the pipe bombs and the machine-gun fire. Not what had hit the Mercedes, but what had missed. Innocent bystanders hurt or killed.

He hadn't lit those fuses or pulled the trigger of that big 240 Bravo, but he couldn't help but feel the weight of those lives. When he closed his eyes, he could see the brief burst of flame and feel the blast wave as a bomb went off. He wondered now, as he had many times before, if there had been another way to get the job done. A cleaner way. He'd never know.

Collateral damage, my ass.

Gantry and McCarter watched him closely.

Peter took a deep breath, then let it out. Kept his eyes wide open.

"I wish it'd happened differently, too," he said. "I have to live with my part of it. You guys do what you have to do."

Gantry and McCarter exchanged glances. McCarter twirled his handcuffs. Gantry gave a small nod.

McCarter said, "We did locate the armored Mercedes SUV that appears to have been involved in the incident. It was set on fire, so there's no physical evidence. The vehicle is registered to a shell company out of Delaware. Local sources, however, link the Mercedes to a man named Robert Kingston, also known as King Robbie, a high-level figure in Memphis crime circles. We're looking for him now."

Peter blinked.

Gantry took up the story. "We also have the red truck that was modified into an improvised assault vehicle, as well as what we believe to be the, ah, remains of Judah Lee Burkitts, who has a history of race-related violence and connections to the white-power movement. That truck was last registered to a man named Carruthers, who was Judah Lee's mentor in prison."

"What about the brother," asked Peter. "Albert Burkitts?"

Gantry shook his head. "I can't say anything about the brother, that's all confidential. For example, his apparent remorse. Or that he's agreed to go to Parchman Farm as a confidential informant on a purely voluntary basis. He'll do life either way. But I can't say anything about that."

"We do have reports of another man's involvement." McCarter twirled the handcuffs a bit more vigorously.

"Thing is, there's a problem," said Gantry. "My superiors ordered me to focus my attention on the jewelry store robbery. I never got the other man's vehicle plate, or saw his driver's license. Technically, I have no idea who the fuck he is." He shrugged. "I don't think I can even give a physical description."

McCarter flipped his cuffs into the air, then caught them and folded them into their leather holster on his belt. "And I never met the man, so I can't say."

Gantry opened the driver's door to his unmarked cruiser. "To be honest, some of us are feeling lucky it wasn't a whole lot worse."

Inside the empty, Nadine and Wanda and June laid out Coyo's body on planks and sawhorses. The slender form was much smaller in death than it had been in life.

They washed the body, then laid it out on a linen sheet and dressed it as if for church, in a crisp white shirt and a new black suit they'd bought in the boys' department at Dillard's. The tie and pocket square were rich purple silk.

In the backyard, side by side, shirtless and sweating under the hot sun, Eli and Lewis dug the grave.

Two shovels. Six feet down, with square, straight sides.

Sometimes they talked, and sometimes they didn't.

When Peter joined the group, the six of them lifted the linen sheet and arranged the finely attired form into the simple pine box that Dupree and Romeo had made. Nadine folded the sheet into a shroud. Peter hammered down the lid. Then the group raised the box to their shoulders, carried it outside, and lowered it gently into the ground.

"He was my best friend." Eli stood at the edge of the hole. Skinny, but not a kid, not really. He'd never been allowed to be a kid. "Rest in peace, I guess."

Taking turns with the shovels, they filled in the grave.

Afterward, everybody went back to The Peabody hotel to wash and change their clothes.

Then they drove to the Lucky Lounge.

Eli stood out back with a cold Coke, waiting for the seats to fill. Dressed in new clothes, he listened to the music of the breeze in the tall grass as Wanda talked with Nadine and Dupree and Romeo about the idea of a tour.

"I was thinking a few small clubs at first." Wanda swirled the Dr Pepper in her glass. She wore her camera bag slung over her shoulder. "Just to see how it goes. I can borrow a van for a few weeks, and Lewis says he knows somebody who can put it together." She looked at Nadine, the worry plain on her face. "You'll come, too, right? If I promise to take more pictures of the living?"

Nadine wore her waitress uniform and her thin black gloves. She brushed her gaze across Eli in a way that was anything but casual. "I suppose," she said. "If I'm invited."

Eli felt the tingle of electric fingers down his spine.

Peter and Lewis and June stood drinking bottles of Ghost River Gold, watching Wanda.

"Thirty-nine thousand dollars." Lewis shook his head. "That's all Albert needed to keep his family farm. This whole thing was about thirty-nine thousand dollars."

"It was about a lot more than that," Peter said. "Did Wanda get her images sent?"

June nodded. "The gallery owner is pretty enthusiastic. Did she ever tell you what happened to her?"

"No," Peter said. "Looks like she's been talking with Nadine, though."

"That young girl?" June looked skeptical.

Lewis said, "She's older than she looks."

Peter thought again about how it had felt when she'd traced her finger across the lines on his palm. Like someone had shaken the cobwebs from his soul.

"What about the gold?" June said quietly.

"Wanda wanted to throw it in the river," said Lewis. "I told her it might be better to put that blood money to use. Give to a community foundation, something."

June turned to Peter. "Have you gotten any closer to figuring out what the fuck you're going to be when you grow up?"

Lewis examined the level of beer in his bottle, then strolled away toward the club.

Peter scratched his chin. "You were the one who sent me to help Wanda, remember? Because I was making you crazy?"

She gave him a sour look. "Now is not the time to woo me with your fucking logic."

"Tell you what," Peter said. "Let me drive you home and we'll talk about it. Take the long way, do a little camping. See if you can stand me for a week."

She looked off into the grass. "What if I can't?"

His stomach twitched and trembled. He thought about the flames blooming when he closed his eyes.

"Then I'll go away for a while. Come back when you're ready. If you'll have me."

"Until some other poor fuck gets in trouble. Then you'll be gone again." She sighed. "I guess you're not going to just start living some kind of normal life."

Peter had known that fact since first contact with the enemy. He was irrevocably changed. The things he'd done, and ordered done, and been ordered to do.

He would never truly fit the modern world again. If he ever had.

"Normal is overrated." He bumped her hip with his. "I never thought you were looking for normal, anyway."

"Seriously," she said, pushing him away. "You can't help yourself. You actually like getting yourself into trouble. You search it out."

He gave her one of Lewis's elaborate shrugs. "Keeps life zesty," he said. "You know I like to be useful. Besides, trouble is how we met. It's romantic, don't you think?"

She rolled her eyes. "You are a real fucking piece of work, you know that?"

"But in a good way," he said. "Right?"

Her mouth twitched, just a little, in what might have been a smile. "We'll see about that."

Eli heard the back door of the Lucky open. He turned to see Saint James leaning out.

"Place is packed to standing. Y'all about ready to get started?"

Eli drained his Coke and caught Nadine's eye.

"Ready when you are."

Author's Note

A few years back, I tried to write a book about Detroit. For various reasons, that book never took off, and I found myself writing about cannabis in Colorado instead. I loved writing *Light It Up*, and I'm very proud of it, but the reasons I wanted to write about Detroit—race, class, and inequality—never went away. *Tear It Down* is, I hope, a better version of what that book might have been.

On the subject of armored cars: please don't try this at home. The Mercedes took a greater beating than any such car would endure, but I hope it made the story more exciting. And please please please don't armor your own hooptie with an eye to shooting up (or blowing up) the town. It never ends well for the guy with the grudge.

As always, I've tried to be faithful to the reality of this book's setting, but I've played a bit with geography and history as needed to suit the story. Remember, this is fiction, y'all.

Acknowledgments

It's important to note that no book is created by its author alone. Many people helped usher this novel into the world in ways both large and small, and I am grateful to all who helped.

First and foremost, thanks are due to Margret and Duncan, who continue to put up with having an unbalanced writer wandering the premises, along with my parents, my brother and sister, and my extended family for their help and support over many years. I love you all more than I can ever adequately express.

Thanks again and always to the members of our armed forces, both veterans and active-duty, who have shared their lives and stories in person or online. As I've noted before, I'm not a veteran myself, and the Peter Ash books are much better for those conversations. If you have a comment or complaint or a story to tell, please find me on social media—see my website, NickPetrie .com, for links.

Thanks also to Danny Gardner for generously reading this book in draft form, preventing me from being an accidental asshole. His help made *Tear It Down* a better novel, and me a better writer. If you haven't read Danny's work, you're missing out on a great storyteller with a unique voice. Any remaining asshole moments are mine alone.

Thanks to Lynsey Addario, a brilliant photographer, whose thoughtful and beautiful memoir, *It's What I Do: A Photographer's Life of Love and War*, provided some of the inspiration for Wanda's character.

Thanks to Sudhir Venkatesh, whose book *Gang Leader for a Day: A Rogue Sociologist Takes to the Streets* provides an entertaining, insightful, and eye-opening view of the daily lives of low-echelon drug dealers. For anyone interested in this topic, it's worth a read.

Thanks to all those who write so bravely and so well about their experiences of war and its aftermath—far too many to list here—who, along with my favorite novelists, continue to teach me how to write. Thanks to the musicians who have given me so much joy and inspiration over the years, and distracted my internal critic so I can put new words on the page while tapping my toes.

Thanks to my friend and neighbor, Dwayne Fulmer of the DEA, for his help with background information on drug transport and criminal databases. Any errors or cheats are mine, not his. Thanks to Dave Kornreich, D.O., orthopedic surgeon and literary consultant—I snuck up on him at a party and he responded with great generosity. Thanks to my dentist, Dr. Stephanie Murphy, D.D.S., for our conversation about radical tooth modification and its consequences. Thanks to Donna at Reed's

Jewelers at the Wolfchase Galleria for the lowdown. Although they have some superficial similarities, my fictional jewelry store is definitely not Reed's Jewelers. (This is not meant to be an exhaustive list—many, many writers and experts have kindly answered my endless dumb questions. You know who you are.)

The dump truck crash was inspired by an article that appeared in *The Journal of Light Construction* many years ago.

Thanks again (and again!) to Jon and Ruth Jordan and the rest of the Crimespree cats for introducing me to the tribe, for their friendship and support, and for general hilarity with coffee and booze and good grub. Thanks to George Easter at *Deadly Pleasures Mystery* magazine and to Mystery Mike Bursaw for being excellent human beings. Thanks to everyone at International Thriller Writers, the Mystery Writers of America, the International Association of Crime Writers, and the Bouchercon crowd for welcoming me with open arms to the permanent floating house party of outstanding conversation.

Repeated and ongoing shouts of gratitude to my agent, Barbara Poelle; my editor, Sara Minnich; and the rest of the Putnam crew who put me out in the world and get me on the bookshelves, including but not limited to Ivan Held, Katie Grinch, Alexis Welby, Ashley McClay, Emily Ollis, Christine Ball, and everyone else on the incredible marketing team and sales force at Putnam—what a crew of smart, talented folks! Thanks also to Steve Meditz, Nancy Resnick, and Kylie Byrd for making this book both beautiful and readable.

I would be remiss if I neglected to mention the many independent booksellers who have put my books in readers' hands. Independent booksellers are the heart and soul of the book business, working long hours because they believe in the power of the printed word. Independent bookstores are on the rise for a reason—they know books like nobody else, and their booksellers turn me on to new authors with each visit. Book people are truly the best people.

These awesome indies are far too many to name individually, with the marked exception of Barbara Peters at The Poisoned Pen in Scottsdale and Daniel Goldin at Boswell Books in Milwaukee, who have been amazingly generous with their boundless energy and exhaustive knowledge. These two will forever define their own categories.

Last but not least, always and forever, thanks to all you readers out there. Without you, I'd just be another lunatic talking to himself.

TURN THE PAGE FOR AN EXCERPT

Peter Ash has no intention of getting on an airplane—until a grieving woman reveals her grandson has been taken to Iceland by his potentially murderous father. When he arrives, Peter is met at the airport by the United States embassy, and it seems Peter's own government doesn't want him there. From a rust-bound fishing vessel to a remote farm a stone's throw from the arctic, Peter must confront his growing PTSD and a powerful snowstorm to save an eight-year-old boy and keep himself out of prison—or a cold Icelandic grave.

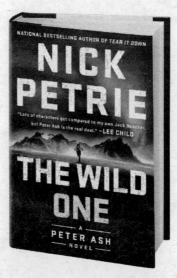

1

Somewhere over Greenland

Peter Ash woke, gasping for breath, from a dream of gunfire. He could still feel the desert heat on his skin, and the smell of spent powder lingered in his nose.

Beside him, his elderly seatmate strained upward, one finger stabbing the call button overhead.

Peter blinked away the nightmare, wondering what he'd said or done in his sleep. He was a tall, bony man with shaggy black hair, a tired face, and the thoughtful eyes of a werewolf five minutes before the change. His green hiking pants were frayed at the seams, his Counterbalance Brewing T-shirt ghosted with old stains.

A beefy male flight attendant advanced up the aisle, broad face expressionless, hands open and ready. Watching him approach, Peter could tell the man had some physical training, and was probably tasked with controlling unruly passengers on this packed transatlantic flight.

Peter raised a hand and caught the other man's eye. "Sorry." It was hard to get the words out, his throat choked with the panic raised by the memories still burned into his brain. His T-shirt was damp with sweat and his mouth was dry as a dust storm. "Just a bad dream. Give me a minute, I'll be fine."

He bent to his bag stuffed under the seat and fumbled the flap as he dug for his pills. His seatmate had shrunk himself against the window, minimizing any contact. Passengers across the aisle were looking anywhere but at him.

"Sir." The flight attendant was almost on him. Peter's shoulders and chest were tight, the cabin of the wide-body jet closing in hard. His fingers closed on the prescription bottle and he straightened up.

"I'm alright." He tried hard to believe it. "I just need my meds."

He fumbled the top off and shook four of the small pink circles into his hand. Then he found the last intact mini-bottle of Reyka vodka in his seat pocket, twisted it open, and swallowed hard, pushing the pills down.

The dreams were new.

He'd come back from Iraq with claustrophobia bad enough to make living outside seem like a good idea. He'd slept alone under the stars or under a rain fly, high above the tree line of one mountain range or another, for more than a year, barely able to manage resupply in small-town grocery stores.

The post-traumatic stress came from kicking in doors in Fallujah, he figured. All those weeks of fighting house to house, room to room, clearing insurgents one doorway at a time.

Along with everything else he'd done.

He called it the white static, that feeling of electric overdrive that sparked up his brainstem, calculating firing angles, searching for exits. Nerves jangling like bare electrodes under the skin, his chest so tight he couldn't breathe, his fight-or-flight reflex gone into overdrive. When he first mustered out, he only had about twenty minutes inside before the static turned into a full-blown panic attack.

In the time since then, he'd made forward progress. He'd made friends with the static, in a way, and a start at a new life. He'd found a veteran's group. He'd met a woman he didn't deserve, a woman named June Cassidy.

But he'd never had dreams, not like this. Not until after Memphis.

Something had gotten knocked loose in him there. Something he'd thought he'd had under control. Now it was roaming around in his head, knocking pictures off the walls, breaking the goddamn furniture.

In retrospect, this plane trip was a bad idea. He'd been in a hurry, had booked his tickets for next-day travel. Seats were limited and the schedule was brutal. He'd started in Portland, Oregon, changed planes and airlines in Minneapolis, then done it again in New York.

Long hours spent in the stale fluorescent clatter of airports, with televisions blaring CNN and some Senate hearing at every turn.

More long hours with his oversized frame jammed into undersized seats, trapped in a cigar tube at thirty-five thousand feet.

His only exercise was pacing the aisles, his only sleep

a few fitful naps. He'd hoped the Valium would help keep the white static at bay, but he'd been stuck inside for too long.

The static was losing patience.

The werewolf was coming.

He touched the little screen on the seatback. The plane icon was over Greenland now. Only ninety minutes to Reykjavík, Iceland, in late December. Where it snowed or rained for days at a time and the sun never truly rose, only brightening the sky for a few hours at midday.

He got up and went to the tiny restroom and splashed his face with water. He didn't look at himself in the mirror. He knew he wouldn't like what he saw there. On his way back to his seat, he plucked two more mini-vodkas from the flight crew's service area and tossed them down in one go.

Maybe the dreams came from the Valium fucking with him. It wasn't supposed to be a long-term solution. He'd read up on the side effects, and they weren't good. He sure as hell wasn't supposed to be chasing it with vodka, although Valium alone had stopped working months ago.

Maybe it was simply the price to be paid for getting back to some kind of meaningful work.

Or maybe he was just running away.

He told himself he'd quit the Valium once he got off the plane. He'd pick up his rental, find a place to park outside the city, and sleep it off, all of it. He had plenty of practice sleeping in a vehicle.

For now, he closed his eyes and drifted.

. . .

The airport's long, narrow halls were packed with people. Peter walked with the crowd to get his heavy pack and duffel, trying not to run, jumping out of his skin with the need to stand under the open sky and feel the wind on his face. Eight in the morning. It would be dark out for a few more hours.

At customs, the female agent behind the glass ran Peter's passport under the scanner. He heard a beep and her cool eyes flickered up at him. "Please wait a moment."

In less than a minute, two uniformed agents appeared as if from thin air, a man and a woman. The man collected Peter's passport. "Sir, please come with us."

His English was excellent, just a trace of an accent. *Sir* became not-quite *shir*, *us* became not-quite *ush*, with a slight whistle to the sibilants. He was older than Peter, early fifties but slim in a crisp black uniform and fresh shave. His uniform had two tags, one in Icelandic on the right breast, LÖGREGLAN, and one on the left that read POLICE. There were no other markings of rank that Peter could see.

The woman was younger than Peter, but not by much. Her tag read CUSTOMS.

Peter took a deep breath and let it out. The white static crackled higher, vaporizing the haze of Valium and vodka. His nerves twanged like a dropped piano. Sweat gathered between his shoulder blades. He wanted nothing more than to get outside. "What's this about?"

The man saw Peter's rising tension and eased away from the woman, opening up the angles, giving himself room.

He moved well enough, but he seemed unconcerned. There were a half-dozen other officers within view.

If he'd known what Peter was capable of, the things Peter had done, the things Peter was contemplating at that very moment, he would have been worried as hell.

The woman smiled with a professional warmth. "Your name is Peter, right? I'm Sigrid. This is Hjalmar. Come with us for a moment, we'll explain everything. Would you like a coffee?"

Peter pulled in another long breath, then bent to pick up his duffel. He already wore the big pack slung over one shoulder. "Sure," he said. "Coffee would be good." Or a double bourbon, neat. Then another, washing down four more Valium.

He needed to get the fuck out of there.

They walked him through a door and down a hallway to a little kitchen alcove with a gleaming stainless-steel machine that could produce a dozen different coffee drinks with the push of a button. She made him an Americano. "Milk or sugar?" The mug was white ceramic, not paper, and warm in his hand. The coffee was better than he expected.

Past the alcove, a bright yellow door opened to a plain white room. It was furnished with a long laminate table and six plastic chairs. Inexpensive stuff, but elegant, lightweight, durable. Interrogation room sponsored by Ikea.

The man, Officer Hjalmar, held the door against the spring and the woman, Officer Sigrid, ushered Peter politely inside. Coffee in hand, he set his pack and duffel on the table. Officer Hjalmar followed and the door closed automatically behind.

It was all very civilized.

Peter thought about how hard it would be to kick his way through the wallboard. With his heavy leather hiking boots, not hard at all. His long leg muscles twitched. He wondered what might be on the other side.

Officer Sigrid gave him the smile again. "Peter, please, have a seat. How is your coffee?" She was sturdy in her black uniform, comfortable in her skin. Everything she said and did was designed to put Peter at ease. It didn't work.

Peter leaned against the wall. "Why am I here?"

"I'm told you had some trouble on the airplane," Officer Hjalmar said. "You were agitated. You shouted."

"I had a bad dream," Peter said. "I'm starting to think I'm still having it."

"You're sweating," Hjalmar said. "Are you nervous about something?"

"I have claustrophobia." Peter hated having to explain it, the weakness it implied. "I get panic attacks in small spaces. Like airplanes. And official rooms with no windows."

The man looked at Peter. "I'm sorry." Maybe some sympathy there, but he was still a cop. "Is that what the medication is for?"

Peter pushed back the shame that washed over him. At his inability to control himself, his inability to live a normal life. Eight years a Recon Marine, the tip of the spear, more deployments than he cared to remember. He was proud of his service, but it had changed him. He was still trying to figure out what he'd become, or was becoming. A work in progress, goddamnit.

But he had no use for sympathy.

"The medication is none of your fucking business," he said calmly. "Again, why am I here?"

There was a knock on the yellow door. A female officer leaned in and said something in Icelandic, a beautiful language. Even that simple sentence sounded like poetry, Peter thought, although he'd probably need two tongues to speak it.

Then the female officer left and a new man stepped in.

He was plump and pink and balding, one of those men who'd been middle-aged since he was seventeen. He wore a dark gray suit with a faint blue windowpane pattern that matched his pocket square and tie. He slung a long gray wool topcoat over a chairback and tucked both hands in his pockets. Not police or military, Peter thought. A civilian. And he'd always been a civilian. Peter could tell by the way he stood, the careless slouch of his shoulders. His soft, useless slick-soled shoes.

The static sparked at the base of Peter's brain, threatening to fill his head with lightning.

He pushed down the urge toward action, that familiar fight-or-flight. It wouldn't help him, not now. Breathe in, breathe out.

The civilian nodded at the officers. "Please. Continue."

Sigrid spoke. "What is the purpose of your visit?"

Peter waved at the big pack filling a chair. "Hiking."

"In winter?" She turned on the smile. "You must be part Icelandic. You are signed up with a tour operator?"

"No. I'm renting a car."

Hjalmar shook his head. "This is not like"—he consulted Peter's passport—"your Wisconsin. Iceland can be quite dangerous, especially in winter."

"Don't underestimate Wisconsin." Peter smiled for the first time. "And I don't mind dangerous, either."

The civilian frowned. The two customs officers exchanged glances.

"Have you come here to die?" Hjalmar sounded concerned for the first time. "Suicide by glacier, or hypothermia? Because we don't want to put our rescue teams at risk, trying to save you."

"I don't want to die," Peter said. "I just want to get outside these walls, see some country. What's going on, here?"

The civilian spoke a second time. "Let's see what's in his baggage, shall we?" He didn't sound Icelandic. He sounded American, like the East Coast. Like several generations of private schools and private clubs and a long history of getting what he wanted.

Peter said, "Who are you?"

The civilian looked amused. "That's not important," he said. "His luggage, please."

The customs officers glanced at each other again.

The man nodded once, just slightly, but he didn't like it.

The woman went to Peter's pack, popped the buckles, loosened the straps. She began to lay out his things on the table. Tent, poles, fly. Stove and pot. Sleeping bag and pad. All the other things he'd need to survive alone in open country. All of it excellent quality, but well-used. She laid everything out neatly. She left the silver emergency blanket and fifty-foot coil of Kevlar-core rope in the top compartment.

"The duffel as well."

The woman set her jaw but moved the yellow waterproof bag to a chair and opened the zipper.

There was something odd here, Peter thought. These cops were annoyed. They didn't like taking this soft man's orders any more than Peter liked being in that room.

This wasn't about some panic attack on the plane.

Sigrid pulled out more hiking gear, along with town clothes and the carry-on he'd shoved inside at baggage claim, a simple daypack with his laptop and charger, a thin insulated jacket, a Ziploc bag of homemade granola bars, his travel documents, his pills, and a few books.

She held up the books. "You are a reader?" Peter nodded. Sigrid smiled. "Iceland is a nation of readers."

Inside his guidebook, she found a photo of a man holding a mop-headed boy in his arms like a happy sack of potatoes. The boy was seven, loose-limbed and cheerful with dirty knees. He looked away from the camera as if already planning his next mud puddle. The man was thirty-three, with a bushy blond beard and a face as empty as a stone. His deep-set eyes seemed too blue to be real.

The civilian stepped forward and tapped the photo with his index finger. "Who's this?"

"A friend," Peter said. "Cute kid, isn't he?"

The civilian's frown deepened, his lips like squirming pink worms. He held out his hand. "Give me your phone."

"I don't think so. I'd like some answers."

The civilian was definitely unhappy now. "Here's an answer for you," he said. "You are not welcome in Iceland. Unfortunately for you, there are no available seats back to the States until late afternoon, the day after tomorrow." He took an envelope from his jacket pocket. "Here is your ticket. You will be on that plane. These officers will see to your safety and comfort until that time, and they will escort you to your seat."

With the flight, that meant three more days stuck inside. Peter felt the static crackle and rise, pushing at the boundaries of his control. But he wasn't going to lose his shit in front of this asshole. He ignored the envelope. "On whose authority, exactly?"

"It's unofficial." The civilian gave Peter a tight smile. "But real nonetheless. You are persona non grata here. Go home."

Breathe in, breathe out. Peter looked at the customs cops. "He can do this?"

They glanced at each other a third time. If something passed between them, Peter didn't see it.

Officer Hjalmar said, "In fact that is a bit unclear. We will require written confirmation from a superior officer."

"Cut the shit," the civilian said. "You have verbal orders. Do as you're told."

It was the wrong response. Officer Hjalmar's face

betrayed no emotion. He simply shrugged. "There are procedures for these things. Forms must be filled out."

Peter pushed down a smile. Insistence on standard procedure was the most elegant form of bureaucratic resistance. As a Marine lieutenant, Peter had used the tactic himself, although not as often as he'd stomped procedure into the dirt in pursuit of his mission and the safety of his men.

"We have no reason to detain him," Officer Sigrid said. "To our knowledge, Mr. Ash has committed no crime. You can see he's in discomfort. He says he's claustrophobic, having a panic attack."

"And you believe him?" Anger and frustration radiated off the pink civilian like an IED's afterglow. The envelope trembled, just slightly, in his manicured hand. Peter wasn't sure why the man was so worked up. He wasn't the one being deported.

"We do things a bit differently in Iceland," the woman said. "We have a great deal of respect for the rights of the individual and the rule of law. We do not detain people without proper cause."

"You should see his file," the pink civilian said. "You'd feel differently."

"But you have chosen not to share that information with us," Officer Hjalmar said.

"This request is unofficial. From one nation to another."

"It is *extremely* unofficial," Officer Hjalmar said. "We will honor your request that he leave the country. But lacking written orders from our superiors, Mr. Ash will be not be detained today." He took the envelope with the ticket. "We will collect his rental car and hotel information. If he does not report here, to our office, four hours before the flight, we will dispatch officers to collect him."

The civilian burned hotter. He took his phone from his pocket. "Give me five minutes."

The woman turned to Peter. "Perhaps you should pack your things."

Into his phone, the civilian said, "Get me the head of the customs police. Yes, even better, the national police commissioner." He listened, his back to Peter and the officers. "Then get his goddamn cell phone and forward me there. Now."

Peter tucked his equipment back into place with the efficiency of long practice. Sigrid took out a notebook and pen. Her smile was still professional, but now it held true amusement. "Your contact information?"

Peter gave her his cell number. "I don't have a hotel room yet."

As Peter zipped his duffel, he heard a phone ring. He turned to watch Officer Hjalmar take his phone off his belt and raise it to his ear. "Já, Hjalmar."

The civilian turned and stared, the phone lowered from his ear. "You're the national police commissioner?"

Hjalmar put his phone away. "Iceland is a small country. Your request is unusual. We take these matters quite seriously."

The pink civilian was turning red. "Do you know who is behind this request?"

"Unfortunately, no. Not officially." Hjalmar turned to

Peter and held out his passport and the envelope with the plane ticket. "I will walk you out."

Hjalmar led Peter past the glass booths and into the airport's modest main hall. Through the glass walls of the atrium, Peter could see snow swirling bright under powerful lights. The white static crackled in response. Sometimes standing by a big window helped the claustrophobia, but Peter was well beyond that point.

It was after ten in the morning and the sky was barely beginning to brighten. Peter was exhausted and hungry and impatient. He wanted badly to walk outside. Hell, he wanted to run. But he held himself there, taking deep breaths. He knew they weren't quite done yet.

Hjalmar watched Peter carefully. "I hope I haven't made a mistake."

"You haven't." Peter stuck out his hand. "I'm Peter. What do I call you?"

"Hjalmar is fine." They shook hands. "We are informal here."

"Who's the guy in the suit?"

"Someone connected to your embassy." The man adjusted his shoulders, as if working out some kink in his back. "There is some weight behind their request. Eventually my government will be forced to honor it. If you do not return when you are due, we will collect you. And we will not be gentle."

Peter nodded. "I'll try to behave myself. But I still don't get why I'm not in a holding cell."

A smile flickered across Hjalmar's face. "Icelanders are independent people," he said. "We do not like being told what to do."

"Huh." Peter watched the snow blowing sideways, drifts gathering in unlikely places. "Me neither."

"You were in the military." Not a question.

"I was United States Marine," said Peter. "Still am, I guess. It's not something that leaves you."

Hjalmar nodded. "I was a ground observer with Norway in the first Iraq war. I had to go, I couldn't help myself. All these years later, I still remember the burned-out Iraqi tanks, the smell of their dead drivers and gunners. Like roasted meat inside a cast-iron pot."

The static foamed and sparked. Peter needed to breathe open air. "Did you become a vegetarian?"

"No," Hjalmar said. "I became a policeman. So I am asking. What is in your file that would concern me?"

"You? Probably nothing."

"Then why don't they want you here?"

"Honestly? I have no idea." For the moment, it was the truth. "Are we done?"

"Yes. I'll see you in two days."

Peter smiled. "Not if I see you first."

Then he stepped forward and the double glass doors slid wide and he walked into the biting, sunless cold. The hard wind in his face and the icy snow falling down the back of his neck felt like some kind of miracle.

NICK PETRIE

"Lots of characters get compared to my own Jack Reacher, but [Petrie's] Peter Ash is the real deal."
—Lee Child